VOLUME 2

Gifted

KINGFISHER
LONDON & NEW YORK

Text copyright © 2013 by Marilyn Kaye
Published in the United States by Kingfisher,
175 Fifth Ave., New York, NY 10010
Kingfisher is an imprint of Macmillan Children's Books, London.
All rights reserved.

Distributed in the U.S. and Canada by Macmillan,
175 Fifth Ave., New York, NY 10010

Library of Congress Cataloging-in-Publication data
has been applied for.

ISBN: 978-0-7534-6789-3

Kingfisher books are available for special promotions and premiums.
For details contact: Special Markets Department,
Macmillan, 175 Fifth Ave., New York, NY 10010.

For more information, please visit www.kingfisherbooks.com

Printed and bound by CPI Group (UK) Ltd, Croydon, CR0 4YY

10 9 8 7 6 5 4 3 2 1

VOLUME 2

Gifted

MARILYN KAYE

KINGFISHER
NEW YORK

contents:

For my goddaughter Rose, her brother Marius,
and their parents, Isabelle Benech
and Laurent Loiseau, with love

For Devlin Burstein

For Baptiste Latil,
who remembers all my stories

Gifted

FINDERS
KEEPERS

CHAPTER ONE

KEN WAS TRYING TO ignore the voice in his head.

Everyone else in the room was involved in a lively debate with Madame, their teacher. His classmates were paying attention, and they actually looked interested. Even Jenna Kelley, who generally affected an expression of boredom, was getting into it.

"What's the big deal, Madame? Okay, so maybe there are bad guys out there who want to get their hands on us. But we can take care of ourselves. We're gifted, for crying out loud!"

"Yes, you have gifts," Madame responded patiently, "but you don't know how to use them properly."

Sarah spoke softly. "Wouldn't it be better if we just didn't use them at all?"

"And let the bad guys use them?" Charles asked. "No way. We have to fight back!"

"Couldn't we just stay away from the bad guys?" Emily

wanted to know.

"That's easier said than done," Tracey pointed out. "I'm with Charles. We have to be prepared to do battle."

Madame was getting frustrated. "But you can't go to battle when you don't know how to use your weapons!"

Ken wanted to be a part of this argument—to listen and maybe even join in. But how could he participate when some old dead guy was yelling at him?

Listen, kid, ya gotta help me! Talk to my grand-daughter—make her see some sense. If she marries that no-good scoundrel, she'll regret it for the rest of her life!

Nobody else could hear the man—only Ken. This was his so-called gift. And he hated it.

This voice was louder than most of the voices he heard. Ken thought maybe the man was hard of hearing. His own grandfather couldn't hear very well and he talked really loudly. Ken had to yell back at his grandfather to be heard.

At least with this old guy Ken wouldn't have to yell. He only had to think his response and the man would hear him. Ken didn't understand how this wordless communication worked. It was just the way it happened.

He "spoke" to the man. Look, I'm sorry, but I can't help you out. I don't even know your granddaughter.

The man replied, I'll give you her address.

Ken wondered if the man could hear his silent groan.

He didn't know what else to tell him.

With other voices he could be tough, even rude, ordering them to leave him alone and get out of his head. But how could he be nasty and disrespectful to an old man?

"Ken? Ken!"

This voice was coming from outside his head. Madame spoke sharply, and to Ken's relief her stern tone drove the dead grandfather away.

"Are you listening, Ken? We're talking about something important."

"I'm trying to listen," he replied.

Her stern expression softened slightly. "Is someone bothering you?"

"He's gone now," Ken told her.

"Good. Then pay attention, because this concerns all of you. Surely by now you've all realized that there are forces in this world who present a grave threat to you. Be aware. Be alert. And never, never let anyone know what you're capable of doing."

From the corner of his eye, Ken saw Amanda yawn. She politely covered her mouth with her hand, but she was directly in Madame's line of vision, and the teacher saw her.

"Am I boring you, Amanda?" she asked, making no effort to hide the annoyance in her tone.

"No, Madame. I just have something else on my mind.

Something I need to tell the class."

"And I'm sure it's something very important," Madame said smoothly. "You'll be able share it with us later. Right now, I need your full attention.

It's very important that you all realize how your gifts could be exploited. I don't want to frighten you, but you need to be aware of the danger. Do you understand this?"

Jenna raised her hand. "Amanda thinks you're exaggerating, Madame."

Madame frowned. "Jenna, I've told you again and again, you are not to read minds in this class." Her eyes shifted to Amanda. "And I am not exaggerating. Perhaps some of you need to recall some recent events. Emily? Emily!"

Ken knew Emily couldn't use hearing voices as an excuse for not paying attention. She was just daydreaming. But not like an ordinary daydreamer might. Emily's dreams had a disturbing tendency to come true.

"Emily!" Madame barked. "Would you mind not thinking about the future and joining us in the present?"

Emily jumped. "Sorry, Madame."

"Remind the class of the potential dangers they could encounter."

"Why me?" Emily asked plaintively.

"Because, if I'm not mistaken, you were the first to encounter a real threat this year."

Madame was rarely mistaken, and Emily knew this. Still, she looked confused. From behind her, Jenna poked her shoulder.

"Serena Hancock, Em. Does the name ring a bell?"

Emily slumped back in her seat. "Oh, right. The student teacher."

"Would you remind the class what Serena did to you?" Madame asked.

Emily was clearly uncomfortable, but she obeyed. "She hypnotized me and tried to make me tell her the winning lottery number for the next drawing."

"And why did Serena choose you as her victim?" Madame prompted her. "Why didn't she threaten Jenna, for example, or Sarah?"

Emily sighed. "Because she knew I could see into the future."

"Precisely," Madame declared. "She knew what you could do, and she wanted to exploit this. Let's move on to another example of a recent threat." She looked pointedly at Jenna.

The goth girl scowled.

Madame spoke briskly. "I know it's a painful memory, Jenna, but it's important that we remember."

Jenna gave an elaborate shrug. "It wasn't painful, just boring."

Ken caught Amanda's eye, and they exchanged knowing looks. This was so Jenna—to act tough, like nothing could really upset her. Not even a man showing up out of nowhere and claiming to be the father who had disappeared before Jenna was even born. Not even when this man turned out to be a fraud, someone who wanted to use Jenna's mind-reading skills to win a lot of money at poker.

"Wait a second," Charles broke in. "What happened to Emily and what happened to Jenna just happened to them. This doesn't have anything to do with the rest of us."

"I disagree," Madame said. "What threatens one of us threatens all of us. I cannot stress this enough. We need to think of ourselves as a team."

Ken hoped his own reaction to that notion didn't show in his expression. He respected Madame and all that, but to call this class a team—that was completely bogus. Ken knew all about teams—as an athlete he'd played on lots of them, including Meadowbrook's soccer team. And he'd been on teams in other classes—working on science projects, stuff like that. Being on a team meant being connected in some way, working together toward a common goal. Looking around this room, he couldn't imagine working with any of his classmates. And he certainly didn't feel connected to any of them. Without the gifts, they had nothing in common. Jenna was a sullen goth girl with a less-than-stellar reputation. Amanda was a superpopular queen bee. Even though he wasn't involved in playing soccer anymore, Ken still considered himself a jock. There was no one else in the class who was even interested in sports.

And each of them dealt with their gift in different ways. Space-cadet Emily sometimes acted like her gift frightened her. Amanda wasn't too crazy about her gift, and Sarah absolutely refused to use hers. Only Charles, who was stuck in a wheelchair, and whiny, wimpy Martin seemed like they enjoyed the powers their gifts gave them.

And what about Carter? Who could have anything in common with a total mystery? The strange, silent boy was little more than a zombie.

As far as Ken was concerned, the only thing they all shared was this class. The gifts—and the students who had them—didn't have any connection at all.

Sometimes, like now, he wondered if Madame had a gift like Jenna's. At that very moment she was looking at him, and she could have been reading his mind.

"I realize that you might not think of yourselves as a team, but that may well be how our enemies think of us. Surely I don't need to remind you of your most recent adventure?" When there was no response to that, she shook her head wearily.

"Or maybe I do. Amanda, would you please refresh our memory?"

Martin piped up. "Why are you asking her? She wasn't even there!"

"Yes, I was!" Amanda snapped.

Martin glared at her. "Hey, I'm not stupid. I would have noticed if you were there. It was me, Tracey, Emily, and Sarah. Oh, and Carter was there for a while at the beginning."

Sarah spoke gently. "I wasn't really there, Martin. Amanda had taken over my body. I didn't get there till the very end."

"I can't believe you didn't know that, Martin," Tracey declared. "Didn't you notice Sarah wasn't acting like herself?"

Jenna snorted. "Are you kidding? Martin never pays attention to anyone but himself."

Charles laughed. "I'll bet Martin was too scared to notice anything."

"I wasn't scared," Martin replied hotly.

"You sure acted like you were," Tracey said.

"Tracey!" Madame said in a warning tone, and the other students frowned at Tracey, too. Teasing Martin was a big no-no. That was when his "gift" came out, and nobody was eager to see mass destruction or suffer personal

8

bodily injury, which might easily happen if Martin's superstrength kicked in. Of course, Tracey wouldn't have to worry if Martin went on one of his rampages. She could always disappear. Personally, Ken thought she had the most interesting gift of all of them.

"Let's get back to the subject," Madame said. "Amanda, could you give us a brief synopsis of what happened to some of you?"

"We were kidnapped," she said, "by this woman named Clare and two men."

Tracey supplied the names. "Howard and George."

"Yeah, whatever," Amanda said dismissively. "They were just flunkies. Clare was in charge. Anyway, they wanted us to rob a bank for them. They took Carter first, then Tracey, Martin, and Sarah. And Emily."

Madame nodded. "And they chose each of you for a reason. Emily could predict the scene at the bank, Martin could break down doors, Tracey could sneak into the vault without being seen. And Sarah could force people to do whatever the robbers needed them to do."

"Except they didn't really have Sarah," Emily noted. "They got Amanda instead."

Jenna laughed. "I almost feel sorry for the bad guys. Can you imagine getting stuck with Amanda? It's not like she could help anyone rob a bank." She paused. "Actually, I take that back. Maybe she would have helped with the robbery if she thought the vault contained shoes. Or handbags. Otherwise her gift is pretty worthless."

Amanda's obsession with fashion was well known, and everyone laughed—except Carter, of course, who never smiled or laughed or showed any emotion at all on his face. Which made Ken think about something that had puzzled him ever since the kidnappings.

"Why did they want Carter?" he asked out loud.

The room fell silent, and everyone turned to look at the figure sitting in the back of the room. As usual, the pale, round-faced boy wasn't perturbed by the sudden attention. His expression was as blank as it always was. Ken knew everyone had to be thinking the same thing: Did Carter even have a gift? Or was he only in this class because he was—well—weird?

Charles broke the silence. "I want to know why they didn't kidnap me. I've got real power."

Charles was known for his bragging, but no one could deny the truth in what he was saying. Being able to make things move with his mind could have made him very useful to someone with criminal intentions.

Emily had an answer for him. "The house didn't have disabled access, Charles. The doorways were too narrow for a wheelchair and you wouldn't have been able to get up the stairs."

"Clearly the kidnappers had done their homework," Madame said. "They knew who they wanted, who they could use. This is what I want to impress upon you. There are people out there who know all about you. And if those people ever got together and pooled their information ..."

Sarah spoke. "You're saying we're all at risk."

"Exactly," Madame replied.

"Except Ken," Charles piped up.

Madame frowned. "Why do you say that, Charles?"

"Dead people talk to him—big deal! How is that going to help a criminal?"

Martin joined in. "Yeah, his gift is totally useless."

"You don't know that," Madame declared. "I'm sure there are people who would find Ken's gift extremely interesting." She looked at Ken, as if she wanted him to back her up.

Ken just shrugged. Because in all honesty, he pretty much agreed with both Martin and Charles on this subject.

Madame continued. "Now, I'd like you all to share your thoughts on how you can best protect yourselves from exploitation."

Several hands went up, but Ken's wasn't one of them. As far as he was concerned, he'd rather learn how to protect himself from his own gift.

From the very beginning, when he realized he had this gift, it had been nothing but a headache.

At first he thought he could use it to help a certain dead person with a problem left unresolved on earth, and he had tried—he'd really tried—to respond to this person's needs. But the result had been disastrous, and now he, Ken, had an ongoing problem to deal with. He hadn't been bothered by it much lately, but there was no telling when the problem would pop up again. Just thinking about the possibility gave him a headache, and he pushed it out of his mind.

Okay, maybe there had been a couple of times when his gift had been useful. He'd been able to alert Jenna to the fact that the man who claimed to be her father was a fraud after Ken got a message from beyond the grave that confirmed it. And he'd learned the whereabouts of a guy who'd helped kidnap some of Ken's classmates when the kidnapper's late mother told Ken where to find her son.

But events like that were rare. Most of the time the voices made demands. And ever since that first demand, the one that turned into a mess, he'd made every effort to ignore them. It wasn't easy. There were so many dead people, so many sad stories. Many of the voices wanted him to communicate a message to someone left behind. A man might ask him to apologize to a friend for something he'd done when he was alive. A woman would ask him to tell her husband that she'd loved him. A thief who'd repented might want him to return money he'd stolen, and other people asked Ken to deliver souvenirs. One time, there had been a man who wanted him to tell the police that his death wasn't an accident—that his ex-wife had killed him.

But Ken didn't want to get involved. He'd done that once, and he was still paying the price. Besides, how could he do what they asked?

Excuse me, miss, but your dead grandfather thinks your boyfriend is no good.

Excuse me, officer, but do you remember the man who died when he fell down the stairs? And you thought it was an accident? Well, I know for a fact that his ex-wife pushed him.

They wouldn't believe him. How could he possibly explain what he knew without telling them how he got the information? And then they'd think he was nuts. Besides, as Madame was constantly telling them, they should never let anyone know about their gifts.

So if Ken couldn't do anything with his gift, his only option was to get rid of it, to make every effort to silence the voices. And he'd been getting a little better at it. Pleading, arguing, ordering the spirits to go away and leave him alone was beginning to have an effect. He had to be tough with them, get angry—even nasty sometimes. He hated being rude, but what else could he do?

Ken . . . Hey, Ken, what's up, man? Are you there? Can you listen?

Ken slumped back in his seat. This was the one voice he could never order to leave him alone.

Yeah, I'm listening.

And as the voice in his head began to talk, Ken's thoughts went back to how it all began for him . . .

Chapter Two

S OME PEOPLE HATED THE first day back at school after summer vacation. Not Ken Preston. Why would he be unhappy about it or unwilling to return to the place where he ruled?

Of course, he wasn't the only king at Meadowbrook. There were plenty of other popular guys.

But in all modesty, he had to admit that he was way up there, on the upper rung of the middle-school social ladder.

"Yo, Preston! Hey, man, what's up?"

Ken saluted the freckled, red-haired boy who strode toward him. "Hey, Jack. How was California?"

"Extremely cool," Jack Farrell told him. "Not much in the way of surf, but lots of action on the beach, if you know what I mean." He whistled.

"I'm telling ya, man, those California girls are a completely different kind of female species."

Ken laughed. In this particular way, Jack had always

been a little more mature than the rest of the gang. "Better not let Lucy hear you say that."

"I just looked, I didn't touch," Jack assured him. "Not like any of them would let me get close enough to do that anyway. Blonds in bikinis are out of my league. What about you? Did you have any adventures with the opposite sex this summer?"

"Not really." They were inside the building now, and Ken lowered his voice. "Well, actually, I kissed Amanda Beeson underwater at Sophie Greene's pool party after school got out last year."

"Oh, yeah? You like her?"

"It was a dare," Ken explained with a shrug. "I barely know her. And I haven't seen her since."

"She's pretty hot," Jack mused.

"Yeah, I guess. Not really my type, though. I think she's kind of a snob."

They rounded the corner to the hall where lockers lined the wall. A whoop went up from three boys gathered at one of the lockers, and Ken and Jack paused to greet them.

"Guess we'll be seeing you two at practice this afternoon," one of them said.

Ken grinned. "Yeah, we thought we might drop by." He and Jack were captain and vice-captain of Meadowbrook's soccer team that year. "See ya there."

They moved on, and Jack stopped at a door.

"Here we are."

Ken opened a notebook and looked at the printout of his class schedule. "Not me. I've got homeroom in 118."

Jack gave a look of exaggerated dismay. "You're kidding! They're splitting us up?"

Ken shrugged. "Guess so. We had a good run, though. Two years in the same homeroom. What else do you have on your schedule?"

The boys compared schedules and discovered they had their lunch period and English class together.

"Excellent," Jack proclaimed. "I'll eat your lunch and you'll write my essays."

"Dream on, pal," Ken responded. "Later." He moved on down the hall to his own homeroom.

At least a dozen students were already seated in the classroom when he entered. A pretty blond girl perked up when she saw him.

"Ken, hi!" She indicated the chair next to hers. "Nobody's sitting here."

Ken couldn't remember her name, but he gave her a friendly smile anyway. He'd been getting a lot of attention like this from girls lately. "Thanks, but I like the back of the room. Less chance of getting called on." He joined the four boys who already lined the wall at the far end.

He was greeted with welcoming smiles and the usual calls of "Hey, man!"

Ken slapped hands as he moved to the end of the row. He knew them all. None of them were on the soccer team, but Ken had never limited his socializing to the jocks. Funny thing, though—when people knew you were an athlete, they thought your only interest was sports.

"You gonna get that lousy team of ours out of the dumps?" one boy asked with a grin.

"Absolutely," Ken assured him. "We're going all the way to the finals this year. Farrell and I have big plans!"

The warning bell sounded and a wave of students rushed into the room, followed by a teacher. Then the final bell rang and the teacher spoke.

"Hello. My name is Mr. Kingston, and—"

That was as far as he got before the intercom on the wall emitted a shrill buzz, indicating that the High and Mighty was about to address them.

First came the voice of the secretary. "May I have your attention for the morning announcements?"

In keeping with tradition, the students in the class yelled out, "No!" Naturally, this had no effect.

The next voice was booming and authoritative. "Good morning, students, this is your principal. I'd like to take this opportunity to welcome you back to Meadowbrook

Middle School."

Since this was the third time Ken had heard Mr. Jackson's first-day-of-school speech, he knew what was coming— the usual exhortations to do well, study hard, behave properly, blah, blah, blah. He tuned out the principal and thought about his own plans for the new school term.

This year, ninth grade, would be his last year at Meadowbrook, and he needed to leave his mark on the middle school. He'd already had two good years here, and he wanted this one to be outstanding.

Next September he'd be a lowly underclassman at Central High School, so he was determined to enjoy this final year of being on top of the heap.

First of all, he'd lead the soccer team to the playoffs, maybe even to the state championship. This would take some real work. He was relying on his popularity with his teammates to keep them enthused and practicing harder and longer than they had the year before. If they had a good season, his reputation could secure him a place on Central's varsity team. Most younger high school players were stuck playing on Central's B-team, but Ken knew they made exceptions for exceptional players. And if he became a star on Central's team, a scout might notice him and he could be up for a college scholarship.

But Ken was a realist. He knew there had to be lots of

soccer players as good as he was, and he knew he couldn't count on soccer to provide him with a college education. He had to keep his grades up, too. What he'd said to that blond-haired girl about sitting in the back of a classroom so he wouldn't be called on wasn't really true. He'd always done pretty well at school, and he was proud of it. If he did really well this year, he could take advanced placement classes at Central, which would give his parents a big thrill.

As for his social life, he had some goals in that area, too. Most of his classmates didn't really go out on "dates"—they just hung out in groups. But lately his friends had started pairing off. Jack and Lucy had been together since last spring. Ken was beginning to think it might be kind of fun to know one girl really well, to talk to her on the phone every night, exchange text messages on their cell phones, and meet between classes. Not to mention what they might get up to when they were alone. Ken grinned to himself. Yes, there were definite advantages to having a girlfriend.

But what girl? Amanda Beeson? Jack was right—she was pretty hot. He didn't much like the clique she hung out with, though. It seemed to consist of a lot of girls who were mean to other girls. And Amanda was rumored to be one of the meanest. He remembered the previous year when she'd been in one of his classes, and she'd said some really nasty things to that strange, sad girl, Tracey . . .

Something. It was weird, but Ken couldn't begin to recall her last name.

Anyway, there were plenty of other girls. And even though Ken would never admit it publicly, he knew many of them wouldn't mind hanging out with him. Like that blond in the front of his homeroom. What was her name? Ken shook his head ruefully. Not such a great start to finding a girlfriend. But someone would turn up in the end.

His first day back at school progressed nicely. Some of the teachers were halfway decent. In his civics class they were going to debate capital punishment. They would dissect crayfish in biology, and in English they were going to read modern novels, so there wouldn't be any of that "thee" and "thou" stuff he hated.

But what he really looked forward to would come after classes were over—his first day as captain of Meadowbrook's soccer team.

After changing into his practice gear, he met with Jack and Coach Holloway in the coach's office for a private consultation. As usual, Coach Holloway looked worried.

"You guys have a lot of work to do. We don't have a decent goalie, and the whole team looks flabby. I don't know how we're going to whip them into shape for the season."

Jack responded in his typically cocky way. "No sweat, Coach. Leave them to us. We can handle them."

Ken was a little less optimistic, especially after they met up with the whole team on the field. A lazy summer filled with too many picnics had taken its toll, and they all looked pretty pathetic.

"You do the pep talk," Jack whispered to Ken.

"Why me?"

"Because people like you better."

Ken grinned. This was true—Jack could be a show off, and he had been known to get on people's nerves sometimes. Ken didn't particularly like public speaking, but he did what he had to do.

"Okay, guys, we've got less than one week to prepare for our first game. We'll be going up against Sunnydale Middle School. Sunnydale made it to the semifinals last year, and I'm sure they think they're going to blow us away. It's going to be a battle, but we can be ready for them. We gotta hit 'em hard and show them there have been some big changes here at Meadowbrook." After a few more encouraging words, he turned the team over to the coach.

"Start off with some laps," Coach barked. "Three times around the field."

This took the wind out of a few boys, but Ken was pleased to see a decent survival rate. After that, Coach put them through a series of grueling exercises, and finally it was time to practice some real plays. The boys split up into two teams, with Ken in charge of one side and Jack taking over the other.

Ken worked on psyching himself up. It wasn't easy seeing your friends—especially your best pal—as your enemy, but that was the only way to get anything out of these mock matches. Squaring his shoulders, he was ready to get down and dirty.

One of the guys kicked the ball, and it flew past him. He took off after it. Glancing over his shoulder, he saw Jack coming up from behind, so he picked up the pace. Then he saw a couple of defenders just ahead, ready to block him. He couldn't let that happen. Quickly he passed to Freddie Ryan, who shot the ball back to Ken as soon as he was clear of the defenders. The pass was high, and Ken turned to head the ball to another teammate.

The last thing he remembered seeing was Jack's face. And then—darkness.

Complete and utter nothingness. No sensations, nothing to see, nothing to hear. No pain either. Just—nothing. He was without form, floating in space.

At some point he thought he felt a prick in his arm, sharper than a mosquito bite. Another time he was vaguely aware of lights. And then some indistinct voices. Hands on his body, something cold pressed against his chest.

And finally, pain. It was almost a relief, because that was

when he knew he wasn't dead.

"Ken? Ken, can you hear me?"

He opened his eyes and saw his mother's anxious face. What was she doing on the soccer field? He tried to sit up, and she rested a hand lightly on his shoulder.

"Don't move, darling. Stay still. George, ring for the nurse!"

George—that was his father. So he was on the field, too. This was all very strange. And why were they calling for a nurse?

Then things began happening quickly. He could hear, he could see . . . he was aware. And he realized he was in a hospital.

Gradually the memory of what had happened started to come back to him. He remembered Jack right behind him, moving fast. Apparently the collision had been pretty bad. They'd both been running at full tilt when they hit each other. Both he and Jack must have been knocked out.

"What time is it?" he asked his mother.

"Almost midnight," she told him. "How do you feel?"

He winced. "Everything hurts."

A nurse appeared. She looked into his eyes, took his pulse, and then gave him a shot. "This is for the pain," she told him. She had a whispered conversation with his parents and then left.

Ken was trying to think, and it wasn't easy. His brain seemed to be operating in slow motion. Practice had started at four. It must have been nearly five o'clock by the time they started the match. His mother had just told him it was midnight. Twelve minus five . . . simple subtraction made his head hurt, but he persevered.

"I've been unconscious for seven hours?"

His mother spoke gently. "It's Friday, Ken. You've been in a coma for four days. You had a concussion, some broken ribs, and you've got some badly torn tendons in your left ankle. But you're going to be okay."

All he really heard was *Friday*. "I've got a game tomorrow . . ." and then the rest of her words sunk in. "I guess I won't be playing."

"No, dear. But you're going to be okay eventually. It will take some time, though."

Was she saying he'd be out for the season? he wondered in dismay. Then he realized he hadn't even asked about the other victim.

"How's Jack? Can he play tomorrow?"

The shot the nurse had given him must have been pretty potent. He drifted off to sleep before he could get an answer, and he wasn't even sure if he'd actually asked the question out loud. Maybe it was the painkilling medication that made his dreams so vivid.

He was back on the soccer field, running after a ball. But every time he got close enough to kick it, the ball moved farther away. He kept running, the ball kept moving. From behind, he could hear Jack's voice. *Ken, wait for me! Wait up, Ken!* Or maybe he was yelling, *Wake up, Ken, wake up!*

And he did.

He was alone in the hospital room now. Light poured in from the window. He lifted his head and tried to sit up, but it was too painful, and his head sank back down on the pillow.

The door opened, and a young woman in a pink pinafore came in wheeling a tray. "Good morning!" she said in a bright voice. "How do you feel?"

"Okay. It hurts a little."

"The nurse is coming around with your medication," she told him. "How about some breakfast? Are you hungry?"

"No," he replied, but she didn't pay any attention to his response. She pressed a button on the bed, and it raised him painlessly into a halfway sitting position. Then she set up a tray over his lap.

He looked at the food without interest. "I'm really not hungry."

"Try to eat a little," she urged him.

Without any enthusiasm, and mainly just to get rid of this perky girl, he picked up a piece of toast and took a bite. The girl smiled with approval and left the room. He took another bite, and to his surprise, he managed to get both slices down. Moments later, an orderly came in with a basin.

Ken suffered through a sponge bath, but at least he was allowed to brush his own teeth. A nurse appeared with some pills for him to take. The pain went away, but he stayed awake. And he actually began to feel almost human.

He must have looked almost human, too, because when his parents arrived they seemed very relieved to see him. His mother began to prattle about the doctor's report, how Ken could probably come home tomorrow or the next day, as soon as he learned how to maneuver some crutches, but his father was oddly silent. And even as his mother continued to prattle, Ken sensed something behind her determinedly cheerful expression.

"What's the matter?" he asked.

His parents looked at each other.

"Is Jack in worse shape than me? Is he going to play tonight?"

His father took his hand. "Son . . . you have to be strong. We have something difficult to tell you."

Ken had a terrible feeling he knew what they were about to say. That he'd never play soccer again. He steeled himself to deal with it.

"What is it, Dad?"

"Jack didn't make it, Ken. He died."

Ken hadn't prepared himself for that.

He couldn't remember the last time he'd cried in front of his parents. Probably not since he was five or six. But he felt absolutely no shame in crying now. Jack was his best friend—they'd been buddies since they were little kids. And now he was gone?

His parents stayed with him and tried to comfort him. Then a nurse came in to give him another shot.

"This will help you sleep," she said.

He didn't want to sleep. He wanted to think about Jack. He wanted to stay awake and ask questions. Why had Jack died and he'd survived? Was he to blame for the collision? But the medication was stronger than he was.

Much later, he opened his eyes to a room that was dark. He could just make out the flowers and balloons that friends and family had sent. He was alone, and he was glad to be alone, because now he had a chance to think.

What had happened? How did it happen? Had Jack suffered? And where was Jack now . . .

He hadn't spoken out loud, and he didn't expect an answer, but he got one.

I'm here.

He didn't see anyone, but he'd know that voice

anywhere. "Jack?"

Yeah, it's me.

Relief flooded over him. "So you're not dead."

Oh, I'm dead, all right. Bummer, huh?

So this was a dream. It had to be a dream.

Ken didn't believe in ghosts.

In case you're wondering, it wasn't anyone's fault. You know how I never learned to fall right. I broke my neck. I guess that's the way the cookie crumbles.

"You didn't deserve to die," Ken murmured.

Whatever. Anyway, just thought you'd like to know, it wasn't your fault.

"Okay. Thanks for telling me."

What a weird dream, Ken thought. I've never had one like this before. It feels so real.

This isn't a dream.

"How'd you know what I was thinking?"

I don't know. I just did. I can't explain. I'm not really talking either. I mean, dead people don't talk, do we? I don't know—it's like you and I are communicating with our minds.

"Oh. I don't get it."

Look, I don't understand it either. But it's kind of cool, huh?

"Yeah, I guess."

You must be tired.

"Yeah, kind of."

Go back to sleep. We'll talk later.

"Right."

Jack's voice faded away and another dream began. This one was a lot easier to deal with. He was a judge in a Miss California beauty pageant. Blonds in bikinis sauntered past him. They were all gorgeous, and he had no idea how he'd pick out the prettiest.

When he opened his eyes again, that perky girl in the pink pinafore was in his room. "Have a nice nap?" she chirped. "It's lunchtime." Once again, she set up a tray on his bed.

He watched as she left the room. Actually, she was kind of cute. Not like the Miss California beauties, of course.

Yeah, I know what you mean. Those California girls—man, they were hot! There was this one on the beach—I know you'll think I'm bragging, but I swear she was looking at me . . .

That was when Ken had to accept the fact that his conversation with Jack wasn't a dream.

It was a nightmare, and it was just beginning.

CHAPTER THREE

AMANDA WAS USUALLY pretty good at hiding her feelings. She'd learned from several bad experiences not to let herself care too much about other people and their problems. And when she felt sorry for herself, or depressed, or angry, or anything like that, she didn't let it show. She was Amanda Beeson, Queen Bee, the prettiest, best-dressed, and most envied girl at Meadowbrook Middle School. She had a reputation to uphold. And feeling sorry for yourself was so not cool.

So throughout the rest of the class, she kept her face fixed in what was a normal expression for her: mildly bored and generally uninterested in anything going on around her. She would not let anyone in this class see how annoyed she was. How they'd hurt her feelings.

Maybe she shouldn't think that "they" had done anything—after all, it was only Jenna who had really insulted her. But the rest of them had laughed, so they were just as guilty.

How *dare* Jenna suggest that her gift was worthless? *Nothing* about Amanda Beeson was worthless. As for her gift—she was a body snatcher, for crying out loud! Jenna could read minds—big deal. Emily could tell the future—so what? Amanda could become another person! And they all knew it.

In this very class, she'd taken over three of them at different times. Tracey, Ken, Sarah—they'd all had personal experience with Amanda's bodysnatching skills. They knew how talented she was, and they should respect her for it. They should have defended her against Jenna's attack.

In all honesty, she had to acknowledge (but only to herself) that she didn't have complete control of her talent. In fact, circumstances often forced her to snatch bodies she didn't want. Like the time when she felt sorry for Tracey Devon, who used to be so pathetic. Who would want to be in Tracey Devon's body?

But Amanda had ended up there, and that was not fun. She still had to feel sorry for someone to become that person, but it was getting easier. She could always find something to pity about a person. After all, each had the misfortune of not being Amanda Beeson.

But while she was very sure that most of the girls at Meadowbrook looked up to her, did any of the students in this class realize how superior she was? She suspected that they didn't. They probably agreed with Jenna. None of them thought she'd be any help in a dangerous situation. And that was so not true. Had Emily forgotten how Amanda-as-Tracey had helped her escape from that insane student teacher? And didn't Ken remember how she'd dealt with one of his voices?

She remembered that experience all too well. The guy's name was Rick. He was a teenager who'd died in the 1960s, and he was lonely. He bothered Ken incessantly. And when Amanda took over Ken's body, Rick talked to her. It didn't bother her so much, though, mainly because she'd fallen in love with Rick.

Ken didn't know about that, of course. All he knew was that somehow Amanda had managed to persuade Rick to leave him alone. And he should be grateful to her for it. Not to mention how she'd transformed Tracey's entire life. That was worth recalling, wasn't it?

As far as she was concerned, she'd done a lot of good for a lot of people with her gift. How could they treat her like this?

Well, they were going to regret it, and soon. Because she was about to make an announcement that would stun them all and make them feel terrible guilt for teasing her.

She'd planned to tell them earlier in the class, but Madame wouldn't let her. The teacher had gone on and on about their enemies and the danger they were in and all that boring stuff. But there were two things she knew for sure about Madame—she was courteous and she was fair. She'd give Amanda her opportunity.

Sure enough, when Madame finally finished nagging them, she remembered that she had cut Amanda off earlier.

"Amanda, you said you had something on your mind. Would you like to share it with us?"

Amanda composed herself. She sat up straight and lowered her eyes. And she spoke quietly.

"This is very hard for me to talk about."

Madame actually seemed concerned. "Go on, Amanda. You're among friends here."

Ha! Amanda thought. But she took a deep breath and spoke solemnly.

"I wanted to let you all know that I'm going to be out of class for a few days." She paused dramatically. "You see, I'm going into the hospital."

She was rewarded with a satisfying gasp. Emily looked positively stricken. Tracey had her hand to her mouth, and even Jenna was taken aback.

"What's wrong with you?" Charles asked.

Before she could answer, Madame spoke. "Yes, I've had a note from your mother. You're having your tonsils taken out."

There was a moment of silence. Then Jenna spoke. "Is that all?"

Amanda drew herself up stiffly. "What do you mean by that?"

Jenna shrugged. "Everyone gets their tonsils out. Well, maybe not *everyone*. But it's no big deal. I mean, it's common."

"It's still an operation," Amanda stated hotly. "Okay, maybe little kids have it all the time, but it's more serious when you're older."

At least Madame backed her up. "Amanda's right. And any stay in a hospital is distressing. We'll miss you in class, Amanda, and we all wish you a speedy recovery. Martin, are you all right?"

Martin was having one of his coughing fits. "Someone must have been eating peanut butter in the cafeteria," he managed to croak.

Everyone knew that Martin was allergic to peanut butter. He couldn't even smell it without getting sick. Madame hastened to his side. "Come along, Martin, I'm taking you to the infirmary."

Amanda couldn't believe it. Martin's stupid allergies were considered more important than her tonsils?

Just as Madame was leaving the room with Martin, the bell rang. Ever since Meadowbrook's reorganization of the class schedule a couple of weeks ago, this class had been moved from just after lunch to the last period of the day. Amanda was pleased with this. The gifted class always put her in a weird mood, and it was a relief to know she could join her real friends immediately afterward.

Normally Amanda would be up and out of there very quickly, but this time there was an odd burning sensation in her eyes, and she stayed in her seat. There was no way she would let anyone see her cry.

Her classmates ran out without a word to her. Except for one. Ken paused by her desk.

"Hey, sorry to hear about that."

Her urge to cry vanished. "What?"

"It's no fun being in the hospital. I know all about that."

She knew he'd been in the hospital for a while after an accident earlier that year. "You understand how I feel," she said softly.

He nodded. "You must be scared."

"I am," she said, and she was actually being honest. She got up, gathered her things, and they left the room together.

"There's nothing to be scared about," he assured her as they walked downstairs. "The nurses and doctors, they're really nice. The worst thing about it is being bored. Bring magazines and books. And make sure your parents arrange for you to have a TV in your room."

"Okay." On the ground floor, he turned in the opposite direction from her locker, but she didn't care. She continued walking by his side.

"But you probably won't have to worry about being bored. You'll get a lot of visitors."

She gave him a sidelong glance. "Really? Do you think so?"

"Well, you've got lots of friends, don't you?"

"Oh, sure. But not in our class."

She was disappointed when he didn't pick up on the hint. She had a thing for Ken, ever since he'd kissed her at her friend Sophie's pool party. She knew that kiss didn't mean anything serious—all the boys were daring each other to do stupid things, like throwing a particular person in the pool or outdoing each other in the number of somersaults they could perform while diving. Silly stuff like that.

But she remembered the kiss. And when she'd been placed in the so-called gifted class, the one thing that had lifted her spirits was the fact that Ken was there.

She had to keep this conversation going. "Did you hear what Jenna said about me in class?"

Ken looked apologetic. "I wasn't really listening."

She knew what that meant—dead people had been talking to him. But she also knew that he didn't like talking about his gift.

"What did Jenna say?" he asked.

"She was talking about my gift. I know she thinks I couldn't help anyone if we were in danger."

"That's not true!" Ken exclaimed. "You could help." He considered it for a second. "For example, you could take over the body of an enemy and stop that person from doing bad things."

There was no way on earth that Amanda would want to do something like that, but she didn't tell him that.

Ken went on. "It's *my* gift that's worthless. At least, it's useless in a crisis."

"I don't believe that," Amanda said stoutly, before it occurred to her that she couldn't think of one possible situation when talking to dead people could help anyone out of a dangerous predicament. "You have a wonderful gift," she said anyway, hoping he wouldn't ask her to elaborate.

"Oh, yeah? What good is it?"

Thinking rapidly, she said, "Um, well, you could bring loved ones together. Maybe there's someone who's desperate to connect with a dead husband or something."

"Yeah, I get requests like that all the time," he admitted. "But I'll tell you something . . ." He stopped walking and looked at her. "This is really awful. But I really don't want to get involved in their lives. Is that terrible of me?"

She could have kissed him right there and then. "No, it's not terrible! I understand completely. It's not like we can solve everyone's problems. I mean, we all have our own problems to deal with, right?"

He gave her a half-smile, and her heart was full. They were bonding!

They'd reached his locker. As he twisted the combination, she considered the possibilities. Would he walk with her to her locker now? Maybe he'd ask her to have a Coke with him at the mall across the street. If not, maybe she could invite him back to her place. But what could she use for an excuse? They didn't have any other classes together—she couldn't pretend to need homework help.

Then she noticed he was frowning. In his hand, he held a piece of paper.

"What's that?"

"I'm not sure. I just found it on the floor of my locker." He showed it to her.

It was an announcement. Or maybe *invitation* was a better description.

SÉANCE.

That was the word in all capital letters at the top. Underneath, it read:

Make contact with those who have passed on. Connect with your loved ones. Ask questions, get answers.

There was an address, a date—today's date—and a time, 8 p.m. On the bottom, someone had scrawled, *Ken, are you one of us? Would you like to meet others who have your gift?*

There was no signature, no name. Amanda looked at Ken. All the color had drained from his face.

"Where did this come from?" she asked.

"I don't know."

"Someone must have slipped it through the locker slot," Amanda said. "Maybe it's a joke from someone in our class."

Ken shook his head. "I don't think so."

She had to agree with him. Their classmates didn't pull pranks.

"Does anyone else know about your gift?" she asked.

"No."

"You don't have any idea who could have put that in your locker?"

"No." He stuffed the note in his pocket. "I gotta go. See ya."

And to her disappointment, he slammed the locker door closed and strode down the hall.

CHAPTER FOUR

WHAT KEN HAD SAID to Amanda wasn't really true. He had a very good idea who could have left that note in his locker. Because there was someone outside of the gifted class who knew what he could do.

Outside the building, the note still in his hand, he paused by a trash can. A friend who lived in his neighborhood waved to him. "Hey, Preston, my brother's picking me up. Want a ride home?"

"No, thanks," Ken called back. "I'm not leaving yet. I've got a couple of things to do." He was about to toss the paper in the trash can, but instead he stuck the crumpled note in his pocket and took off.

Actually, he felt like thinking and he needed to be alone for that. He headed around to the back of the cafeteria, where there was a bench under a tree, and sat down. Much as he didn't enjoy reliving the past, he was going to have to let his mind wander back to those days after the accident.

41

He was allowed to go home three days after he regained consciousness. His parents came for him. Even though he had been issued crutches, hospital regulations insisted he leave in a wheelchair. His parents followed as a nurse wheeled him out into the parking lot.

"Happy to be going home, Ken?" the nurse chirped cheerfully.

"Yes," Ken replied. *What a stupid question*, he thought. Of course he was glad to be going back to his own bed, his mother's cooking . . . and maybe an end to those disturbing conversations with his dead friend.

It was just so—so strange, having Jack in his head. It didn't feel right. But what could he do? His best friend was dead. The least he could do was listen to him.

Grabbing his crutches from his dad, he got out of the wheelchair and hobbled into the car. As his parents got in, he noticed for the first time that they were very dressed up for a weekday afternoon. His mother wore heels and a black dress with a small strand of pearls at her neck. His father wore a dark suit with a white shirt and black tie.

"Where are you going?" he asked them.

His parents exchanged meaningful looks. "It's where we've been," his mother told him gently. "Jack's funeral was this morning."

"Oh."

"Later, we're going over to his house to pay a condolence call," she went on.

"I guess I should go, too," Ken said.

"If you like, you can come with us," his mother said.

"But we'll understand if you don't feel up to it," his father added.

He knew he should go. He'd known Jack's family for a long time. But all he could think about right now was the way they'd probably look at him. He was alive and their son was dead. Maybe they would even hold him responsible for the collision.

He could get out of it—he knew that. All he had to do was say he felt tired, or that his ribs hurt. And that was what he planned to do. Someday, maybe in a week or two, he would stop by and see them. Apologize. It was the least he could do.

His father helped him out of the car while his mother adjusted his crutches. He winced as he limped into the house, keenly aware of the dull ache in his chest from the broken ribs. Slowly, he managed to get down the hall and into his bedroom. His mother fussed over him, adjusting his pillow, bringing magazines, asking if he was hungry.

"I had your prescription filled, so tell me if you're in pain," she said.

At the same time, another voice spoke.

Hey, Ken. Can you talk?

His heart sank. But what could he say? "Sure."

He didn't realize he'd spoken out loud until his mother came closer. "Here are the pills, and I'll get you some water."

"I'm not in pain," Ken said.

His mother looked confused.

Ken? Are you there? I gotta ask you something.

"Wait a second."

Now his mother was concerned. "Ken, are you all right?"

"I'm fine, I'm fine," Ken said quickly. "I—I think I'm going to sleep awhile."

His mother gave him one more worried look and finally left the room.

Ken sat up and listened. Was Jack still there?

Yeah, I'm here.

That was when he realized he didn't have to speak out loud to communicate with Jack. He only had to direct his thoughts.

I've got a favor to ask you.

What?

It's about Lucy.

What about her?

I bought her this gift, from California. It's a bracelet made out of seashells. I was going to give it to her the day I got back, but we had a fight.

What about?

Stupid stuff. I kept talking about the cute girls on the beach in California, and she got jealous.

What do you want me to do?

Could you give her the bracelet? It's in the top drawer of my desk, in my bedroom. And . . . and tell her I'm sorry about the fight. She'll understand. Will you do that for me?

Yeah, okay. Hey, Jack . . .

What?

What's it like, where you are?

It's okay. I can't really describe it—you wouldn't understand. I'll check with you tomorrow and find out what Lucy said, okay?

Tomorrow? Ken thought in alarm. *I have to do it by tomorrow?*

But there was no response. Jack was gone. Ken sank back on his pillow and wished he could make some sense out of this. He'd always been a pretty down-to-earth guy. Sure, he enjoyed psycho-thriller movies as much as any of his friends did, but he'd never been really scared by them because he didn't believe in that spooky stuff.

He still didn't believe in it. So how could he explain hearing Jack's voice? Was he just imagining these conversations? Had his brain been damaged in the accident?

The doctor had said all the tests and scans were fine, but doctors could make mistakes.

Only he *felt* fine, too, except for the pain in his ribs and his ankle. His head didn't hurt at all. And he couldn't have been imagining Jack's voice. It was just too real.

So now what? He had to find the bracelet Jack had told him about. Deliver it to Lucy. And tell her Jack was sorry.

Would Lucy think he'd lost his mind? Possibly. He didn't really care, though. He'd never told Jack this, but Lucy wasn't one of his favorite people in the world. He'd always thought she was kind of shallow—one of those girls who thinks only about herself. The kind of girl who was accustomed to always getting what she wanted. Having seen her flirt with other guys at school, he'd wondered how much she really cared about Jack. But Jack liked her, so Ken had to be nice to her.

The truth of it was, he had to do this for Jack, whether he wanted to or not. He got out of bed and went to the door.

"Mom? When you and Dad go to the Farrells'—could you let me know? I'd like to go with you."

★ ★ ★

As Ken had expected, the scene at the Farrell house was pretty grim. There was a black wreath on the door. Jack's mother, her eyes red, hugged him, and Jack's father put an arm around him. Neither of them acted like Ken was responsible for Jack's death, and Ken was ashamed for even thinking they might.

There were other people at the house, too—Jack's friends from school and other adults who were neighbors and friends. A lot of people brought food, and the big dining room table was covered with cakes and pies. It could have been a party, except that there was no music, no laughing. And no one was having a good time.

Ken chatted quietly with a couple of friends, but all the time he was thinking about how and when he could get into Jack's bedroom. Should he come up with an excuse? He could say he wanted to get the tennis racket he'd loaned to Jack. But that would sound kind of cruel, like he was afraid he'd never get the racket back now that Jack was dead. Maybe he could say he wanted to borrow a book, but that didn't seem right either. Jack wasn't much of a reader.

It might be best just to sneak into the room. There were plenty of other people there—no one would notice if he went missing for a little while. And there was a bathroom right next to Jack's bedroom—he could say he was going there if anyone asked.

In the end, he didn't have to invent an excuse. Jack's

father took him aside.

"Ken, you were Jack's best friend, and we'd like you to have something to remember him by. When you have a chance, go into his room and choose something—anything. His jacket, maybe. Or the karate trophy. Whatever you want."

Ken nodded. "Thank you, Mr. Farrell."

On his crutches, he hobbled down the hall to Jack's room. Once inside, he closed the door and went over to Jack's desk. Just as Jack had told him, the seashell bracelet was in the top drawer. He shoved it into his pocket.

But what if Mr. Farrell wanted to see the souvenir he'd chosen? He looked around the room. There was a stack of old comic books on a shelf. He and Jack had been Spider-Man fanatics when they were little kids. He took an issue off the pile and left the room.

When he returned to the living room, he saw that some people had left and others had arrived. And among the new arrivals was Lucy. He stood back and watched her for a while.

He had to admit, for a pretty girl she looked pretty awful. Her normally pale face was even paler than usual, and there were dark shadows under her red eyes. Clearly, she'd been crying a lot and hadn't had much sleep. So maybe he'd been wrong about her feelings for Jack. She certainly looked grief-stricken, like someone who'd lost the love of her life, and his heart ached for her.

He adjusted his crutches and limped over to her.

"Hi, Lucy."

She managed a small, woebegone smile. "Hi, Ken. How are you feeling?"

"Okay. How are you?"

She shrugged. "Well, you know . . ."

"Yeah. I know. Look, Lucy, I need to talk to you. It's kind of personal." He glanced around. The room was getting crowded, and he didn't want anyone else hearing what he had to say. "Um, do you want to go outside for a minute? Get some air?"

She followed him through the kitchen and out the back door. Fortunately, there was no one else in the backyard.

But how to begin? How was he going to tell this unbelievable tale?

"I know how awful this must be for you," he said.

"Tell me about it," Lucy said. "You know, Ken, this was going to be the best year of my life. Jack was the coolest guy I ever went out with. I mean, he was cute, he was vice-captain of the soccer team . . . all my friends were jealous. I'd already bought a dress to wear for the eighth-grade dance . . ."

A tear trickled down her cheek. "I can't believe this

happened to me."

"You could still go to the dance," he said, and he immediately wanted to bite his tongue. What a lame thing to say.

She sighed. "With who?"

He figured she probably meant something like she wouldn't want to go with anyone but Jack.

"I still don't understand how he died," she murmured. "He just fell down." She looked up.

"You crashed into him, right?"

"Well, we sort of crashed into each other," Ken said.

"But you're not dead."

He bit his lower lip. "I'm really sorry, Lucy."

"Sorry you're not dead?"

"Well, no, but . . ."

"Sorry you didn't look where you were going?"

Ken felt sick. "Lucy, I don't think it was my fault. The coach, the doctor—everyone said it was an accident."

She shrugged. "Whatever."

"Jack doesn't blame me," he blurted out, needing to convince her he wasn't in the wrong.

"How do you know?" she asked sharply.

This wasn't how he'd wanted to bring it up. But he had to tell her sooner or later. "Because . . . because he told me."

Her eyebrows went up. "Before he died?"

"No. After."

She stared at him a moment. "I don't understand."

"Neither do I," Ken admitted. He took a deep breath. "Lucy, I know this is going to sound pretty bizarre, but . . . Jack's been talking to me."

Her eyes widened. "You mean—you've seen his ghost?"

"No, it's not like that. I hear his voice. In my head."

She blinked. "He—he contacted you from beyond the grave?"

Ken nodded. "He started talking to me while I was in the hospital. I don't understand it—maybe it's because we collided, but . . . he's able to talk to me. I know this sounds totally crazy . . ."

Lucy gazed at him thoughtfully. "Not really. Lots of people believe in stuff like that. My mother went to a medium once. Do you know what a medium is?"

"No."

"It's someone who's in contact with the spirit world. My mother said the medium put her in touch with her great-great-grandfather." She smiled. "There'd always been a rumor in the family that he'd buried some treasure during the Civil War. She wanted to know where it was."

"Did she find out?"

Lucy shook her head. "It turned out to be a legend. Too bad, huh?"

"That's . . . interesting," Ken said.

"What did Jack tell you?" she asked. "Did he say anything about me?"

"Yeah. He wanted me to give you this." He reached in his pocket and pulled out the bracelet. "He got it for you in California."

"Oh, wow!" Lucy exclaimed. "It's really cute." She put the bracelet on. "How does it look?"

"Fine," Ken said quickly. "And he wanted me to tell you he was sorry about that argument you guys had just after he came back from California."

"Okay." She admired the bracelet on her arm. "At least now I have something to remember him by. Thanks, Ken."

"You're welcome."

"And if you talk to Jack again, tell him . . . tell him I forgive him. About the fight."

"Okay, I will."

"I want to go and show off the bracelet to my friends," she said, and turned to go back to the house.

"Lucy, wait!"

She turned back. "What?"

"Um, listen, you can't tell anyone how I knew about the bracelet. How Jack's been talking to me. Everyone will think I'm nuts."

Lucy nodded. "You're probably right. I mean, people

just aren't very open-minded about this kind of thing. Don't worry, I'll say Jack mailed it to me from California and it just arrived today."

"Thanks a lot," Ken said fervently.

She smiled, cocked her head to one side, and gazed at him oddly, like she was scrutinizing him or judging him. Which wasn't surprising, Ken thought, considering what she'd just learned about him. Then, without saying anything else, she ran back into the house.

When Ken went back inside, he was grateful to find his parents ready to leave. He said his goodbyes to the Farrells, and once he was in the car he told his parents he was really tired so they wouldn't talk to him.

What a relief to have that over with! Now he could give Jack an honest report. He'd given Lucy the bracelet, apologized on Jack's behalf, and Lucy had seemed pleased with the gift. Maybe . . . maybe this would put an end to Jack's communication.

And then he felt terrible. Jack was *dead*. The least Ken could do for him was listen. Maybe he'd get used to it. He'd *have* to get used to it. He could never tell his best friend to stop talking to him.

He really was tired, he realized when he got home. Once he was in bed he considered taking a sleeping pill, but he figured he was so wiped out he'd fall asleep without one.

Ken?

Oh, no. Jack wasn't supposed to contact him till tomorrow.

I'm kind of tired right now, Jack.

What did you call me? My name isn't Jack.

Ken frowned.

Who is this?

I'm Arthur. Arthur Penfield. I'm dead. And I was wondering if you could get a message to my brother.

Ken sat up, his heart pounding furiously.

Wait a minute—you've got the wrong guy. I don't know anyone named Arthur Penfield.

No, we've never met. I died before you were born.

Then—why are you contacting me? Talk to one of your own friends!

None of my friends have your gift. You're one in a million, son. You're going to be hearing from a lot of us.

Suddenly, Ken didn't feel very well. What was this Arthur guy talking about? What gift?

"Leave me alone!"

He didn't realize he'd spoken out loud until his door opened.

"What's wrong, Ken?" his mother asked. "Darling, you're sweating! We shouldn't have let you come with us tonight. It was too soon for you to be out and about."

Worriedly, she put a hand on his forehead.

Oh, if only he could blame this on a fever! If only he could tell her what was happening. Yeah, right. He'd be back in a hospital before dawn. And possibly in a straitjacket.

"I'm not feeling so great, Mom," was all he could say. "Could I have one of those pills now?"

He wasn't actually in any pain. He was just hoping the pill might put him to sleep immediately. Because he didn't really want to hear from any more dead people tonight. Or ever again.

But he had a very, very bad feeling about this. He didn't think there was any kind of pill that was going to put an end to these strange communications.

CHAPTER FIVE

In the months that followed the accident and Jack's death, Ken didn't see much of Lucy. She was a year younger, in the eighth grade, so they didn't have any classes together. And fortunately, since Meadowbrook was a pretty big school, you didn't run into the same people every day in the hallways. If he did run into her and they made eye contact, they just mumbled vague greetings. She never asked him any more questions about Jack, and he suspected that she didn't think much about her late boyfriend.

But she was the only one, outside of his gifted classmates, who had been told about his "gift." And so, after getting his thoughts together, he got up from the bench and went in search of her.

He remembered that Lucy was a cheerleader, and he knew that the cheerleaders practiced almost every day after classes were finished, so he headed to the gym. When he got there, the cheerleaders had just started to gather.

He spotted Lucy outside the gym entrance, talking to Simon Dowell. Simon was on the soccer team, but Ken had never known him very well.

He ambled toward them. "Hi, guys."

"Yo, Preston," Simon muttered. He didn't look too thrilled to see Ken. But Lucy didn't seem to mind the interruption.

"Hi, Ken!"

He tried to sound casual. "Lucy, can I talk to you for a second?"

"Sure!"

Ken glanced at Simon. "Um, it's kind of personal." He hated saying that—he knew it made him sound secretive and mysterious—but he couldn't talk about Jack in front of Simon.

Lucy looked surprised, and Simon was clearly annoyed. Ken realized Simon must have been flirting with Lucy, and he groaned inwardly.

Now Simon would think Ken was trying to make a play for her.

"It's about a class," he added quickly, which was another stupid thing to say since he had no classes with Lucy. But Lucy actually smiled.

"Excuse me, Simon," she said, and moved away. Ken followed her to a relatively private corner of the gym.

Lucy smiled prettily. "What's up, Ken?"

Ken took the crumpled paper from his pocket and unfolded it. "I was wondering if you know anything about this."

Lucy took the paper. "Séance," she read out loud.

"Shh!" Ken hissed. He glanced around nervously. "Just read it to yourself, okay?"

She did. From the way her brow furrowed as she read, Ken knew this was the first time she'd seen the announcement.

"I don't get it," she said. "Why are you showing me this?"

"Well, you're the only one I ever told about Jack talking to me. So I thought, maybe, well . . . you might have put this in my locker. Because you thought I'd be interested."

She looked at him blankly for a second, and then her expression cleared. "Oh, right. You told me Jack talked to you after he died, didn't you?"

"He told me to give you the bracelet, remember?"

"I remember. Do you still talk to Jack?"

"Once in a while."

"How's he doing?"

"He's all right. I mean, considering the fact that he's dead."

Lucy nodded. "It's funny—back when you first told me

about that, I thought you'd just imagined Jack talking to you. I mean, you'd had a concussion, right?"

"Yeah."

"But it's for real," she said thoughtfully. "What do you and Jack talk about?"

He was beginning to feel even more uncomfortable. "Stuff. So, you didn't give me this announcement about the séance?"

She shook her head. "Sounds cool, though. Can I come?"

"Um, I don't even know if I'm going." He shoved the paper back in his pocket. "See ya, Lucy."

"Wait!" Lucy called.

"What?"

"Tell Jack I said hi, okay?"

"Yeah, sure."

Ken hurried off, feeling frustrated. So Lucy hadn't slipped this note in his locker. Then who? At home in his room, he put the crumpled paper on his desk and smoothed it out.

SÉANCE.

Could someone from his gifted class have put it in his locker? But why wouldn't that person just tell him?

Ken, are you one of us? Would you like to meet others who have your gift?

Madame was always saying there were other people who knew about them. Bad people. But maybe they weren't *all* bad. And maybe, just maybe, there really were other people out there who had this ability to communicate with the dead.

He had to wonder—did it bother them as much as it bothered him? How did they deal with it? Could they offer any advice on how to control it? He was pretty sure by now that he'd never be able to get rid of it, but maybe there was a way to turn it on and off.

He wouldn't have any problem getting out of the house tonight. It was a Friday, and it wasn't unusual for him to go out, joining some friends who went to the bowling alley practically every Friday night. He glanced at the address on the announcement. This place wasn't far from the bowling alley. He wouldn't even have to lie to his parents, really— he could stop by the alley on his way back from the séance.

His cell phone rang. "Hello?"

"Hi, Ken, this is Amanda."

For reasons of safety, in case they got into trouble, Madame had insisted that all members of the gifted class exchange phone numbers. But he'd never had a call from Amanda before.

"Ken, are you there?"

"Oh sure. I'm sorry, I guess I was daydreaming."

"The voices?" Amanda asked sympathetically.

"You know how it is," he mumbled. She really did, too, because of that brief period when she'd taken over his body. He still felt a little embarrassed when he thought about it.

"What's up?"

"I was just wondering . . . are you going to that séance tonight?"

"I'm kind of thinking about it," Ken admitted.

"Would you like some company?"

He was surprised. "You?"

"Yes," she replied. "And you'd be doing me a favor. I'm a little nervous about going into the hospital on Sunday. I'm trying to keep busy so I won't think about it."

Ken considered it. He'd actually been feeling a little warmer toward Amanda lately. She seemed less snobby than she used to be, more interesting. And earlier today, when they'd talked about their gifts, he almost felt like they understood each other.

Hey man, what's going on?

It was Jack. *Hang on a sec*, Ken told him, and spoke into the phone.

"Okay. I'll come to your house and pick you up at 7:30."

After he hung up, he wondered if maybe he should have told her to meet him somewhere. Picking her up at her house made this seem almost like a date.

You've got a date? Who with?

He'd forgotten Jack was there.

Amanda Beeson, he replied. *Only it's not really a date. We're just going to the same place.*

But I heard you—you said you'd pick her up at home. That makes it a date.

Ken grinned.

Well, maybe that's not so terrible . . .

I had a feeling you guys would get together eventually. Where are ya going?

To a séance. Where people try to make contact with the dead.

He could hear Jack chortle. *You're kidding. You believe in that garbage?*

I just thought it might be interesting.

Yeah, okay. Hey, you seen Lucy lately?

Yes, today. In the gym.

Even from beyond the grave, he could hear the wistfulness in Jack's tone.

Is she hanging out with anyone?

I'm not sure. I think maybe Simon Dowell is into her.

Simon Dowell? That scumbag?

Why do you call him a scumbag?

Don't you know his reputation? I used to think he was making up the stories he used to tell about all the girls he's been with, but maybe it's true. Anyway, I don't want him messing around with

Lucy—he's bad news.

There's not much you can do about it, Ken pointed out.

Yeah, I know. But you could.

Ken's heart sank. *What do you mean?*

Could you keep an eye on her? Distract her?

And how am I supposed to do that? Jack, you don't want me to go out with Lucy?

No, no, nothing like that. Be kind of a big brother to her. Just—just hang out with her a little. Let her know what a jerk Dowell is. C'mon, Ken, do this for me. Please?

Okay, okay.

And don't let her know I put you up to this! She'll think I'm jealous and it'll just make her more conceited.

Yeah, yeah, whatever. Listen, I've got to go—we'll talk later.

Jack "hung up," or whatever it was he did to cut the communication. Ken flopped down in a chair. Now what? Would he really have to hang out with Lucy? He supposed it wouldn't be the end of the world, to get together with her once or twice and warn her off Simon Dowell. But what if Amanda saw him with Lucy?

He had to smile. Amanda wouldn't care, would she? It wasn't like they had a relationship.

Not yet.

The address for the séance turned out to be an apartment building. Examining the announcement again, Ken saw that there was a number next to the address—46.

"I guess this must be the apartment number," he told Amanda.

Amanda was looking at the list of names next to buttons outside the front entrance. "There's no name next to forty-six."

Ken pressed the button. He expected to hear a voice asking him to identify himself. Instead, a buzzer indicated that the door had been unlocked.

Silently, they went inside. To the left of the entranceway, there was an elevator. Inside, buttons were labelled 1 through 5. Ken pressed 4.

The elevator doors opened onto a hallway. They didn't have to look at the numbers on the doors to find number 46—the door to it opened immediately.

The figure inside spoke sweetly. "Welcome. You may enter."

Ken felt Amanda take his hand, and he couldn't blame her. The woman looked very unusual. She wore a long, flowing robe, dark green with little golden sparkly things all over it. Over her head was some kind of veil—layers of silky stuff—and it completely covered her face. Tiny slits gave her the ability to see Ken and Amanda, but they couldn't make out her face at all.

They went inside the apartment. The interior wasn't as spooky as its inhabitant. There was a living room, with a sofa and a couple of armchairs. Just off the living room was the dining area with a round table, but it wasn't being used for dining at the moment. Three people were sitting there—two women and a boy. Ken didn't recognize any of them.

"Join us," the veiled woman said as she went to the table. There were three empty chairs. Ken took the seat next to the boy, and Amanda sat beside one of the women. Then the veiled woman sat down.

"I am Cassandra," she said. "I am your medium. You will talk to me, and I will attempt to reach the spirits you wish to contact. But I must warn you, your first attempt at contact may not be successful. It takes effort and practice to communicate with the spirit world. You must be determined and you must be patient. Much depends on the need and willingness of your loved one in the spirit world to speak to you. They may need to be persuaded, and I will try to persuade them. But there are no guarantees."

Amanda spoke. "Will we get our money back if we can't make contact?"

The woman turned toward her. "Have I asked you for any money? I do not charge for my work. That would be wrong. I have a gift, and it is my responsibility and obligation to share this gift freely."

That was interesting, Ken thought. So this séance thing wasn't a scam. Maybe this medium, Cassandra, could actually do what he could do. The only difference was that she probably had more control of her gift. And she seemed to be pleased to have it.

"Before we begin attempting contact," she continued, "we need to establish a connection among ourselves. Each of you will introduce yourself and explain what you hope to accomplish here." She turned to Amanda. "You may begin. What is your name?"

"I'm Amanda." She hesitated. "Do I have to give my last name, too?"

"No, that won't be necessary—not if you don't want to," the medium said smoothly. "We respect each other's privacy here. Why have you come to the séance, Amanda? What do you hope to accomplish?"

Ken looked at his classmate worriedly. Had she guessed she would have to say something? What would happen if she told them she just came to keep him company? Would she be thrown out?

But Amanda was cool. "I've been thinking about my great-grandmother lately. I'd like to talk to her."

"For any particular reason?" the medium asked.

"Well, I never knew her—she died before I was born—and I just want to say hi."

Ken gave his name. "Um, there's no one in particular I'm trying to reach. I was just wondering if any of my ancestors wanted to contact me."

The medium appeared to accept that. "All right." She turned to the woman who was sitting next to Amanda. "And you are . . . ?"

"Margaret." She spoke barely above a whisper. "I want to talk to my mother." There was a catch in her voice.

Ken looked at her. She wasn't very old—just in her twenties, he'd guess. Which meant her mother must have died young. She certainly looked depressed. She had long, limp brown hair, with bangs that hung over the thick brown-framed glasses that covered her eyes. She was pasty-pale.

The medium must have picked up on the sadness in her tone. She responded gently.

"Did you lose your mother recently, Margaret?"

"Yes. She died only two weeks ago. I—I miss her so much!"

"I understand," the medium said. "I hope we'll be able to reach her. Next?"

The woman sitting by Margaret looked completely different. First of all, she didn't seem miserable at all. Her heavily made-up green eyes sparkled, and her face was framed by carefully styled silver-gray curls. Long dangly hoops hung from her ears, and she wore an orange shawl over a purple dress.

"I'm Dahlia," she said brightly. "At least, that's my name *now*. I believe this is my fourth life, but it may be my fifth. In my previous reincarnations I've been called Maria, Constance, Genevieve—"

The medium interrupted her. "Yes, well, we'll call you by your current name. Why are you here, Dahlia?"

"Well, my memory isn't what it used to be," the woman said. "And I don't want to forget all the friends I've made in my other lives. I'd like to make contact with them and reminisce about old times."

"But how do you know they're in the spirit world?" the medium asked. "Perhaps, like you, they've been reincarnated, too."

Dahlia shook her head. "No, very few people are like me. Oh, I'm not the only person in the world who has lived many times, but there aren't many of us who have been regularly reincarnated. And if any of my old friends were alive in another shape or form, I'd know it. I'd *feel* it."

Ken wished he could see the medium's expression. This woman sounded like a real nut. He glanced at Amanda, and then quickly looked away. He had to avoid making eye contact with her or they'd both start laughing out loud.

Cassandra turned to the boy sitting next to Ken. "Would you like to introduce yourself?"

"I'm Stevie Fisher." The boy sounded nervous.

He was thin and fair-haired and looked a couple of years younger than Ken.

"Who would you like to contact, Stevie?"

"My dad."

"When did your father die?" the medium asked.

"A couple of months ago. It was a car accident."

"And is there a particular reason you want to contact him?"

Stevie nodded. "I have to ask him something."

"Yes?" the medium prompted him.

The boy brushed a lock of hair out of his eyes. "Well, a few days before my father had his accident, I was in a store with him. And my dad bought a lottery ticket. I don't know why—he didn't usually buy lottery tickets. Maybe he just felt lucky . . ." His voice trailed off.

"Go on," the veiled woman said.

Stevie sighed. "The day the winning numbers were announced, he was at work. He called home, all excited, and told my mother he'd won! And the jackpot was two million dollars!"

Ken gasped. He knew about the weekly lottery, of

course, but he'd never bought a ticket. And he'd never known or met anyone who had actually won.

Stevie continued. "But . . . he was in an accident on the way home. He died right away. And we don't know where the ticket is."

"Maybe it was in his pocket," Ken suggested.

"No, we thought of that. But the police only found his wallet."

"Maybe someone else found the ticket and took it," Dahlia said.

Again Stevie shook his head. "No one ever claimed the prize. We think the ticket is somewhere in the house, but we've searched everywhere and we can't find it."

"Oh, well," Dahlia said. "Who needs two million dollars anyway?"

"We do," Stevie said simply. "Well, we don't need *that* much, but we need money. See, my father didn't have any life insurance. Or any savings. I've got two little sisters, and one of them isn't even school age, so my mother has to stay at home and take care of her. When I get home I watch her, and Mom goes to clean other people's houses. But she doesn't make much money, and we can't pay the rent on our house. The landlord says we have one more month, and then he's throwing us out."

It was a long speech for a young boy, and it couldn't

have been an easy one for him to make. For a moment, everyone was silent.

Finally, the medium spoke. "You want to ask your father where he put the lottery ticket."

Stevie nodded. "I have to help my family. I don't want us to end up homeless."

Ken was overcome. What a burden for a kid to carry on his shoulders.

"Then we need to reach your father," Cassandra said. "And we have to make contact within a month. I suggest we get started." She gazed around the table.

"Please join hands and close your eyes. The séance begins."

Chapter Six

E VERYONE'S EYES WERE closed—except Amanda's. She didn't want to miss a thing.

Ken had obeyed the medium's instructions, which was fortunate for Amanda, because he wouldn't be able to see how she was staring at him. He really was so good-looking. And even though he didn't play soccer anymore, he still looked like an athlete. She'd been after him for ages, and now they could be on the verge of a real relationship! A happy little thrill rushed through her. Even the prospect of a hospital stay and an operation didn't upset her as much now.

The medium spoke.

"We have come together to seek advice from those who have left us behind," she intoned.

Amanda envisioned herself sitting up in bed in the hospital wearing her new lacy light blue nightgown, her hair pulled back with a matching headband, smiling as Ken walked into her room. Bearing armfuls of flowers, of course.

Maybe a box of candy. She didn't mind giving up her tonsils at all if it meant getting a relationship with Ken started.

As for this séance thing, she wasn't sure what she thought about it. The medium looked spooky, but she spoke nicely to everyone. That Dahlia woman, with her crazy clothes and makeup, was seriously goofy. Margaret . . . she was just plain sad. And not just because her mother had recently died. She looked terrible, in a bulky gray sweater that was too big for her. It hung over a long, wrinkled, faded black skirt. You couldn't even tell what kind of figure she had. And that hair—had the woman ever been to a salon? Okay, maybe not lately, because she was mourning her mother . . . but that hair looked like it had never been touched by professional hands. And those glasses she wore were absolutely gross. Nobody wore tortoiseshell frames anymore.

The medium was still talking. "We know there is a world beyond our own, a world of mystical mystery and energy that we can never understand. And in this spirit world, there is great wisdom."

Amanda tuned out again. What about that kid, Stevie? She had serious doubts about him. He might look young and innocent, but that story of his was just too crazy to be true.

Cassandra continued, in a soft monotone. "We seek you,

oh spirits who dwell beyond our comprehension. We bid you come closer to accept our pleas."

Yeah, whatever, Amanda thought. She was still more interested in scoping out Stevie. What was his deal? Why would he make up a story like that? She couldn't think of a reason. Unless, maybe, he was hoping someone somewhere had lost a winning lottery ticket, and some dead person would tell Cassandra where it was. It seemed like a far-fetched scheme, though.

Cassandra's voice rose. "I am being contacted! A spirit from the world beyond wishes to connect with one of our group."

Dahlia let out a little squeal. "Is he on a horse?"

"No . . . and it's not a 'he.' It's a female spirit."

Amanda caught the flash of disappointment on Stevie's face.

"Maybe it's my former mother-in-law," Dahlia mused. "Is she wearing a hoop skirt? It was during the Civil War. I was a Yankee from up North married to a Southern boy, and his mother just hated me. It would be just like her to start haunting me now."

"No," the medium said, and her voice was a little sharper this time. "It's not your mother-in-law. Please, I must have quiet. We could frighten her away. She will not come closer and identify herself unless we remain silent."

Silence reigned at the table. Amanda wondered if Cassandra was really making contact with a dead person. She wished she knew what Ken was thinking. She'd have to wait till they left before she found out if he believed the medium was for real or not.

"She is coming closer!" the medium exclaimed softly. "She is speaking to me . . ." She gasped. "It's your mother, Margaret."

"Mama?" the woman murmured.

"Yes, yes, she is here, Margaret. What would you like to tell her?"

"I miss you, Mama . . . Oh, why did you leave me?"

Amanda could hear the pain in her voice. She couldn't imagine how she'd feel if her own mother died.

Cassandra spoke. "She says it was not her choice to leave you, Margaret."

"You were the only person I could trust, the only person I loved." Now Margaret was weeping. "I can't bear this! I want to be with you."

Amanda drew in her breath. This was so hard to hear. The poor woman—she was so sad!

"Your mother says not to think like that. You mustn't die—this is not your time. You must live and keep her memory alive."

"But I'm all alone," Margaret said, weeping. "You were

the only person who cared about me, the only one who loved me. I'm so lonely now ..."

There was a lump in Amanda's throat, and for a moment she thought she was going to burst into tears herself. And she wasn't even thinking about how badly dressed Margaret was. This woman had absolutely nothing going for her. She was suffering, she was utterly despondent. Her words, her tears—they'd brought a cloud of sadness into the room and it was descending on Amanda ... Wait—she recognized this feeling. She'd had it before.

Ohmigod, ohmigod, oh no, oh no, this can't be happening, not here, not now ... She closed her eyes and concentrated fiercely. *I don't care about Margaret, she means nothing to me, I feel nothing for her* ...

But it was no use. She could feel it happening. And when she opened her eyes, she could feel bangs tickling her forehead and she was looking through thick tortoiseshell frames. She was looking through someone else's eyes. Margaret's eyes.

Nobody else had noticed. Their eyes were still closed, but it wouldn't have mattered if they'd been watching her. This had happened before and no one had been aware, except her.

Actually, there *was* one other person whose eyes were open. The person who looked like Amanda. Who wasn't even really a person, just some sort of automatic fake Amanda, programmed to act like her. Flesh and blood, but more like a robot than a human being.

"Your mother has to go now, Margaret," the medium said. "But she'll come back another time to talk to you again. Do you have anything to say before she leaves?"

There was a silence. It took Amanda a few seconds before she realized *she* had to respond for Margaret.

"Uh . . . bye."

"She is gone," Cassandra said. "And I'm afraid there are no other spirits waiting to speak with us tonight. But do not despair. This is just the beginning. The spirits have been called, and they will respond. We will meet again on Monday evening."

Amanda-Margaret rose quickly. She had to let Ken know what had happened to her. But that woman Dahlia clamped a hand on her arm.

"You poor dear, I feel so sorry for you. Why don't we go out and have a nice cocktail together?"

"Sorry, no—I can't," Amanda said, pulling free with some effort. She turned—and saw Ken with Other-Amanda, walking out the door. She took off after them and ran out of the apartment . . . only to see the elevator doors closing behind them. Frantically, she looked for the stairs. She flew down the four flights, but when she arrived at the hallway she was greeted by an open elevator, with no one inside.

She went outside, with absolutely no idea where she was going. Her heart—Margaret's heart—was pounding furiously, and she took deep breaths to keep her rising panic under control. She heard voices behind her and hurried around to the side of the apartment building, where no one would see her. She had to collect her thoughts, figure out what she was going to do.

She found a bench and sat down. That was when she realized that Margaret's purse was still slung across her chest. She opened it and found a wallet. Inside the wallet there was a driver's license. In the dark the photo wasn't clear, but she could make out a name—Margaret Robinson—and an address. There were keys in the bag, too. So Margaret probably came here in a car . . . but there were more than a dozen cars parked along the curbs of this street. How would she know which one was Margaret's?

And what did it matter even if she could identify Margaret's car? Amanda didn't know how to drive.

She explored the pockets in the wallet. Well, that was a relief—there had to be at least fifty dollars in it. She had an address, keys, and money for a taxi. So at least she could get home.

She walked down to the first major street and flagged

down a taxi. Giving the driver the address she'd found, she leaned back in the seat and considered her situation. So, now she had become a depressed and badly dressed woman living a sad and lonely life. Why couldn't she snatch the body of someone *cool*?

At least Margaret didn't live in a dump. The taxi pulled up in front of a modern building in a decent part of town. Amanda paid the driver and got out. One of the keys unlocked the front door, and she found the name Robinson on one of the mailboxes in the hall. Noting the apartment number, she took the elevator up to the third floor.

In the séance, Margaret had talked about being so alone. That meant she probably didn't have roommates. That was good—Amanda wouldn't have to start communicating like Margaret right away. Another key opened the apartment door. Feeling along the wall, she located a light switch and flicked it.

She was pleasantly surprised by what she saw. She'd imagined Margaret living in a place that looked as depressing as she did. But this apartment was very nice. It wasn't a grand, fancy place, but it was modern, well furnished, and even trendy. There were hanging plants, a colorful rug on the floor, pictures on the walls. A big framed poster from a rock concert hung over the sofa. Funny—Margaret hadn't seemed like the kind of person who went to rock concerts. There was a framed photograph on an end table showing five good-looking people in their twenties on what looked like a tropical beach. Friends of Margaret's? But then why was she so lonely?

Amanda moved into what she thought would be a bedroom. She was right, and once again, it was a stylish room. There was a bright blue-and-white duvet on the big four-poster bed, big fluffy pillows, and a large white dressing table with a matching chest of drawers. A huge full-length mirror was on the wall, and there was a big walk-in closet. That got Amanda's full attention. She went inside, switched on the light, and gasped. Margaret had clothes, and lots of them. On a wall were shelves covered with shoes. Checking things out, Amanda could see that the clothes and shoes weren't the best brands. Most were from discount stores that sold cheaper versions of the hot new looks, but the things she found were a lot better looking than the awful baggy sweater and wrinkled skirt she had on now.

Why was Margaret wearing this? Just because she was in mourning for her mother? It seemed to Amanda that you didn't have to dress like an old bag lady just to show you were sad about your mother's death.

She wandered over to the mirror and examined herself.

Taking off the glasses, she found her reflection disturbing. Not just because Margaret was so drab—it was something else. That pasty skin—it didn't look natural. She rubbed Margaret's cheek, and then looked at her hand. It was stained with white powdery stuff. Peering closer at her reflection, she saw a spot of normal-looking skin on her cheek.

Hurrying into the bathroom, she took a washcloth and scrubbed her face. More powder came off, and more real skin was visible. It wasn't just ordinary skin either. Margaret had a nice golden tan! Why had she covered it? Maybe she thought it would look wrong to have a tan so soon after her mother's death.

It wasn't just puzzlement that made Amanda scratch her head. It had been itching for a while now, and after scratching harder, she realized why. Margaret was wearing a wig.

This was getting weirder and weirder. When Amanda took the wig off, Margaret's own hair turned out to be a much nicer shade of light brown with some blond streaks—the kind that must have been put in by a good hairdresser. The hair had been flattened down by the wig, but once Amanda poked at it with a comb for a while, she could see that Margaret had a cute layered bob. And when she took off the baggy sweater and skirt, she discovered that Margaret had a good figure, too.

Rummaging in Margaret's chest of drawers, she found skinny jeans and a tight-fitting top. A box on top of the dressing table contained lots of makeup, all good brands. She applied eyeliner, mascara, a little blush, and a rose-pink lipstick. Then she stepped back from the mirror and examined herself again.

Margaret was cute! If she'd looked like this at the séance Amanda would never have felt so sorry for her, not even with her sad story. Well, okay, she might have felt a little sorry for her because her mother had died, but not so much that she'd do a body snatch.

She went back into the living room and looked at the photo on the end table again. Now she recognized Margaret as one of the attractive young people on the beach. That was probably where she'd gotten her tan. She took the wallet out of Margaret's bag and examined the driver's license again. She could see the photo clearly now, and Margaret looked pretty much like Amanda had just made her look. So Amanda hadn't given her a makeover—this was how Margaret normally dressed. Exploring further, she found a couple of credit cards in the wallet, too.

It dawned on her that it might not be so awful being Margaret Robinson for a little while. She wouldn't mind living in this apartment. And she was 25 years old! She could go to clubs and hang out in places that would never let a thirteen-year-old in.

And there was something else—if she remained in this body up to Monday, Other-Amanda would have the operation in her place! Yes, there was a lot about this situation that could work to her advantage.

A phone rang. It sounded like a cell phone, so she dived back into Margaret's purse.

"Hello?"

"Hi, Margie, it's me." The voice was a woman's.

Amanda tried to sound casual. "Oh, hi. How are you?"

"Fine. Well, burning up, actually. It's ninety-nine degrees here, and our air conditioner's broken."

Amanda didn't know what the temperature was outside, but she was very sure it wasn't anywhere near 99 degrees. It had been cool when she left the séance.

"Where are you?" she asked.

The woman sounded amused. "Where do you think I am? Miami, of course. You'll be coming down to visit next month, won't you?"

"Um, I guess. I'll try."

"You *must* come," the woman said. "It's been too long. We'll send you money for a flight. Daddy and I want to see you. Wait, he wants to say hello."

A man spoke. "Margie, listen to your mother. We'll expect you in December."

"Okay. I have to go now. Bye."

"Here, say goodbye to your mother."

"Bye, Margie!" the woman trilled.

Amanda swallowed. "Bye . . . Mom."

They were disconnected. Amanda just stood there for a minute, still holding the phone. Daddy. *Mom.*

What was going on here?

Chapter Seven

*S*O HOW DID IT GO *with Amanda?*

Ken yawned. It was Saturday morning, he was still in bed, and for once he didn't mind having a chat with his old friend.

I don't know. She was sort of weird.

How do you mean, weird?

Well, like, at first things were really good. I mean, we were kind of connecting, you know? We talked a lot on the way there. And during the séance I couldn't even look at her because I was afraid we'd start laughing. I thought things were going pretty well for us.

Cool.

But then things changed. After the séance, coming home, she barely spoke to me. I asked her if she wanted to get something to eat, but she said she wasn't hungry. So I took her home. And she didn't invite me to come in.

Did you kiss her?

I didn't even get a chance. The second we arrived at her

place, she went inside and closed the door. She didn't even say goodbye!

That's pretty weird. Maybe she's just not into you. Hey, what are you doing today?

I don't know. I haven't thought about it.

Why don't you go to the pool?

The indoor pool at the community center? Nah, it's too crowded on Saturdays.

Oh, c'mon, you could use a good swim. Work out your frustrations over Amanda. And you'd be doing me a favor.

How's that?

Lucy goes to the pool every Saturday. It'll give you a chance to talk to her. Find out what's going on between her and Dowell.

Ken sighed. Well, if he was going to help Jack he'd have to talk to Lucy sooner or later, and he might as well get it over with. The pool was as good a place as any.

When he arrived, he saw that the pool wasn't as crowded as he'd expected. He didn't see Lucy around so he decided to make the most of it. He dived in.

The thing he liked best about swimming was that he could put his mind on automatic pilot and let his thoughts wander. And his thoughts went back to Amanda. He hoped she didn't go to the pool on Saturdays. Nah, the public swimming pool was probably beneath her.

She'd really been a major disappointment, he thought as he swam his laps. He'd been feeling positive about her at the séance, and when the séance was over he'd looked forward to discussing what they'd just observed and comparing their reactions.

But Amanda had been totally uninterested in having any kind of conversation. When he tried to talk to her, she acted like the whole thing had been boring. She just kept shrugging her shoulders and saying, "Whatever." He'd asked her if she was worrying about her operation, and all she said was that she hoped she could get a manicure at the hospital! She was like a different person from the one he'd gone to the séance with. Maybe Jack was right, and she just wasn't into him. Maybe she'd decided his "gift" really did make him a freak.

When he emerged from the pool, he saw that Lucy had arrived. She was setting down her bag beside a table and chairs, and she was alone.

He ambled over to her.

"Hi."

She looked up. "Oh, hi, Ken. How's Jack?"

"Fine," he murmured, hoping no one he knew could overhear their conversation.

She pulled out a chair for herself and one for Ken. "Sit down."

He did.

"I was just wondering, what's it like, talking to a dead person?"

Ken couldn't meet her eyes. "It's hard to describe."

"Did you contact more dead people at the séance?" she asked.

"Some people did. Not me."

"Do you ever talk to dead people besides Jack? Anyone famous?"

"No, nobody famous. Listen, Lucy, I really don't like talking about this, okay?"

She nodded. "I can understand that. Because most people aren't as open-minded as I am. They'd think you were nuts."

He couldn't argue with that. Just then, Lucy's purse started to beep.

"Ooh, I've got a text message," she said. She fumbled in her bag and pulled out her phone. She punched some buttons and looked at the screen. "Yea!" she exclaimed.

"Good news?" Ken inquired politely.

"Simon Dowell wants to know if I'll go to the basketball game with him on Tuesday evening."

"Oh." He scratched his head. "Are you going to go?"

"Sure. Why not?"

"Um, well . . . you know, Simon has a reputation. I've

heard he's kind of a player, if you know what I mean. Do you really like him?"

Lucy shrugged. "He's okay. But if you don't think I should go out with him, I won't."

He wished he could tell her it was *Jack* who was concerned, not him. "Well, I can't tell you what to do. I just wanted to warn you."

"Thank you, Ken. Listen . . . what are you doing later?"

"Later?"

"Mm. Like, tonight."

"Tonight?" he repeated stupidly.

"I thought maybe you'd like to come over to my place." She lowered her eyes demurely. "My parents are going out."

Ken swallowed. "Uh, thanks, but, no, um, I have to do something. See ya, Lucy." He jumped up and hurried to the boys' locker room. Once he was safe in all-male territory, he leaned against the wall and let out the breath he'd been holding. *Oh, great.* She thought he was interested in her— and not in a big brother way. What had Jack got him into? Man, if his best friend wasn't already dead, Ken would have killed him.

Maybe Jack heard his thoughts, because he didn't try to contact Ken the rest of the weekend, and Ken could think about more important subjects. Like the next séance on Monday.

He'd decided he was definitely going back. That Cassandra, the medium—Ken didn't have any experience with mediums, but she seemed like the real thing. Her voice, when she related the messages from Margaret's mother, sounded sincere to him. Like she was really listening to another voice, and like she really cared.

That poor Margaret! He hoped the medium would be able to help her. Maybe if she knew her mother was okay, in heaven or whatever, she'd feel better and be able to get on with her life. The older woman, Dahlia—she seemed a little nuts, but it was possible she actually had experienced other lives. Lots of intelligent people believed in reincarnation.

But the one who had really touched him was Stevie. The boy really cared about his family, and he was desperate to help them.

Ken was dying to talk about this, to share the experience. But he couldn't tell his friends—they'd just laugh. And how could he explain his own interest without revealing his gift? Lucy knew about it, but he was afraid to talk to her about anything. She'd only think he was coming on to her. So for once he was really looking forward to the gifted class. His classmates were the only people he could tell.

He arrived early at class that Monday. Emily was the only other student already there.

"I bought a get-well card for Amanda," she told Ken. "Will you sign it?"

Ken grimaced. Of course he'd have to sign it—it would be childish and mean to refuse. And it wasn't as if he wanted her to die, or suffer terribly. But what would he write?

Emily had already contributed her message. "Hi, Amanda, we miss you!!! Get well fast!!! Love, Emily."

After thinking a moment, he scrawled, "I hope you feel better soon. Best wishes, Ken Preston."

It was the kind of thing you'd write on a card that was going to someone you barely knew. But that was how he felt about her now.

He sat at his desk and waited impatiently for the others to arrive. Emily made each of them sign the card, and when Madame arrived she had to sign it, too.

As soon as the bell rang, his hand flew up. So did Tracey's. Madame called on her first.

"Madame, could we take up a collection to send Amanda some flowers?"

"That's a nice idea, Tracey," Madame said.

Charles didn't think so. "Her family's rich. They can afford to buy her plenty of flowers."

Madame frowned. "That's not the point, Charles. We want Amanda to know we're thinking about her."

Martin raised his hand. "*I'm* not thinking about her."

Jenna turned to him. "Just fake it, Martin. It's the right thing to do."

"I think she likes roses," Tracey said. "Yellow ones would be nice."

"Roses are really expensive," Emily said. "I don't know if we'll be able to collect that much money. Are tulips in season now?"

Ken slumped in his seat. Personally, he felt like agreeing with Charles and Martin. But mainly he wanted this discussion of flowers to end so he could bring up his news.

Finally the money was collected and Emily said she'd go to the florist and see what kind of flowers they could buy. The second she finished speaking, Ken put his hand up, and Madame nodded to him.

"There's something I want to tell the class about," he said. "Last Friday night I went to a séance."

"What's a séance?" Martin asked.

Madame answered for Ken. "It's a ritual where people try to contact friends and family who have passed on." She frowned. "What were you doing there, Ken?"

"I just thought it would be interesting," he said. "To meet people who do what I do."

Now Madame looked seriously concerned. "Did you participate in the séance, Ken? Did you let people know about your gift?"

"No, no, nothing like that," he assured her. "I was just listening. Anyway, there was this kid—"

He was interrupted before he could get any further. "Are you nuts?" Jenna asked. "Those things are scams."

"You don't know if that's true," he declared. "Hey, if *I* can talk to the dead, there must be other people who can do it."

But Madame was shaking her head. "That's not necessarily true, Ken. Your gift may be unique."

"I don't think so," Ken argued. "This medium, Cassandra, she wants to help people. She doesn't even charge money for coming to the séance."

Madame didn't look convinced. "I'm sorry, Ken, but I don't think it's a good idea for you to attend meetings like that. You'll be urged to join in. You may feel compelled to share your gift."

Ken scowled. "I can control myself, Madame."

"That's not true," Jenna interjected. "You're always saying how you can't control your gift."

Ken glared at her. "I meant, I know how to keep my mouth shut."

"I'm sure you do," Madame said smoothly. "But Ken, you'll encounter temptations. Perhaps a participant in the séance will be desperate to contact a deceased loved one and you'll actually receive a message from that person who's passed on. You'll want to relay the message."

She had a point, and Ken found it extremely annoying. It was as if she didn't trust him to behave properly. And his classmates weren't sympathetic either.

"Do you understand what we're saying, Ken?" Madame asked.

He shrugged. "Whatever."

But that evening he told his parents he was going to the library. Instead he went back to Cassandra's apartment.

He got there early, but he wasn't the first to arrive. Dahlia was already there, having an intense conversation with Cassandra.

"I knew Cleopatra very well, you see. I was one of her handmaidens. And I told her over and over again, 'Cleo, Mark Antony is worth a dozen Caesars.' But would she ever listen to me? That woman had a mind of her own. She could be so stubborn."

He really didn't want to get caught up in this conversation, and he was relieved when Stevie arrived next.

"Hey, how's it going?" he asked the younger boy.

Stevie didn't look any more cheerful than he'd looked at the last séance.

"Okay, I guess," he said. "Mom took Dad's old clothes to a secondhand shop and sold them. We didn't get much, though." He smiled sadly. "It's not like he wore designer clothes."

Ken nodded sympathetically.

Stevie continued. "I've been trying to get a job delivering newspapers, but you have to be twelve and I'm only eleven." He looked at Ken hopefully. "Do you know anyone who would hire me?

I'm very mature for my age. I could run errands, mow lawns, carry groceries . . ."

"I'll ask my mother," Ken promised him. "Listen, I get a pretty decent allowance. I could give you a few bucks . . ."

Stevie shook his head violently. "I won't take charity," he stated firmly. Ken could see that he was trying to look older than his eleven years. It made Ken hurt inside. He wished the medium would pay more attention to the boy and less to the lady with the past lives. Dahlia just wanted to say hi to old friends, but Stevie was in serious need of help.

Another woman walked in, and it took Ken a minute to realize she was Margaret. She looked completely different tonight. Her hair was shorter, she wore jeans, and she was—well, kind of pretty! He was amazed. Had that brief message from her mother completely changed her life?

Cassandra seemed very surprised to see her, too. She ushered them all to the table, but she kept looking at Margaret with a puzzled expression.

They joined hands and the medium began. "Oh spirits, hear our fervent plea. We are in great need of your presence. Please speak with us tonight."

The group was silent, and Ken concentrated very hard. Maybe something would happen for Stevie tonight.

"A spirit is approaching," the medium said. "I am getting a message."

Ken held his breath. *Oh please*, he thought, *let it be Stevie's father.*

After a moment she added, "It's a man," and his heart leapt. Come on, Mr. Fisher, Stevie needs you.

Then Cassandra said, "He's carrying red roses," and Dahlia let out a squeal.

"It's Vladimir!" she cried out. "He always brought me red roses."

Ken opened his eyes. "Who's Vladimir?"

"My lover, in Russia," Dahlia said. "Before the Revolution. Does he have a message for me?"

"Yes," Cassandra said. "He wants you to know he waits for you in eternity."

"Oh, how lovely," Dahlia said happily. "I have such wonderful memories of my time with Vladimir. I'm so happy to know he still thinks of me."

Ken couldn't help rolling his eyes, and then he realized Margaret was looking straight at him. And she was smiling! He was so surprised that he couldn't even smile back at her. He closed his eyes.

The medium had more words from Vladimir for Dahlia—mushy stuff that almost made Ken blush. Finally Vladimir made an exit, and Cassandra was available to hear from another spirit.

"Margaret, your mother is here."

"Oh, yeah?"

"She wants to know if you've been taking your vitamins."

"Uh, sure."

"She wants you to know she's watching you, Margaret."

"Okay."

"And thinking about you."

"Great," Margaret said. "Tell her I'm thinking about her, too."

Ken opened his eyes again. There was no sign of a tear on Margaret's face. He noticed that, above the veils, the medium's eyes were open, too.

Ken didn't blame her. This was a completely different Margaret from the one they'd seen the previous Friday.

"Well," Cassandra said finally, "your mother is very pleased to see you're feeling better. She wants to say goodbye now."

"Bye, Mom," Margaret said.

The medium noticed that Ken's eyes were open, and

she frowned. Obediently, he closed them.

"Someone else is coming," Cassandra said. "I think it may be Cleopatra, Dahlia."

Ken uttered a silent groan. Where was Stevie's father? Didn't the man realize how desperately Stevie needed to talk to him?

He made a decision. As soon as the séance was over he was going to have a private conversation with the medium. Despite Madame's warning, he was going to tell her about his gift.

Because together, if they joined forces, they just might be able to help Stevie.

Hey, man, what's up?

Jack, not now! I'm in the middle of a séance. I'm trying to concentrate!

But did you talk to Lucy? Did you tell her not to go out with Simon?

Yeah, I told her.

Thanks, pal. Look, could you do something else for me? You've still got my iPod, right? I left it at your place a couple of days before I died, remember?

I think so. Why?

Could you give it to Lucy for me? And tell her it's from me?

Okay, okay. Jack, listen, I gotta go. I really want to concentrate on this séance.

Sure, man. See ya.

Ken opened his eyes for a minute, and realized that Cassandra's eyes were open, too. And she was looking straight at him. Maybe she'd sensed he hadn't been paying attention. Obediently, he closed his eyes and thought about Stevie's father.

But Cleopatra was the last dead person to speak to them that night.

Chapter Eight

AMANDA WAS RELIEVED WHEN the medium turned her attention to Dahlia.

It wasn't easy, pretending to talk to Margaret's dead mother. Especially when she knew Margaret's mother wasn't dead at all.

What was Margaret up to, anyway? She'd been in Margaret's body for almost three days now, and she was no closer to an answer. But she wasn't letting the question drive her crazy. She was having too much fun for that.

Bored with the conversation between Dahlia and Cleopatra, she closed her eyes and let her mind drift back, to remember and relive the very interesting weekend she'd just enjoyed . . .

Once she recovered from the shock of learning that Margaret wasn't a drab, depressed woman with a dead mother, she explored the apartment to learn who she really was. Unfortunately, Margaret didn't keep a diary—at least, Amanda couldn't find one. There were photos—more of Margaret on the tropical beach, plus pictures of her at what looked like a party. She didn't see any pictures of her alone with a guy, so she assumed Margaret didn't have a current boyfriend. She was glad—it might be hard to fool a boyfriend into believing she was really Margaret. In fact, she decided it would be best to spend the next few days on her own and try not to encounter any of Margaret's close friends. Having seen the credit cards in the wallet, she knew she could have a very nice time all by herself.

After a good night's sleep in Margaret's comfy bed, Amanda woke feeling refreshed and ready to begin her new life as a 25-year-old adult. Having watched a great many television shows about young single women, she had some good ideas as to how she could spend the weekend.

From Margaret's closet, she selected leggings, a tunic top, and a pair of stilettos. It was the very first time she'd worn heels this high, and she felt positively glamorous. Once outside, she walked to the closest bus stop. She would have preferred to take a taxi, but she'd already made a dent in Margaret's cash resources. There was an ATM card in the wallet, but she didn't know Margaret's PIN, so she would have to be careful with the money. It was a good thing she had the two credit cards.

A *very* good thing. Because her first stop was the mall.

There were many stores she liked, but Unique Boutique was her favorite. It had the trendiest clothes in town, and a notice in the window assured her that Margaret's credit cards would be accepted. She spent a few minutes just looking at the window displays, reveling in the knowledge she could have anything she wanted.

Does Margaret ever go to this store? she wondered. She doubted it—she hadn't seen anything in her closet with the labels carried here. Unique Boutique was probably too expensive for Margaret. But that was what credit cards were for—to buy things you couldn't afford, right?

It was funny—people thought Amanda's family was rich and that she could have anything she wanted. But that wasn't exactly true. Maybe her parents were rich, but they didn't spend all their money on her. And contrary to popular opinion, she wasn't spoiled—at least, she didn't consider herself spoiled. Her parents didn't give her everything she wanted, like her own credit cards. She had to ask for stuff, and sometimes they said no. And she didn't have many items from Unique Boutique.

But there was no one to say no to her today. She didn't have to get anyone's permission to buy anything. She could have it all.

Like that unbelievably cute slinky red party dress with the wide black belt . . . She could just hear her mother saying, "Amanda, you do not need another party dress." Amanda smiled happily and went into the store. She found the dress in her size, didn't even look at the price tag, and headed to the dressing room.

There, she encountered an unusual problem. The dress didn't fit. She couldn't even zip it up. What was going on here? She didn't think she'd gained any weight . . .

Then it hit her, and she groaned. Of course the dress wouldn't fit her. She'd chosen the size that Amanda Beeson wore. Margaret was taller, wider in the hips, and much bigger on top.

Well, it wasn't such a terrible problem. All she had to do was change back into her clothes, return to the rack, and pick out some larger sizes to take back to the dressing room to try on. But then something else occurred to her. Amanda Beeson wouldn't be emerging from this spending spree with a new wardrobe. Margaret Robinson would.

It wasn't like Amanda was going to be Margaret forever. She didn't know how long she'd be in this body—she'd been in Tracey for two whole weeks, after all—but now, after three big bodysnatching experiences, she was pretty sure she'd be able to get back into herself when she wanted to get out of Margaret. All it seemed to take was a little physical shake-up. Just last month, a slip on a freshly waxed floor had got her out of Sarah. She planned to stay in

Margaret until Other-Amanda got out of the hospital and recovered and Margaret's life stopped being interesting.

But the realization that Margaret would be keeping the fabulous clothes she bought had taken much of the joy out of her plans for the day. Maybe she could buy the clothes in her own size and figure out a way to take them with her when she returned to her own body. But that would be sort of like stealing . . .

In the end, she halfheartedly bought the slinky dress and a cashmere sweater. After another hour of wandering around the mall, her feet hurt and she was forced to buy a pair of sneakers in Margaret's size. Stilettos were not meant for shopping, she decided.

The day improved considerably when she decided to indulge in expensive treats that she could enjoy while she was in Margaret's body. She went to an expensive salon and got a few more blond streaks added to brighten Margaret's hair. She treated herself to lunch at a chic café and then went to her mother's own favorite day spa for a facial, a massage, and a manicure. From there she went to the cosmetics counter at a major department store and had a complete makeover.

Then it was happy hour—at least according to those single-girl TV shows she watched. She took the bus back to Margaret's apartment to change clothes. Putting on the slinky dress, she slipped the stilettos back on and went out to a nearby bar she'd read about in a magazine. The article said it was the hippest place in town.

She liked the look of the bar—all black and silver and glass. It was elegant and stylish. The customers looked nice, too—well dressed and good-looking. There were little pedestal tables with high stools alongside them, and behind the bar, a very handsome man was mixing drinks.

Amanda went to the bar and sat on a stool. The bartender smiled at her and asked, "What can I get you?"

She hadn't even considered what she'd drink. She'd look like an idiot if she ordered a Coke or orange juice or something like that in this kind of place. They might not even have drinks like that here.

Back home, her parents sometimes had a glass of wine with dinner, and her father had let her taste his wine a couple of times. She'd never really liked the taste—sort of like grape juice, but sour.

Maybe now that she was in an adult's body she would like it.

"I'd like a glass of wine, please," she said.

"Sure, what kind? A white wine? We've got a fruity Chardonnay, and a nice crisp Chablis.

Or a Pinot Grigio, if you like that. It's very dry." Amanda just stared at him blankly.

"Would you prefer a red?" he asked. "We have an excellent Merlot, and a hearty Burgundy."

This was way too complicated. Amanda thought frantically. What did her father order in restaurants, before the meal?

"Um, I changed my mind. I'd like a martini, please. Very dry."

"Coming up," the bartender said.

Amanda looked around. A man sitting alone at one of the high tables caught her eye. To her surprise, he grinned and winked at her. It made her distinctly uncomfortable. He was *old*—at least thirty. What was he doing winking at a thirteen-year-old?

He doesn't know you're thirteen years old, she reminded herself. Quickly, she looked away. The bartender set a frosted glass with a long stem in front of her.

"One very dry martini," he announced. "I threw in two olives. No extra charge." Then *he* winked at her. All this winking was giving her the creeps.

And she hated olives. When the bartender wasn't looking, she fished them out with her fingers.

Then she held the drink to her lips and took a tentative sip.

It was *disgusting*. How did adults drink these things? It was all she could do not to gag.

Suddenly, she realized that the man who had winked at her earlier had come to the bar. There were several empty places, but he took the stool right next to her.

"Hi," he said. "Good to see you again."

Oh no! It was somebody who knew Margaret.

She should never have gone to a bar so near Margaret's apartment.

"Um, nice to see you, too," she murmured.

His eyebrows went up and he seemed pleased. "Yeah? The way you blew me off last time, I didn't think you'd be so happy to see me."

He whistled to the bartender and indicated Amanda's martini. "I'll have one of these," he said. "And put them both on my tab."

Amanda's brow furrowed. "You don't have to pay for my drink. I've got my own money."

"My treat," the man said. "Now, let's get to know each other."

Amanda fumbled in Margaret's bag and took out what she hoped would be a large enough bill.

"No, thank you," she said quickly, putting it on the bar. "I have to go."

"You just got here!" The man's protests rang in her ears as she fled the bar. Okay, maybe she wasn't ready for this kind of adult life.

But she still had the credit cards, and she'd found another card in Margaret's wallet—a video-store membership. She could still be an adult, in a different way. She used the credit card to buy food she normally never ate—fried chicken wings, French fries, and sugar-packed soft drinks. Microwave popcorn with butter. And real ice cream, not that reduced-fat stuff they always had at home. After all, she didn't have to worry about gaining weight—these calories weren't going into *her* body!

At the video store she picked up movies that she wouldn't have been allowed to see in a theater. Not dirty stuff—just sophisticated films that were rated 18 and over. She brought her goodies back to Margaret's apartment and had a very enjoyable evening all by herself.

She told herself that on Sunday she'd do more "adult" things, like go to a really fancy restaurant. Get a pedicure, or maybe have her legs waxed. Find a club where she could dance.

In the end, she spent all of Sunday doing what she'd done on Saturday night—eating junk food and watching movies. And totally enjoying herself. This was the kind of adult life she could handle.

On Monday morning she learned what Margaret did for a living. The phone woke her at 7 a.m.

"Miss Robinson, this is Eastside Elementary School.

We have a teacher who just called in sick. Could you substitute today?"

Amanda wasn't even tempted. "Oh, I'm very sorry, but I'm sick myself. I'm about to have my tonsils out."

She didn't even have to lie! Because right now, at the hospital across town, someone who looked like Amanda Beeson—who *was* Amanda Beeson, physically at least—was being put to sleep before her operation.

Yes, it had been a very pleasant weekend. But now she had to return to the present, and she looked at Ken across the table. His eyes were shut tightly, and he was gripping the hand of the young boy, Stevie.

"I can't seem to reach your father, Stevie," the medium said, "but I can feel him getting closer. We'll try again tomorrow."

Ken opened his eyes. He glanced at Margaret, but his eyes didn't linger. *He doesn't have a clue*, Amanda marveled. Wait till he hears this is *me*!

Once again, she didn't get the opportunity to tell him. When they rose from the table, Cassandra spoke to her.

"I must have a word with you, Margaret," she said. "Could you stay for a minute?"

"Okay," Amanda said. "I just need to—" But by then, Ken was already out of the apartment. Stevie was gone, too.

Cassandra waited until Dahlia had left and then she turned to Amanda. Her tone changed dramatically.

"What do you think you're doing?" she asked shrilly. "What's the matter with you?"

Amanda was startled. "Huh?"

"Look at you! Nobody's going to believe you're a grieving daughter! And you didn't behave today the way we practiced. Do you want to blow this whole thing?"

"What do you mean?"

"I brought you in on this to make it look like a real séance. You're supposed to be looking for your dead mother and I'm pretending to talk to her for you. You were fine last week—why are you screwing up tonight?"

As she spoke, Cassandra tugged at the scarves that veiled her face.

"I—I don't know . . ." Amanda sputtered, but she didn't finish the sentence. She was suddenly speechless.

Because the last scarf had come off, releasing long, thick blond hair, and Amanda recognized the face that had been hidden. The last time she'd seen that face, its owner had been hypnotizing Emily in an effort to learn the next week's winning lottery number.

Cassandra the medium was Serena Hancock, the student teacher.

CHAPTER NINE

KEN HAD WANTED TO stay behind and talk to the medium, but Stevie looked so upset when he ran out that Ken had to go after him. On the street in front of the medium's building, he could see disappointment written all over the younger boy's face.

"Are you okay?" Ken asked.

"Yeah . . . well, no, not really. I thought she would have made contact with my father by now."

"It's not that easy," Ken said. "Sometimes the spirits of dead people are totally open to communicating. You don't even have to look for them—they're there. Others are harder to find. Your father might not even be aware that he can get a message to you."

Stevie looked at him curiously. "How do you know so much about it?"

Ken couldn't meet his eyes. "I've read a lot."

Stevie stared at the ground. "My youngest sister, Dena, she keeps getting these rashes. My mother thinks she might be allergic to something, and she wants to take her to a doctor for tests. Only we can't afford it. We don't have any health insurance. And my other sister, Cindy . . . she's growing so fast, and now she's complaining her shoes are too tight. Only there's no money to buy her a new pair."

Ken could see he was close to tears. "Listen . . . you know the public library, on Slater Street?"

"Sure."

"Well, I need a bunch of books for—for an English assignment," Ken said. "And I don't have time to go there. If you could go for me and check out the books, I'd pay you for your time."

Stevie gazed up at him. "Really?"

"Yeah. Here, I'll give you a list." Ken reached into his backpack. He didn't really have an assignment, but his English teacher had given everyone in the class a list of "suggested reading"—not required—which meant nobody was going to read the books. But Stevie wouldn't know that.

He handed the list to the boy.

"If you could get me, like, five of these and bring them to the séance tomorrow night, I could give you forty dollars." He'd been stashing portions of his allowance every week for the past month, trying to save up for an iPhone. There had to be at least forty dollars in his desk drawer.

"Maybe more," he added.

"Just to go to the library and check out books?" Stevie asked.

"Yeah. You'd be doing me a big favor. Like I said, I don't have the time. It's worth the money to me."

Stevie's eyes were shining. "Hey, thanks! See you tomorrow."

Ken watched as he took off. Forty dollars, maybe fifty. That wouldn't pay for new shoes *and* a visit to the doctor. And it wasn't like Ken could provide money like that on a regular basis. Stevie and his family needed more. They needed that lottery ticket.

He was about to climb into bed that night when he remembered Jack's latest request. Opening the drawer of his desk, he poked around through the junk he stashed in there and finally found the iPod Jack had left behind. So he'd have to talk to Lucy again. At least this time he could make it clear that he was only doing this for Jack, and she'd realize that Ken wasn't interested in her in that way.

He went to sleep thinking about Stevie, and he was still thinking about him the next morning. By the end of the afternoon, when he entered the gifted class, he'd made a decision.

He wanted to talk about it, but he didn't get the opportunity right away. Emily was practically bursting with news.

"Tracey and I went to see Amanda at the hospital yesterday evening," she told Madame and the class.

"How is she feeling?" Madame asked.

"The girl we saw is feeling okay," Emily said, "but it wasn't Amanda."

"It was that fake Amanda who takes over when the real Amanda is in someone else's body," Tracey reported.

"Are you sure?" Madame asked.

Emily nodded vigorously. "She had that blank expression, like there weren't any thoughts in her head. And she kept looking in a mirror and putting on lip-gloss."

"And filing her nails," Tracey added.

"Sounds exactly like the real Amanda to me," Jenna commented.

"Nah, I could see the difference," Tracey said.

"I had the real one in me, remember? I can't explain it, but I could feel that it wasn't really her."

"Does she know where the real Amanda is?" Sarah asked.

Tracey shook her head. "No. I even tried asking her, but she just looked at me like I was speaking a foreign language. It was definitely the robot Amanda, or Other-Amanda—whatever you want to call her."

Jenna snorted. "That is *so* Amanda."

"What do you mean, Jenna?" Madame asked.

"She'll do anything to get out of doing something she doesn't want to do. She does a body snatch so she won't have to go through the operation. She makes Other-Amanda have it instead."

Ken agreed. "Yeah, she's pretty selfish."

Madame smiled slightly. "Oh, I don't know if what she did was so terrible. Whatever takes over Amanda's body when she's not there—it's not a real person. It's like an impression of Amanda. I don't believe it has any feelings."

Jenna shrugged. "Okay, maybe the fake Amanda doesn't care if she has an operation. I don't think the real Amanda cares whether fake Amanda feels it or not, as long as *she* doesn't have to suffer."

"I think," Madame said slowly, "that you're being a little hard on her, Jenna. But there's something else about this situation that I find interesting. Sarah, do you know what I mean?"

"Yes," Sarah said. "It's getting easier for Amanda to snatch bodies. Last month she took over my body because she was afraid she'd be kidnapped. But when she took over Tracey, it wasn't like that."

Tracey nodded. "She didn't want to be me but she felt sorry for me, so the body snatch just happened. Why would she feel sorry for Sarah? She just wanted to get out of her

115

own body, so she picked Sarah's."

"But we don't know that for sure," Madame pointed out. "The only person who knows is Amanda. Ken, do you have an opinion about this?"

"No," Ken said quickly. As far as he knew, the others weren't aware that Amanda had taken over his body for a while, and he wanted to keep it that way. But in the back of his mind he'd always wondered—why had Amanda done that? Had she felt sorry for *him*?

"What does it matter anyway?" he asked.

Madame replied, "It matters because we need to be aware of what we can and cannot do, so that we can rely on each other in the future."

Ken grimaced. She was going to start talking about the dangers they faced again. And he had something more important to tell them.

"I've found a way I could use my gift to help someone," he announced.

"How's that, Ken?" Madame asked.

He told them about Stevie, Stevie's dead father, the missing lottery ticket, and the plight of the boy's family. "I'm thinking . . . if I work with the medium, if we put our heads together, maybe we can reach Stevie's father and find out where the lottery ticket is."

Madame frowned. "Ken, we've talked about this before

and I thought I'd made myself clear. You cannot tell anyone about your gift."

"But why not? Okay, I can understand why most of you have to keep your gifts secret, but bad guys have never been interested in me! Nobody's tried to get me to help rob a bank or anything like that. My gift doesn't have any value for criminals. Why can't I use it to help someone?"

"What about the rest of us?" Charles protested. "If you tell the world about what you can do, it could lead people to this class. We could all be in danger."

"Charles is right, Ken," Madame declared. "Revealing your gift can have serious consequences. If you can help Stevie without giving anything away, that's all right. But you can't tell Stevie or this medium what you can do."

Ken slumped in his seat. He wasn't going to continue arguing this. If he could help Stevie on his own he would do it, no matter what Madame said. Would he be putting the whole class at risk? Maybe Madame was exaggerating.

But what did it matter, anyway? He had no idea how to contact Stevie's father. He'd never contacted *anyone*. They came to him.

That appeared to be the case with live people, too. He'd completely forgotten about Lucy and Jack and the iPod, but when he left the gifted class, he found her waiting for him in the hallway.

"I always wondered what goes on in that class," she said. "Do all of you talk to dead people?"

"No. Look, I've got something for you."

She beamed. "Really?"

He reached in his backpack and pulled out the iPod. "It's from Jack. He told me to give it to you."

"Oh. Well, tell him thank you."

"Sure. I'll see you around."

"Ken!"

"What?"

"I did what you told me to do."

"What are you talking about?" he asked.

"I told Simon I didn't want to go out with him."

"Oh. Okay, good. I'm sure you'll find someone else to hang out with."

She smiled coyly. "I think I already have. Can we go to the basketball game tonight?"

Damn. "Uh, gee, I can't go to the game, Lucy. I've got plans tonight. Bye."

At least he didn't have to lie this time. There was no way he was going to miss the evening's séance.

When he arrived that evening, Stevie was already there, and he presented Ken with a stack of books he'd checked out from the public library. Ken handed over forty-seven dollars, all the money he'd found in his dresser drawer.

Stevie was thrilled.

"You know, Ken, I can do stuff like this for you every day," he said eagerly.

Ken forced a smile, and nodded. "Yeah, we'll see." He could always make up errands to run. But where would he find the money to pay Stevie for them?

Crazy Dahlia was there, too, and Margaret. Ken absent-mindedly noticed that she didn't look quite as good as she had the day before. Not as bad as she'd looked the first time he saw her, though. Her hair was kind of messy, and she had on those big brown glasses again. But she wasn't as pasty-pale.

Just as Cassandra called them to the table, there was a knock on the door.

"Well, it seems we have another participant tonight," the medium said.

"I'll get the door," Dahlia offered.

Ken, Cassandra, and the others took their seats at the table. A moment later, Dahlia returned with the new person. Ken choked.

"Jenna!"

"Hi, Ken," Jenna said in an artificially bright voice. She turned to the others. "Ken is in my class at school. He was telling us about the séance, and it sounded so interesting, I just had to come."

She must have followed him, Ken realized. And he didn't believe a word she'd just said. Jenna was not the kind of person who would believe in mediums and séances.

He couldn't see Cassandra's veiled face, but he could tell by her tone that she wasn't thrilled with this new addition to their group.

"My dear, a séance isn't for everyone. Do you have an open mind? Are you willing to connect with the spirit world? Will you be able to receive the spirits?"

"Actually, I was thinking I'd just watch this time," Jenna said.

The medium shook her head. "I'm afraid that's not possible. You can't simply observe a séance. Your mere presence could ruin the event. You could distract and interrupt the mood and frighten off any spirit who wishes to address someone."

"Then I'll join the group and participate in the séance," Jenna said.

"No, I cannot allow that," Cassandra declared. "I'm sorry, my dear, but I can feel that you are a nonbeliever. Please leave now."

When Jenna didn't move, the medium did. She came around the table and faced Jenna.

"This is my apartment, my home. If you do not leave, I will call the police."

Jenna gave up and went to the door. Cassandra waited until she was out of the apartment before returning to the table and beginning.

"Join us, spirits, in our quest to find answers . . ."

Thank goodness there was nothing for Dahlia that evening, but Margaret's mother returned.

"Your mother wants to know how you're feeling, Margaret."

"I'm sad," Margaret said. "I miss you very much, Mama. I think about you all the time."

It was pretty much the same thing she'd said last Friday, but Ken thought there was something different this time. Maybe it was her tone—she didn't sound like she was going to burst into tears. In fact, her voice was almost wooden, like she'd memorized and rehearsed these lines.

"Your mother wants you to stay busy, Margaret," the medium told her. "That's the only way to get over your grief. She suggests that you find an interesting club to join. Bird watching, perhaps."

"Bird watching?" Margaret exclaimed. "Ick! Are you for real?"

Cassandra's voice was steely. "This is your mother addressing you, Margaret."

"Oh, right," Margaret said. "Sorry, Mom, I'll think about it."

"Your mother's leaving us now, Margaret."

"Don't leave, Mama!" Margaret cried out. "Stay here, please. I'm begging you, don't go away, I'm so lonely and sad, I need you . . ."

Cassandra almost sounded impatient. "She can't stay, Margaret. She'll be back tomorrow. Now let's try to call another spirit to us. Let us all be very quiet and concentrate very hard."

Ken began a silent chant. *Mr. Fisher, Mr. Fisher, Mr. Fisher, Mr. Fisher . . .*

"A spirit approaches," Cassandra intoned. "It is a man. He is calling a name. I'm having difficulty hearing him . . . Oh spirit, please, speak louder . . . Mr. Fisher, is that you?"

"Dad?" Stevie cried out.

"Shh," the medium murmured. "Again, spirit, again, who do you wish to contact?" She drew in her breath. "Your son? Your son . . . Stevie?"

Holding Stevie's hand, Ken could feel the boy's grip tighten.

"Do you have something you want to say to Stevie? Do you have a message for him?"

Ken couldn't breathe. Or maybe he was just feeling the tension in the boy sitting next to him.

"What is the message? Oh spirit, I cannot hear you! Your voice . . . it's too faint! Repeat! Repeat!"

And then Cassandra sighed. "He's gone."

"Oh, no!" Stevie cried out. "Dad, come back!"

"I'm sorry, Stevie. It wasn't a good connection. But don't despair! We've made contact. He'll come back. Maybe I'm just not strong enough. If only there was another medium here, someone else who is also sensitive to the spirit world. Perhaps together we could forge a pathway."

That was all Ken needed to hear. "Can I talk to you privately, Cassandra?"

"Of course, Ken," the medium said. To the others, she said, "The séance is over. We will meet again at the same time tomorrow evening."

Dahlia and Stevie went to the foyer, and Dahlia opened the door. Jenna practically fell in, as if she'd been leaning against it.

"What are you doing here?" Cassandra demanded to know. "I told you to leave!"

"I was waiting for Ken," Jenna said. "I thought we could walk home together. Come on, Ken."

Ken glared at her. "I need to talk to Cassandra."

"Ken, don't tell her anything! I read her mind. She's a fake!"

"How dare you?" Cassandra cried out. "Get out of here now!"

"I'm not leaving without Ken," Jenna yelled.

Ken turned to the medium. "I'm sorry about this. I'll get rid of her." He grabbed Jenna's arm and dragged her out the door.

"Ken, I'm serious," Jenna hissed once they'd reached the hall. "I don't know who she really is, or what she's up to, but she's not a medium. This is a fraud."

"You're just saying that to keep me from helping her find Stevie's father," Ken accused her. "You don't want me to tell her what I can do."

"It's not just that! I'm telling you, Ken, I swear, I saw something in her mind. And she's not telling the truth."

Ken couldn't remember ever hearing Jenna sound so fervent before.

"Ken, just do me one favor, okay? Don't tell her today. Think about it."

"I'm not going to change my mind, Jenna."

"Just wait till the next séance," she pleaded. "It's not like anything can happen now. Okay? Please?"

"What difference is one day going to make?"

"I don't know! I just feel like—like it will make a difference."

That sounded pretty lame to Ken, but he'd never heard Jenna sound so frantic. If it really meant that much to her . . .

He went back into the apartment, where Cassandra

and Margaret were talking.

"Um, I have to go."

"I thought you wanted to talk to me privately," Cassandra said.

"It can wait till tomorrow," Ken said.

Chapter Ten

THE WOMAN WHO HAD been calling herself Cassandra pulled off her veil and cursed as the door closed behind Ken.

"I think we're all right," she told Amanda. "I kept my mind completely blank all the time that girl was in the room."

Amanda reminded herself that she wasn't Amanda. "Why?"

"She can read minds," Serena said. "But I blocked her from getting into mine."

"You can do that?"

"I learned how when I studied hypnosis," Serena Hancock informed her. "You concentrate on a little phrase called a mantra. Some people do this for meditating, to clear the mind. It can work when you're around mind readers, too. When I was student teacher in her class, I was able to hide my thoughts from her." She started toward the kitchen. "I'm going to fix myself a martini.

Do you want one?"

Amanda shuddered. "No, thanks." She followed Serena into the kitchen. "You can't really make contact with spirits, can you?"

Serena stared at her. "Are you being funny? Of course not! You know that."

Margaret would know that, Amanda thought.

"Oh, sure, but I was just wondering. Maybe, after doing this for a while, you might have developed the gift."

Serena began mixing her drink. "It doesn't work like that. You've either got it or you haven't. It's too bad, though. If I could connect with dead people, I wouldn't need Ken. I hope he's not going to be a problem. I think he really wants to help Stevie. He seems like the caring type."

"Yeah, Ken's like that," Amanda said. Once again Serena looked at her oddly, and Amanda tried to recover. "I mean, that's how he's been acting here." Mentally, she scolded herself. She *had* to remember who Serena thought she was. It wasn't easy. She was still reeling from the revelations of the evening before.

"Don't you want anything to drink?" Serena asked.

"Just water," Amanda said. "I . . . um . . . I'm on a diet. Excuse me, I'm going to wash my hands."

It was just an excuse to be alone in the bathroom for a few minutes. She put the lid down on the toilet and sat there.

She had to admit, Serena had designed a very clever scheme. Fortunately, when Amanda had learned who Serena was the night before, the shock had left her speechless and she was able to learn a lot about the plan by just listening to Serena talk about it.

She gathered that Margaret and Serena were friends from back in the days when they'd studied to become teachers at the same university. Teachers didn't make much money, and Serena wanted a lot more than she earned. And it appeared that Serena was still obsessed with getting her hands on a winning lottery ticket.

From what Amanda had figured out, Serena had learned about Stevie's plight from another friend, Jane, who taught at a different school. Stevie was in Jane's class, and he'd confided in his teacher. Jane was so moved and saddened by the story, she'd mentioned it in passing in a conversation with Serena. And Serena—without telling Jane, of course—came up with a plan.

Having done some of her student teaching at Meadowbrook in the gifted class, she'd learned about their special gifts. She knew what Ken could do, and she thought he'd be able to get in touch with Stevie's father. So she set herself up as a medium, contacted Stevie and Ken, and enlisted Margaret to help her out by acting like a satisfied client. This would hopefully convince Ken that "Cassandra" was a legitimate medium. And as payment, Margaret would get a cut of the money from the lottery ticket.

What Amanda hadn't figured out yet was how Serena would find out the location of the lottery ticket before Ken told Stevie. And she was afraid to ask because she was sure Margaret already knew.

She was also curious about Dahlia's role in all this. But she didn't even have to ask about that. When she returned to the living room, the martini seemed to have put Serena in a talkative mood.

"This is going even better than I expected," Serena mused. "We really lucked out when Dahlia showed up. That was a good idea you had."

What idea was that? Amanda wondered. "You think so?" she asked carefully.

"Obviously—Dahlia would never have turned up if she hadn't read the ad you put about me in the newspaper." Serena laughed. "What a crackpot. She really believes she had these other lives. And she's so gullible! She's falling for everything I've told her."

Amanda got it. Dahlia was giving the whole scam more credibility.

"Ken is totally sympathetic to Stevie," Serena continued. "Tomorrow I'm going to tell him I sense that he has a special connection with the spirit world. I'll ask him to help me locate Stevie's father."

She yawned and set down her empty glass. "I can't keep my eyes open."

"I'm tired, too," Amanda said quickly. "I guess I'd better be going home."

"By the way," Serena said, "you were better tonight. But you need to be a little more emotional about your mother, the way you were last Friday."

"Okay," Amanda said.

"Oh, and I need you to do me a favor." Serena went to a desk and took a piece of paper from a drawer. "Go to the pharmacy tomorrow and get this prescription filled."

"What is it?" Amanda asked, taking the paper.

Serena rolled her eyes. "What do you think?" She walked Amanda to the door. "See you tomorrow. And try to be a little more pathetic, okay?"

On the way to the bus stop, Amanda paused under a street light and tried to read the prescription. The handwriting wasn't easy to read, but she could tell it was one of those medical words that didn't mean anything in regular English. Beziterol or Besiteral—something like that. She had no idea what it was for.

Thank goodness for the Internet. As soon as she was back in Margaret's apartment, she sat down at Margaret's laptop and went online. On her third attempt at deciphering the word, she hit the jackpot.

The search engine had taken her to a dictionary of drugs. She skipped over the chemical words and came to a definition of Besiterol that she could understand.

"A highly potent and fast-acting insomnia medication. To be used with extreme caution."

Amanda didn't think Serena had insomnia. She'd been falling asleep tonight after one martini. And then it clicked—Amanda knew how Serena was going to find out the lottery ticket's location before Ken gave the information to Stevie. Somehow she'd get this medicine into Stevie, and he'd fall asleep while Ken talked to his father. And if Ken didn't willingly offer Serena the information, she could always hypnotize him to get it.

Amanda didn't know what amazed her more—Serena's evil mind or her own brilliance at figuring it all out. And those classmates of hers thought she was worthless! Well, she'd show them what she could do.

Now she was glad she hadn't been able to tell Ken that she'd snatched Margaret's body. They'd all be surprised and impressed with Amanda when she exposed this nasty scheme all by herself.

Chapter Eleven

K EN HAD NO FAITH in what Jenna had told him about the medium. He wasn't stupid. He knew exactly what she was trying to do, and this had nothing to do with anything she claimed to find in Cassandra's mind. Jenna just didn't want him to reveal his gift, and she'd say anything to keep him from helping out at the séance. He'd been furious at her when she stormed into the séance, but after sleeping on it, and thinking about it, he wasn't angry anymore. He thought he knew why Jenna had tried to stop him from getting involved.

She was scared. She believed all that stuff Madame said about the enemies who were out to get them, and Ken supposed there could be some truth in it for some of the people in the gifted class.

But the bad guys weren't out to get *him*.

What bad guys?

Ken frowned. *Jack, I wish you wouldn't just jump into my head like that. I'm entitled to my private thoughts.*

Hey, man, we never had secrets from each other. What bad guys are you thinking about?

Madame says we can't let anyone know about our gifts because there are bad guys out there who want to use us.

What could they use you for?

Not a clue.

Besides, who's going to believe you can talk to dead people?

Lucy believes, Ken pointed out.

Yeah, I bet that's just because she wants *to believe so she can keep in touch with me. I don't think she'll ever get over me.*

Uh, Jack . . .

What?

I'm sure Lucy misses you a lot, but she's getting on with her life. I mean, she wants to go out with other guys.

Not Simon Dowell!

No . . .

Who, then?

Ken sighed. *Me.*

You're kidding!

Honestly, Jack, I tried to play the big brother role, but I guess she misinterpreted it. She thinks I want to go out with her.

Do you?

No! But how am I going to let her down easy?

There was a long silence before Jack responded again.

You could.

I could what?

Go out with her.

Are you crazy?

Really, Ken. I don't want her to go out with jerks, guys who are going to put the moves on her. I trust you. And if the other guys think she's with you, they won't bother her.

Jack! I don't want to go out with Lucy!

Why not? You don't like that Amanda chick anymore, right? And there's nothing wrong with Lucy. Don't you think she's hot?

She's okay, she's just not my type. Jack, I don't want to start anything with Lucy.

Aw, c'mon, be a pal. You don't know how rough it is for me, thinking about her, not knowing what she's doing, who she's seeing . . . Can't you do this for me? Please?

It was Ken's turn to plead. *Can we talk about this later, Jack? I've got stuff to think about for school.*

Okay, okay. But remember, you're my best pal. Don't let me down.

Jack was gone, and Ken could get back to his own thoughts. What had he been thinking about before Jack interrupted? Right, the bad guys. The ones who were *not* out to get him.

It was like he'd said in class—his gift just didn't have any criminal potential. And despite what Madame had said, he honestly didn't think that talking about his gift would endanger anyone else in the class. He just had to convince

Jenna that this was true and assure her she had nothing to worry about.

He was prepared to do that in the gifted class that day. He even hurried to class so he could take her aside and have time to talk to her before Madame arrived. But when he arrived at room 209, he changed his mind—even before he went in.

Through the glass window in the door, he could see a few students were already in the room. Jenna, Emily, and Tracey were huddled together, obviously having a private conversation. And Ken had a pretty good feeling he knew what it was about. Jenna was trying to get the girls to gang up on him, to stop him from going to the séance and offering to help the medium. He sighed in exasperation. What did they think they could do? Tie him up and sit on him?

No, it was more likely that they were planning to hound him and nag him till he broke down and gave in. Or threaten never to speak to him again. Or cry? No, not those three.

Like he cared anyway. Like these girls were more important than a kid whose family was about to lose their home. As far as Ken was concerned, Jenna, Emily, and Tracey were being selfish—more concerned with their own safety than with the suffering of others. And the minute they started bugging him, he was going to tell them that.

He opened the door, looking at them in scorn as they practically jumped out of their seats. The three of them wore almost identical guilty expressions. Ken went to his seat and opened a book. But before he began reading, he gave each one of them a long, hard glare.

It was pretty effective. The girls didn't approach him.

Jenna didn't even bring up the subject in class. Actually, she didn't have a chance—Charles and Martin got into an argument about some stupid thing. Martin felt like Charles was making fun of him, and his gift came out. When he attacked Charles, Charles made a light fixture fall on Martin's head. Even though neither of the boys was seriously hurt, it was utter chaos in the classroom. But at least it kept everyone's attention off Ken.

He was still concerned about Jenna's efforts to stop him, and when he arrived early at the séance that evening, he spoke to Cassandra before the others arrived.

"If that girl comes by here tonight, don't let her in. Actually, if *any* girls come by, don't let them in."

Since he couldn't see Cassandra's face, he had no idea if she was puzzled by his demand. She didn't act disturbed. In fact, she changed the subject.

"I'm glad you're here early, Ken," she said. "There's something I want to talk to you about." She motioned for him to sit on her sofa, and she sat by his side.

She spoke softly. "Ken, I hope this won't sound presumptuous. I haven't known you very long, and yet I feel as if I *do* know you. In a unique way."

Ken stared at her. "I—I don't know what you mean."

She continued. "I believe we may have something in common. Something very deep and profound."

Ken swallowed hard. He didn't know what to say.

"I believe," Cassandra said, "that you may have a special awareness of the spirit world. As you know by now, I am receptive to their messages, and thus I am highly sensitive to others who are receptive. I think you and I may have similar gifts."

Ken nodded. "I was going to talk to you about that tonight. Sometimes, dead people contact me."

The medium nodded. "I suspected this might be the case. And tonight, Ken, I may need your help."

"With Stevie?"

She pressed her hand gently on his. "Oh, I was right—you *are* perceptive! I so desperately want to help this boy find the lottery ticket. But you see"—she lowered her head—"I must confess that while I do have a gift, I am not the strongest medium in the world. And for some reason I'm finding it very difficult to communicate with Mr. Fisher, Stevie's father."

"Do you actually think I can help?" Ken asked. "I've

never even tried to contact spirits. They come to me."

"If spirits can find you, you can find them," Cassandra said. "With my assistance, of course. Will you try? For Stevie's sake?"

Ken nodded. "Absolutely." Then he asked, "Could we keep this just between us? I don't want everyone to know I have a gift. No offense, but I don't want to get into the medium business."

"Don't worry," Cassandra said. "They won't even be aware of what's going on. You just pass whatever you learn on to me."

Margaret arrived at the apartment at that moment, followed by Stevie and then Dahlia.

"Margaret, could you help me in the kitchen for a minute?" Cassandra asked. The two women disappeared into the other room.

"How ya doing?" Ken asked Stevie.

Stevie actually smiled. "That money you paid me . . . my mother was able to buy Cindy some shoes from the thrift store. They're not new, but at least they fit her and they don't hurt. And she found some cream at a pharmacy that's helping Dena's rash."

"That's great," Ken exclaimed. "So things are better, huh?"

Stevie nodded, but his smile faded. "But the landlord

came around again. He's only giving us another week to get the rent money together."

"Well . . . maybe by then you'll have the money," Ken said. He didn't tell the boy about his plan to help the medium because he didn't know if it would work, and Stevie had already had enough disappointments in his life.

Margaret and Cassandra returned, and to Ken's surprise, Cassandra was holding a tray with glasses. Margaret carried a pitcher of red stuff.

"This is homemade strawberry punch," Cassandra announced. "I have a good feeling about tonight—that it's going to be special. So I thought we'd have a little pre-séance celebration."

"Shouldn't we have the celebration after the séance?" Ken asked. "I mean, if it's successful?"

"One has to establish the ambience for success," Cassandra declared as she set the tray down. "Success is more likely to come when the appropriate feelings are in the air."

Her reference to "feelings" bothered Ken. He looked at the punch suspiciously. "Is there alcohol in this?"

Cassandra let out a tinkling laugh. "Of course not, Ken. I would never serve an alcoholic beverage to young people. I don't even drink alcohol myself—mediums rarely do. We are afraid it could dull our senses and make us less accessible to the spirits."

He felt foolish for having asked. He should have known Cassandra would be the responsible type.

"Margaret, will you pour?" Cassandra asked.

Margaret picked up the pitcher and turned her back to the others to face the coffee table.

Ken approached her.

"Can I help?" he offered.

"No!" Cassandra answered for her. "Margaret can do it herself. *Aaah!*"

Surprised by the strong reaction, Ken turned to Cassandra. But she wasn't protesting his offer of assistance. The scarves that covered her face were coming off. And they weren't just falling—it was as if invisible hands were ripping them from her.

Invisible hands . . . that could mean only one thing. One person. "Tracey!" Ken yelled in outrage. She must have followed him! But in an instant his fury turned to something else. Something more closely related to utter shock.

The medium's face had been exposed, and he recognized her.

"You!" he cried out.

At that very moment there was pounding on the door. "Go away!" Serena Hancock shouted.

"Police! Open this door immediately or we'll break

it down!"

"Good heavens!" Dahlia exclaimed. "Isn't this exciting?" She went to the door and opened it.

Two uniformed police officers strode in. Ken gaped, and his mouth dropped even farther when, just behind the policemen, Emily and Jenna entered. And then Tracey was there, too.

Emily pointed at the student teacher medium. "That's her! That's the woman who threatened me two months ago at Meadowbrook!"

"She's crazy!" Serena screamed.

"I recognize her, too," Jenna declared.

"So do I," Tracey cried out.

"So do I," Ken echoed in a whisper. He was still in a state of shock. But somehow he managed to blurt out, "I think there's a scam going on here."

One of the police officers produced a pair of handcuffs. As he was locking Serena's hands together behind her back, the woman yelled, "I'm not going down alone for this." She jerked her head at Margaret. "She's in on it, too! Margaret Robinson!"

"That's not true!" Margaret declared hotly as the other officer began to cuff her. "I'm not even Margaret!"

But the police weren't giving either of them the opportunity to protest further. The two women were hustled out the door, leaving behind three stunned seekers of guidance from the spirit world—and three girls with expressions that were just a little bit smug.

Chapter Twelve

AMANDA WASN'T SURE IF she was frightened or furious or some combination of the two. Sitting on a bench, her back pressed against the wall, she tried in vain to calm down. This just couldn't be happening.

She was in jail. Amanda Beeson, Queen Bee of Meadowbrook Middle School, was behind bars. Okay, it wasn't Amanda Beeson's body in the holding cell, but it was Amanda Beeson who felt imprisoned.

She wasn't alone. Serena was there, too, pacing the floor, muttering to herself. And there were four other women, none of whom looked very nice. They weren't pacing or shaking or acting nervous, though. In fact, they all looked like they'd been in prison before. One of them was even sleeping!

Serena-Cassandra glared at her. "Stop crying!" she snapped.

Amanda hadn't even realized there were tears running

down Margaret's face. She certainly had every right to cry. She didn't deserve to be here! She'd even tried to stop Serena's evil scheme from succeeding. The prescription Serena had given her . . . Amanda had had it filled at a pharmacy, but only so she could see what the pills looked like. Back at Margaret's place, she'd emptied the pills into the sink and replaced them with similar-looking little white mints that wouldn't do anyone any harm. While Serena would think Margaret was dropping a sleeping pill into the glass meant for Stevie, he would simply receive a glass of punch with a little mint flavoring. He wouldn't fall asleep. Ken would tell him where the lottery ticket was, Amanda would reveal herself and expose the scheme, and she'd be a hero!

But instead she was one of the villains. A common criminal. Was this the kind of person Margaret was? She wondered if Margaret had ever been in jail before. Maybe Amanda should be acting a little more nonchalant about all this. But what did it matter now? She actually wanted the guards to know she *wasn't* Margaret!

Unfortunately, she really didn't know how she was going to convince them of that. Had anyone ever used bodysnatching as an excuse to be released from a prison? She seriously doubted it. No one would believe her.

There was only one way out of this mess. She had to get

out of Margaret's body and back into her own, which at that very moment was probably lying in her nice, soft bed being waited on and coddled by her mother.

She took some deep breaths and tried to think rationally. How had she gotten out of bodies before? Falling, hitting her head—it was usually something like that. When she had been invisible Tracey, an accidental kick in the head had sent her back into herself. During the bank robbery, when she was Sarah, a slip on the floor did the trick.

Tentatively, she leaned back and tapped her head against the wall. Nothing happened. Her head didn't even hurt. She forced herself to bang her head a little harder.

One of the other prisoners, a hard-looking woman with bright red hair, stared at her. "What are you doing?"

"Nothing," Amanda said quickly.

The woman snickered. "It's not going to work, you know."

"What?"

"Hurting yourself to get out of here. You'd have to spill some serious blood. And even then you'd only end up in the clinic here. You'd still be behind bars."

Amanda remembered another kind of shock that had worked in the past.

She thought back to when she occupied Ken's body. During that time, she formed a—a relationship with a dead boy named Rick. When Rick had said he wouldn't contact her anymore, she'd been really upset. That strong feeling had pushed her out of Ken and back into herself.

But here she was in jail. Wasn't that shocking enough to get her out of Margaret? Apparently not.

She tried banging her head again, but she was beginning to think she would never be able to hurt herself enough to provide an adequate physical shock. The redheaded woman glared at her.

"Hey, stop that. I told you, it won't work."

Amanda ignored her and kept thumping her head.

"You're annoying me," the woman growled. "If you don't stop, I'll *make* you stop."

The threat in her tone sounded very real. Amanda stopped. What else could she do to cause herself pain?

She tried pinching her arm. She dug her manicured nails in so hard, she actually saw a tiny drop of blood. But it didn't hurt all that much.

Maybe she needed that mean-looking woman to carry out her threat. The thought of being attacked was so scary, for a moment she thought it might get her out of Margaret. But no such luck. She was going to have to get really and truly beaten up.

She started thumping her head again. The redhead turned to her with a look of fury. But at that moment, a guard appeared.

"Hey, Cassidy."

Cassidy turned out to be the redheaded woman.

"Yeah?"

The guard opened the door. "Your lawyer's here." The woman hurried out.

"I want to make a phone call!" Serena demanded. "I know my rights—I'm entitled to a phone call!"

"Yeah, yeah, I'll be back in a minute," the guard muttered.

Amanda noticed that Serena's hands were clenched into fists. And it dawned on her that she could probably get Serena mad very easily, just by confessing who she really was.

And Serena would believe her. She'd been in their class, and even though she hadn't paid much attention to Amanda when she was there, she must have learned about all the gifts. If Amanda could get her good and mad right now, Serena might just go over the edge and slug her—or at least slap her. Really, really hard. And as much as Amanda didn't want to experience that, it could work.

"Serena?"

"What?" Serena snapped.

Amanda got off the bench and came closer to Serena, within slapping distance. "I've got something to tell you."

But that was as far as she got. The guard reappeared.

"Okay, Hancock, you can come and make your phone call."

"About time," Serena muttered. To Margaret-Amanda, she said, "I'll get us out of here."

Great, Amanda thought dismally. And then what? She *had* to get out of this body! She knelt down by the wall and started banging her head again, harder this time.

"Hey, you're going to hurt yourself!" another prisoner yelled. "Guard! Guard!"

The guard reappeared.

"I think you'd better do something about this nut case," the prisoner said.

The next thing Amanda knew, she was being dragged out of the cell by two guards, one holding each arm. And then she was in another cell, a smaller one, all by herself. One of the guards spoke to the other.

"Keep an eye on her till I can find something to tie her to the bed."

The other guard pulled up a chair just outside the cell. "Don't move," she ordered Amanda.

Amanda didn't move. She couldn't. She was in a total state of shock. And yet the feeling still wasn't strong enough to get her out of this body.

This couldn't be happening . . .

Chapter Thirteen

KEN WAS DEPRESSED.

So the whole séance thing had been a scam. Cassandra was Serena Hancock, still trying to get her hands on a winning lottery ticket. That woman Margaret—she must have been her accomplice. Ken assumed the whole dead-mother thing was a made-up story so the medium could seem authentic.

Was Dahlia in on it, too? Maybe, maybe not. In the confusion with the police, she'd taken off. The person he was really concerned about was Stevie. He had disappeared, too, before Ken could talk to him. The poor kid . . . He must have been totally freaked out when he realized it was a scam.

"Or maybe little Stevie was part of the scam," Jenna said.

"Stop reading my mind," Ken barked. They had stopped at the bowling alley, where there was a café. Jenna, Tracey, and Emily were celebrating their successful mission with ice cream. Ken had a glass of water.

"Sorry," Jenna said.

He looked at her stonily. "You should be. Why didn't you tell me what you were planning to do at the séance?"

"I wanted to tell you," Emily reported, "but Jenna said we couldn't trust you not to warn the others."

Ken hadn't taken his eyes off Jenna. "Maybe if you'd just told me the medium was really Serena Hancock . . ."

"I didn't know for sure," Jenna said. "Her mind was really hard to penetrate. Not like yours, Ken. You're totally transparent."

"Jenna!" Tracey exclaimed in disapproval. She turned to Ken. "Jenna said this was the only way. She said you were so into the séance thing, we had to shock you into seeing the truth."

Ken grimaced. "Oh, really? And since when is it Jenna's business to shock me into seeing things?"

"Oh, for crying out loud," Jenna said airily. "You should be thanking me, Ken. You could have been totally suckered into their little con game. You were really falling for it! You know, I saved your—"

He wouldn't let her finish. "Just shut up, Jenna! And for your information, Stevie was not part of it. He's eleven years old!"

"So what?" Jenna countered. "I once saw a documentary

on TV about criminals under the age of twelve."

"Well, Stevie isn't one of them. He was an innocent victim."

"How can you be so sure of that?" Jenna shot back. "Did you read Stevie's mind?"

Ken knew he wasn't a violent person, and he'd definitely never hit a girl. But right now, he was feeling very close to a complete change of character, so he did the only thing he could think of doing. He turned away from the girls and headed to the exit.

"Ken! Ken, wait up!"

He turned to find Lucy coming toward him. Could the evening get any worse?

"Do you like bowling?" she asked. "I love to bowl! Maybe we could bowl together sometime soon. Like, what are you doing this weekend?"

"Lucy, could you bug off? Can't you take a hint? I don't want to go out with you!" And he stormed out the door.

Once outside, he started walking, fast. He knew he'd been horribly rude and unkind to Lucy, but he felt propelled by an anger that was out of his control. He wasn't sure if he was more angry at himself or at Jenna— himself for being so gullible, Jenna for sticking her nose in his affairs. And for suggesting poor Stevie was part of the whole nasty business . . .

He slowed down. What she had said to him . . . "Did you read Stevie's mind?" Was she saying that she *had* read his mind?

But how could Stevie be in cahoots with Serena? He was looking for his father's lottery ticket, and he only went to Serena because he thought she was a real medium who could contact his father.

Unless . . . unless . . . the kid in the séance wasn't really Stevie Fisher. Maybe he'd just heard about the situation, and he was pretending to be the boy whose father had died. Or maybe he was some kind of juvenile actor whom Serena had hired to play Stevie. And they were both waiting for Ken to make contact with Mr. Fisher so they could steal the lottery ticket before the real Stevie found it.

There was only one way Ken could know for sure. He had to find the kid who called himself Stevie Fisher.

He looked at his watch. It was almost nine o'clock and this was a school night, which meant he was expected to be home at ten, and he had no idea where Stevie Fisher lived.

But he had his cell phone. And his cell phone had Internet access.

He took it out of his pocket, hit the web button, and got a search engine. But now what? He doubted that

Stevie had a phone number listed under his own name, and he didn't know the name of Stevie's mother or his late father. Fisher was a common name—there could be hundreds of them.

And then he had a better idea. He went to the town newspaper's website, which had its own search capability. He typed in the name Fisher and added the word that just might give him the Fisher he was seeking: *obituary.*

Bingo! There it was—an obituary from two months ago. Melvin Fisher, age 42, of 72 Apple Creek Road. Killed in an automobile accident.

What did people do before cell phones? Ken wondered. Within seconds he had a map on the little screen and directions to Apple Creek Road.

When he arrived, he found a dead-end street lined with small cottage-style homes. He approached the door of number 72, but he didn't get close enough to knock.

A window opened and a voice called out, "What are you doing here?"

Ken sighed with relief. The boy he knew as Stevie Fisher was looking through the window.

"I just wanted to see if you were okay," he said. "You disappeared when the police arrived."

"No kidding," the boy said. "I didn't want them thinking I was one of you people."

"What do you mean?" Ken asked, walking toward the window.

"Don't come any closer or I'll call the police myself!" Stevie yelled. "How come you're not locked up?"

"Because—because—" Ken sputtered, "I wasn't in on it! I thought it was a real séance, too!"

"Yeah, right. Just get out of here." Stevie slammed down the window.

Ken couldn't believe it. Stevie thought *he* was in league with the fake medium. Now he was even more depressed.

He was late getting home, but fortunately his parents were caught up in watching a soccer game on TV and hadn't noticed the time.

"Join us," his father called from the den. "It's a terrific game."

"No thanks," Ken said. "I'm kind of beat. I'm going to bed."

He knew his parents were probably looking at each other in bewilderment and that his mother was wondering if he was sick. He knew they didn't think anything was more important to him than soccer, even if he didn't play anymore himself. He loved his parents, but there was so much they didn't know about him.

In his room, he flopped down on the bed and stared at the ceiling. He certainly hadn't lied to his parents about being tired. He was thoroughly, utterly exhausted by the bizarre chain of events that had made up the past few hours. He hoped he would be able to fall asleep easily. He didn't want to think about this crummy day.

Ken?

Not now, Jack. I'm beat. And I've had a really bad day.

I just wanted to tell you . . . I'm sorry.

About what?

About what I asked you to do for me. About going out with Lucy.

The experiences of the past couple of hours had practically erased Jack's request from his memory. And he flushed as he recalled how awful he'd been to Lucy at the bowling alley.

Jack . . . I really don't want to do that.

It's okay. I shouldn't have asked you.

He sounded . . . different. Not sad, not happy, just sort of . . . calm.

I've been thinking a lot, Jack went on. *And I've been getting some help.*

From who?

I can't really say. You wouldn't understand.

Ken had a sudden image of Jack surrounded by a bevy of kind and wise angels. Jack was right—wherever he was right now, Ken could never understand.

So, it's okay if I don't go after her?

Yeah. You see, I've got to let go.

Of Lucy?

Of everything. I have to let go of my life. And I have to stop asking you to live a life for me. I gotta get into where I am now.

So—you're not going to talk to me anymore? With a pang, Ken realized that he would miss hearing from Jack.

Oh, we can still talk. I'm just not going to be asking you to do me any more favors.

Oh. Okay.

You said you had a really bad day. What happened?

Long story. Can I tell you tomorrow? I need to get some sleep.

Sure. And if Lucy keeps coming on to you, feel free to blow her off.

I already did, Ken thought dismally. He wondered if he could drum up the energy to sit down at his computer right now and compose an apologetic e-mail to her.

Hello, can you hear me?

He thought Jack had gone.

Yeah, I hear you.

Excuse me, I'm sorry to disturb you . . .

Well, it definitely wasn't Jack. He'd never be so polite.

I need your help. It's important.

Look, I'm sorry, but this isn't a good time, okay? Would you mind going away?

Please, young man, you could save my family!

Right. They were always dramatic, these spirits or ghosts or whatever they were.

Another time, okay?

It won't take long. I just want to tell you where I left a lottery ticket . . .

Chapter Fourteen

AN HOUR LATER, WHEN the guard finally returned, Amanda did something she'd done only once before in her life, when she'd wanted her parents to buy her real diamond studs for her pierced ears.

She begged.

"Please, please, please, don't tie me up! I promise I won't hit my head against the wall again! Honestly, I swear to you, I won't!"

The guard didn't even look at her. She spoke to the other guard.

"Let her out. She made bail."

Amanda jumped up. "You're kidding! Who bailed me out?"

But these guards apparently never shared any more information than they absolutely had to. The guard opened the door, and Margaret-Amanda made a hasty exit. She was directed down a hall and told to go through the last door on the right.

She was clinging to one big hope—that Jenna had read her mind when she was in Cassandra-Serena's apartment. Jenna was the only person who just might know that the Margaret Robinson who was arrested at the séance was really Amanda Beeson. And Amanda made a promise to herself. If this was the case, and Jenna had arranged to get her out of jail, Amanda would never be mean to Jenna again. She would never criticize her or laugh at her behind her back—or in front of her either. She'd even persuade her own personal friends to let Jenna into their clique.

But she started regretting her promises even before she reached the door. Jenna would never fit into Amanda's clique. She had the wrong style, the wrong personality, the wrong everything.

So it was almost a relief when she walked through the door and found that Jenna wasn't waiting for her. But someone else was.

"Come on," Serena said, leading the way out of the room and down the hall, toward the main doors. "I've got a taxi waiting for us outside."

"Who bailed us out?" Amanda asked.

"Very funny," Serena snapped. "Really, Margaret, I'm not in the mood for jokes."

Amanda was on the verge of telling her that she wasn't Margaret, but she didn't think this was the right time or

159

place. Serena probably wouldn't slap her right in front of a police station, and even if she did there was no guarantee it would send Amanda back into her own body. Besides, the idea of a taxi taking her back to Margaret's apartment was a lot more appealing than walking or looking for a bus stop.

They settled into the back of the taxi, and Serena gave the driver an address that was unfamiliar to Amanda. It was neither Serena's address nor Margaret's.

"Where are we going?"

"Where do you *think*?" Serena retorted. "Honestly, Margaret, what's the matter with you? Did one hour in a jail cell turn your brain to mush?"

Amanda managed a weak smile. "I guess I'm just a little tired."

"Yeah, me, too," Serena said, sinking back in the seat. "Not to mention extremely aggravated. I really thought we'd score tonight. We were so close! I could taste that lottery ticket!"

"Yeah, me, too," Amanda murmured.

"I can't believe Ken went and told his idiot classmates about the séance," Serena went on. "When I was the student teacher in that class they barely talked to each other—they were like strangers."

She was right, Amanda realized. A lot had changed since those days when she herself had first entered room

209, just before Serena appeared as a student teacher. Not that she would call any of them her best friends now or even invite them to a party.

But they'd shared some very peculiar stuff, and they'd helped each other in and out of some very weird situations. A strange sort of bond was forming. She just had to be very careful that the rest of Meadowbrook Middle School never found out, or else her reputation would be in tatters.

"Do you think Stevie will ever find the lottery ticket?" she asked Serena.

"Who knows?" Serena shrugged off the question. "Who cares? It won't be ours." She sighed. "Well, it's no big deal. It would have been nice to have the two million, but we've got bigger stuff in the works."

Amanda choked back the words *We do?* Apparently, she and Serena were connected well beyond the séance scheme. What kind of terrible activities were next on the agenda?

This wasn't the life for her. Among the many fantasies Amanda had entertained for her future, being a criminal just wasn't one of them. All the money in the world wasn't worth the churning, sickening feeling she had right now in the pit of her stomach.

But if she was stuck in Margaret Robinson's body, what were her options? Serena was dangerous. She wasn't just going to let Margaret walk away from a life of crime. In the back of her mind, she started considering the various possibilities. Those parents in Florida . . . She could go down there and stay there, far away from Serena Hancock. It wouldn't be easy pretending to be Margaret in front of Margaret's own parents, though. She'd managed to do it with Tracey's parents, but that hadn't been so difficult since Tracey's parents had never paid much attention to her. From that phone conversation she'd had with Margaret's mother, she got the feeling they were a lot closer. Mrs. Robinson might be able to see that a stranger was occupying her daughter's body.

If she could find the PIN for Margaret's ATM card, she could take all her money—but how much money would a substitute teacher have? She could buy a flight with one of Margaret's credit cards and flee the country, but that meant having a passport, which meant providing documents like birth certificates—assuming Margaret didn't have a passport already. She had no idea how to get her hands on stuff like that, and she hadn't found a passport on any of her hunts through Margaret's apartment. And even if she did make it to, say, France, what would she do there? She couldn't even speak the language.

Suddenly she felt like she was going to throw up. But she was too scared even to do that.

The taxi pulled up at an ordinary medium-size house

on a tree-lined street. Amanda started to breathe a little easier. This didn't look very scary. Serena turned to her.

"Ready?"

For *what*? Amanda wanted to ask. But she just managed a weak smile and nodded.

"Remember," Serena said as they went up the path to the front door, "we're members of the team, too. And they've all had missions that didn't work out. The big project is still on schedule. I realize that this is the first time you'll be meeting them, but don't let them intimidate you."

"I won't," Amanda whispered.

"And let me do the talking."

Amanda was perfectly willing to go along with that.

Serena had a key to the front door. They walked into a foyer that led into a bland, ordinary living room.

"Hello?" she called out.

"We're in here." The voice was masculine and deep. Amanda thought it sounded vaguely familiar.

She followed Serena into another room, where three people sat at a dining table. And none of the three was a stranger to Amanda.

The first one she recognized was Clare. Her hair was blond again, the way it had been when Amanda-as-Sarah had been kidnapped by her.

Next to her was the man she knew as Stuart Kelley, who had claimed to be Jenna's father.

And on the other side of Clare sat Mr. Jackson, the principal of Meadowbrook Middle School.

None of them looked at her with any particular interest. Why would they? They'd never seen her before—or so they thought.

But Amanda had seen all of them before, in different places, and in circumstances that were completely unconnected. Or so she'd thought. And the realization of what she was now seeing stunned her. She was dizzy, her head was spinning. Reeling, actually. She didn't think that she'd ever had a greater shock.

Which could explain why she suddenly found herself lying in her very own bed with a very sore throat.

Chapter Fifteen

WHEN HE WOKE UP the next morning, still dressed in the clothes he'd worn the day before, Ken's first action was to check to see if an open notebook lay on the nightstand by his bed. With enormous relief, he found it.

So it hadn't been a dream. And he'd done the right thing—he'd written the instructions down.

He read them over and over, until he committed them to memory.

It was early—his alarm wasn't set to go off for another two hours. This was good news because he had a lot to do before school started. As he took a shower and changed his clothes, he went over the plan. He would go back to the Fisher house and catch Stevie before he left for school. He'd tell the boy how he'd had a message from his father, and he'd show him where his father had left the lottery ticket. He bet Stevie would be really surprised to know that his father had a secret place where he kept important things—under a loose floorboard in the back of a rarely visited closet full of old junk.

Stevie's mother could cash in the lottery ticket and save the family home. Little Dena could see a real doctor about her rash, and Cindy could have a new pair of shoes. And best of all—for Ken at least—Stevie would know that Ken was a good guy, that he had never been a part of Serena's scheme to steal the ticket. Maybe he and Stevie would remain friends and Ken could be like a big brother to him.

There was only one small problem. Two, actually. First of all, Stevie wasn't going to be very happy to see Ken back at the Fisher house. Ken was going to have to do a lot of fast talking to persuade Stevie to let him in.

But it was the second problem that really made him nervous. To accomplish this task, he would have to let Stevie know about his gift.

He'd argued with Madame and others in the class about this. He hadn't believed that his gift had any value to whatever enemies the class had, and he'd been sure that none of the others in the gifted class would be in danger if he revealed his gift.

Well, events of the past week had proved he was wrong about the first part of his assumption. Bad people *had* tried to use him. And if he could be wrong about that, he could be wrong about putting the class in danger.

But Stevie needed that ticket. And now that Ken knew where the ticket was, how could he do nothing? How could he let Stevie and his family suffer—lose their home, live in poverty—when they didn't have to?

His mother was in the kitchen when he came downstairs.

"What are you doing up so early?" she asked him.

At that moment, Ken learned that he wasn't such a bad liar after all. "I've got a meeting at school with my science project group."

His mother was impressed. "Well, you kids must be excited about this project if it's getting you out of bed. What is your group doing?"

He couldn't lie *that* well. He looked at his watch. "Oh wow, I'm late. I'll tell you about it later, Mom."

"Don't you want something to eat?" his mother called after him, but he just yelled back another whopper.

"No, thanks, I'm not hungry." And he was out the door.

But now what? He still hadn't figured out how he was going to fix Stevie's problem.

His cell phone rang. He flipped it open and held it to his ear.

"Hello?"

"Ken, this is Tracey. I hope I didn't wake you up."

He scowled. What did *she* want? He was still very much annoyed by the way the three girls had behaved. "No, I'm up. What do you want?"

"I couldn't sleep. I felt so bad about yesterday. We shouldn't have made those plans without telling you."

"It was Jenna's idea, wasn't it?"

"Yeah, but Emily and I went along with it, so we're just as guilty."

Ken doubted that. He knew how pushy Jenna could be. And Tracey sounded really sorry.

"It's okay," he relented.

"I wish I could make it up to you," Tracey said, sounding sincere.

Ken stood very still. A brilliant idea had struck him.

"Actually, Tracey, you can. If you're really sorry, you can help me do something right now."

He told her all about his visit to Stevie's house the night before and explained that he now knew where the ticket was. Then he told her his idea.

Ten minutes later, they met up at a corner halfway between their two homes.

Tracey was nervous. "It doesn't always work, you know. I mean, I'm getting better, but sometimes I just can't do it. And even when it does work, I never know how long it will last."

But she completely understood why he'd come up with his plan. And she was willing to try as hard as she could to make it happen.

When they arrived at Apple Creek Road, Ken pointed out the house.

"I can't walk through walls, you know," Tracey reminded him. "I'm going to have to wait for someone to come in or out."

Ken looked at his watch. "Stevie should be leaving for school pretty soon. Can you get ready now?"

He told her about the closet and the loose floorboard. Tracey nodded.

"Okay. Here goes," she said. She stood very still and closed her eyes.

"What does it feel like?" Ken asked curiously.

She opened her eyes. "Be quiet. I have to concentrate."

"Sorry," Ken said.

He'd never seen the process in action before. Tracey had developed her gift back when her parents ignored her and she felt invisible. She was a much happier person now, and Ken knew it had to be difficult for her to recapture the feeling of being a nothing, a nobody.

But she did it. Right there, before his eyes, she began to fade. It was positively eerie, like watching a special effect in a science fiction movie. And then she wasn't there.

"Tracey?" he asked.

She must have already taken off. He looked at the house

across the street. He couldn't see her, of course, but if she was following the plan she was waiting just by the door.

Something could still go wrong, and Ken knew it. Maybe Stevie had already left for school, or maybe he wasn't going to school today. Maybe nobody would go in or out of the house at 72 Apple Creek Road all day. Maybe, maybe, maybe . . .

But he could stop tormenting himself. The door of the house opened. Ken ducked behind a tree and peered through the branches. A woman stood there—Stevie's mother, Ken guessed. She had a small child in her arms. That had to be Dena.

An older girl appeared at the door, and then Stevie was there, too. They kissed their mother.

Then they started walking away, the mother went back inside, and the door closed.

Ken let out the breath he'd been holding.

There had been plenty of time for the invisible Tracey to get inside. Now she had to stay invisible long enough to accomplish her mission and get herself back outside.

Ken stared at the house, even though there wasn't really anything to look at. It was weird, not having a clue as to what was going on inside.

An eternity seemed to pass. He kept looking at his watch, and he could see that only a few minutes had gone by, but it felt like much longer.

The door to the house opened again, and Mrs. Fisher came out. She was holding little Dena's hand. With the other, she locked the front door. Oh no! Ken thought. Would Tracey be trapped inside until someone came home?

"I'm here."

He looked in the direction of the voice.

"Tracey?"

Even though he couldn't see her face, he could hear the excitement in her voice.

"I found it, Ken! It was right where you said it would be, under the loose floorboard in the closet."

"What did you do with it?"

"I put it on the refrigerator door, under a magnet. They can't miss it."

Ken frowned. "Isn't that a little obvious? I mean, wouldn't they have noticed it before?"

"Haven't you ever searched everywhere for something and then found it, right in plain sight?"

She had a point.

"I guess we better get to school. We've got a long way to go."

"Yeah, okay."

"And you can come back now," Ken added. "Nobody's watching."

"Actually . . . I can't."

"What do you mean?"

"Well, it's weird. I'm getting better and better at disappearing when I want to, but it's not so easy to make myself reappear. It's like the invisibility has to wear off on its own."

"How long does that take?"

"I never know exactly. But it's usually within an hour or so. I should be okay by the time we get to school."

Ken found it surprisingly easy to talk to an invisible Tracey as they walked back to Meadowbrook. He considered holding his cell phone to his ear, so anyone passing by wouldn't think he was talking to himself, but he was too happy to really care.

"So, things are going to be all right for Stevie and his family," he said.

"Yeah. Of course, Stevie won't ever know that you found the ticket for him. He'll still think you're one of the bad guys who tried to steal it."

"I know. I'll just have to live with that." He was disappointed, but he knew it was for the best because this way he didn't have to tell Stevie about his gift. "Speaking of bad guys . . . do you get freaked out when Madame keeps talking about how much danger we're in?"

"Not so much," Tracey replied. "Not for myself, at least.

If I can disappear, no one can really hurt me. I worry about everyone else, though."

"Including me?"

"Sure. You didn't think bad guys would be interested in your gift, and look what just happened."

"So I suppose we really should try to keep our gifts secret."

"Absolutely," Tracey declared. And then she laughed.

"What's so funny?"

"I'm thinking about kids at school—regular people, not criminal types. If they found out what each of us can do . . ."

"How do you think they'd react?" Ken asked.

"Well, unless they see us in action," Tracey said, "we've got nothing to worry about."

"What do you mean?"

"Think about it, Ken. Hi, guys, guess what I can do? I can disappear! You know Jenna Kelley? She can read minds. Emily sees into the future, and Ken talks to dead people."

"I think I get your point," Ken said. "They wouldn't believe it." He remembered Jack telling him the same thing.

"Exactly. I mean, I wouldn't go around talking about what we can do. But if a rumor starts spreading around school, well, I don't think we have anything to worry about. By the way, do you know where Amanda went?

The real Amanda?"

"No. Maybe she'll be back at school today and we'll find out."

"I think it could be fun to live someone else's life for a while," Tracey said. "If you could be anyone else for a week, who would you be?"

They were able to entertain each other with candidates all the way back to Meadowbrook. Tracey wanted to go into space as an astronaut or be a jockey on a horse that could win the Kentucky Derby. Ken admitted to a secret dream of performing as a hip-hop artist. They were so caught up in their fantasies that Ken completely forgot he was talking to someone who wasn't visibly there. He only remembered as the school came into view.

"Better lower your voice," he cautioned Tracey as they approached the building. "Actually, it's still early. There aren't many people around. But we probably ought to stop talking before anyone notices us."

"They can't hear me," Tracey told him. "You're the only person who's ever been able to hear me when I'm invisible."

"I guess I'm just more sensitive to people who aren't really there," Ken replied.

"I can't believe I'm still invisible," Tracey grumbled. "I hope I'm back by this afternoon—I've got an appointment for a haircut."

Ken didn't reply. He'd just spotted Lucy standing alongside the stairs leading up to the main entrance. She was alone, and when she spotted him, she waved.

He winced. He hadn't written that apologetic e-mail yet. He was going to have to apologize in person. Well, so be it. He squared his shoulders and started toward her. It dawned on him that Tracey might still be by his side, and he should tell her to go on, that this was something personal. But now it was too late. Lucy would be able to see him speaking to no one if he did talk to Tracey.

He tried to put his companion out of his mind and focus on the girl in front of him. "Hi, Lucy. Listen, I want to apologize for last night. I was in a really bad mood about something, and I took it out on you. I'm really sorry."

She didn't seem upset. "That's okay, I forgive you," she said with a smile. "As long as you take me to the eighth-grade dance this weekend."

"I'm in the ninth grade, Lucy."

"I know that! But we're allowed to bring people from other grades as our dates."

He took a deep breath. "Listen, Lucy . . . you're a cute girl and all, but—well—I'm sort of into someone else."

He could have sworn he heard a sharp intake of breath, like a gasp, and it hadn't come from Lucy. Damn!

Tracey was still there. And now she'd want to know whom Ken was talking about.

Lucy didn't seem to care. "Well, she's out of luck, whoever she is. Because I want you to be into me."

Ken shifted his weight from one leg to the other. This was not going to be easy. "Like I said, Lucy . . . you're really nice, and I know Jack was crazy about you, but I'm just not interested in you in that way. I hope we can be friends, but . . ." His voice trailed off as her expression changed. There was something cold in her face now.

"Don't forget, Ken, I know something about you."

He looked at her stupidly. "Huh?"

"I know what you can do. How would you feel if I told people that you talk to dead people?"

It was Ken's turn to gasp. "Lucy! You wouldn't do that, would you?"

"Not if you go to the dance with me. And other places."

It took Ken a moment to respond. "Are you—are you trying to blackmail me?"

Lucy laughed, but it wasn't a pretty laugh. There was something very mean about it. "I never thought I'd have to threaten a guy to go out with me, but I'll do what I have to do. I want you to be my boyfriend, Ken. I think we'd be good together, and once you get over your hang-ups about me being Jack's ex-girlfriend, you'll be happy with me."

"Lucy, this has nothing to do with Jack. No offense, but I'm just not into you!"

Her voice hardened. "Then get into me. Or everyone at school is going to know about your weird conversations."

He couldn't believe what he was hearing.

"You'd really do that?"

"Sure."

He looked at her thoughtfully.

"Well?" she asked, smiling.

He smiled back. "Go right ahead."

Her smile faded. "What?"

"Tell them. Tell everyone I hear dead people. Write an article for the school newspaper. Or announce it over the intercom."

She was speechless. Ken's smile broadened.

"Because it's not like anyone's going to believe you," he said. "I gotta go. Hope you find someone to take you to the dance."

He knew Tracey was by his side as he walked into the school. She was still invisible, but he could have sworn there was a huge grin on her invisible face.

CHAPTER SIXTEEN

EVEN WITH HER SORE throat, Amanda had never before been so incredibly happy to be back in her own body. She felt so good, she insisted on going back to school. And for the first time ever, she was impatient to get through the day so she could go to the gifted class.

She had so much to tell them! Even Madame would be impressed with her adventure. Of course, Jenna would claim to be the hero, since she had organized the revelation of the medium's true identity. But Amanda could top that. She had the most amazing, stupendous news of all. There was a conspiracy, just as Madame had suggested. People who'd tried to use the gifted students were working together. And their very own school principal was part of the gang.

Just before class, she went into a restroom to touch up her lip-gloss and brush her hair. She wanted to make a grand entrance, so she stayed there until the warning bell rang and then dashed down the hall.

She entered just as the final bell rang. From her desk, Madame looked up and smiled.

"Welcome back, Amanda! How are you feeling?"

"A little tired," Amanda said, "but not from the operation." She addressed the whole class. "You'll be surprised to learn I haven't been spending the past few days in bed."

Jenna spoke. "We're not surprised. Tracey told us."

Amanda stared at her. "Tracey told you what?"

"Emily and I went to visit you at the hospital," Tracey said. "We knew it wasn't really you."

Amanda hadn't realized Tracey was there. Neither had Madame.

"Tracey! Where did you come from?"

The newly visible Tracey explained. "Ken wanted to help his friend from the séance, Stevie, find his father's lottery ticket."

Ken picked up the story. "His father spoke to me last night and told me where the ticket was. I wanted to tell Stevie myself, but I came up with a better plan that meant I didn't have to reveal my gift. I asked Tracey if she could turn herself invisible, get the ticket, and put it somewhere the family was bound to see it."

Madame looked pleased. "Very good, Ken.

You managed to keep the secret *and* help Stevie's family. Well done!"

Now everyone was congratulating Ken and Tracey. Amanda was starting to feel as if *she* were invisible.

"Isn't anyone interested in knowing where I went when I left my body?" she asked loudly.

"Let me guess," Charles said. "Someone who wasn't getting their tonsils taken out."

"No kidding," Jenna remarked. "You know, Amanda, I never thought you had a very useful gift—at least not for helping anyone else—but it certainly works for *you*. You can get out of doing anything you don't want to do."

Amanda was furious. "For your information, Miss Know-It-All, I happened to be at Ken's séance!"

Ken was clearly startled. "You're kidding! Who were you?"

Gratified by the attention, Amanda preened. "Margaret Robinson, the woman who claimed her mother had just died. But who turned out to be Serena's pal!"

"Serena?" Madame asked.

Ken broke in. "Serena Hancock, that girl who did student teaching here. She was the fake medium."

"Good grief!" Madame remarked. "She's certainly determined to get her hands on a lottery ticket."

Amanda was about to announce that there was much

more to it than that when Madame turned back to her.

"Amanda, if you took over the body of someone involved in this business, you must have realized right away that it was a scam."

Amanda nodded proudly. "I did, and—"

But Madame wasn't finished. She spoke sternly. "Then you should have come directly here and told me! You put yourself in grave danger, not to mention Ken."

"And us," Jenna piped up. "Me and Emily and Tracey."

"Why did you do that, Amanda?" Madame wanted to know. "Why didn't you tell us what was going on?"

Jenna jumped in again. "Because she was probably having too much fun being an adult. What did you do, Amanda? Shop till you dropped?"

That got a laugh from several classmates.

"Now, Jenna," Madame reprimanded her, "let's hear Amanda's side of the story."

But Amanda was no longer interested in telling them what she'd learned. They were making fun of her, criticizing her, treating her like a villain! And the way Ken was looking at her now, like she was scum! She was hurt, and she was furious. These people—they didn't deserve to know what she knew.

She made a decision. She was *not* going to tell them about the conspiracy, about Mr. Jackson—about anything.

She'd keep it to herself. And they'd all be sorry for having picked on her like this.

Because with the information she had, she'd be the one who would save them all from whatever those bad people were planning. She'd be the biggest hero of all. She'd be worshiped and adored and respected. Which was what she deserved.

But for now . . .

"My throat hurts," she announced. "Can I go to the infirmary and ask the nurse to call my mother? I think I should go home."

Madame was immediately sympathetic. "Of course, Amanda. We can discuss this another time, when you're feeling better."

And with her head high and her secret intact, Amanda left the room.

Gifted

Now You
See Me

CHAPTER ONE

"TRACEY!"

Her mother's voice rang out loud and clear from the kitchen. Curled up with a book on the living-room sofa, Tracey responded.

"What?"

"Tracey! Have you seen my purse?"

Tracey raised her eyes up from the page and surveyed the room.

"It's under the coffee table!" she called back.

"Tracey!" Now her mother sounded annoyed. "Tracey, answer me!"

Tracey frowned. Was her mother developing a hearing problem? She was about to yell back even louder when the front door opened and her father came in and walked right past Tracey without even greeting her. That was when Tracey realized that sometime in the past half-hour, she'd gone invisible.

She wished she could understand how and why this

had happened. It used to be so simple. Years of feeling unimportant and not worthy of attention had caused her to go invisible on a regular basis. She didn't feel that way about herself anymore, but occasionally she could make herself go invisible by recalling how she used to feel. It wasn't always a reliable process, but she'd been getting better and better at controlling her gift. Still, every now and then it just happened—she would disappear, and she wasn't sure why. Maybe this time it was caused by the book she'd been reading, *Jane Eyre*. The character of Jane had just been sent away to a horrible boarding school, and she was lonely. Maybe Tracey was simply feeling sad for the character . . .

Her father had gone into the kitchen, and she could hear her parents' conversation.

"Have you seen my purse?" her mother asked.

"No, did you lose it?"

"I don't know. I don't think so—I had it this morning. But I've looked all over the house! The seven are at their swimming class. I have to pick them up in ten minutes, and I can't find my purse!"

So *that* was why the house was so quiet, Tracey mused. Her little sisters, the identical septuplets collectively known as the "Devon Seven," weren't at home.

"What am I going to do?" her mother wailed. She sounded on the verge of hysteria, which didn't really alarm Tracey. Mrs. Devon had a tendency to become terribly dramatic very easily.

Reluctantly, Tracey put her book down. *Come back,* she ordered herself. But of course, it wasn't that easy. She concentrated on feeling good about herself. *People pay attention to me, my parents care about me, I have friends.* It didn't work—she was still invisible. She really had to work harder on controlling her gift, practice more, learn how to concentrate harder. But meanwhile, her mother needed her purse.

Tracey got up, retrieved the purse from under the coffee table, and ambled into the kitchen. Her mother was still ranting.

"My car keys are in the purse! How can I pick the girls up without car keys?"

"Take my car," Mr. Devon suggested.

"But my driver's license is in my purse! I can't drive without a license!"

Tracey planted herself in front of her mother and dangled the purse in the air. Her mother didn't blink.

"Where did I leave that purse?" she fretted.

Tracey hadn't been thinking. Of course, if she was invisible, and the purse was in her hands, then the purse

189

was invisible, too. She dropped the purse onto the kitchen counter.

"Isn't that your purse?" her father asked.

Mrs. Devon turned and gasped. "It wasn't there two seconds ago!" Then she shrieked. That was when Tracey realized she had become visible again.

This wasn't the first time she'd suddenly appeared in front of her parents, and her parents knew about her so-called gift, but her mother couldn't get used to it.

"Tracey, don't *do* that!" she cried out.

"Sorry, Mom, I didn't mean to scare you." Tracey glanced at the clock on the wall. "I gotta go—I'm meeting Jenna and Emily at the mall. I'll be home before dinner."

"But will we actually see you later?" her father wanted to know.

Tracey just grinned and took off. She was heading to the big mall, not the one across from their school, so she had to take a bus. She supposed she could have asked her mother to drop her off on the way to pick up the seven, but she wasn't in the mood to listen to her go on and on about her disappearing act. She had to admit, though, it was kind of nice hearing her parents express a desire to see her. There was a time when that hadn't been the case at all.

Thank goodness she was meeting two friends from her gifted class, where every student had an unusual skill. Even though their abilities were different, they had some of the same problems. She didn't have to explain or apologize to *them*.

Jenna Kelley and Emily Sanders were waiting for her at their usual meeting place, in front of the bookstore. They made an unlikely pair, Tracey thought as she approached them. Jenna was a goth goddess— black spiky hair with long bangs that gave her a witchy look. Pale complexion, eyes circled in black eyeliner, purple lips, and a variety of piercings. Black skinny jeans and a black T-shirt with white letters that read "Stay Out of My Way." If you didn't know her, you might think she was dangerous.

Emily's plain, long brown hair, soft dreamy expression, and unmade-up face made her look at least three years younger than her 14 years. *Her* jeans were baggy, and her T-shirt was a washed-out pale blue.

And how would Tracey herself fit into the odd combo? As she passed a store, she glanced at her own reflection in the window and caught a glimpse of a small, slender girl with blond hair that skimmed her shoulders. Not a lot of makeup—just a little green eyeliner to make her pale eyes sparkle and a wash of pink lipgloss on her lips. It was still a pleasant surprise to see how much better she looked now than she used to. Lately, she was happy just to be able to see herself at all.

Her friends were pleased to see her, too, though Jenna glanced pointedly at her watch.

"You're five minutes late," she declared.

Tracey grinned. "Just be glad I'm here at all. I disappeared for a while today."

"Without trying?" Emily asked.

Tracey nodded. "Yeah. It was kind of freaky. Of course, I wasn't as freaked out as my mother was when I reappeared right in front of her. She practically fainted!"

Jenna made a "humph" sound. "Serves her right. The way she's treated you, she deserves to be freaked out."

Tracey brushed that aside. "That's all in the past, Jenna. And look on the bright side. If my parents hadn't ignored me all those years, I might never have developed my gift."

"But it still wasn't nice, the way they behaved," Emily murmured.

She was right, Tracey thought. The Devons had been normal, attentive parents to her when she was very young. But something happened when she turned eight. That was the year the Devon Seven were born.

They weren't the first septuplets in the world, but they were the first identical set of seven girls. Her family became famous, and Tracey could remember being just as excited as everyone else about the remarkable birth of her sisters.

192

But then things changed.

She supposed it was normal for her parents to become completely preoccupied with the newborn girls. But was it normal for them to completely forget their oldest child?

It wasn't like those terrible stories of child abuse you read about in newspapers. They didn't yell at Tracey, or hit her, or refuse to give her food. It was more like Tracey just wasn't there anymore, like she'd ceased to exist. And Tracey found herself responding by simply fading away.

At first, it was just in her mind—it was her own attitude that made her feel "invisible" to people outside her own family. If she didn't deserve attention at home, why should she expect anyone else to notice her? That was the kind of vibe she gave off, and people reacted by not giving her any consideration. At school, teachers never called on her. On the street, people would bump into her and then look surprised, as if they hadn't realized anyone was there. In stores, she couldn't get a salesperson to help her.

It got worse and worse. Since no one seemed to care about her, she stopped caring for herself. And as bizarre as it sounded, it seemed inevitable that she would become physically, as well as emotionally, invisible.

But all that had changed. Tracey had learned to assert herself and demand the attention she deserved as a human being. She could still disappear, sometimes on purpose, but she didn't have complete control over her gift. Neither did Emily or Jenna, but they were all learning more and more about what they could do. Emily had learned how to examine her visions of the future, so she could understand what she was actually seeing. As for Jenna . . .

"Read any interesting minds lately?" Tracey asked her as they strolled through the mall.

"Nothing worth talking about," Jenna said. "But I was thinking the other day—you know what would be cool? If I could hang out at police stations and check out all the people who are arrested and tell the cops whether or not they really committed any crimes. Or go to trials and read the minds of the defendants. I'd be able to tell the judge if they were guilty or not, and they wouldn't even need a jury."

"Dream on," Tracey commented. "You think the judge would believe you?"

"And since when do you want to help police officers?" Emily wanted to know. "You're always saying you don't like cops."

"And even if the police believed you, Madame would kill you," Tracey added.

Jenna made an elaborate "who cares" gesture. "Big deal."

Tracey and Emily exchanged knowing glances. Jenna liked to act tough, as if she wasn't scared of anything or anyone, but her friends knew better. All the students in the gifted class had a healthy respect for Madame. She was one of the few people they could totally trust with the knowledge of their gifts, and the only one who really understood the gifts and what they meant.

Madame was always telling them to keep their gifts secret, and for good reason. They'd all had experiences with some real low-life types who wanted to use their abilities for less-than-noble purposes.

Jenna glared at them both. "I know what you're thinking."

Emily gave her a reproving look. "Jenna, you're not supposed to try to read our minds."

"Didn't have to," Jenna declared. "It's all over your faces—you think I'm showing off. But I'm telling you, I don't care what Madame thinks."

"And you'll never know, will you?" Tracey said. "You can't read Madame's mind, right?"

"Not if she knows I'm around," Jenna replied. "You know, I've finally figured out why some people are a total blank to me. If they know what I can do, they can figure out how to block their thoughts from me. That's why I could never read my mother's mind. She always knew about me." She sighed. "I used to think it was because we're related. And I thought that was why I couldn't read that—that man's mind. Because I believed he was my father."

Tracey knew who she was talking about. A man had turned up one day over a month ago and claimed he was Jenna's long-lost father. At first she believed him, and she was thrilled. But he wasn't her father; he was of no relation to her at all. Somehow, he'd learned about her gift. And all he really wanted was for Jenna to read minds for him so he could win at poker.

"He knew what you could do, so he blocked you," Emily said.

Jenna nodded. "What I always wondered was, how did he find out about me?"

Neither Tracey nor Emily could answer that. And Tracey was more interested in learning something else.

"So, how do *we* block you?"

Jenna grinned. "You'll have to figure that out for yourselves."

"It's easy," Emily informed Tracey. "I've been practicing. You get the feeling she's poking around in your head and you just shut her out. It's like an instinct or something."

Jenna gave her a sour look. "Thanks a lot. I don't care, anyway. I mean, it's not like you two ever think about anything worth hearing."

"That's right," Tracey said cheerfully. "Besides, we always

end up telling each other what we're thinking."

"That's true," Emily noted. And even Jenna had to agree with that.

Tracey agreed, too, and she felt pretty good about it. It was *nice* having friends she could be so open with, friends who understood what you were all about. Their parents knew about their special talents, but they couldn't really understand, since they didn't have these gifts themselves. That was what made the gifted class so special. They could talk freely about their abilities, and everyone could relate to them. They could be appreciated and respected by one another.

Okay, maybe "everyone" was an exaggeration. Tracey spotted someone just a short distance in front of them who'd never expressed much appreciation or respect for any of her classmates.

Jenna saw her, too, and groaned. "Uh-oh, watch out. The Evil Queen and her Evilettes are here."

Amanda Beeson was looking into the window of a new boutique, Apparel, with her pals Nina and Britney.

"Gee, from a distance, they almost look like human beings," Jenna commented.

"Oh, come on, Jenna, they're not that bad," Tracey remonstrated. "Okay, Nina and Britney are pretty snotty, but Amanda can be okay sometimes."

"Yeah? Like when?"

Tracey turned to Emily. "Don't forget, she was the one who saved you when you were trapped in the closet at school with that awful Serena. Remember?"

Emily shuddered. "I'm not likely to forget that. But it wasn't Amanda who burst into the closet, it was you."

Tracey shook her head. "Amanda had taken over my body, and she was in control. So it was really her."

"Oh yeah, that's right," Emily murmured.

"I don't care. I think she's positively despicable," Jenna declared. "She didn't do a thing to help Ken in that séance scam, remember?"

It was less than two weeks ago, so Tracey wasn't likely to have forgotten the event already—they'd been discussing it ever since. Ken's so-called gift was the ability to communicate with dead people. Looking for someone who might understand what he could do, he'd gotten involved with a fake medium. Amanda had taken over the body of another séance participant. Amanda could only do this when she felt sorry for someone, so this woman must have seemed pretty sad. But even when Amanda learned that the participant was the medium's partner-in-crime, she'd done nothing to stop the scam from moving on.

"That was pretty weird," Tracey admitted. "Especially because I always thought Amanda was into Ken."

"Amanda is into Amanda," Jenna declared. "It must have been really horrible for you, having Amanda in your head."

"I don't know," Tracey answered honestly. "I don't remember anything. It's like I was asleep."

"She'd better not ever try to take over my body," Jenna declared.

"I doubt that could happen," Emily said. "She has to feel sorry for someone before she can take over their body. Why would she ever feel sorry for you?"

"Because I can't afford the clothes in Apparel," Jenna replied. "Not that I'd ever want any of them. And you know what? I don't buy that business about Amanda feeling sorry for people. She's a selfish snob, and she never thinks about anyone but herself."

"That's not true," Tracey said. "When she had my body, she did a lot for me. She got my parents to pay attention to me. She bought me decent clothes, she got me a haircut . . ."

Jenna snorted. "Only because she was afraid she'd be stuck being you forever."

Tracey wasn't so sure about that. Even though she hadn't been aware of Amanda's intentions when Amanda was inhabiting her body, she couldn't help feeling that the girl might have had some kind motives. She was about to tell Jenna this when she noticed that Jenna was staring at

Amanda in a particular way that Tracey recognized.

"Are you reading her mind?" Tracey asked.

"Yeah, she's thinking about trying on the skirt in the window. Thrilling, huh?" But then her expression changed. "Whoa, wait a second."

"What is it?" Emily asked.

"She's got a secret. It . . . it has something to do with, with . . ." she squinted in her effort to concentrate. Then her eyes widened in surprise. "She's thinking about Mr. Jackson!"

Tracey was startled. "As in, Principal Jackson?"

"What kind of secret could she have about Mr. Jackson?" Emily wanted to know.

They weren't going to find out—at least, not that day. Amanda spotted them.

"Damn, she's learned how to block me, too," Jenna muttered.

Tracey laughed. "What did you think she'd do? 'Hi, Jenna, welcome to my private thoughts.'" She smiled at Amanda, but all she got back was a blink of recognition before Amanda moved hurriedly away, with Nina and Britney at her heels.

"She really is a snob," Emily remarked. "She won't even speak to us."

"It's just because she's with her friends," Tracey said.

"She knows Nina would say something mean to us. I think she's trying to protect us from being insulted."

Both Jenna and Emily gazed at her as if she was out of her mind.

"Why are you always defending her?" Jenna asked.

"I don't know." Tracey sighed. "I guess I can't help thinking there's something good in Amanda." The expressions of disbelief on her friends' faces remained intact, so she changed the subject.

She turned to Emily. "Got any predictions to make?"

"About what?" Emily asked.

"Anything."

"It doesn't work like that," Emily said. "I have to be thinking about something in particular."

"Think about me," Jenna suggested. "Is anything interesting going to happen to me this week?"

Obediently, Emily looked at Jenna in that peculiarly dreamy way she took on when she was trying to get an image of the future. Her eyes glazed over.

"Well?" Jenna asked impatiently. "Can you see me?"

"Yes." Emily's brow furrowed. "With . . . with a knife in your hand."

"Good grief!" Tracey exclaimed. "Is she pointing it at someone?"

"No. She's just holding a knife."

Tracey looked at Jenna with concern. After all, her friend did have a reputation. When she'd first come to Meadowbrook straight from some sort of place for delinquent teens, she'd been observed with trepidation by students and teachers.

Jenna just shrugged. "That makes sense."

"It does?" Emily asked. Now she was looking nervously at Jenna, too.

Jenna nodded. "I'm fixing dinner tonight, and I'm making tuna salad. I'll be chopping onions, celery, carrots . . . yeah, I guess I'll be holding a knife for at least half an hour."

Tracey immediately felt guilty for having even considered that Jenna might be planning to do something criminal with a knife. Jenna didn't hang out with gangs anymore, and even though she retained her tough-girl demeanor, she hadn't been in any serious trouble. Tracey was absolutely, positively, no-doubt-about-it certain that Jenna had completely reformed.

Still, it was reassuring to know that Jenna's knife would be used for strictly nonviolent purposes.

Chapter Two

WHAT A DIFFERENCE a few months could make, Jenna thought as she strolled into room 209 on Monday afternoon. She remembered the first day she'd entered this classroom and how angry, depressed, and scared she'd been. She'd just been let out of that place she'd been sent to after her arrest for drug possession. Harmony House . . . a fancy name for what was really a jail for teenagers. She'd been taken away from home and forced to spend three months with thieves, gang leaders, addicts . . . when *her* only real crime had been hanging out with people like that.

Not that home had been such a great place to be, either. Her mother was rarely there, and when she was at home, she was drunk. Welfare checks were spent on booze and who knew what else, and Jenna could recall many nights when she went to bed hungry.

So release from Harmony House wasn't any great relief. She went back to Brookside Towers, the depressing low-income housing development she'd been living in with her mother for two years. Her mother was still drinking, still partying. The apartment was a mess, her *life* was a mess, and she had to keep that fact a secret from the social workers or she'd be sent into foster care. She'd already endured foster care twice temporarily, and she didn't plan to go through that again.

By order of the judge, Jenna had been transferred to this school, Meadowbrook, and as if that wasn't bad enough, she also had to report to a school counselor every week. But the counselor, Mr. Gonzalez, wasn't such a bad guy. He didn't know about Jenna's ability to read minds, but he must have suspected there was something uniquely odd about her because he sent her to see Madame. Jenna had been furious—she'd been branded as a "problem" again, and now she had to attend a "special" class with other problem students.

So the first time she entered this classroom, she was in a very bad mood. The so-called gifted class could only make her already wretched life even worse.

But then things began to turn around for her. Aspects of her life started to improve. Her mother went into a rehab program, and now she'd been sober for over a month. She'd gotten a job, too.

Even her home was better. The residents of

Brookside Towers were demanding long-overdue improvements to the development, and the city council was actually responding.

And the gifted class turned out to be nothing like what she'd expected. Her classmates weren't "problems"—not in the traditional sense. They had "gifts," too. And despite her usual efforts to remain aloof and disagreeable, Jenna found herself fitting in—and even making friends. It wasn't in Jenna's nature to show her feelings or admit them to anyone, but deep in her heart she knew she was as close to being happy as she'd ever been.

Not that she was great friends with *all* her classmates. She glanced at Martin Cooper, who sat over by the windows. He was looking at her right now with fear in his eyes.

"You'd better not be reading my mind," he said to her in an accusing tone.

Jenna shook her head wearily. The little wimp. He was the eternal victim, always expecting to be picked on and bullied. His only satisfaction came when he was teased so much that his gift emerged—and an incredible physical strength made him capable of causing serious damage.

"Out of my way," barked a voice behind her. Jenna stayed right where she was, knowing full well that Charles Temple could easily maneuver his wheelchair around her. She wondered if being unable to walk was the reason he could be so aggressive and argumentative. She assumed it was the source of his gift—telekinesis—the ability to make things move with his mind.

Sarah Miller was already in her seat, of course. Jenna always thought of her as "Little Miss Too Good to Be True." How else could she criticize someone who was always sweet? It was still hard to believe that Sarah had potentially the most dangerous gift of all of them—the ability to make people do anything she wanted them to do. Not that Jenna had seen much evidence of this amazing gift. For some mysterious reason, Sarah didn't want to use her talent.

Ken Preston looked up and caught her eye. "Hi," he said. The greeting wasn't expressed very warmly, but Jenna was just pleased to be acknowledged by him. She and Ken had experienced some conflicts recently, and she didn't want him to hold anything against her. He wasn't a close friend like Emily or Tracey, but she thought he was an okay kind of guy. Also, since that séance experience, he was pretty down on Amanda, and any enemy of Amanda's was a friend of hers.

She plunked down in the seat next to his. "Hi. What's up?"

"Not much," he said. "You?"

"Nothing special," she replied. They both fell silent. Jenna tried to think of a way to keep the conversation going.

"Heard from anyone interesting lately?" she ventured.

He seemed to be considering the question. "Well, there's this lady who was watching some series on TV before she died, and she's always asking me to find out what's happening on it. So I started watching the show, but it's really stupid and I hate it."

Jenna shrugged. In her opinion, Ken was just too nice to the dead people who communicated with him. Of all the gifts, Ken's was the one she'd least want to have. "So tell her to leave you alone." She turned away from him and pretended to gasp. "Hey, what's Carter doing?"

Ken's eyes widened, and he turned swiftly to look at the boy who sat at the back of the room. "What are you talking about?"

Jenna grinned. "Gotcha."

Carter Street was the mystery of the gifted class, a mute, blank-eyed boy who seemed to be more of a robot than a human being. He did what he was told to do, but he never responded or took any initiative, and his expression was always the same—empty. No one knew his real name or where he came from or if he had any kind of gift at all. Jenna wasn't even sure what he was doing in the class.

Emily and Tracey came in, but Jenna couldn't say anything more than "hi" because Madame was right behind them, and the bell rang. Madame took her usual place behind her desk at the front of the room, and she gave them her usual smile of greeting—but the smile looked a little tense to Jenna.

Her eyes scanned the room. "Where's Amanda?" she asked.

Nobody responded, and Madame frowned. She was big on punctuality.

"I've got a task for you today," the teacher continued. As usual, there were a couple of groans, and as usual, Madame ignored them. "I want each of you to make a list of all the people who know about your gift. Include parents and any other family member who is aware of what you can do."

"Why?" Ken wanted to know.

Jenna half-expected Madame to snap something like "Because I told you to"—but that was how other teachers would respond to a question like that. Madame wasn't like other teachers.

She seemed to be taking her time and considering her answer carefully. Finally, she spoke.

"It's important for all of us to be aware of who knows about the gifts. You all know by now that there are people out there who want to use you, to utilize your gifts for their own purposes. We have to keep track of all potential . . . potential problems."

"But you said we have to include our parents," Sarah

said. "You don't think *they'd* want to use us, do you?"

"Not intentionally," Madame said quickly. "But they might slip and reveal something to someone who—who shouldn't know about you. They may already have done so."

"Why do you think that?" Tracey asked.

"Because you've all had experiences that lead me to believe that you've been observed. That you're being watched."

Martin went completely white. "You mean, some-one's spying on us?" He looked around nervously. "Right now?"

At that moment, the door opened and Amanda walked in. Actually, *sauntered* in would be a better way of describing her entrance, Jenna thought. Most students entering a classroom late would shuffle in with their head down. Amanda was practically strutting.

Madame looked at her and raised her eyebrows. Amanda smiled brightly and didn't even bother to apologize for her tardiness.

"I have an excuse," she proclaimed and handed a folded piece of paper to the teacher.

Madame opened the note and looked at it.

"I can't read this signature," she said.

"It's from Mr. Jackson," Amanda said. "I've been working in the office. You see, I'm his new student assistant."

Jenna couldn't blame the cool, calm, and collected teacher for becoming momentarily speechless. This was pretty shocking news, considering who it was coming from. Jenna knew of other students who worked as assistants—in the cafeteria, the gymnasium, and the library. But Amanda Beeson was the last person in the world who would be expected to take on a job like that. Students did jobs like that to get extracurricular credits or to build up experiences that would make it easier to get part-time paying jobs when they were in high school. Amanda was only interested in social extracurricular activities, and it was unlikely that she'd be thinking about working for money when she got into high school. Her parents were either rich or very generous. In any case, Amanda certainly didn't need to work for spending money.

She assumed Madame was thinking the same thing. "Why have you suddenly decided to become a student assistant, Amanda?"

Clearly, Amanda hadn't anticipated the question. "I . . . I just think it's good to learn office skills," she finally replied. "I mean, you never know when you might, um, need them."

Madame eyed her curiously, but she didn't press the issue. "Take a seat, Amanda," Madame said. "And please make it clear to Mr. Jackson that I expect my students to be here on time."

Jenna and Emily exchanged looks. They knew why Madame sounded a little huffy about Mr. Jackson. She hadn't been too thrilled when the principal foisted a student teacher on the class. Especially when that student teacher turned out to have aspirations other than teaching . . .

Madame repeated the day's assignment to Amanda, and everyone went to work on their lists. Jenna's was pretty short. There was her mother. She was pretty sure her mother wouldn't have told anyone else, even if she was drunk. And then there was that man who called himself Stuart Kelley and claimed to be the father she'd never known. He could have told other people, she supposed. But how many people would believe someone who claimed he knew a mind reader? That was the benefit of having the kind of weird talents they all had—people didn't believe their gifts were possible.

She added names she was pretty sure were on everyone's list—the people who had tried to force some of her classmates to rob banks for them. Clare and those two men who'd been with her. Serena, the student teacher, of course. But that was about it. She'd never told any of the cops or social workers or judges she'd encountered in her brief career as a supposed juvenile delinquent. Or any of the foster families she'd been forced to live with back when her mother went on one of her binges.

Madame collected the lists, and they spent the rest of the class time discussing the names on them.

"Charles, you have two brothers in high school," Madame noted. "Do you think that they might talk about you with their friends?"

"No," Charles said. "They're ashamed of me."

Madame looked at him doubtfully, but she didn't pursue the subject. "I see that all of you put Ms. Hancock on your lists," she commented.

"I didn't," Jenna protested. "Who's Ms. Hancock?"

"Serena, the student teacher," Sarah reminded her.

"Oh, okay, I forgot her last name. If it *is* her real last name."

"You shouldn't forget anything about that woman," Madame warned her. "She's dangerous. She learned about your gifts when she was here. And she utilized that knowledge to get Ken involved in that séance scam."

Jenna didn't miss the way Ken shot a dark look at Amanda before responding to Madame's comment.

"There's something I still don't understand about that," he said. "I know she was the one who invited me to the séance. But what I can't figure out is how she got the invitation into my locker. We've got pretty tight security here. It's not like someone can just walk into the school and put notes in lockers."

"Maybe she got someone to do it for her," Emily suggested. "Someone who could get past security. Someone who actually belongs here."

A silence fell over the room, and Jenna assumed her classmates had the same thought running through their minds as she had. The bell rang.

"We'll continue this discussion tomorrow," Madame said and dismissed the class.

Outside the classroom, Jenna paused at the water fountain. Emily and Tracey waited for her, and Ken joined them.

"What do you think?" Ken asked the girls. "Is there a spy at Meadowbrook?"

Emily considered this. "It seems to me that if one student knew about us, everyone would know about us. You know how rumors spread around here."

"Not necessarily," Jenna remarked. "Not if that student wanted to do something more important than just spread gossip about us. Like, pass information to our enemies."

"Exactly," Ken said. "If someone is working with *them,* she wouldn't want other kids at school to know what she knows."

Tracey frowned. "Why do you think it's a 'she'?"

Ken shrugged and didn't answer, but Jenna read his mind

before he could block her. "You think Amanda's the spy."

"That's ridiculous," Tracey said. "Why would Amanda do something like that?"

"Maybe because she's a terrible person?" Jenna suggested. "Maybe because she's a snob who thinks she's better than the rest of us?"

"It's gotta be someone in our class," Ken said. "No one else could know so much about us."

Tracey shook her head. "You think we're the only ones who know where your locker is, Ken? I've seen you hang around there with your pals. Maybe one of them is working with Serena and put her note in your locker."

"But does anyone else know that Jenna's father disappeared before she was born?" Ken asked.

Jenna shook her head. "So that guy who said he was my father had to learn about me from someone in our class."

"That still doesn't mean the spy is Amanda," Tracey pointed out.

"She knew Serena was posing as Cassandra-the-medium and she didn't tell anyone," Ken offered.

"Maybe she was afraid of Serena," Tracey murmured.

"She's working in the office," Emily pointed out.

"So what?" Tracey asked.

Jenna answered for Emily. "So, she has access to all kinds of personal information about us. I'll bet that's why she took the job, so she could pass it on."

Tracey groaned. "Come on, you guys. You're just ganging up on Amanda because you don't like her. Okay, maybe someone in our class is a spy. Let's think of who else it could be."

Emily spoke. "Martin?"

Ken looked at her in disbelief. "That weasel? He wouldn't have the guts."

"I'm not so sure about that," Tracey said. "All that 'scaredy-cat' stuff could be a big act. He's totally self-centered. Think back to when we were kidnapped. He was completely willing to go along with those guys. I think he'd sell us out to anyone who paid attention to him."

"I guess you have a point," Jenna said grudgingly.

But Ken was more stubborn. "I still think it's Amanda."

"Whoever it is, we need to know," Jenna declared. "So what are we going to do?" She looked at Tracey. "You got any ideas?"

Tracey nodded. "I think I'm going to do a little spying myself." She grinned at the others briefly and then scrunched her face as if she was concentrating very hard.

And before their very eyes, she disappeared.

CHAPTER THREE

SOMETIMES IT WORKED, just like that. Would she ever figure out the logic of her gift? Tracey couldn't take time to think about it now: she had to move. Fortunately, Martin was a slow walker, and she caught up with him just outside the school. Of course, he had no idea she was walking alongside him. Tracey was pretty sure Martin hardly ever had anyone visible walking beside him, never mind *invisible*.

She'd never seen him hanging around with other kids at school. She supposed that wasn't so weird—after all, until a couple of months ago, Tracey didn't hang out with anyone at school, either. She'd been as much of a loner as Martin seemed to be. But there'd been good reasons for Tracey's isolation.

Maybe Martin had reasons, too, but maybe they were bad ones. Maybe right this minute he was on his way to meet Serena, or Clare the kidnapper, or some other person who was interested in gifted students for all the wrong reasons.

If so, Martin wasn't in any rush to get there. He walked slowly, head down, shoulders slumped, dragging his feet.

As they walked, Tracey took the time to give Martin a long, hard look. She'd never paid much attention to him in class—he was so irritating, everyone tried to ignore him. But now that he was silent, she was able to actually see him—and she was mildly surprised by what she saw. Physically, he really wasn't that awful.

Whenever she envisioned Martin—which wasn't often—she always thought of him as being a puny kid, sort of a less-than-life-size scarecrow. But she realized now that he'd been growing, and he was several inches taller than she was. He was thin, but not totally scrawny. His hair was still fair, but he couldn't have had a haircut recently. The straight blond strands fell down his forehead and almost into his eyes, which were very green—funny how she'd never noticed that before. If she hadn't known him, she'd almost think he was kind of cute.

But she *did* know him—he was Martin Cooper, whiny and fussy and annoying. And possibly a traitor to his class.

On a leafy, residential street, he turned and made his way up the driveway of a house. A plump, fair-haired woman

217

was on the front steps, and she looked anxious. When she spotted Martin, she hurried forward.

"There you are, honey! You're late, I was getting worried." She enveloped Martin in a tight hug.

Well, he was loved, Tracey thought. Clearly, he didn't have the kind of problems Tracey used to have. But what was all this business about being late? Okay, Martin had walked slowly, but he'd come directly home.

Mrs. Cooper ushered her son into the house, and Tracey followed close behind.

"You know how I worry when you're late," the woman said to Martin.

"I'm not late," Martin protested weakly.

"You're usually here at three thirty-five," his mother said. She looked at her watch. "It's three forty-two!"

Seven minutes late, Tracey thought. This lady was kind of obsessive. She looked around the living room they were walking through. Everything looked very clean and neat. There was a sofa, easy chairs, the usual stuff—the only things in the room that seemed a little odd were the pictures on the walls. They were all photos of Martin, from birth to his most recent school picture.

He was an only child, that much was obvious. In a few of the pictures, Martin was posing with his mother, but there was no sign of a father. Was Mrs. Cooper a widow or divorced? Divorced, Tracey decided. Otherwise, there'd be some indication of the other person who'd helped produce Martin.

Pleased with the conclusions she'd come to by way of observation, Tracey was beginning to think she might make a pretty good spy. She followed Martin and his mother into a large, country-style kitchen.

"Wait till you see the snack I have for you today!" Mrs. Cooper announced. She lifted the lid off a cake tin. "Chocolate with butterscotch icing! What do you say to that?"

"Thank you, Mom," Martin said automatically, but there wasn't a lot of enthusiasm in his tone. He allowed his mother to lead him to a chair at the kitchen table and practically place him on it. Then she stepped back and gazed at him with worry.

"You're looking a little pale, darling. Do you have a fever?" She placed a hand on his forehead. Martin flinched, but he didn't push the hand away. Finally, his mother removed it. "No, I don't think so. But I want you to take it easy today, dear. No running around, all right? You know how sports tire you out. You're just not suited to strenuous exercise."

Good grief, Tracey thought. This woman wasn't just a little obsessive, she was a nervous wreck.

Martin picked up the knife that lay next to the cake tin and started to cut a slice of cake. His mother squealed.

"Honey, be careful! That's a very sharp knife. Here, let me cut the cake for you. There's milk in the refrigerator."

Martin relinquished the knife to his mother, got up, and went to the refrigerator. Back at the table, he looked at the unopened carton of milk for a few seconds and then touched the cap.

"I can't get this open," he whined.

"You didn't even try!" Tracey exclaimed, forgetting herself. Fortunately, no one could hear her.

"I'll do it for you," his mother said.

She treats him like a baby, Tracey realized. So that's how he acts. This was confirmed to her when his mother unfolded a napkin and actually tucked it into his neckline, like a bib. And Martin let her.

While Martin ate, his mother hovered over him and kept up a nonstop stream of chatter. "Now, when you've finished with your snack, we'll go to the supermarket. Unless you're too tired, of course. But we're almost out of the cookies you like so much. And maybe we can stop at the hair salon—your grandfather keeps telling me your hair is too long." She leaned over and brushed a lock off his forehead. "Though I think it looks sweet. I remember your first haircut, when you were two. I cried!"

Tracey was beginning to feel nauseous. This was too, too sickening.

When he finished his snack, Martin made no move to take his plate and glass off the table. Why should he? His mother automatically took them away and began washing them at the sink. Without even thanking her, Martin got up and went into the living room. Tracey followed him.

He plunked himself down on the sofa, picked up a remote control from the coffee table, and pointed it toward the TV. Tracey was surprised to see that he surfed the channels all by himself and didn't demand that his mother do it for him.

He let the screen rest on what looked like a rerun of an old series. After a few minutes of watching it with him, Tracey recognized it—*The Incredible Hulk*. That figured. Martin would appreciate the story of an ordinary man who could turn into a violent superhero.

The front door opened, and a man came in. Martin's eyes didn't leave the screen, but Tracey looked at the newcomer with interest. He seemed pretty old, with hair that was almost completely white and a lot of lines on his face. But he looked like he was in good shape, and when he spoke, his voice was strong.

"Can't you even say 'hello' to your grandfather, boy?"

Martin's lips formed the shape of "hi," but Tracey couldn't hear anything. Mrs. Cooper came into the room.

"Hi, Dad. Martin, are you ready to go to the super-market? Oh dear, you *do* look tired. Maybe you should stay at home. Dad, could you watch Martin while I do some shopping?"

"Good grief, Linda," the man said. "He's almost fourteen years old! He doesn't need babysitting."

The woman gazed at her son fondly. "He'll always be my baby. Well, I'm off—back in an hour or so."

Once she'd left, the man took the remote control and switched the TV off.

"Hey, I was watching that," Martin protested.

"It's too nice outside to be watching television," his grandfather replied. "Let's go kick a ball around in the backyard."

"I don't want to go outside," Martin said.

"C'mon, it's good for you."

"I'm tired," Martin whined.

"Don't give me that nonsense," the man barked. "You're too young to be tired."

"But Mom said—"

"I don't care what your mother said! Get your lazy butt off that couch and come outside with me!"

Martin blanched, and Tracey flinched. She could sort of

understand the man's frustration with Martin, but he could have been a little gentler in his persuasion methods.

At least he'd scared Martin into getting up. Tracey followed them through the kitchen and out the back door. The grandfather jogged over to a ball lying on the grass and kicked it in Martin's direction. When it flew past him, Martin ducked and made no effort to go after it.

"Kick it back!" the old man ordered him.

Slowly, Martin ambled toward the ball.

"Run!" his grandfather yelled.

Martin may have picked up the pace a bit, but any increase in speed was imperceptible to Tracey. And when he reached the ball, he barely tapped it with his toe.

"You call that a kick? Put some muscle into it!"

This time the ball actually moved a few feet. The man ran toward it and gave it a fierce kick. The ball hit Martin in the stomach, and Martin let out an ear-shattering wail.

"Ow, that hurt!"

Tracey couldn't tell if Martin was really suffering or if he was just putting on one of his acts. In any case, it made no difference to the grandfather.

"Stop complaining, you little brat! You're a big baby. Grow up, you stupid child!"

Martin froze. The man continued with his tirade.

"You know what? You're pathetic! How did I end up

with such a lousy grandchild? You make me sick!"

Tracey watched Martin in alarm. The boy was becoming flushed, and his breathing had become so labored she could hear it from where she was standing at the edge of the yard. Then his whole body began to tremble.

She knew what this meant. Martin's gift was emerging, just as it always did when he was teased or taunted. Frantically, she turned to the grandfather. Was he aware of Martin's ability? Did he know that any minute now Martin would be able to beat the man to a pulp?

And what should *she* do? How could she stop Martin, rescue the old man, put an end to this? Madame could control Martin with a sharp look, but Tracey wasn't Madame. Besides, Martin wouldn't even be able to see any sharp look Tracey could muster!

But to her amazement—and relief—Martin didn't explode into a fury of superstrength. She watched with interest as his face contorted into an expression of intense concentration. And after a moment, his complexion returned to its normal color, his breathing calmed, and his body was still. Then he ran back into the house.

Now she was confused. Why hadn't Martin attacked the man? Was he able to control his gift? She wished Jenna were there. She could have read Martin's mind and explained why he was acting like this.

The back door had been left open, so Tracey didn't have to wait for the grandfather to let her back inside. She hurried after Martin.

He wasn't in the kitchen or the living room, so she went upstairs. In the hallway she could hear sobs coming from behind a closed door. Usually, Martin's self-pitying tendencies annoyed her. This time, to her surprise, she found herself feeling sympathy for him.

As long as the door remained closed, however, there was nothing she could do about it. She couldn't walk through walls. She'd just have to wait for Martin to come back out.

Fortunately, he didn't seem to need much crying time. After a few minutes, he emerged. He went into the bathroom, splashed some water on his face, and came out. Tracey followed him down the stairs.

He went directly to the front door. His grandfather was in the living room, and he bellowed, "Where do you think you're going?"

Martin didn't reply. He left the house, and Tracey left with him. He wasn't dragging his feet this time. He was walking as if he had a purpose, some place to go. Even while invisible, Tracey could feel her heartbeat quicken. Was this it? Was Martin on his way to meet their enemies?

They were coming up to a playground, and this appeared to be Martin's destination. Tracey looked around, wondering if she'd spot Serena, Clare, or any of the people she and the other gifted students had encountered in the past. But all she saw was the kind of people one would expect to find in a playground—some little kids with parents over by the seesaw and swings, and a group of teenage boys on the basketball court.

The latter group was the one Martin approached. He planted himself on the court just in front of the boy who held the ball. Like the other guys in the group, the player looked around 16 or so. All the boys were bigger than Martin.

"What do you want?" the boy holding the ball asked.

"I want to play with you guys," Martin said.

Oh no, Tracey thought. She didn't have to be Emily to see what the immediate future held for Martin. The boy would tell him no. Beat it, kid. Get lost, jerk. Something like that. Martin would refuse, maybe try to take the ball. The other guys would jeer. And Martin's inner superhero—or in his case, supermonster—would come out.

But the older boy just shrugged. "Sure. I need another guy on my team. Go take a position over there."

Was she crazy, or was that disappointment she was seeing in Martin's eyes? He scowled.

"Forget it," he muttered and walked off the court.

His next stop was a picnic table just a few yards away,

where a group of men were playing cards. A couple of them looked kind of rough, and there was a bottle of cheap whiskey on the table. Tracey got nervous.

Martin tapped one man on the shoulder. "I want to join your game."

A grizzled face turned to him. "You play poker, kid? Sure, take a seat."

Once again, Martin's face fell. "Never mind." And he walked away.

Now Tracey understood. Martin didn't want to play basketball or poker. He wanted to be teased, taunted, brushed aside. He wanted those older boys who played basketball, the men at the poker table, to mock him, make fun of him, laugh at him. Then his so-called gift would be summoned. Martin had been looking for a way to be strong, to assert himself in the only way he knew how.

But then, why did he resist the gift when it started to emerge in his backyard? Okay, maybe he didn't want to hurt a blood relative. This was interesting, she mused. It meant that Martin actually had some con- trol of his gift—it seemed like he could stop his gift from taking him over, but he still couldn't make it happen by himself—she knew how frustrating that must be for him because she sometimes had a similar problem. It also meant he had feelings, that he wasn't just this whiny wimp who didn't care about anyone but himself. So there might be more to Martin than any of his classmates ever suspected.

But as she walked alongside him while he dragged himself slowly home, she was pretty sure that whatever else Martin might be, he wasn't a spy.

Chapter Four

IN MOST OF HER classes, Jenna sat at the back of the room, where she wouldn't be noticed and the teacher would be less likely to call on her. If she got bored—and this happened frequently—she could amuse herself by reading the minds of her classmates. Outside the gifted class, she could benefit from the fact that no one knew what she could do and no one could block her. In her last class, she'd been nicely entertained by a student's memory of a family trip to New York City.

But this was her English class, one of the few classes where Jenna sat closer to the front and paid attention. She'd always been a book person, and in this class, they'd been given some good stuff to read. And Ms. Day, the teacher, had a way of getting the students to talk about the literature they'd been assigned. Right now, they were reading *Jane Eyre*, and even though the language was old-fashioned, Jenna liked the heroine. For someone who'd had a crummy childhood, Jane was actually a pretty gutsy girl, and Jenna could relate to her. She was looking forward to discussing chapter four today.

But it was not to be. On this Tuesday, Ms. Day was absent, and a substitute teacher was taking her place. Mr. Roth was a frequent substitute at Meadowbrook, and Jenna slumped back in her seat when she saw him at Ms. Day's desk. It was always the same when Roth took over a class. Jenna prepared herself for 50 minutes of utter boredom.

First, the substitute glanced at the lesson-plan book. "You're supposed to discuss chapter four of *Jane Eyre* today. Let's see . . ." he looked at the roster. "Johnson, Alex. Summarize chapter four."

A boy responded. "Uh, I didn't get a chance to read it."

Roth scowled. "Kitchens, Laurie. You summarize chapter four."

A girl squirmed in her seat. "Um, I *did* start reading it last night, but I—I fell asleep before I could finish it."

Jenna, who rarely volunteered in class, was almost ready to raise her hand and offer a summary, but Mr. Roth had apparently already given up.

"Well, you can't discuss it if you haven't read it. So, you can all use this class time to read chapter four."

The girl sitting next to Jenna raised her hand. "What if we've already read it?"

"Then read it again," Roth stated. "Or read chapter five." With that, he opened his briefcase, took out a newspaper and unfolded it.

Students used the unexpected free time for a variety of purposes. Industrious ones started home-work assignments. One girl began filing her nails, while a couple of boys put their heads down on their desks and closed their eyes. Jenna had no desire to attack homework or sleep, so she scanned the minds of selected classmates for something interesting to entertain her.

. . . *I'll go to Gametown after school and see if the new Infernal Toxic Battleground Warriors game is in yet* . . .

. . . *I wish I had my iPod* . . .

. . . Jane Eyre *is boring. Why can't we ever read anything good? Something with vampires* . . .

Jenna uttered a silent groan. There wasn't anyone in this class worth spying on . . .

But that brief thought led her to something actually worth contemplating—the spy in the gifted class. Someone was taking the information learned in the class and passing it on. How else would people like Serena, Clare, and Stuart Kelley know so much about them?

It had to be Amanda. Everyone else could be eliminated for one reason or another. Emily and Tracey were completely out of the question, of course. It couldn't be

Ken—if he could feel guilty about ignoring the voices in his head, he wasn't the type to betray his classmates. And according to what Tracey had told them at lunch today, the guilty party wasn't Martin.

Sarah . . . ? Maybe all that niceness was just a mask. No, Jenna couldn't suspect Sarah. She might make fun of Sarah, calling her Miss Perfect or something like that, but deep down she instinctively knew that Sarah was a genuinely good person. There was a bit of mystery to her, that was true, but it seemed to be something personal and private. She wouldn't do anything that would hurt anyone else.

They could forget about Carter—he couldn't even communicate. For a brief time, when she first entered the class, she'd toyed with the notion that Carter's oblivious attitude was an act. But once, when Charles had one of his tantrums and sent books flying off shelves, everyone else in the class had covered their heads. Carter hadn't even flinched until Madame had instructed him to duck. No, the guy was truly out of it.

What about Charles? He could be pretty nasty . . . but she remembered how he'd helped her and Ken rescue the kidnapped students. Someone in cahoots with the bad guys wouldn't have done that.

No, it had to be Amanda. Before she came to the gifted class, none of them had been threatened by outside forces.

Amanda had no real friends in the class, so she had no sense of loyalty to anyone. Tracey had said she thought there was some sort of romantic connection between Amanda and Ken, but from the way Ken talked about Amanda now, any friendship they might have had was finished.

And now Amanda had chosen to work in Mr. Jackson's office.

Jenna had always harbored uncomfortable feelings about Mr. Jackson, and not just because he was the school principal. There was something about him that gave her the creeps.

Madame had assured the class that no one else at Meadowbrook knew about them. The administration thought the students in Madame's class had some unusual aspects to their personalities or learning skills and that was why they'd been brought together for a class under her supervision. None of them, not even the principal, was aware of what they could do. Mr. Jackson knew they had "gifts," but he thought they were little personality quirks and talents. Not weird supernatural stuff.

And yet, the way Mr. Jackson looked at them . . . Surely he suspected something. It was Mr. Jackson who had brought Serena to their class as a student teacher. It was Mr. Jackson who had accepted the man who called himself Stuart Kelley as Jenna's father. Jenna had no difficulty picturing the principal and Amanda working together to exploit the gifted students.

The gifted class met right after this class. That meant Amanda should be working in the office right now.

The one good thing about substitute teachers was the fact that they were more gullible than real teachers. Jenna got up and went to the desk.

Mr. Roth looked up from his newspaper with annoyance at being interrupted. "Yes?" he asked testily.

"I need to go to the nurse," Jenna said.

His eyes narrowed with suspicion. Jenna elaborated.

"I think I'm going to throw up."

That comment set Roth in motion. Frantically, he grabbed an excuse pass from the top drawer and practically threw it at her.

Once out in the hall, Jenna knew she needed to figure out another story right away. It wasn't like she could walk into the office and just hang out. She needed a reason for being there. But what possible excuse could she have for going to the office? She could claim that Mr. Roth sent her for some classroom supplies . . . but then she'd be handed the supplies and sent back to class. She needed to stay in the office for a while so she could observe Amanda and figure out what she was up to. This was not going to be easy . . .

But she was in luck. There was a lot going on in the office when she arrived, and she didn't have to provide an excuse, at least not right away. A counselor with a red face was demanding to see Mr. Jackson immediately. The custodian was complaining about something nasty in a bathroom, while two teachers were arguing over the use of some video equipment. And a couple of boys who'd obviously been in some sort of fight (and who wanted very much to continue fighting) were being held apart by another teacher.

Ms. Simmons, the head secretary, was yelling at them all, telling them to sit and wait until Mr. Jackson could see them. Amanda was behind the desk, in front of a computer screen, and not paying any attention to what was going on.

Jenna approached cautiously and tried to get a better look at what Amanda was doing without letting Amanda get a glimpse of her. She couldn't see what was on the screen, but she could get into Amanda's mind, which was even better. There, Jenna could not only get a vague image of the screen, but she could also get a sense of how Amanda was responding to what she saw.

Amanda was looking at an e-mail inbox. Her own? No, not unless Amanda normally received e-mails with subjects like "Budget request for physical education equipment" and "Board of Education Meeting

Schedule." It had to be Mr. Jackson's e-mail. And if Amanda had access to the e-mail account of the principal, wasn't that an indication that they were pretty chummy?

Now she needed to know what Amanda was thinking about the e-mails she was reading . . .

"Hello, Jenna, what are you up to?" Mr. Gonzalez, the counselor she saw regularly, was standing there. "Not in any trouble, I hope!" He said this with a broad smile, showing that he was just teasing her.

Jenna forced a smile, but it wasn't easy because Mr. Gonzalez had a booming voice and she knew that Amanda must have heard him. She didn't even have to look at her classmate to confirm this. Her connection to Amanda's mind had been severed.

At that moment, Mr. Jackson came out of his office. "Who's next?" he called out. Several of the office occupants clamored for his attention, and Jenna decided to take advantage of the moment to explore the principal's thoughts.

But as hard as she tried, she couldn't penetrate his mind. Then she was aware of Mr. Jackson staring straight at her, and there was a flash of something in his expression that she couldn't interpret.

"What are *you* doing here?" he demanded to know.

Jenna looked around for an excuse. "Uh, Mr. Roth

needs a stapler."

Mr. Jackson took one off Ms. Simmons's desk. "Here."

Jenna took the stapler from him. "Thank you," she said, hoping she sounded polite and casual, but her stomach was suddenly in knots. There was something about the way Mr. Jackson was looking at her . . .

Hurrying out, she tried to dismiss this sudden sense of apprehension that had come over her. Why hadn't she been able to get even a glimpse of the principal's thoughts? And why had he glared at her like that? It wasn't like he could know she'd been trying to read his mind.

Unless . . . unless he knew what Jenna was capable of doing, and he'd blocked her. He'd know because Amanda had told him. Which was precisely the kind of thing a spy would do.

Back in the English class, Mr. Roth was still reading his newspaper and the students were still doing whatever they'd been doing when she left. Jenna took her seat, stuck the stapler in her backpack, and opened *Jane Eyre*.

Much as she liked the story, it was hard to concentrate. Her thoughts kept going back to the scene in the office. Now she was more convinced than ever about Amanda. She couldn't wait to get into the gifted class and share her news with Emily, Tracey, and Ken.

But there was nothing she could do right now, and there

were still 30 minutes of this class left to go. She plunged back into *Jane Eyre*.

The story grabbed her this time, and soon she was completely absorbed in it. The next time she glanced at the clock, she was surprised and pleased to see there were only about five minutes left before the bell would ring. But as it turned out, she didn't even have to wait that long to leave the room.

The door opened, and Amanda walked in. With an air of importance, she strode briskly up to Mr. Roth and murmured something to him. The teacher looked at the class.

"Jenna Kelley?"

Jenna looked up. "Yes?"

"You're wanted in the office."

Jenna frowned and looked at Amanda, but Amanda's expression didn't give her any hint as to why she was being summoned. She picked up her backpack, stopped at the desk to get another hall pass, and left the room. Amanda was right behind her.

"What's going on?" Jenna asked her.

"Not a clue," Amanda replied. "Ms. Simmons told me to come and get you. I just follow orders."

I bet you do, Jenna thought sourly. They walked along in silence for a moment. At the end of the corridor, however, Amanda turned right instead of left, which was the direction to the office.

"I don't have to go back to the office," she offered by way of explanation. "Mr. Jackson said I could go on to my next class."

Jenna doubted that Amanda was actually going to appear early for the gifted class. She'd undoubtedly use this time to go into a bathroom, where she could fuss with her hair and her makeup and admire her own reflection for as long as possible. Jenna had once read a biography of a famous female spy named Mata Hari. *She* paid a lot of attention to her appearance, too. Maybe it was a female spy thing.

As she approached the office, the reason for her summons dawned on her. The stapler she'd borrowed—Ms. Simmons wanted it back. She took it out of her backpack, and when she entered the office, she held it out to the secretary.

But Ms. Simmons barely glanced at the stapler. Her disapproving eyes were on Jenna herself, and Jenna thought the secretary looked just a little too harsh, considering the situation. So she'd kept the stapler for half an hour—big deal.

Ms. Simmons nodded toward Mr. Jackson's closed door. "You're wanted in there," she told Jenna.

Jenna's forehead creased in puzzlement. Now what? But

Ms. Simmons offered no further explanation. Jenna crossed the reception area and rapped on the principal's door.

"Come in," the principal called.

Jenna opened the door. And then she just stood there, her hand still on the doorknob. It was an unexpected and unsettling scene that greeted her.

Mr. Jackson sat at his usual place, behind his massive desk. On the chair facing him sat Jenna's mother. By his side stood a uniformed police officer. Jenna wasn't sure who looked more frightening—the cop with his stern expression or her mother, who had tears in her eyes.

"Oh, Jenna," her mother moaned. "Why did you do this?" She couldn't seem to bring herself to even look at Jenna as she spoke.

Jenna stared at her in utter bewilderment. "Why did I do what?"

Mr. Jackson had no problem looking at Jenna. "You know our policy about weapons," he said.

"No," Jenna replied honestly.

"It's in the student guide," the principal snapped.

Yeah, like anyone ever reads *that,* Jenna thought, but she decided it would be wiser not to say it out loud.

"We have a 'no-tolerance' policy," the principal continued. "Do you understand what that means?"

Jenna nodded slowly. "I guess it means nobody should

240

bring any kind of weapon to school, right?"

"That's right," Mr. Jackson said. "It doesn't matter if it's an assault rifle or a slingshot." He opened his drawer. "Or a knife."

It was a big, sharp knife, the kind that Jenna imagined would be used for carving meat. Jenna stared at it blankly.

"Where did that come from?"

"Your locker." He placed the knife down in the center of his desk. "Unfortunately for you, we held a random locker search today."

An odd, shivery sensation went up her spine. "I—I've never seen that knife before in my life."

"Of course you haven't," Mr. Jackson said with a sneer. "It just sprouted legs and walked into your locker. It even knew your combination."

Jenna turned to her mother. "Mom, I swear, it's not mine! I didn't bring a knife to school."

"I want to believe you, Jenna . . ." her mother began, and her voice broke.

Mr. Jackson finished the sentence for her. "But she can't, because we have the evidence. I'm sorry, young lady, but you're in serious trouble."

"Are you suspending me?" Jenna asked.

"Given your history, I don't feel suspension is an adequate punishment," the principal declared.

"You are being sent back to Harmony House for an indefinite period."

Jenna froze. She opened her mouth to protest, but no words came out.

And she wasn't only mute. She had difficulty hearing, too. Vaguely, she was aware of being told that the police officer would escort her to Harmony House, but the sound seemed to be coming from very far away. Her mother was saying something, too, but the words made no sense at all. Maybe because she was crying as she spoke.

Then she was in the hallway, with the policeman's hand on her shoulder. The bell must have just rung, because there were people in the hall, and she knew they were looking at her. Strangely enough, she wasn't upset, she wasn't humiliated. She didn't care. How could she?

She'd gone completely numb. She was too shocked to feel anything at all.

CHAPTER FIVE

TRACEY WAS IN THE bathroom when three girls she didn't know made a noisy entrance. They were talking loudly and excitedly.

"I saw it all!" one of them told the others. "Police officers took her away! Five or six of them! And she was in handcuffs!"

"No way!" another one exclaimed.

"Really, I swear!"

"What did she do?" the third girl asked.

"I don't know, but it's serious. They don't call the police for cutting a class."

Uneasily, Tracey turned to the group. "Who are you talking about?"

"You've seen her around," the girl told her. "She's that goth girl. I think her name's Jeannie or Janie, something like that."

"Jenna," Tracey said. "Jenna Kelley." She slung her backpack over her shoulder and left the bathroom.

In shock, she managed to get up the stairs without tripping. This had to be a mistake. Maybe the girl in the bathroom hadn't understood what she saw. Or maybe there was another goth girl at Meadowbrook. She told herself that when she walked into room 209, Jenna would be there, just as she always was. She even concocted a story that would account for what the girl in the bathroom had seen: a police officer had been invited to speak in Jenna's last class and Jenna was simply escorting him to the door. There had to be a reasonable explanation . . .

But when she walked into the class, her heart sank. Emily's woebegone expression said it all.

"Do you know about Jenna?" Emily asked her.

Tracey sank into her seat. "I heard people talking. They said she was arrested. Is it true?"

"It's something like that," Emily acknowledged. "I know a policeman took her away. I don't know what she did, but it has to have been something really bad."

"But maybe, maybe it wasn't because of something *she* did," Tracey said. She thought frantically. "Maybe . . . maybe her mother was in an accident, and the police came to take her to the hospital."

"There's nothing wrong with Jenna's mother."

Tracey and Emily turned to see Amanda sauntering into

the room. "How do you know?" Emily asked.

"Because she was in Mr. Jackson's office. First she came, then the policeman came, and then Ms. Simmons sent me to get Jenna out of class." Amanda sat down and whipped out her makeup bag.

"But *why?*" Tracey wanted to know. "What happened?"

Amanda examined her own reflection in a little compact mirror. "Well, Mr. Jackson did a locker check today. He might have found something in Jenna's locker."

"Like what?" Charles asked. "Drugs? Guns?"

"I don't know," Amanda replied as she applied lipgloss.

Ken's eyes narrowed. "Are you sure about that?"

Amanda snapped the compact shut. "Just because I work in the office doesn't mean I know everything that goes on in there. All I know is that Mr. Jackson suddenly decided to do some random locker searches, and when he came back, he wanted to see Jenna."

"It was a knife," Sarah said softly.

Everyone turned in her direction. "How do you know?" Tracey asked her.

"I saw it," Sarah said. "I'd just been excused from class to get some water. Mr. Jackson and a policeman were in the hallway. Mr. Jackson opened a locker and took out a big knife. I didn't know whose locker it was." She shook her head sadly. "I can't believe Jenna would bring a weapon to school."

"Why not?" Amanda asked. "I mean, she was a juvenile delinquent, right?"

Emily looked stricken. "That's not true!" She amended that. "Okay, maybe it was a little bit true, but she's not like that now. You don't know anything about her, Amanda."

"I know all I want to know," Amanda murmured. She took her cell phone out of her bag and began composing a text message.

"You reporting on this to someone?" Ken asked her.

Amanda looked at him. "*What?*"

But then Madame walked in. Everyone turned to her expectantly.

"Madame, did you hear about Jenna?" Emily asked.

The teacher nodded. "I don't have all the facts. I've been told that something unacceptable was found in her locker during a routine security search."

"Was she suspended?" Tracey asked.

"I believe so," Madame replied. "As I said, I don't have all the facts yet." Tracey knew Madame had to be upset about this. But being Madame, her tone was calm and unemotional.

"I know we're all upset, but we can't jump to conclusions. Try not to listen to any gossip you might hear. And I don't think we should discuss this in class until we know more about the situation. Today, I suggest we spend the class time practicing our relaxation techniques."

As usual, Martin and Charles groaned, but Tracey could see the point of this. The exercises—in breathing and meditation—were supposed to help them control their gifts. Today, the soft music and Madame's soothing voice would help calm their feelings.

But even as they went through the motions of the exercises, Tracey's mind continued to race.

She knew all about Jenna's past, how she used to practically live on the streets. Anything was better than staying at home with an alcoholic mother who used the apartment as "party central" for her drinking buddies. Jenna hung out in train stations and bus stations with people who wouldn't be considered good citizens. Pickpockets, druggies, people with actual criminal records . . . they weren't exactly Jenna's friends, but they accepted her as another troubled soul with nothing to do and no place to go.

Tracey knew Jenna herself had never been violent, and she never took drugs or did anything illegal. But she liked to act tough, she hung around with tough people, and she had gotten into trouble because of them.

But that was then, and this was now. Jenna's life had

changed dramatically. She had a home with a sober mother, she had friends, she no longer saw her old street gang. She wasn't looking to get into trouble, and there was absolutely no reason for her to bring a knife to school.

So why did Mr. Jackson find a knife in Jenna's locker?

Ken thought he knew. The second they were dismissed, he motioned for Emily and Tracey to join him in the hallway.

"It's a setup," he declared. "Jenna didn't bring a knife to school. Someone put a knife in Jenna's locker."

"But why would anyone do something like that?" Emily asked in bewilderment.

"To get rid of her," Ken said. "And I know who that someone is." He looked past the girls. They both turned to see Amanda sweep by them.

Ken waited until Amanda was beyond hearing before he spoke again. "I've got it all figured out. Amanda knows Jenna thinks she's the class spy."

Tracey broke in. "How could Amanda know that? Jenna never accused her."

"She didn't have to, not out loud," Ken said. "Haven't you seen the dirty looks Jenna's been giving Amanda?"

Jenna gives lots of people dirty looks, Tracey thought. But maybe Ken had noticed something she hadn't.

"Besides, maybe Jenna *did* say something to Amanda," Ken continued. "Anyway, Amanda had to get Jenna out of her way. So she plants the knife, she sends Mr. Jackson an anonymous note telling him that Jenna has a weapon, and Jenna's suspended."

Emily gazed at him thoughtfully. "Ken, have you been reading a lot of detective novels lately?"

Ken ignored that. "Think about it—it all makes sense. Working in the office, Amanda could get her hands on Jenna's locker combination. And it would be easy for her to slip a note under Jackson's door when no one was looking."

Tracey had to admit there was logic in what he said. But . . .

"You can't prove this, Ken, can you?" she asked.

"Maybe I won't have to," he said. "If we can get her to confess."

"How can we get her to do that?" Emily wanted to know.

Ken smiled grimly. "I've got a plan. What means more to Amanda than anything else?"

Tracey blanched. Surely Ken wasn't suggesting that they threaten to destroy the contents of Amanda's closet.

But Emily understood. "Her reputation. Being cool."

Now Tracey got it. "Right, she has to be the queen bee, everyone's supposed to look up to her."

"Especially her pals," Emily added. "What did Jenna call them? The Evilettes."

"Exactly," Ken said. He glanced at his watch. "I bet she's still at her locker—that's where she meets her friends after school. C'mon, let's go."

On the way there, he explained his plan. Personally, Tracey thought it sounded a little cruel, and it certainly wasn't going to be easy for them to pull it off. But if it could bring Jenna back, she supposed it was worth a try.

As Ken suspected, Amanda was still at her locker, with two of her friends, Nina and Katie. Amanda was tapping her foot impatiently.

"Where is Britney?" Tracey heard her say as they approached. "We're going to be late for our manicures."

"Hey, Amanda," Ken called out. Emily and Tracey said nothing, but it didn't matter. The three girls only had eyes for the boy. Even though Ken was no longer a top athlete at Meadowbrook, his good looks and general popularity still made him a catch.

"Hi, Ken," they chorused with identical flirty smiles on their faces.

He focused on Amanda. "Listen, Amanda, I have to tell you something."

She cocked her head coyly. "What?"

"Martin's got a thing for you."

Her forehead puckered. "Who?"

"Martin Cooper, from our class. Jenna told me. She has a way of, you know, finding things out, and she said he definitely likes you. She meant to tell you today, but like, she didn't get a chance. Anyway, I thought I'd pass it on."

Nina giggled. "Martin Cooper? That little wimp?"

And Amanda rolled her eyes. "What makes you think that I would care if Martin Cooper likes me?"

Now Ken's face reflected confusion. "But—but you told me, remember? You said you kind of liked him. So I thought you'd want to know that the feeling is mutual."

Amanda's mouth dropped. "I never said anything like that!"

"Oh, was it supposed to be a secret?" Ken asked. "Sorry." With that, he turned away and started toward the door. Tracey and Emily followed. But Tracey couldn't resist turning around to get a glimpse of Amanda's reaction.

The girl looked positively shocked. But what was even more interesting were the faces of her friends. They were both staring at Amanda as if they'd just learned she had a contagious disease.

Chapter Six

THE LOBBY OF HARMONY House hadn't changed since the last time that Jenna had seen it. The same puke-green walls, the same row of orange plastic chairs, the same stupid poster proclaiming, "Today is the first day of the rest of your life." The other people in the lobby might not have been the same ones who were waiting the last time she was here, but they fell into the same categories. Angry boys, sullen girls, unhappy parents, bored social workers . . .

Jenna sat on one of the orange chairs and stared at the poster. If the rest of her life was going to be like today . . .

The policeman sitting next to her interrupted her thoughts.

"Looks like it's going to be a while."

Jenna said nothing.

"By the way," the officer said, "my name is Jack. Jack Fisher."

What was she supposed to say now? He already

knew *her* name. And "pleased to meet you" didn't seem exactly appropriate, given the circumstances.

"You've been here before," he said.

Jenna didn't look at him as she responded. "How did you know?"

"I've read your file," he said. "I have to say, I was kind of surprised . . ."

This time she actually glanced at him. "About what?"

"You didn't seem like a repeat offender. Actually, it didn't seem like you committed much of an offense to begin with. They didn't find any drugs on you, did they?"

Because I wasn't doing any drugs, Jenna answered silently. But her response to the cop was simply a shrug.

"In fact," he continued, "it sounded to me like your biggest crime was being in the wrong place at the wrong time, with the wrong people. Am I right?"

Again, she only shrugged.

"I talked to your counselor at school, that Mr. Gonzalez," the cop remarked. "He said you've been doing pretty well at Meadowbrook since you started there."

This time she didn't even bother to shrug.

"So what happened?" he asked. "Why did you have that knife?"

Jenna couldn't hold back any longer. "What do you want me to say, that I was framed?" she asked. "That someone set me up? Isn't that what all the criminals say?"

Jack Fisher didn't blink. "Sometimes it's true."

It wasn't what she'd expected to hear from him, and for a moment, she was tempted to say more. But what if she came right out and accused Amanda Beeson? What good would that do? Amanda, who came from a "good" family, who was one of the most popular girls at school, versus Jenna Kelley, who lived in the projects, with no father, a recovering-alcoholic mother—a girl with a "file." Who'd come out on top?

But even though Amanda was superficial and selfish and full of herself, it was hard to believe that she could be this downright evil. Then again, if she was spying on their class and working with serious bad guys, it made sense.

Still, it had come as a complete shock, that scene in Mr. Jackson's office. Her mother . . . she'd been so upset. Would this incident make her start drinking again?

She could feel tears forming in her eyes. She needed to brush them away, but she didn't want to draw attention to herself.

But Jack Fisher was watching her. "Are you feeling sorry about something?" he asked softly.

Jenna turned to him and spoke fiercely. "I have nothing to be sorry for." She clenched her fists. If there was anything worse than a regular cop, it was a cop who pretended to care.

A voice from the other end of the lobby called out, "Jenna Kelley?" Jenna rose.

"Would you like me to come with you?" the cop asked.

Jenna shook her head. "I know the routine." She turned her back on Jack Fisher, but he touched her shoulder.

"I'm the police liaison for Harmony House," he told her. "So I'll be seeing you."

It was on the tip of her tongue to reply, "Not if I see you first," but all she managed was, "Whatever." And she took off for the registration ordeal.

Entering the office, she saw that prissy, white-haired Ms. Landers was still the so-called director, sitting behind a desk. The woman gave her a sad smile.

"I wish I could say it's nice to see you again, Jenna."

Jenna slumped into the seat facing her. She knew what was coming next—the "welcome to Harmony House" speech, which was supposed to assure you that this wasn't a prison; to consider your stay here as an opportunity to search your heart and soul; to come to an understanding of why you're here; to exorcise bad habits; to explore other ways of expressing yourself; blah, blah, blah. It was all crap, of course. The prisoners were called "residents," not inmates, and there were "resident assistants" instead of wardens, but there were bars on the windows and guards stationed at the doors. They called Harmony House a rehabilitation center, but it was no better than a prison.

After the speech came the rules, and those hadn't changed, either. The demerit system—any infraction of the rules would result in demerits, issued by the resident assistants. The accumulation of demerits would result in the loss of privileges.

Girls were confined to one side of the building, boys to the other, and the only interaction would take place at mealtimes or in the TV lounge or at scheduled "activities." Jenna recalled a compulsory "disco night" and shuddered. No phone calls or visitors for the first 48 hours, which was fine with Jenna—she wasn't feeling very sociable.

When Ms. Landers finally finished, Jenna thought she'd be released to go to her room, but she'd forgotten another Harmony House ritual.

"Now, you'll see Dr. Paley for your intake interview," Ms. Landers informed her.

There hadn't been a "Dr. Paley" the last time she was here. It had been a Dr. Colby then. But now that she'd been reminded of it, Jenna knew what was coming.

Dr. Paley was a smiling, plump, bald man in a white coat.

"Hello, Jenna," he said jovially. Jenna grunted in return.

Dr. Paley didn't seem dismayed—she figured he probably never got much more than a grunt from the young people he dealt with here.

With a nurse by his side, he listened to Jenna's heart, took her pulse and blood pressure, looked in her ears and down her throat—all the usual stuff. Everything must have checked out okay because he kept smiling.

When he finished, he told the nurse that she could leave and invited Jenna to take a seat across from him at his desk.

"Let's have a little chat," he said, opening a folder, which Jenna presumed was her file. Jenna didn't bother to stifle her groan. The last time she'd been here the doctor had only been interested in her physical state. This was something new.

"You're a shrink," she muttered.

His perpetual smile broadened. "Well, I'm a medical doctor who specializes in mental as well as physical health. I provide therapy for the residents here."

"There's nothing mentally wrong with me," Jenna declared. "I'm not crazy."

"You don't have to be crazy to benefit from therapy," the doctor said. "You've been sent here, to Harmony House, which indicates that you have some problems that need to be examined and resolved. I believe the best way to deal with problems like yours is to talk about them."

Yeah, like you have any idea what my real problems are, Jenna thought bitterly.

The questions started.

"How's life at home, Jenna?"

"Fine."

"I see that your mother's been through a rehabilitation program. How do you feel about that?"

"Fine."

"And I see you started a new school recently. How is that going for you?"

"Fine."

"Have you made friends there?"

"Fine ... I mean, yes."

He turned a page in her file. "I see you're taking geometry, English, geography . . ." he paused. "What's this 'gifted' class?"

Jenna sat up straighter. "It's just this little special class for kids who are . . . gifted."

"Gifted in what way?"

Jenna tried not to squirm. "Different ways."

"What's your gift? Are you a computer genius? Do you play a musical instrument?"

"No. It's not that kind of a gift." She knew he wouldn't be satisfied with that, so she tried to remember what she'd once heard Tracey tell someone. "Actually, I don't know why they call it 'gifted.' Each student has something—something sort of unusual going on. Like one guy, he's in a wheelchair. And there's another guy who used to be a big athlete, but he had an accident and he can't play sports anymore."

The doctor nodded. "And what's unusual about you?"

"I'm a juvenile delinquent."

"I see . . ." He eyed Jenna sharply. He wasn't smiling now. "I'd like to hear more about this class."

Jenna shifted in her chair. "I'm kind of tired."

The smile returned. "Of course—you should go to your room and get settled. We'll talk another time."

Finally, she was released. When she left the doctor's office, a woman wearing a tag identifying her as a "resident assistant" escorted her to her room on the second floor.

"You're lucky," the woman told her. "We're not completely booked right now so you don't have a roommate."

That was a major relief. The last time Jenna had been here, she'd been stuck in a room with a 12-year-old shoplifter who cried incessantly. Jenna thought she was incredibly stupid—what good would crying do in a place like this? If you were stuck here, you just had to grit your teeth and get through it. She'd tried to be a good role model for the girl, acting tough and invulnerable, but the girl never seemed to pick up on Jenna's example. At least this time she wouldn't have to put up with anyone's tears.

The room looked just like the room she'd had the last time. Twin beds, a white dresser, two desks. The only difference was the picture on the wall. In the last room, she'd had a cutesy picture of puppies. This time, she had kittens.

She threw herself down on one of the beds and stared up at the ceiling. Now what? She had no computer, no TV, no music ... She remembered that there was a little library downstairs, by the dining hall. She could go and check out a book.

But there was no time for that now. A bell rang, signaling dinner time. Jenna had no appetite, but she knew she had to show up for the meal. It was one of the rules. She still didn't know how long she'd have to stay here, but she had no intention of extending the time by breaking any of the rules.

In the dining hall, she picked up her tray and went to an empty table. Unfortunately, it didn't stay empty. A girl who looked a little younger than Jenna joined her.

"Can I sit here?"

Jenna shrugged. Her shoulders were definitely getting a workout today.

The girl sat down. "I haven't seen you around before," she said. "Is this your first day here?"

Jenna nodded.

"It's not so bad," the girl said. "I mean, I was really scared at first. Some of the kids are *mean*, you know? Like, they've done violent things. All I did was break into a car with some friends and take it for a ride. We didn't hurt anyone."

Jenna gritted her teeth. Oh no, this one was a talker. She had to get rid of her.

"What did you do?" the girl asked.

"They found a knife in my locker at school," Jenna said.

"A pocket knife?"

Jenna shook her head. "No, a great big butcher's knife."

"What were you going to do with it?"

Jenna met her eyes. "Cut up some people who were getting on my nerves." While she spoke, she fingered the cutlery on the table. The "knife" was a plastic thing and couldn't do any damage, but the girl got the hint.

Alone again, Jenna pushed the food around the plate and kept an eye on the clock. In 20 minutes she'd be allowed to leave. She set her expression in a scowl that she hoped would keep all potential tablemates away.

After a while, a guy ambled toward her. With his zits and his sandy hair pulled back in a ponytail, he looked young, but not young enough to be one of the inmates. When he got closer, she saw that he had on one of those "resident assistant" tags.

"You Jenna Kelley?" he asked.

She deepened her scowl. "Who wants to know?"

He smirked. "Peter Blake, resident assistant." He indicated his badge. "Can't you read?"

Jenna glared at him. "What do you want?"

"Just to say 'hi.' Welcome to Harmony House." He pulled out a chair and sat down. "What are ya in for?"

Jenna considered possible responses and settled on "Weapons."

Peter nodded, and Jenna could have sworn he almost seemed impressed. He probably thought she was referring to guns. Well, let him think what he wanted to think.

His next question was unexpected. "You got friends?"

"Yeah, why?"

"They can't visit for forty-eight hours," he told her.

"I know that. I've been here before."

His eyebrows went up. "Oh, yeah? Then you probably know the game. How things work here. Demerits, privileges . . ."

"I know the rules," she said shortly.

He grinned. "Sure you do. After a couple of days, you can have visitors. I bet you've got cool friends."

"Yeah, they're okay," Jenna acknowledged. What was he getting at?

"Are they cool enough to do you some favors?"

262

Still puzzled, Jenna asked, "What kind of favors?"

"Oh, come on," he said, "I thought you knew the game."

"What game are you talking about?"

Peter Blake rolled his eyes in exasperation. "Your friends do favors for you. You do favors for me. I return the favor."

"I don't know what you're talking about," Jenna declared.

He grinned. "You will. I just want to know if you're going to play along."

Jenna still didn't understand what he was suggesting, but she was pretty certain it wasn't something on Harmony House's list of rules and regulations.

"I'm not playing at anything," she said flatly. "I don't owe you any favors, and I don't want any from you."

He raised his eyebrows. "Yeah? Well, don't say you weren't warned." He got up. "See ya around."

Weirdo, Jenna thought. What did he want, assault rifles? And what would she get in return—extra helpings of dessert? What a jerk.

But at least he'd helped her pass the time. She could leave the dining hall now.

She stopped at the little library to find something to read, and she was almost pleased to find a copy of *Jane Eyre*. It was funny, in a way. One of the only advantages of being sent here was the fact that she wouldn't have any homework assignments. Actually, she would *get* the assignments—the school would send them to Harmony House. But it wasn't like she had to do them—no one would be checking on her. And yet here she was, voluntarily taking on the task she'd be doing at home.

Back in her room, she settled down on the bed and opened the book. She'd read enough of the book to know that Jane had endured some pretty rough times in a boarding school that was like a jail. Now Jenna could identify with the character even more.

But it was hard to concentrate on reading. Her mind kept going back to the events of the day. Tracey and Emily—all the students must know by now what had happened to her. Madame, too. What were they thinking of her?

And her poor mother, who was trying so hard to make up for the bad times. But here was her daughter getting into trouble again.

Could she ever convince them that she'd never brought a knife to school? That the whole thing had been a setup? That Jenna Kelley was not a committed criminal?

Over and over, she re-lived the scene in Mr. Jackson's office. Finally, she put the book down, turned over, and buried her head in the pillow. It seemed she would have to put up with someone's tears after all.

Her own.

Chapter Seven

WAITING FOR THE SCHOOL bus on Friday morning, Tracey moved away from the other kids and took out her cell phone.

"Hello?"

Tracey tried to sound natural. "Hi, Amanda, it's Tracey!"

"What do you want *now*?"

Tracey couldn't blame her for sounding annoyed. This was the fourth time she'd called in three days. In the background, she heard another voice—Nina's or maybe Britney's.

"Who is it?" And she heard Amanda respond, "Nobody." Tracey talked fast before Amanda could hang up.

"I just wanted to remind you to save a seat for me at lunch. I'm planning to sit with you."

"Stay away from me!" Amanda shrieked. And Tracey was disconnected.

Relieved that her morning obligation was finished, Tracey tossed the phone back in her bag. But she still had the lunchtime duty to do—and she wasn't looking forward to *that*.

It was one of Ken's ideas. Yesterday, Tracey had picked up her tray in the cafeteria and carried it over to the table where Amanda and her friends always ate lunch. Britney, Nina, and Katie were already there, but Amanda hadn't arrived yet. The three Evilettes stared at her as if an alien had just landed at their exclusive gathering place.

"Amanda invited me to join you guys," Tracey had explained.

"She *did*?" Katie asked in disbelief.

"When?" Nina wanted to know.

"Oh, we were on the phone last night for ages," Tracey lied. "We talk all the time, you know. Anyway, she said she wanted me to sit with you all from now on."

Amanda arrived with another of her friends, Sophie. She was clearly taken aback to find Tracey at *her* table.

"What are you doing here?" she asked bluntly.

Nina answered for her. "Tracey said you invited her."

"I did no such thing!" Amanda exclaimed.

"Don't you remember?" Tracey asked. "Last night, when we were talking on the phone, you said—"

Amanda didn't let her finish. "I didn't talk to you on the phone last night! I've never called you in my life!"

Tracey had tried to look concerned. "Are you okay,

Amanda? Are you having memory problems?"

At that point, all the girls were looking at Amanda. Amanda was speechless.

Tracey had spoken sadly. "Are you ashamed of us being friends, Amanda?" Then she rose, picked up her tray, and walked away.

She had no idea what happened at the table after she left, but she suspected that it hadn't been too comfortable for Amanda. Today, Tracey planned to arrive at the table after Amanda, and she would thank Amanda for having called last night to apologize for her rude behavior.

Ken had also given Emily jobs to do. Yesterday, she'd passed a note to Nina in a class they had together.

Nina, if you see Amanda next period, could you tell her she can borrow my yellow sweater this weekend. She's been begging me to lend it to her.

Despite the fact that Tracey wasn't crazy about these efforts to destroy Amanda's reputation, she had to laugh at the notion of the well-dressed queen bee wanting to wear anything of Emily's.

The bus arrived. Tracey hurried to climb on so she could get a seat in the back, where the driver wouldn't see her on the phone. They weren't supposed to use their cell phones on the bus, but if he couldn't see her she'd be okay. The passengers never told on each other.

She got her seat and took her phone out again.

"Good morning. Harmony House."

"Hello, can I speak to Jenna Kelley, please?"

"I'm sorry, Jenna can't come to the phone."

Tracey frowned. This was the same response she'd been getting each time she tried to call her. "Well, can you tell me when visiting hours are?"

"I'm sorry," the voice on the other end said again, "but Jenna isn't permitted visitors."

"Why not?" Tracey demanded to know.

"Have a nice day," the voice replied, and the line went dead.

This was too frustrating. Even prisoners in real jails were allowed to have visitors.

When Tracey met Emily a few minutes later on the steps of Meadowbrook's entrance, she learned that Emily had been getting the same information from Harmony House.

"I can't believe that no one is allowed to have visitors in that place," Tracey fumed.

"Maybe Jenna doesn't want visitors," Emily suggested. "You know how she doesn't like people to feel sorry for her."

Ken was waiting for them just inside the building. He didn't bother with greetings.

"What did Amanda say when you called her this

morning?" he asked Tracey.

"What she said when I called yesterday," Tracey said. "'Stay away from me.'" She sighed. "Ken, how much longer do we have to do this? I hate going to that table at lunchtime. They don't want me there, and I don't want to be there."

"I'm going to try to get her alone this afternoon," Ken said. "I'm going to tell her we'll stop if she'll confess to what she did to Jenna."

Emily was looking at Ken quizzically. "Ken," she began, and then she bit her lip.

"What?" he asked.

Emily hesitated. "I don't know how to say this, and— and I know it's none of my business, but . . ." She looked at Tracey. Tracey had a feeling she knew what Emily was about to say, and it was something Tracey had been wondering about herself.

"Go ahead," Tracey said.

Emily spoke carefully. "I used to think . . . well, we all used to think that there was something going on between you and Amanda. Like, you were sort of interested in each other, you know what I mean?"

Ken didn't say anything.

Emily went on. "But now . . . it's like you totally hate her."

Ken shrugged. "Sure, I hate what she did to Jenna. And the way she put us all in danger when she was involved in the séance."

Tracey took over. "Are you sure it's not something else, too? Like, maybe you're going overboard because you still have feelings for her."

Ken glared at her. "And maybe you're defending her because she took over your body and got you a nice haircut." And he took off before she had a chance to deny it.

"I'm going to the bathroom before class," Emily told Tracey. "Want to come with me?"

Tracey shook her head. "I want to find Madame. Maybe she can talk to those Harmony House people so we can visit Jenna. See you in class."

"I won't be there—I've got a dentist appointment," Emily told her. "I'll call you tonight."

Tracey hurried upstairs to room 209. Madame wasn't there, but someone else was.

The Queen of Mean, who could usually be found wherever she could see and be seen, and who was always surrounded by friends, was hidden away in an empty classroom and all alone. And she didn't look mean today. People who were truly mean didn't bury their faces in their hands.

"Amanda?" Tracey murmured.

Amanda looked up. Instantly, her expression changed— but now she seemed more frightened than mean.

"Leave me alone!" she hissed. "Stop bothering me!"

Tracey took the seat next to her. Ken had said he'd talk to Amanda later, but Tracey figured this was as good a time as any to hit her with the ultimatum.

"Look, Amanda, you can make us stop bugging you right now. All you have to do is come clean about Jenna."

"What are you *talking* about? I didn't do anything to Jenna!"

She seemed honestly and sincerely bewildered. Ken would say that Amanda was putting on a good act, but Tracey wasn't so sure.

"We think you set up Jenna to get her into trouble. You work in the office, which means you can get your hands on the list of locker combinations."

Amanda still looked confused. Tracey was going to have to spell it out for her.

"You put the knife in Jenna's locker."

Amanda's eyes widened. "Why would I do that?"

"Because . . . because she was on to you. And you wanted to get rid of her."

Amanda didn't blink. "On to me about *what*?"

Tracey took a deep breath. "We think you're the spy, Amanda. We think you're the one who's communicating with our enemies: Serena, Clare—all those people who want to use us."

Amanda gasped. "Are you nuts? Why would I do something like that?"

"Because . . . because . . ." Tracey tried to think of a way to explain their suspicions that wouldn't be too hurtful. It was impossible, so she told the truth.

"Because you're selfish," she said finally. "You don't care about anyone—you only think of yourself. You think you're better than the rest of us."

Amanda's eyes narrowed, but she didn't deny any of the accusations.

"And you took that job in Mr. Jackson's office so you could find out more about us," Tracey finished.

Now Amanda became annoyed. "Is that what you think?"

"Well, you don't need the job. And I seriously doubt you're interested in learning office skills. So what other reason could there be?"

Amanda's lips tightened. Tracey got the feeling there was something she wanted to say but that she was keeping it inside.

"It's not just me," Tracey added. "Jenna, Emily, Ken . . . we all think you're spying on us."

"Ken . . ." Amanda murmured. "So that's why he's been acting so mean."

"That's why we've *all* been acting mean," Tracey corrected her, but she could tell it was only Ken that Amanda cared about.

"If he only knew why I took that job, he'd feel so bad about treating me like this," Amanda declared hotly.

Tracey blinked. "Then why don't you tell him? I mean, *us*? You could tell me right now why you took that job."

For once, Amanda seemed uncertain. She bit her lip and rapped her manicured fingernails on the desk. Finally, she spoke.

"Can you keep a secret?"

"That depends," Tracey said carefully. She hated the idea of swearing to secrecy before she knew what the secret was. What if Amanda was up to something that might put all the gifted students in danger?

"I'm not going to tell you unless you promise not to tell anyone," Amanda stated. "Not your friends, not Madame, not anyone."

Tracey was torn, but she knew that if she didn't give in, she'd learn nothing. "Okay, I promise. Why did you take the job in the principal's office?"

Despite the fact that they were alone in the classroom, Amanda lowered her voice.

"Remember when I went into the hospital last month

273

to get my tonsils out?"

Tracey nodded.

"Well, you know that wasn't me in the hospital."

Tracey nodded. "Like I told you when you came back to school, Emily and I went to visit you at the hospital. We could tell it wasn't you."

"And you remember who I was when I was out of my body."

Again, Tracey nodded. "You were the woman who was working with Serena on that séance scam. I forget her name."

"Margaret. And when I was in Margaret's body, Serena took me to a meeting. And you know who else was there? Clare, the woman who kidnapped us. And that man who claimed he was Jenna's father."

"So there really is a conspiracy," Tracey murmured in wonderment.

"Someone else was there, too," Amanda said. She did another of her dramatic pauses.

"Who?" Tracey asked impatiently.

"Mr. Jackson."

Tracey drew in her breath sharply. Nobody liked Mr. Jackson, and Jenna was always saying he gave her the creeps. But this was a little hard to believe.

"But Madame says he doesn't know about us!" Tracey

exclaimed.

"Madame doesn't know everything," Amanda countered. "I'm pretty sure it was Mr. Jackson who planted the knife in Jenna's locker."

"But—why?"

"If he's in on the conspiracy, then he knows about Jenna's gift," Amanda said. "Jenna was in the office earlier that day, and Mr. Jackson saw her. Maybe he was thinking about us, and he was afraid Jenna read his mind. So he had to get rid of her. I can't prove it, but he did leave the office just after Jenna was there, even though there were all these people waiting to see him."

"Maybe he had to go to the bathroom," Tracey offered weakly.

Amanda gave her a skeptical look. "Yeah, sure. And maybe he went to the cafeteria kitchen and picked up a knife."

Tracey's head was spinning. But everything Amanda said made perfectly good sense.

"What did Madame say when you told her about Mr. Jackson?" Tracey wanted to know.

"I didn't tell her," Amanda replied. "And you're not going to tell her, either."

"But Amanda, this is important! If our own principal is working against us, we're in danger right here at school!"

Amanda agreed. "And I'm going to prove it. All by

myself. That's why I'm working in the office—so I can watch him, so I can listen in on his meetings and phone calls and read his e-mails. I want to get real evidence."

"But you've already got evidence," Tracey protested. "Even if you can't prove that he put the knife in Jenna's locker, you know he's guilty of *something*. You saw him with your own eyes. Well, Margaret's eyes. He was meeting with people who have tried to get to us. That proves he's a bad guy."

"It's not enough," Amanda said. "Who's going to believe that I was in someone else's body?"

"Madame would."

Amanda shook her head. "That's not enough. Look, Tracey. You said I think I'm better than the rest of you. Well, socially, that's true. I am."

Tracey rolled her eyes. "You're not exactly modest, Amanda."

Amanda ignored that. "But you guys look down on me! You think my gift is worthless. You think I can't do anything important. Well, I'm going to show you I can."

So *that* was what this was all about. It wasn't enough for Amanda to be the prettiest, the best-dressed, the most popular girl at Meadowbrook. She wanted to be queen of the gifted class, too.

"Amanda, that's stupid!" Tracey declared. "We should

276

all be working together on this."

"And let someone else get the credit? Forget it!" Amanda began counting items off on her fingers. "It was Jenna who figured out that Serena was hypnotizing Emily to get winning lottery numbers. Ken saved Jenna from going off with that man who said he was her father. Charles got the gun away from Clare in the bank robbery. *You* pulled the scarves off Serena at the séance. Well, now it's *my* turn to be the hero."

"But this is too dangerous!" Tracey protested.

Amanda looked at her watch. "The bell's about to ring." She got up. "So now you know I'm not the spy, and you'll stop hassling me, right?"

"But how am I going to persuade the others to stop if I can't tell them what you're up to?"

"Find the real spy," Amanda said. She started out of the room but paused at the door and looked back. "Did you say you visited me at the hospital?"

Tracey nodded. "With Emily."

Amanda frowned. "Did anyone see you there? Were any of my real friends visiting?"

"Not while we were in the room."

"That's a relief," Amanda said and left.

Tracey didn't even feel insulted—by now, she was used to the way Amanda protected her social reputation.

Besides, she was still reeling from Amanda's revelation, and she couldn't give much thought to anything else.

Mr. Jackson, their very own principal! He wasn't exactly loved by the students, but he was an important man in a highly respected position. He was an educator! How could someone like that be a criminal?

She supposed it was possible that Amanda had just made up the story to throw suspicion off herself. But Tracey didn't think so. Amanda just didn't seem like she had that much imagination. And it *was* Mr. Jackson who had brought Serena into their class . . .

It was all beginning to make sense. If they had been in on this together since the beginning, Serena would have told Mr. Jackson what she'd learned about their gifts. But Serena wasn't around anymore, and someone was still feeding Mr. Jackson information. Someone in the class.

But if Amanda wasn't the spy, then who was? There was still one person she considered to be capable of treachery—Charles. Now was as good a time as ever to check out *his* private life. So, just before the gifted class, she ducked into the bathroom.

Taking a deep breath, she closed her eyes and conjured up an image of her former self, friendless and lonely. She dredged up sad memories of isolation, alienation, feeling worthless and unimportant. She concentrated intensely on the emotions she'd known back then and the sensation of not being seen. She visualized herself fading away, and then she started to feel it. The sensation of being weightless, lighter than air . . .

She opened her eyes and looked at the mirror over the sink. There was no reflection. She was getting better and better at this! Pleased with herself, she left the bathroom, went upstairs, and positioned herself outside room 209, where she could hear what was going on.

There wasn't much to hear, though. Apparently, Madame had set them to work on some sort of writing assignment, and her classmates were industriously scribbling away in silence. So she amused herself by roaming around the building, dancing in front of oblivious hall monitors and peeking through classroom windows. She considered going to the office and checking out Mr. Jackson's activities—but there was always the chance she might inadvertently reappear. She couldn't risk it.

She came back to room 209 just before the bell rang. When the door opened, Charles was the first to emerge. That wasn't unusual—he could make that wheelchair go very fast, and the others stepped aside to let him pass. Tracey was never sure if that was because they were trying to be kind or if they were afraid he'd run them over. She suspected that Charles would prefer the latter reason.

Ken was right behind him. She thought she might tell him what she was up to. It was comforting to know he could hear her when she was invisible, when no one else could. His ability to hear the voices of dead people seemed to extend to invisible people as well, at least in Tracey's case. But Ken brushed by her so quickly, she didn't have a chance to speak to him, and Charles was moving in the opposite direction.

People jumped out of the way as his motorized chair tore down the hall to the elevator. As far as Tracey knew, he was the only student permitted to use it. She hopped in with him and rode down to the main floor.

She'd never paid attention to how Charles got home. Today, for the first time, she noticed the white van parked just in front of the exit. A man stood by the vehicle, and when Charles appeared, he opened the back door. A ramp slid out, and the man pushed Charles's chair up into the van. Tracey stayed close behind and got inside just before the man closed the door.

It wasn't until the van pulled away that she got a look at Charles's face. It was red, and she wondered why. Was it from the exertion he'd expended hurrying out of school? Or maybe he was embarrassed by the van and the assistance he'd needed to get into it.

Funny how she'd never thought about how Charles

might feel, being unable to walk. She didn't even know how the situation came to be—if he'd been in an accident or something like that. It dawned on her that she'd never had any sort of private conversation with Charles. She didn't think anyone in the gifted class knew much about him. She doubted that anyone had ever been invited to his home.

It was a very nice house, all on one level but large, with a fine, freshly mowed lawn. At the end of the driveway, she saw a couple of bicycles leaning against the garage wall and a basketball net hanging over the door. She remembered Madame saying something to Charles about having brothers. Hadn't Charles said that they were ashamed of him?

The man pushed Charles out of the van and started wheeling him up the driveway. "Beat it!" Charles growled. "I can do it." The man released him and Charles took control of his chair. But instead of continuing up the driveway, he turned the chair so it rolled over the grass, making ugly tracks on the lawn.

"Charles!" Tracey exclaimed, forgetting for a moment that he couldn't hear her. Not that it would have made Charles move back onto the driveway. He had a tight smile on his face that made her think he was messing up the lawn on purpose.

The woman who opened the front door obviously thought so, too.

"Charles!" she cried out. "Stop that! Look what you're doing to the grass!"

Charles rolled himself up the ramp and right past her without a word of greeting or apology. Then he turned to the right, accelerated, and sped into what looked to Tracey like a very formal living room with a white carpet—over which there were now streaks of brown and green from the wheels of Charles's chair.

"Oh, Charles!" There was a note of resignation in the woman's voice, which led Tracey to believe this wasn't the first time Charles had pulled a stunt like this.

Charles stopped in the middle of the room and looked at a fancy vase filled with flowers on a pedestal. The vase rose up, moved toward Charles, then fell and broke, sending flowers and shards of glass all over the floor.

"Charles, why are you doing this?" the woman wanted to know.

Charles ignored her. He crossed the room, raced down a long hallway, and turned into a room. The door slammed shut before Tracey could reach it.

Astonished, she looked back at the woman to catch her reaction to this little performance. At first, she'd presumed this was Charles's mother, but now she realized she must be someone who worked here. Probably the person who would have to clean up the mess. She wondered what would happen when the woman reported Charles's behavior to his parents.

She couldn't get into Charles's room now because he'd closed the door. The front door was still open, though, so she went out to check if she could look into Charles's window and see what he was doing.

But something else distracted her. A couple of boys were now on the driveway, shooting baskets. As she moved closer, she saw the family resemblance. Both boys had Charles's red curls and freckles. They were close in age, maybe 15 and 16.

She wondered if they were both on the basketball team at the high school. Tracey didn't know much about basketball, but they looked like they played pretty well—most of their attempts sent the ball through the basket.

But then one of the boys threw the ball toward the basket, and it veered off in another direction. The other boy grabbed the ball, tossed it, and it went straight up in the air, so high that it disappeared. Then it came down so fast that both boys scampered away to avoid getting hit on the head by it.

They both looked annoyed but not surprised. "Charles!"

one of them bellowed.

That was when Tracey noticed an open window, and Charles looking out of it.

"Charles, knock it off," the taller boy called out.

"Make me!" Charles responded. To Tracey, he sounded like a five-year-old.

The other boy moved toward the window and spoke calmly. "Why don't you come out and play with us?"

"Yeah, I'll run around and chase the ball like you," Charles said sarcastically.

"You can play in your chair," his brother said. "You know there are whole teams who play basketball in wheelchairs. I've seen them on the Sports Channel."

"If I can't play like a normal person, I don't want to play," Charles replied.

The boy sighed. "Okay, don't play. But you don't have to mess up our game, okay?"

Charles uttered a word that would have sent him straight to Mr. Jackson if he'd said it at school. The ball flew up from the ground and settled on the roof of the house.

"Thanks a lot, Charles," one of the boys muttered. Charles's window slammed shut.

Maybe he'd be coming out of his room now, Tracey thought. As she started back toward the door, a car pulled into the driveway. The boys got out of the way, and the car went into the garage. A few seconds later, a nice-looking woman with a shopping bag in her hand emerged.

"Hey, Mom," the boys called out to her.

"Need a hand?" one of them added.

"No thanks, dear, I can manage," she said cheerfully. She paused and looked at the lawn. The cheerful expression vanished. "Oh, no. Charles must be in one of his moods."

The woman Tracey had seen earlier opened the door for Charles's mom. "I'm so sorry, Mrs. Temple. I couldn't stop him. I'm cleaning the mess in the living room now."

"I'll help you," Charles's mother said.

Tracey skipped on ahead of her so she could get back inside the house. She was interested in seeing how Mrs. Temple was going to deal with Charles's behavior. Would he be grounded, lose privileges?

But Mrs. Temple didn't even go to Charles's room. She disappeared for a few minutes, and when she returned she was carrying a vacuum cleaner. She joined the other woman in the living room.

This must be normal behavior for Charles, Tracey realized. His mother was upset, but she didn't seem at all surprised by the mess he'd made.

Tracey stood there, watching the women clean the carpet and waiting for Charles to come out of his room. Suddenly, out of the blue, a dish came floating across the room. It carried a stack of cookies, and as it whizzed past her, cookies fell off and dropped on the carpet. Mrs. Temple sighed and put the vacuum cleaner down. Picking up cookies along the way, she kept pace with the plate. Tracey went, too. When the plate reached Charles's door, it opened. Mrs. Temple went in, and Tracey followed.

Charles was on his bed, watching TV. He barely glanced at his mother. He made the plate settle on his lap, took a cookie, and crammed it into his mouth.

This was something new, Tracey realized. Charles had summoned the plate from another room that was not in his line of vision. She'd never before seen Charles move something without being able to see it. So his gift was evolving and changing, too, like hers. But he hadn't shared this with the class.

"Charles, I want to talk to you," his mother said.

Charles didn't respond. His mother took the remote control and switched off the TV. *That* got a response.

"Hey!"

For a moment, Tracey felt like she was watching a replay of what had gone on in Martin's house. There was a big difference, though, between Martin's bullying grandfather and Charles's mother. Mrs. Temple sat on the edge of her son's bed and gazed down at him with serious concern.

"Charles, why do you do these things?" she asked him.

"What things?" he mumbled.

His mother's voice became sterner. "Things like ruining the lawn, when you could have gone up the driveway to the back door."

"I just wanted to see what it felt like, to be on the lawn. I would have walked on it but I can't walk, in case you haven't noticed."

"Why did you make the vase fall?"

"Because I wanted to smell the flowers. Only I couldn't because I can't stand up."

She indicated the plate of cookies. "You summoned your snack here, and now there are cookies all over the floor. Were you just too lazy to go to the kitchen for them?"

"I'm not lazy!"

"Then why did you use your gift?"

Charles pressed his lips together tightly, as if he was trying to keep the words from coming out. His mother waited, but when he still didn't respond to her question, she sighed and shook her head.

"I don't know what to do with you, Charles."

He had an answer for that. "Just leave me alone."

Silently, Mrs. Temple rose and left the room. Tracey remained. Was Charles like this all the time at home? she wondered. Or was this an especially bad day for him? She recalled the expression on his face when he saw his brothers playing basketball. She couldn't be absolutely, positively sure, but she thought maybe she knew why Charles acted like this. He felt helpless, and he used his gift to feel powerful.

He wasn't helpless, of course. Being in a wheelchair might give him a disadvantage, but lots of people had disadvantages. Charles used his gift so he wouldn't have to deal with the fact that he couldn't walk. He was hung up on being helpless.

She could understand because she'd given in to helplessness herself. She blamed her parents for ignoring her—but what had she done to help herself? She'd wallowed in self-pity. Amanda had shown her how to break out. And it wasn't just the clothes, the haircut, the makeup. It was learning to stand up for herself.

That was what Charles had to do—stand up. He couldn't do it physically, but it was Charles's attitude that kept him down, not his legs.

He wasn't the class spy. He was just another sad kid who wanted to be like everyone else. And she could help him. She couldn't take over his body like Amanda had taken over hers. But she could talk to him, she could be a friend, and maybe he'd open up to her. His family loved him, but they couldn't understand his needs. She could—because she'd been there.

She wanted to help him, and she had to do it *now.* When else would she be able to corner him alone like this? If she could make a real connection with him, maybe she could encourage him to connect with the gifted class, open himself up to the group experience. She knew she couldn't appear right in front of him, so she dashed out of the room and out of the open front door.

Behind a bush where she knew she wasn't visible from the house, she closed her eyes and concentrated on becoming visible. She envisioned herself as real and solid and commanded her body to reappear. When she felt nothing happen, she gritted her teeth and worked harder, concentrating, focusing, directing all her mental energies into becoming herself. She couldn't remember the process ever taking this much energy before.

Opening her eyes, she realized why. She was still invisible.

And she began to get nervous.

CHAPTER EIGHT

◆

JENNA SANK INTO THE chair in the lounge and looked at the TV screen without even seeing what was on it. She supposed she could take advantage of the fact that for once she was alone in the lounge and could watch something she wanted to watch. But she wasn't in the mood for TV.

She wasn't in the mood for anything. It was 5 P.M. on a Friday afternoon, and she'd been at Harmony House since Tuesday. What would she be doing if she wasn't here? Waiting for her mother to come home from work and thinking about what they might have for dinner. Maybe throwing some things in a backpack for one of the regular Friday night sleepovers at Tracey's. Checking online to see if there were any good movies playing in town.

Instead, she was imprisoned in a facility for bad teenagers, and she wasn't bad. And right now, all the really bad teenagers were enjoying visits from friends and families, while she, Jenna Kelley, who had done absolutely nothing wrong, was all alone.

That Landers woman had said she couldn't have visitors or phone calls for the first 48 hours. Those 48 hours were over 24 hours ago, and she'd had neither a visitor nor a phone call.

Peter Blake, the creepy resident assistant, came into the lounge.

"It's visiting hours," he announced.

"Yeah, I know," Jenna muttered.

"Guess you didn't get any visitors," he commented.

Jenna didn't think she needed to dignify that with an answer.

He turned to leave but looked back at her from the door. His lips curved unpleasantly into a smile that was more like a sneer. "I wonder why."

So did Jenna. Not one visitor, yesterday or today. Not from her mother, not from Tracey or Emily. She'd harbored a faint hope that Madame might have come to visit her. Okay, maybe she acted like she didn't care what Madame thought about her, but deep in her heart she did trust the teacher, and she thought the teacher trusted her. But now she had to wonder if maybe Madame thought she belonged in this prison.

At first she was surprised by the lack of calls and visits—

now she was depressed. Did they all believe she'd really come to school armed with a butcher's knife? Had they all abandoned her? Was her very own mother on the phone right now to social services telling them to keep her daughter forever?

It hurt, bad. Even during the worst times of her life, when her mother was drinking and Jenna was basically living on the streets, she couldn't remember feeling so low. So alone.

This morning, she'd had another meeting with that doctor, Paley. He'd asked her if she was making friends here at Harmony House. She'd lied and said yes, just to get him off her back. It wasn't like she could tell him she'd read a few minds and realized there wasn't anyone here she wanted to make friends with. So many of them were like the people she'd known before, on the streets.

She didn't even have to read minds to know that some of them were just deadly dull. Every day, there were "group" sessions she had to attend. Around ten residents gathered with a counselor to talk. What they mostly did was complain and find other people to blame for their situations—usually a mother or a father. It was boring.

So she'd been hanging out by herself, eating alone, not making any effort to connect with anyone. She supposed there had to be some decent people here, but she just couldn't get up the energy to make the effort to find them.

She'd been almost glad when another resident assistant, Carrie, told her yesterday she was getting a roommate. But when the new girl, Kristy, arrived, Jenna could see right away that her life was only going to get worse.

She didn't look terrible—in fact, she was something of a goth herself, with dyed black hair and several prominent piercings. She even had tattoos, something Jenna hadn't gotten into yet. But the minute Carrie left them alone together in the bedroom, Kristy reached into her bag and pulled out a cigarette.

Jenna didn't want the new girl to think she was some sort of goody-goody, but once Kristy lit up, the smell was too seriously disgusting.

"Um, I'm pretty sure that's against the rules," she murmured. "Not that I care about rules," she added hastily, "but someone's going to smell the smoke in the hall and you'll get into trouble."

No sooner had the words left her mouth than there was a sharp rap at the door and Carrie entered.

"No smoking," she declared and pointed to the very visible sign of a cigarette with a big X over it on the wall. She took the cigarette from Kristy and then, without even asking permission, she went into Kristy's bag. Removing the pack of cigarettes, she said, "You're getting a demerit for that."

"Like I care," Kristy muttered, as soon as Carrie left. She then began to regale Jenna with her reasons for being at Harmony House. It seemed that Kristy had been part of a gang that was robbing convenience stores. She went on and on about how cool it was to hold a gun and scare the wits out of some guy behind the counter at two in the morning.

She didn't say if she'd ever actually used the gun, and Jenna suspected she hadn't because Kristy seemed like the type who would brag about it if she'd shot someone. As her tales went on, Jenna wondered which was worse— someone who wept over her crimes or someone who boasted about them. The latter, she decided. Her former roommate at Harmony House may have gotten on her nerves, but this one was truly creepy.

Fortunately, her new roommate discovered that some old pals of hers were in residence at Harmony House, and she spent the rest of the evening in search of them. Kristy slept late and skipped breakfast that morning— which resulted in another demerit—and Jenna didn't even have to eat lunch with her today in the dining hall. Kristy spent her lunchtime at the table famous for hosting the most serious offenders.

But Jenna couldn't avoid her forever, and she

wasn't surprised when Kristy ambled into the lounge. Of course, she wouldn't have any visitors—she was still in her first 48 hours. Without even asking Jenna if she was watching whatever was currently on the TV, Kristy picked up the remote control and started hitting channel buttons. Then she reached into her pocket and took out another pack of cigarettes.

As she lit up, Jenna spoke.

"There's a resident assistant around," she warned Kristy.

Kristy glanced at her briefly. "That Peter guy, right?"

Jenna nodded.

Kristy uttered a short laugh and took another drag. Jenna wondered if the girl was really as tough—or as stupid—as she acted. With nothing else to do, she poked around Kristy's mind.

. . . hate this place . . . maybe it won't be so bad . . . can't make phone calls, that sucks . . . gotta figure out a way to get in touch with Pete . . . tell him to come on Monday and bring E . . .

E . . . she *could* be referring to a person whose first initial was E. But it was more likely she was talking about the drug ecstasy. Oh, great, Jenna thought. Cigarettes were bad enough. Now this idiot was going to try to get high in here.

The smell of the cigarette was making her nauseous. Another resident, a boy, came into the lounge, and Jenna looked at him hopefully. Maybe the smell would bother him, too, and together they could get Kristy to put out the cigarette.

But the boy wasn't staying. "You guys seen Peter?"

"He's around somewhere," Kristy said.

The boy seemed a little nervous as he touched the pocket of his jeans. "Well, if you see him, tell him I've got something for him."

Puzzled, Jenna couldn't help wondering why the boy looked so uneasy, his eyes darting around the room. One quick sweep of his mind gave her the answer. He was carrying a bag of weed.

That was when it hit her. Peter Blake was using residents to get drugs. He was telling them to get their visitors to smuggle the junk into Harmony House. Maybe he was bribing them with extra privileges—like giving Kristy the right to smoke. Or it could be blackmail. He'd discover someone breaking a rule and make a deal— no demerit in return for a favor.

And this would explain why she, Jenna, had no visitors. She leaped up and went out into the hall and down the stairs to the office of Ms. Landers.

"Hey, you can't just go in there!" the secretary exclaimed. But Jenna walked right past her and opened the door to the director's office.

The director wasn't alone. That cop, Jack Fisher, was sitting on the other side of her desk. Ms. Landers looked up with annoyance written all over her face.

"Young lady, you do *not* barge into my office like that!"

Jenna ignored that. "I want to know why I haven't had any visitors," she demanded.

The woman's expression didn't change, but at least she answered her. "I explained this when you entered. The accumulation of demerits results in the loss of privileges. Five demerits means no visitors or phone calls for twenty-four hours."

Jenna's eyebrows went up. "I have five demerits?"

"Six, I believe. Let's see . . ." she turned to her computer and hit a couple of keys. "Sneaking over to the boys' dormitory wing. Picking fights. Smoking in your room."

As she continued with her litany of fabricated violations, Jenna wanted to hit herself on the head for being so incredibly stupid. Peter had asked her if she had friends who would do "favors." She didn't know what he was talking about, but he'd assumed she was refusing to ask her friends to bring in drugs, or what-ever else he asked residents to smuggle in for him. So he'd made up infractions for her and given her demerits. It was a punishment for not cooperating.

She should have figured this out that first day, in the

dining hall. But what could she have done about it? There was no way she'd ask her friends to do something like that. Her friends couldn't do anything about it, anyway! She tried to picture Emily looking around a bad neighborhood for a drug dealer.

"If you feel these demerits are unwarranted, you may appeal them," the woman said. "But not at this moment— I'm busy. You can make an appointment with the secretary."

Jenna left and passed the secretary without bothering to make an appointment. What good would it do? She couldn't tell Ms. Landers about Peter Blake. She wouldn't believe her. And if she directed Ms. Landers toward the others who were being threatened or bribed, they'd only deny it. And how would she prove she was telling the truth? Admit to having read their minds?

Outside the office, she paused in the empty corridor and leaned against a wall to gather her thoughts for a moment. She'd been screwed, that's all there was to it. And there wasn't a thing she could do about it.

"Are you okay, Jenna?"

She hadn't even heard Jack-the-cop come out of the office.

"I'm fine," she said shortly.

He reached into his pocket and pulled out a pack of chewing gum. "Want some gum?"

"No."

She knew how rude she must sound, but what did it matter? He'd heard Ms. Landers's report on her. He knew she was nothing but trouble.

But she could have sworn she saw something else in his eyes. And just out of curiosity, she peeked into his head.

. . . surprised . . . she doesn't seem like the type . . . is she covering for someone? Wish I could get her to open up to me . . .

She must have been staring at him, because he cocked his head to one side and smiled. "Want to talk?"

She *did*—but not to him. Not to a cop. She didn't care how much sympathy she saw in his eyes or read in his mind, she couldn't trust him.

"No," she said and walked away. But just as she was about to turn the corner, she looked back at him. Somehow, she managed to get one more word out.

"Thanks."

Chapter Nine

I N THE KITCHEN AT home, Tracey sat on the counter—a position that was forbidden in the Devon home. But it didn't matter because her mother couldn't see her.

Her mother stood just a few feet away, with the phone in her hand.

"Tracey isn't here, Emily," she was saying. She laughed nervously. "Actually, she might very well be here, but she's not available, if you know what I mean. I haven't seen her since she left for school yesterday."

There was a pause, which Tracey assumed meant that Emily was responding. Then her mother spoke again.

"No, I'm not worried. Not yet. I mean, this has happened before. I'm sure she'll turn up eventually."

Eventually. That was the key word. Tracey hadn't gone this long without reappearing since—since the days before Amanda changed her. At least now her parents actually noticed that she wasn't visible. That was definitely an improvement.

Her problem now was figuring out how to share what she'd learned from Amanda yesterday. The only person she'd be able to communicate with was Ken. But every time she'd tried to defend Amanda, everyone had told her she was being silly. They all thought that just because Amanda had inhabited Tracey's body and improved Tracey's life, Tracey had some dumb notion that she owed Amanda something.

But there was one other possible connection—Jenna. Could Jenna read the mind of an invisible person? Jenna could read people's minds when she couldn't see them, but Tracey couldn't recall any circumstance when Jenna had read her mind when she was invisible. Maybe if Tracey *thought* about what she'd learned from Amanda, Jenna would "hear" her. Their gifts were constantly developing, evolving—she'd seen Charles display an aspect to his gift she'd never seen before. It was possible that her own gift, and Jenna's, too, had potential they hadn't yet discovered.

But only if Jenna knew that Tracey wanted her mind to be read. Tracey had to get close enough to Jenna to give her some kind of signal, to let her know. And how could she get close to her when she wasn't permitted any visitors?

Tracey had to laugh at herself. What an idiot she was!

301

She was invisible—she didn't need anyone's permission to visit Jenna.

She had to take three buses to get to Harmony House, but her biggest problem was not the distance or the time it would take to get there—it was getting on and off each bus. If no one else was waiting at the bus stop or getting off there, the bus wouldn't stop or open its doors. Fortunately, this happened only once, and then someone came along, which enabled her to get on the next one. The positive aspect was the fact that she didn't have to pay for the ride—but being a basically honest person, she didn't feel very good about it. Riding the bus free seemed like stealing. But she couldn't waste energy feeling guilty about it—she had no other option.

Jenna's residence didn't look like a prison. The brick building was painted white, and it was set far back on a green lawn. The sign on the lawn read "Harmony House," not "Detention Center" or anything like that. There were bars on the windows, but they'd been painted white, too, and shaped in a design that made them look more like window decorations. Tracey suspected that the two men who were standing on either side of the front door were guards, but at least they weren't dressed like guards, and she couldn't see any guns. They could have been doormen at a hotel.

When someone came out, she slipped inside. Now the place looked more like an institution, with its sickly green walls and the lobby that seemed more like a waiting room. But Tracey had no time to waste on criticizing the décor. She had no idea if she might suddenly become visible again. This was a pretty big place, and she had no idea where Jenna might be.

Luckily, it was dinner time, and she followed people who all seemed to be heading in the same direction—a dining hall. And there she found Jenna, sitting alone at a table.

From a distance, Tracey studied her friend, and her heart ached for Jenna. She wore that dark, angry face that Tracey remembered from when she first saw her, the day Jenna entered the gifted class. Her expression had softened considerably since then. Even when Jenna was doing her "I'm-tough-as-nails" thing, she didn't look so—so enraged. And something else, too. Sad. In Tracey's opinion, sad was worse than angry.

She moved closer and closer, until she was at the table, standing right in front of Jenna.

Jenna, it's me, Tracey.

But Jenna's expression didn't change. Tracey wasn't surprised. If Jenna didn't know she was there, she wouldn't try to read Tracey's mind. How could she let Jenna know of her presence? She considered various possibilities.

Recalling her mother and the purse, Tracey took a salt shaker from another table and placed it in front of Jenna. But the sudden appearance of the salt shaker didn't grab Jenna's attention. Obviously, her mind was elsewhere.

Tracey removed her own headband from her hair. It was something she wore a lot, and maybe Jenna would recognize it. She dropped it, and it landed right on top of Jenna's sandwich.

Jenna saw it, but her reaction wasn't what Tracey expected. She snatched up the band and stood up.

"Whoever threw this at me, you're in trouble!" she yelled.

A couple of kids giggled, but the people sitting closest to Jenna just stared at her blankly. Jenna walked over to the trash cans and dropped the headband in one.

Tracey watched her mournfully. It had been one of her favorites. But she should have known that Jenna wouldn't notice what other people wore, not even her closest friends. Jenna was the opposite of Amanda— she didn't care about stuff like that.

She'd probably know what she herself was wearing, though. Jenna's necklace, a thick silver chain with a dangling pendant of a skull, was one she wore frequently. Moving around the table, Tracey quickly lifted the necklace over

Jenna's head and dropped it in front of her.

Jenna whirled around. But no one could have approached her and gotten away so quickly. She picked up the necklace and examined the clasp. Then she shrugged and put it back around her neck.

What else could she do, Tracey wondered. Gather up plates and bowls and dump them on Jenna's table? That would get Jenna's attention, but it would attract attention from the others in the dining hall, too. She was getting desperate—she had to talk to Jenna. She had to share this information; she wanted Jenna's advice and opinion. Jenna would know what Tracey should do. She had to make contact with her. She needed her friend!

Suddenly, Jenna's eyes widened. "Tracey?" she whispered.

Yes! Yes, it's me, I'm right across the table from you. How did you know I was here?

Jenna put a hand over her mouth and spoke so softly that Tracey had to lean across the table to hear her.

"I don't know, but it happened once before, when Emily was trapped by Serena at school. I guess she was trying so hard to make contact with me that I actually heard her."

Just like me, Tracey said with feeling. *I've got to talk to you.*

"What's going on?" She'd taken her hand away from her mouth, and a couple of kids at the next table glanced at her curiously. Jenna quickly speared a carrot from her plate, stuck it in her mouth and chewed furiously.

Just listen. I've learned something. This wouldn't be breaking the promise she'd made to Amanda . . . because she wasn't "telling" the secret—she was only thinking it.

Silently, Tracey recalled the story Amanda had told her about Mr. Jackson. *She's telling the truth, Jenna. I'm sure of it. And it all makes sense, when you think about it. The spy is reporting to Mr. Jackson. That's how he found out about our gifts.*

"So it was Jackson who put the knife in my locker?"

I think so.

"But who's the spy?" Jenna asked. "Who's telling Jackson about us?" Realizing she was talking out loud, she clapped a hand over her mouth, but it was too late. People turned to look at her. And one guy with a bad complexion and a ponytail sauntered over to her.

"Talking to yourself, Jenna?" he asked unpleasantly.

Jenna glared at him. "Does that get me another demerit?"

"No," the guy said. "Just a report to Dr. Paley."

Can we go someplace private? Tracey asked.

Jenna rose and picked up her tray. Tracey followed her as she left the tray by the trash cans and went out of the dining hall.

"We're going to my room," Jenna murmured as they

walked.

But they weren't going to get any privacy there. A girl was lying on one of the twin beds and smoking a cigarette.

Jenna spoke. "Get out of here with that cigarette or I'll ram it down your throat."

The girl smirked. "Is that a threat?"

"No," Jenna said. "It's a promise."

Tracey was impressed. She knew Jenna could act tough, but she'd never heard her sound quite so scary.

The girl got the message. Once she was out of the room, Jenna threw herself on the other twin bed. "That threat's going to get me another demerit. Which will probably mean another day of no visitors."

Is that why they've been telling us you can't have visitors? Because you've got demerits?

Jenna nodded. "Only I didn't earn them."

Tracey was shocked to hear the story about the assistant who was blackmailing residents. *Can't you tell someone about him?*

"He'll only deny it. And how am I going to explain why I know about all the other kids he's using?"

But this has to stop! He'll keep making up stories about you, you'll get more demerits, and, and . . .

Jenna finished the thought for her. "And I'll never get out of here."

Just as she'd never heard Jenna sound as fierce as she had moments earlier, she'd never heard her sound so flat and resigned as now. She preferred the fierce Jenna. Maybe now Jenna needed Tracey as a friend even more than Tracey needed Jenna.

That's not going to happen. I'll get the proof we need. I'll get you out of here. I promise, Jenna.

There was a knock on the door, and then it opened. A young woman poked her head in.

"It's time for your group session, Jenna."

Jenna groaned. "Can't I skip it today?"

"Sure," the woman said, "if you don't mind getting another demerit. Oh, and Dr. Paley wants to see you tomorrow."

"I just saw him this morning!" Jenna exclaimed.

The woman shrugged. "Well, he wants to see you again tomorrow."

"Boy, Peter works fast," Jenna murmured.

The woman's brow furrowed. "What do you mean?"

"Nothing." Jenna got up and went to the door. Tracey followed her.

You want me to stick around?

Jenna shook her head. The woman looked at her curiously. "Are you all right, Jenna?"

Jenna almost smiled. "No. But I will be."

Yes, Tracey thought fervently. *Yes, you will, Jenna.*

Outside Harmony House, Tracey went to wait at the bus stop. Looking back at the building, she had the same thought she'd had when she arrived.

No, it didn't look like a prison. But a place didn't have to look like a prison to be a prison. A prison didn't even have to be a place. A secret was like a prison—it could keep a person trapped in the same way. Jenna, Tracey, Emily . . . all of Madame's students were imprisoned by their secret gifts.

Somehow, Tracey was going to get Jenna out of Harmony House. She'd find the real spy, and the spy would lead her to the proof about Mr. Jackson and the knife. Jenna would be released; she'd be free. But could any of them ever feel completely—really and truly—free, free to do whatever they wanted, free to be themselves?

No one else came to wait at the bus stop, and the bus was approaching. Tracey could only hope that someone was getting off at this stop so she could get on. No, she wasn't free to do whatever she wanted.

Chapter Nine

W HEN TRACEY ARRIVED HOME, she could hear the Devon Seven and her mother in the kitchen.

"Where's Tracey, Mommy?" one of them asked. Tracey was pretty sure it was Brandie. The others chimed in.

"Where is she?"

"I want Tracey to play with us!"

"We can't find her, Mommy!"

Mrs. Devon looked frazzled. "She's—she's out, girls, she's busy. Go outside and play. Tracey's coming home soon."

As soon as the kitchen was vacant, the woman sank down into a chair. "Tracey?" she called out weakly. "Are you in here?"

Her mother looked really upset.

"Tracey . . . I'm sure you're fine, you're just being invisible, but . . . I'm worried! What if you're hurt? Maybe you've run away from home . . ." She gasped as another thought must have occurred to her. "Maybe you've been kidnapped! Oh, Tracey, sweetheart, if you're here . . . I know I wouldn't be able to hear you if you spoke, and I know you can't write me a message, but . . . could you just give me a sign, so I know you're all right? You're not usually invisible for this long."

Once again, Tracey marveled at the irony of it all. Not so long ago, she could have disappeared for a lot longer than a couple of days and her mother wouldn't have even noticed. Now she was worried . . . Tracey wasn't sure which feeling was stronger—her pity for her mother or her satisfaction at the change in family relationships.

It was the pity that made her go back into the living room, pick up her mother's purse from the coffee table, and bring it into the kitchen. When the purse appeared in front of her mother, Tracey was rewarded with a sigh and smile of gratitude.

"Thank you, dear," her mother said humbly. Tracey left and went up to her room. She had some thinking to do before she made her next move to fulfill her promise to Jenna.

Okay, so Mr. Jackson was the major bad guy at Meadowbrook, the numero uno villain. But how was he getting his information about the gifted students? Someone was telling him what went on in class.

Tracey refused even to consider the notion that Madame

would betray her students. The teacher was beyond any suspicion, and she was sure her classmates would agree with her. So it had to be one of them. From what she knew, and what she'd observed, she could eliminate herself, Jenna, Emily, Amanda, Sarah, Ken, Martin, and Charles. Which only left Carter.

But how could Carter be a spy? The boy didn't speak; he didn't write; he couldn't communicate at all. He was practically a zombie.

She searched her memory for what she knew about him. Supposedly, he was found wandering on Carter Street. He carried no identification, and the police had no reports of any missing boy who fit his description. Social services had taken over his care, and he'd been placed in a foster home. That was all she knew.

From her desk drawer, she retrieved the Meadowbrook Middle School Directory and looked up his name. The foster family was named Granger, and they lived not too far from her own house.

The address turned out to be a medium-size, very ordinary-looking cottage-style house on a tree-lined street. The sun was setting, and the lights were on inside. She waited on the front steps for a while, but no one came in or out. Fortunately, the curtains weren't drawn, so she walked around the house and peeked in at each window.

She found Carter in what was clearly the dining room of the house. He was sitting at a table with two other young boys, a man, and a woman. She assumed the adults were the Grangers. The two younger boys didn't look at all alike, nor did they look like the adults, so she thought they might be foster children, too.

The Grangers certainly fed their foster kids well. The table was laden with food—roast beef, bowls of vegetables, a big tossed salad. She couldn't hear any conversation, but she could see lips moving as the family talked. It seemed to her that they were having a lively conversation. Of course, Carter wasn't participating in it. He ate, slowly and rhythmically, but he stared straight ahead, not making eye contact with anyone else at the table. It was the same way he behaved at school. She saw the woman bend over and speak to him, but Carter didn't respond.

It dawned on her that she was hungry. Eating while invisible wasn't easy. Even if she could get herself inside the house without anyone noticing a door opening, she couldn't very well join them for their meal. There were too many people at the table, and someone was bound to notice if food started to disappear.

So she stood there, suffering hunger pangs, and waited for the meal to end. Only, what did she expect to happen after that? The boys would probably watch a little television and go to bed. There wouldn't be much to see through the windows. She had to find a way to get inside the house and into Carter's room. Maybe there she'd find something interesting about Carter, some clue as to whether or not Carter had a secret life as a spy.

Fortunately, when dinner was over and the table was being cleared, she observed the woman saying something to Carter again. He got up and left the dining room. Skipping over to the next window, Tracey could see him scraping leftovers from the plates into the trash can in the kitchen. Then he took out the garbage-packed liner and went to the back door.

Tracey hurried to position herself by the back door, and as soon as Carter opened it, she slipped inside. While Carter took the garbage to the outdoor garbage can, she did a quick survey of the kitchen. A platter of leftover roast beef slices hadn't been put away yet.

A benefit of being invisible meant she didn't have to think about manners. She snatched up a slice of meat and practically crammed the whole piece in her mouth. Then she took a second slice. Mrs. Granger came in and picked up the platter. Looking at the remains of the meat, her brow furrowed for a minute, as if she'd realized there was less there than she thought there should be. Finally, she shrugged and wrapped the slices.

Carter returned.

"Could you help me load the dishwasher, Carter?" the woman asked.

Carter didn't say yes or no, but he opened the door of the dishwasher and began loading items. He was just like he was at school, obeying without communicating.

Tracey left the kitchen and went down a hallway that she presumed would lead to bedrooms. One bedroom held a big double bed, and she assumed that was the master bedroom. Another bedroom had bunk beds and toys strewn on the floor.

She decided that the third bedroom must be Carter's. It held one single bed, a desk, a bureau, and a bookshelf. Everything was impeccably neat and tidy.

With no one else in there, she had the freedom to open drawers. All she found there were clothes. Desk drawers contained pencils, a ruler, ordinary school stuff. She couldn't find any notes or letters.

Next, she checked the books on the shelves. She tried to remember if she'd ever seen Carter reading, but no image came to mind. Actually, the books all looked pretty new and untouched. She opened a few in the half-hearted hope she might find a note tucked inside, but she had no luck.

It was frustrating. There had to be something in this room, but she couldn't tear it apart and make a mess. She'd have to wait until Carter came in and hope he would reveal something to her. To pass the time, she took one of the books from the shelf, a biography of Helen Keller. Maybe the Grangers had given it to him in the hope that he might find something in common with a person who overcame disabilities. She sat at Carter's desk and started to read.

Once she sat down, she realized how exhausted she was. It had been a long day. The life of Helen Keller was intriguing, but Tracey was too tired to get caught up in it. She put her head on the desk and closed her eyes.

It was amazing how easily she fell asleep in such an uncomfortable position. When she opened her eyes, the room was completely dark. Rising from the chair, she saw Carter in bed, sound asleep.

The whole house was silent—everyone must be asleep, she thought. The bedside clock told her it was midnight. Well, at least she could get out without anyone seeing a door open by itself. She just hoped there was no alarm system.

Suddenly, making barely a sound, Carter sat up in bed. For a second, Tracey thought he was looking straight at her and that maybe she'd become visible. A glance at the mirror over the bureau told her that this hadn't happened.

Carter got out of bed and gathered up the clothes he'd been wearing earlier. Politely, Tracey averted her eyes while he dressed. He then walked out of the room.

Was he sleepwalking? Tracey wondered. She followed him down the hall and into the living room. Silently, he opened the front door.

On the street in front of the house, a black car was waiting. A man stepped out from the driver's side, and without speaking, he opened the back door. Carter got in, with Tracey close behind.

The driver took off. He said nothing to Carter, and he seemed to know where he was going. The ride took about 20 minutes and brought them to a residential area on the other side of town. The car pulled up in front of a house on another tree-lined street. Again, the driver got out and opened the door.

Carter walked to the front door. Tracey hung back for a moment to get a good look at the house so she could identify it later. It was white, smaller than Carter's house, but well kept and nice looking.

She'd expected Carter to knock or ring a bell, but someone must have seen him approach from inside. The door opened, and Carter went in. Tracey raced forward, but she was too late—the door had closed by the time she reached it.

Furious at herself, she raced around the house, looking for another way to get inside. There was a back door, but it was locked.

So she was in the same position she'd been in back at Carter's house, and she was forced to do what she'd done there—look for a window that would give her a view of what was going on inside. Again, the people were in the dining room and sitting around a dining room table. But they weren't eating.

She could identify all of them. Clare, the woman who'd been in charge of the bank robbery. Serena, the student teacher and fake medium. The man who called himself Stuart Kelley and claimed to be Jenna's father. And Mr. Jackson.

Carter was offered the chair at the head of the table. Serena seemed to be talking to him—at least, she was looking at him and her lips were moving. And then Tracey saw something she'd never seen before.

Carter's lips were moving. With the window closed, Tracey couldn't hear anything, but it was obvious that Carter was speaking. And whatever he was saying had the full attention of the others.

Clare was taking notes. Mr. Jackson was nodding. Stuart Kelley appeared to interrupt at some point to ask a question. Carter responded.

At first, Tracey was stunned. Then, when she recovered from her surprise, she was furious. That weasel, that little fake—he was pretending to be a zombie and all the time he was perfectly capable of communicating. He must have an incredible memory, too. She'd never seen him write anything down in class, but he was obviously able to remember everything he heard there so he could report to this evil gang. At least, that's what Tracey assumed he was doing—telling the others what went on in the gifted class. But what else could intrigue this band of conspirators?

If only she could read lips! What was Carter telling them? How were they going to use the information?

Oh, how she wished *she* could communicate right then and there. She'd call her classmates, she'd call Madame at home, she wouldn't care if she woke them all up. She'd tell them where she was, they could join her, and together they could confront these people.

She couldn't tell them while invisible, of course. She wasn't physically capable of doing that. But maybe she could *show* them. From her bag, she drew out her cell phone. On the menu, she clicked on the camera function.

The phone in her hand was invisible. Maybe any picture she took with an invisible camera wouldn't be seen. But she couldn't waste time pondering the logistics of invisibility. She maneuvered the phone until she thought it was in the right position to catch the image of the table and the people around it—and clicked. In this darkness, it wouldn't be a great picture, and it wouldn't prove that Carter could talk.

But it would show that Mr. Jackson was in league with those other villains. And that was a start.

CHAPTER ELEVEN

A T TEN O'CLOCK ON Saturday morning, Jenna found herself facing Dr. Paley in his office. Behind the desk, the round-faced man gazed at her steadily. Jenna stared right back at him.

The doctor wasn't smiling quite as broadly this time. "I don't usually come in to Harmony House on Saturdays," he said. "But I thought it was important to see you as soon as possible."

Jenna affected a look of wide-eyed innocence. "Why?"

"I think you know," he said.

Of course she knew, but she wanted to hear it from him. She couldn't defend herself until she knew exactly what that creep Peter had said. So she simply shrugged.

Dr. Paley gave in. "When I checked my messages this morning, there was a new and urgent report about you. You've been observed talking to yourself."

Jenna said nothing.

"And your expression indicated that you were listening

to another voice. As if someone else was with you."

Jenna remained silent.

"You don't deny it?" he asked.

Jenna chose her words carefully. "I don't remember doing anything like that."

Dr. Paley looked at his notes. "You appeared to be carrying on a conversation in the dining hall, and you were alone."

Jenna shrugged. "I was probably daydreaming."

Dr. Paley studied her thoughtfully. "Who were you talking to, Jenna?"

What would he say if she replied "my invisible friend"? The thought made her smile.

"This isn't a laughing matter," he said.

Jenna shifted uncomfortably in her chair. "Sorry. I guess I was just daydreaming again."

"You don't strike me as a daydreamer," he said. He looked at his notes again. "I see you've amassed a lot of demerits. Smoking, picking fights . . ."

She tried to stop the fury from rising inside, but it was impossible and she knew it came out in her voice. "I've never smoked a cigarette in my life," she declared hotly. "And I haven't picked any fights. Not here, at least."

"Then why do you have all these demerits?"

"It's all made up, I shouldn't have those demerits.

Someone's out to get me." And then she wanted to kick herself. Now he was going to think she was paranoid.

"Who's out to get you? Ms. Landers? Other kids?"

She shook her head.

He looked at the file. "I see all these demerits were reported by the same resident assistant."

She couldn't stop herself. "Peter Blake."

"Is that who's out to get you?" When she didn't reply, he asked, "Why would he make up these things about you?"

"Because he's a slime bucket," she muttered.

A brief smile flickered across the doctor's face. "That may well be—I don't know the young man. But why would he pick on *you*?"

She was so sick of this, of beating around the bush, avoiding the questions. Of being Peter's victim. "Because I wouldn't tell my friends to bring me drugs so I could slip them to him. He's punishing me by giving me demerits, thinking I'll give in eventually. And it's not just me." She hesitated.

"Go on."

"I'm not paranoid. That's what he does, you see. And if you do what he wants, he'll even look the other way if you break the rules."

Dr. Paley's bushy eyebrows shot up. "He's doing this

with other residents as well?"

She nodded.

"You've seen him do it?"

She hesitated. "No, not exactly . . ."

"So they've talked to you about it? What do they say about it? Are they angry?"

"No one talks about it," she told him, and then realized her mistake.

"Then how do you know this is going on with people other than yourself?"

She had known all along that it would come down to this. She knew because she could read his mind, but there was no way she could explain that, and now she was just sounding paranoid. "I—I just know. That's all."

His voice became gentle. "Jenna, if there's something you're not admitting, you mustn't be afraid to tell me. You have to trust me. Have you ever heard of doctor-patient confidentiality rules? Anything you say in this office to me, anything you don't want revealed to anyone else, remains strictly between us."

Jenna looked away. A full moment of silence passed. Then Dr. Paley sighed deeply.

"Jenna, if you can't offer any explanation for your behavior, then I have no alternative. You're demonstrating feelings of paranoia. You're talking to yourself. You're hearing voices. These actions are evidence of serious mental problems, the kind of problems we aren't capable of dealing with here at Harmony House."

Jenna looked at him. "What do you mean?"

"I'll have to consider recommending that you be sent to another facility."

Jenna drew in her breath. "What kind of facility?" she asked, but she had a sinking suspicion she already knew the answer to the question.

"An institution that can provide the kind of therapy we're not equipped to handle here."

Jenna put it more bluntly. "A nuthouse. You want to commit me to an insane asylum."

"A mental hospital," he corrected her. "You've said you're not a juvenile delinquent, and I believe you. But you've got serious issues that need to be addressed."

"I'm not crazy!" Jenna cried out. "It's just that I'm different!"

"How?"

"Because—it's because—I can—" she clenched her fists. She couldn't say it. If he thought she was crazy now, what would he think if she told the truth?

"Tell me, Jenna," he said urgently. "What makes you different? Jenna, I don't want to send you to a mental hospital. But you have to give me an explanation, or I won't have any alternative. Tell me! What can you do?"

"I can read minds!" Jenna cried out. Then she buried her face in her hands.

It was out. She'd said it. And now he'd pick up the phone and call for an ambulance. She'd seen movies, she knew what would happen next. Men in white jackets would put her in a straitjacket and carry her away . . .

When nothing happened right away, she took her hands from her eyes. He was looking at her seriously, but she didn't see alarm in his eyes. It was more like interest . . .

"I knew there was more to your case than meets the eye, Jenna," he said.

"You did?" she asked stupidly.

He nodded. "I didn't know what, or why, but I could sense you had something extraordinary about you."

Was he putting her on? Trying to make her dig a deeper hole to sink into?

"Why did you think that about me?" she asked.

"It's an instinct," he said simply. "Years of working with young people have given me a sense of what people are all about. You have a gift."

"Why did you call it that?" she asked sharply.

He didn't answer. "Tell me more about your gift."

"It's just something I can do," she replied.

She wanted to look away again, but there was something

326

about his gaze that held her.

"What am I thinking about right now?" he asked.

Still suspicious, Jenna eyed him warily. Then she began to concentrate.

It was almost too easy, like he was putting his thoughts out there in writing, in big black and white letters. "You're thinking about food. Chinese food. You're thinking about getting sweet and sour pork for lunch from a Chinese restaurant when you leave here." After a second, she added, "and cold sesame noodles."

He nodded. "Very good. You're absolutely right."

"I know," she said. But she thought his reaction was strangely calm. "Aren't you shocked?"

"No," he said. "I've done a lot of research into these kinds of extrasensory abilities. Some people have gifts that simply can't be explained scientifically. There are people who can see into the future, people who can move things with their minds . . ."

"I can't do that," Jenna said quickly.

But her expression must have told him something. "Does this have anything to do with your special class, Jenna? The one called 'gifted'?"

Jenna didn't know what to say. It was one thing to give away her own secret. How could she betray her classmates?

"I can't talk about that," she said.

He didn't press her. "I understand." He closed her file. "I'm going to look into this resident assistant. His name is Peter Blake, right? He cannot be permitted to continue in his position. His contract must be terminated immediately."

"You said you'd keep my secret!" Jenna exclaimed.

"And I will," the doctor assured her. "I can investigate this without revealing my sources."

"But he'll know it's me who told on him," Jenna protested. "The other kids—they don't mind what he's doing to them. He'll tell them it's me who got him fired. I could be in danger here!"

"I realize that," he said. "Which is why I'm going to recommend that you be given an early release from Harmony House."

"An early release?" Jenna repeated in disbelief.

He nodded. "There will be some paperwork involved. But I can make some calls, pull some strings. And with any luck, you'll be home tomorrow."

Home. Tomorrow. Jenna gazed at him in wonderment. So Madame was wrong. There were people in this world who could be trusted with their secret gifts. Not many, of course.

But she'd just found one.

Chapter Twelve

TRACEY WAS WIPED OUT. Did invisibility drain her energy in some special, highly complicated cellular way? she wondered. No, she was pretty sure she was just exhausted in the normal way. After all, other physical sensations remained behind when her physical self wasn't present. She got hungry, she got thirsty, she had headaches . . . why wouldn't she be tired? And now, at ten o'clock in the morning, after spending the night in an unusually uncomfortable position, she had every right to be extremely beat.

When she'd left the house-of-the-bad-guys, it was almost one in the morning. She'd taken a few more photos with her phone, and then the group inside disbanded. Only Clare remained in the house. She must live there, Tracey thought.

She'd made her way back to her own house, and there she encountered a problem she hadn't counted on. The house was dark—everyone was in bed—so she assumed she could walk right in. What she hadn't considered was the fact that her security-conscious parents would have locked the doors from the inside. And then it started to rain.

Invisibility did not protect her from natural forces, and Tracey felt cold and wet. She found shelter in the backyard, in the septuplets' playhouse. It was a bigger-than-average playhouse, but it hadn't been set up for sleeping, and Tracey had to attempt to sleep on a hard wood floor. It was not a restful experience.

Now, stiff and sleepy, she sat on the steps in front of Ken's house and tried not to doze off. The rain had stopped. There was actually some sunshine, and she figured Ken wouldn't stay inside all day. She just hoped he wasn't the type who slept till noon on weekends.

He wasn't. Just half an hour later, the front door opened, and Ken emerged. Unfortunately, he wasn't alone. A man she assumed was his father walked alongside him, and they headed toward the car on the driveway.

"Ken!" she called. Ken stopped, turned, and looked around.

"It's me, Tracey. I'm still invisible. I'm on your steps."

"Ken?" his father asked. "Are you coming?"

"Yeah, sure." Ken mouthed some words. Tracey couldn't figure out exactly what he was telling her, but she knew from his fierce expression that it had to be something like "shut up" or "beat it."

"Ken, it's important! I've found out something about the conspiracy. And I know who the real spy is. Ken, *please*, talk to me!"

He and his father had reached the car, and Mr. Preston was opening the door on the driver's side. But Ken didn't move.

"Ken, let's go!" his father said.

"Um . . . you go, Dad. I've changed my mind."

His father looked confused. "I thought you wanted me to drop you off at Mike's."

"I'm going to take my bike. It's okay, you go on."

His father still looked puzzled, but he shrugged, got into the car, and took off. Ken waited until he was out of sight before he joined Tracey on the steps.

"I'm not sitting on you, am I?"

"Believe me, you'd know if you sat on me," Tracey said. "I still have feelings."

"Okay, so what's so important?"

"Look at this." Tracey put her cell phone down on the ground, where it magically appeared for Ken. "Click on the photos and tell me what you see."

"Not a thing," Ken replied. "Your battery's dead."

Tracey groaned. Of course, she hadn't been able to recharge it the night before. "Well, I'll tell you. It's a photo of Carter with Clare, Serena, that Stuart Kelley guy . . . and Mr. Jackson. *Our* Mr. Jackson. And Carter's talking to them."

She'd made an impression—she could see it on his face. She told him the whole story—how she'd followed Carter to the house and watched the proceedings through a window.

"He's the spy, Ken, not Amanda. That whole zombie business, it's a big act he's putting on. He sits in our class and pretends he can't communicate, and then he goes and reports on us to these people. That's how Jackson knows about us. *He* put the knife in Jenna's locker because he was afraid she was reading his mind and he had to get her out of the picture."

"How do you know that?" Ken asked.

She remembered her promise to Amanda. "Well . . . it makes sense, doesn't it?" She hurried on. "Other things make sense, too, Ken. Like when we were kidnapped, Carter was taken first, remember? They got information out of him about the rest of us. Then, after they took me and Emily and the others, they sent him back because they didn't need him."

Ken didn't say anything.

"Don't you believe me?" Tracey asked him.

"Are you sure about Jackson? You said yourself, you

332

were looking through a window. Maybe it was someone who just looks like Mr. Jackson. I mean, I'm not crazy about the guy, but he's the principal of a middle school, for crying out loud!"

"He's definitely involved with this conspiracy," Tracey insisted. "I'm not the only one who's seen him with those other creeps. Amanda said—" She caught herself just in time and stopped.

Ken rolled his eyes. "I should have known Amanda had something to do with all this. Did you two cook up this story together?"

"Ken! Amanda is not the spy, I swear to you!"

"How can you be so sure about that?" he countered.

Frustrated, Tracey wanted to scream. *This* was exactly why a person shouldn't promise to keep secrets.

"You see?" Ken said triumphantly. "You're not really sure, are you? You don't want to admit that Amanda can be this evil."

"And you don't want to admit that you have a thing for her," Tracey shot back. "You're still upset that she didn't tell you about Serena in the séance. You're letting your personal feelings get in the way of logic, Ken!"

"That's bull," Ken muttered.

"Oh, come on, Ken, get real! You like Amanda. You've always been into her. You're just trying to get back at her for not acting like she's into you! Which, by the way, I think she is."

Ken looked away, as if he didn't want to confront something he knew was true.

"Talk to her," Tracey pleaded. "Tell her . . ." She tried to think of a way to clue him in without breaking her promise. "Tell her to tell you what she told me."

"Forget it," Ken said. "I'm not talking to her." He stood up. "I have to go."

Helpless, Tracey watched him walk away. Now what? She was on her own.

Yawning, she decided to go home and get some sleep. There, she could plug in her phone, recharge it, and be all set to go back to Clare's house. She walked back to her house, trying to form a plan.

She didn't know the conspirators' schedule—if they met daily or if Carter met with them every night at midnight. But if Clare's house was their headquarters, there had to be items lying around that could provide evidence. So even if there was no gathering of bad guys today, she'd accomplish something.

On her own. Totally on her own, by herself. And, as she lay on her bed thinking about the task before her, she was scared. Okay, she was invisible. Nobody could really hurt her if she couldn't be seen, right? But even so, she was afraid.

She tried to shake off the fear and concentrate on the job she had to do. First, she had to get into Clare's house. If there was no meeting and people weren't going in and out, how could she carry out any investigation? For that reason, she decided to go to Clare's earlier, in the afternoon, when hopefully the woman might leave or come home and open a door for her.

Reasonably refreshed, with her fear on a back burner and with a fully charged cell phone, she left her room. She felt pretty focused, but even so, she couldn't help picking up on the family conversation going on in the living room.

For once, the Devon Seven were quiet. Her parents were talking to them.

"Girls, we know you miss Tracey," her father was saying. "Your mother and I miss her, too. But even if we can't see her, we know that she's here."

Her mother spoke up. "George, you're confusing them. They can't understand Tracey's gift."

Tracey had to smile. Her mother was right—how could the five-year-olds understand her gift, when she couldn't understand it herself? Impulsively, out of the septuplets' eye range, she picked up her mother's purse. The sudden disappearance of her purse caught the woman's attention. Tracey then placed it back down. Her mother smiled.

"But you don't have to worry, girls," she said. "Tracey's

all right."

Was she? Tracey wondered. Was she really all right? She'd never been invisible for this long before, and although she hadn't tried to reappear today, she had the feeling it wouldn't work if she did. And here she was, all alone, ready to embark on what could possibly be a very dangerous mission. She didn't know *what* she was.

All she knew for sure was that she'd made a promise to Jenna, to get her out of that awful place. She needed to be able to prove Jenna's innocence, and from what Amanda had told her, the evidence could only come from Mr. Jackson.

It took her a while to find Clare's house. And when she thought she'd found it, she was actually at the house next door. She realized this when a car pulled into the other house's driveway and Clare got out.

Tracey tore across the lawn, determined not to get shut out this time. Clare was talking on her cell phone, and when Tracey caught up to her, she was able to hear her side of the conversation.

"I'm telling you, she's been released! No, I don't know why, but we have to talk about this, today. And bring the kid."

There was a pause.

"Good grief, you're the principal, you can come up

with an excuse. Tell the parents it's a special school activity or something. Or you're taking him to see a specialist. Come up with something—just get over here."

The kid—she had to be talking about Carter, Tracey thought. And the "she" who was released—was that Jenna? Had she left Harmony House? Clare shut off her phone as she went into the house, and Tracey slipped in alongside her.

Clare went through the living room, but Tracey paused and gazed around. It looked like such an ordinary living room—there was a modern sofa, a couple of chairs, a coffee table, but the only piece of furniture that grabbed her eye was a desk.

She went on through the dining room and spotted Clare in the kitchen. She was making coffee, and Tracey hoped she wasn't going to bring it into the living room. Clare might not be able to see her, but if Tracey wanted to open drawers or move things around, she needed to do it when Clare wasn't in the room.

She eased open the desk's file drawer slowly, trying not to make any noise. A row of folders greeted her, and she knelt down to read the tabs on them. Bills . . . receipts . . . banking . . . They were the same kinds of labels she'd see if she opened her parents' desk at home. Except for one.

She was amazed to see that Clare hadn't even tried to

disguise the subject of the folder. It was right there, printed in black ink on a white tab: "Gifted."

She went to take another quick look in the kitchen. Clare was sitting at a little kitchen table with her cup of coffee, and she'd opened a newspaper. It looked like she'd be occupied for a while.

She pulled the folder out and set it on the desk. Taking a deep breath, she opened it.

The first page could have been some sort of application form. It bore the heading "Amanda Beeson." A small head-and-shoulders photo of her classmate was attached. It looked like it could have been a recent school photo.

Data about Amanda included her address, phone number, parents' names and occupations, and her date and place of birth. Then there was physical information.

Height: 5 ft., 2 in.

Weight: 110 lb.

Hair: Light brown.

Eyes: Blue.

So far, this could have come directly from some file at Meadowbrook Middle School.

But the next piece of information was something Tracey never expected to see neatly typed in black and white on an official-looking document.

Gift: Ability to transfer consciousness into another body.

Characteristics: Subject must experience a sensation of pity for the person in the body prior to transfer. Subject is without personal consciousness but remains physically unchanged, with all natural abilities intact. Subject appears to be operating through a remote memory of typical behavior patterns. All consciousness of the subject is in the new body. Consciousness of person who normally inhabits body appears to be in a sleeping state.

Limitations: Subject exhibits some control in taking over a body but has not yet achieved the ability to release body at will.

Project potential: Could replace heads of state and others in a position of decision-making in order to establish an environment suitable for project.

Tracey turned the page. The next document was devoted to Martin. There was all the basic information, but Tracey ignored that.

Gift: Ability to develop superstrength.

Limitations: Subject must feel ridiculed for strength to emerge.

Project potential: Battle.

She read Jenna's page next.

Gift: Ability to read thoughts of other human beings.

Characteristics: Subject must want to read the thoughts and must be able to concentrate. Object of mind-reading will not be aware of the process.

Limitations: Subject appears to be able to employ gift at will. Object who is aware of subject's gift may be able to mentally block the process.

Project potential: Ability to determine loyalties and emotional states. Revelation of confidential information. Verification of intent.

Verification of intent . . . Tracey assumed that was just a fancy way of saying Jenna would know if someone was telling the truth.

The document devoted to Sarah was particularly intriguing. Under "Limitations," it stated: *Subject has personal reasons for not wishing to exercise her gift. Must ascertain the nature of the reasons and resolve her reluctance so that gift may be exploited.* And under "Project potential," there was only one word: *Unlimited.*

There was a knock on the door. Hastily, she closed the folder and shoved it back in the file. She barely got the drawer closed before Clare entered the room and went to the door.

Serena-the-student-teacher-alias-Cassandra-the medium was at the door, along with the man Tracey knew as Stuart Kelley.

"What's so important that we had to come rushing over here?" Serena demanded to know.

"It's the Kelley girl. She left Harmony House this morning."

Stuart's eyebrows shot up. "She escaped?"

"No, she was released early."

"Why?" the man asked.

"I don't know," Clare replied. "The investigator just knew she'd left. I'm hoping the kid knows something."

"How could he know anything already?" Serena asked. "It's Saturday—there's no school."

Clare ignored her. "Here they come now."

Mr. Jackson and Carter arrived, and within seconds they were all at the dining-room table. Mr. Jackson looked tense. Carter had no expression at all. Tracey took out her cell phone and began moving around the table, snapping photos.

"I can't have her back at the school," Mr. Jackson said flatly. "She's too dangerous. I can't be constantly thinking about what I'm thinking about."

"But you can block her," Clare pointed out.

"Not if I don't see her," he said. "She's got a way of sneaking around. I have more than three hundred students at the school. I've got people running in and out of my office all day. I can't know where she is every minute."

"I don't understand why you're so anxious about her," Serena said. "You don't even know for sure if she's interested in reading your mind."

"I didn't like the way she was looking at me in the office the other day," Mr. Jackson grumbled.

"You're the principal—it's natural for her to hate you," Stuart said. "A kid like her, she hates any kind of authority. Look, I know her better than the rest of you. I was almost her father. Just because she gives you dirty looks doesn't mean she knows anything about you."

"These kids aren't idiots," Mr. Jackson declared. "They're going to put two and two together. They know you were a fraud. They know Clare's out to get them, and they're suspicious of Serena . . . They're going to start connecting the dots."

Clare interrupted. "But they don't know about you. They have no idea you're involved."

"I'm not so sure about that," Mr. Jackson muttered. "The Beeson girl—she's working in my office. She could be snooping around."

Serena frowned. "Which one is she?"

"The body snatcher," Clare told her.

Serena's face cleared. "Oh, right. She came to one of my séances with Ken."

Clare's eyebrows went up. "You didn't tell us that."

Serena shrugged. "It was only the one time—she never showed up again."

But Clare still looked disturbed. She turned to Carter, who hadn't said a word. "Did Amanda say anything about the séance in class?"

342

In Tracey's view, Carter looked exactly the way he would look if someone at school asked him a direct question. He just stared into space, not even acknowledging that he'd been addressed.

Clare appeared irritated. "Haven't you brought him out yet?" she asked Serena.

"You haven't given me a chance, have you?" Serena snapped. She pulled her chair around so she could face Carter directly. She stared at him, so hard that Tracey could actually see her pupils enlarge. She didn't blink at all. Then she began murmuring softly. Tracey couldn't make out the words.

She spoke directly into the boy's ear, her voice soft and rhythmic. Tracey moved closer, but even when she was practically on top of them, she couldn't under-stand what Serena was saying. It was like gibberish, the same nonsense words over and over in a monotonous tone.

It was a good thing nobody here could hear her, because her gasp would have been audible. The change in Carter's expression was dramatic. It was like a curtain had been lifted from his eyes. She hadn't been able to see this when she watched through the window last night, so she was completely startled.

"We want to ask you about Amanda," Serena said to him. "She came to one of the séances. Did she say anything about it in class?"

For the first time, Tracey heard Carter's voice. It was slightly high-pitched, which made him sound very young. But other than that, it was normal.

"Not just one séance," he said. "She went to all of them. Amanda was Margaret."

Serena drew in her breath sharply. "Amanda took over Margaret's body?"

"Yes," Carter replied. "She felt sorry for her. She didn't want to be Margaret, but it happened."

"Margaret . . ." Mr. Jackson repeated and frowned. Serena turned to him.

"My friend, who was helping me out. She pretended to have just lost her mother. She came to a meeting— you met her. She was freaked out. She couldn't handle that stay in jail. She was a nervous wreck, remember?"

"Whatever happened to her?" Stuart asked.

"She had some sort of breakdown, and now she's living with her parents in Florida." Suddenly, Serena gasped. "Ohmigod, it's all starting to make sense! Her behavior at the séance . . ."

It dawned on Tracey that she should be recording this conversation. Hurriedly, she fumbled with her cell phone, looking for the little icon that would turn the phone into a recorder . . .

And it slipped out of her hand.

"What's that?" Clare asked.

They were all staring at a cell phone, which had suddenly appeared on the floor. Serena reached down and picked it up.

"It's not mine," she said.

Tracey tried not to panic. Okay, they had her phone. They'd see the pictures she'd taken. They might even be able to figure out that the phone belonged to her. But it wasn't like they could do anything to her—they couldn't even see her . . .

Then her stomach turned over. Because they weren't looking at the phone anymore. They were looking right at her. And they could see her.

345

CHAPTER THIRTEEN

JENNA'S MOTHER WAS TRYING very hard to grasp the situation. "But why would the principal want to get rid of you, Jenna? You haven't been in any trouble since you started at Meadowbrook."

"He's afraid of me, Mom," Jenna explained. "Because I can read minds. I don't know what he's thinking about that's so bad, but he doesn't want me to find out."

"Why don't you just tell him you won't read his mind?" Mrs. Kelley suggested.

"I don't think he'd believe me," Jenna said.

"Oh, dear," her mother sighed. "Jenna, couldn't you just stop reading minds? It's not really a very nice habit, is it?"

Jenna smiled. Her mother meant well, but she was no Dr. Paley. She'd never be able to understand.

The doorbell rang. "That must be Emily," Mrs. Kelley said. "She called earlier and I told her you were coming home."

But it was a different classmate who stood in the

doorway.

"Ken!"

"Emily called and told me you were home," he said. "I have to talk to you about something."

"Come on in. Mom, this is Ken Preston, from my class at Meadowbrook."

"Hello, Ken," her mother said brightly. "Would you kids like something to eat? There are cookies . . ."

"No, thank you, Mrs. Kelley," Ken said politely. "I just need to talk to Jenna about something. I won't stay long."

"I'll give you two some privacy," Mrs. Kelley said and disappeared into the kitchen.

"She's nice," Ken said.

Jenna nodded. She could remember a time when she would never have willingly allowed a classmate to meet her mother. She could also remember a time when the mere notion of Ken Preston showing up on her doorstep would have boggled her mind.

Now she wasn't boggled, but she was puzzled. "What's up?"

"Tracey's been invisible for a while," he began.

Jenna nodded. "I know. She came to see me at Harmony House."

"Well, she came to see me this morning. And she

347

says . . ." He frowned. "This is going to sound crazy. She claims she spied on a meeting. That Clare woman, Serena, the guy who said he was your father . . . and Mr. Jackson!"

Slowly, Jenna nodded. "That doesn't sound so crazy to me."

"But you haven't heard the rest of it. She says Carter's the spy, not Amanda. She says she actually saw him talking at this meeting."

"Wow!" Jenna breathed. "I wouldn't have guessed *that*."

"You believe her?" Ken asked.

"Tracey doesn't lie, Ken."

Ken frowned. "She said I should talk to Amanda. And to ask Amanda to tell me what she told her. Does that make sense to you?"

"Yeah."

Ken pulled out his cell phone and just looked at it for a moment. "She's gotta hate me. I mean, I haven't exactly been very nice to her." Then, with a less-than-enthusiastic expression, he hit a number.

Jenna grinned. "You got her on speed-dial, huh?"

"Forgot to take her off," he mumbled. "Hello, Amanda? This is Ken. Yeah. Um . . . are you busy? I mean, like, could I come by and talk to you about something? Okay."

He put the phone back in his pocket. "I'm going over

there now."

Jenna grabbed her jacket. "I'm going with you."

He didn't protest. In fact, Jenna could have sworn she saw relief in his eyes. She couldn't blame him. She wouldn't want to face an irate Amanda alone, either.

And she was glad Ken was by her side when Amanda opened the door. The look Amanda gave Jenna was a lot scarier than the one she gave Ken.

"What's *she* doing here?" Amanda wanted to know.

"Don't worry, Amanda, I'm not armed," Jenna said.

Amanda sniffed, but she stepped aside and let them both in. Before Ken could say anything, she made a statement.

"I am *not* the spy."

"I know, I know," Ken said. "Tracey told me."

That didn't seem to make Amanda any happier. "Oh, so you believe Tracey but you wouldn't believe *me*."

"I *want* to believe you, Amanda!" Ken exclaimed. "It's just that, I don't know, you get me all mixed up!" Suddenly, his face was red. Jenna had the feeling he'd just admitted something he didn't want to say.

And Amanda went pink. "You mix me up, too!" she blurted out. "I mean . . . Oh, never mind, just forget it."

Ken looked like he was about to smile, but then thought better of it. "Well, for cryin' out loud, Amanda, what was I supposed to think? I find out you were at that séance all the time, knowing full well that it was a scam, but you let me go on and make a fool of myself believing that woman was a real medium. I was pretty pissed off at you!"

"Aw, you can't blame her, Ken," Jenna broke in. "She got to be a twenty-five-year-old woman for a weekend. It opened up new shopping opportunities."

Amanda glared at her, and Jenna actually backed down. "Sorry. I'm sure you had other reasons."

"No kidding. Look, I know what you guys think of me. You think my gift is worthless and I only think about myself. I wanted to show you that maybe I had something to offer. Like, I could find out more about these people who are out to get us. And I did."

"What did you find out?" Ken asked.

Amanda smirked. "Wouldn't you like to know."

"Oh, go ahead and tell him, Amanda," Jenna said.

Amanda narrowed her eyes. "Did Tracey tell you? She promised to keep it a secret."

"She didn't have to tell me. I read her mind."

"She wouldn't tell me, either," Ken said. "Tracey told me to ask you to tell me what you told her." He grimaced. "Did that make sense?"

"I guess so," Amanda replied with clear reluctance. She paused dramatically. Jenna had an enormous urge to scream, "Spill the beans, Amanda," but she managed

350

to keep her mouth shut. She knew the girl would want to make the most of this moment.

First, they had to hear the tale of her two hours in jail as Margaret, her desperate attempts to get back into her own body, her fear of never seeing the light of day again, blah, blah, blah. Someone bailed both her and Serena/Cassandra out of jail, and they went immediately to a meeting in a nondescript suburban house on an ordinary tree-lined street.

"And there they were at the dining table, the conspirators," Amanda said. "Clare, the kidnapper. Stuart Kelley. *And . . .*" she paused dramatically.

Jenna couldn't stand it any longer. "Mr. Jackson."

Amanda's eyes shot daggers at her, but she was distracted and rewarded with Ken's wide-eyed reaction.

"So it *is* true?"

Amanda nodded solemnly. "He's one of them, Ken. The second I saw him, the shock sent me right back into myself. But I decided I was going to find out more about this. That's why I took the job in his office, so I could spy on him. On *Mr. Jackson*, Ken. Not you guys."

Ken offered a weak smile. "Okay, I was wrong about you. I'm sorry."

Amanda affected the look of a martyr. "I just wanted to prove to you all that I could do something to help us."

"Did it ever occur to you that we could have all worked together and accomplished more?" Jenna asked.

Amanda made a face at her. "Look who's talking. Miss Sociability. Since when have you been into teamwork?"

"Since I came to grips with reality," Jenna shot back. "You should give it a try sometime." She turned to Ken.

"Can I use your phone? I want to make some calls."

CHAPTER FOURTEEN

OW LONG HAD SHE been here? Lying on a bed, Tracey stared at the ceiling and realized that she'd completely lost track of time. She had a vague memory of being brought into this bedroom, but when? She felt dizzy and disoriented. Had they given her some kind of drug? Or was she just suffering from the shock of suddenly finding herself made of flesh and blood and bones again?

The clouds in her head began to float away, and she started thinking more clearly. Serena had probably hypnotized her, and she was just now coming out of it.

She was quite a hypnotist, that Serena. Tracey always thought hypnosis could only happen if the subject cooperated, if the subject was willing to be put under. Tracey certainly hadn't given permission.

And what kind of hypnosis had she been using on Carter? From what she'd observed, it was like he was in a constant state of hypnosis, and she brought him out of it only when they wanted information.

But all these questions could be put on hold. Right now she had to concentrate on getting out of there.

She got off the bed and grabbed onto a bedpost as a fresh wave of dizziness swept over her. Her legs were trembling, too. But the sensations passed, and she made her way to the door. She wasn't surprised to find it locked. Of course, she was being held prisoner. And even if she went invisible, she couldn't get through a locked door.

But they'd come in here sooner or later, she assumed, and if she was invisible, she could slip out while the door was open. She tried to concentrate, to pull up the feelings that could make her disappear.

You're worthless, you're alone, nobody sees you, nobody cares about you, you're depressed . . .

It wasn't working—she was still all there. Maybe Serena had given her some posthypnotic suggestion . . .

There were windows in the bedroom. She went over to them and examined the latches.

With the sound of a lock turning, she faced the door. Clare stood there. "What are you doing?"

What could Tracey say—"Admiring the view?" It was a stupid question.

"I'm trying to get out," she replied.

"Well, you can't," Clare said. "Come with me."

The others were still at the dining-room table. "You're slipping, Serena," Clare announced as she pushed Tracey toward the table. "She's already awake."

Serena frowned. "It's not easy with these kids. They're not normal. Their brains don't work like other people's. I'm going to have to develop some sort of special individualized hypnotic program for each of them."

Stuart indicated Carter. "You didn't have any problem with *him*."

Serena gave him a withering look. "Of course not. He isn't gifted."

Now, that was interesting, Tracey thought. She'd always wondered about that. So he hadn't been put in their class because he was like the rest of them. He'd been placed there simply because he was strange, weird, not normal. Which, when she thought about it, was like the rest of them . . .

Stuart was looking at her nervously. "Is she trying to disappear?"

"She shouldn't be able to," Serena said. "I gave her a posthypnotic suggestion."

Clare grimaced. "What makes you think that's going to work any more efficiently than your hypnosis?"

"I'd like to see *you* do a better job," Serena retorted.

Mr. Jackson spoke up. "Don't bicker. We need to

concentrate on how we can make this work for us."

"What's the problem?" Stuart asked. "We were going to take them all eventually, anyway."

"But not yet," Clare snapped. "Nothing's in place. We're not ready for her."

They were talking about her like she wasn't there. In a way, this could be good for her, though. If she could feel like she wasn't there, maybe in another moment or two she *wouldn't* be there.

But instead of feeling depressed, she felt annoyed with them. Did they think she was stupid? "Are you talking about the project?" she blurted out.

That got their attention. "What do you know about the project?" Clare asked sharply.

Uh-oh! Tracey offered a weak smile and hoped it looked mysterious.

"I don't like this," Stuart declared. "She knows too much."

"And she could disappear any minute," Clare added.

Serena agreed. "So what are we going to do with her?"

Only Mr. Jackson seemed calm. "She's not going to disappear."

"How can we stop her?" Stuart wanted to know.

Mr. Jackson's smile was extremely unpleasant. "I'm going to tell her exactly what will happen if she does." He addressed Tracey directly.

"Do you love your little sisters, Tracey?"

Tracey stared at him blankly.

"And what about your parents, Tracey? Do you love them?"

Mutely, she nodded.

"And you wouldn't want anything terrible to happen to them, would you?"

Tracey found her voice, but it was trembling. "You're a very bad person."

Mr. Jackson shrugged. "Good, bad—it's all relative."

"Besides," Tracey continued, trying very hard to steady her voice, "I can't always control my gift. Do you think I wanted to appear in front of you today?"

"But you're getting better and better," Mr. Jackson said. "That's what your special class is all about, isn't it?" He nodded toward Carter. "That's what he's told us. You practice, you work at gaining control. Madame's doing a good job with you, isn't she?"

Tracey could feel her own breathing become harder, faster. Was it possible that Madame was involved in the conspiracy? The one person they all completely trusted, the one who knew them better than their own families—was she part of this? Her heart was thumping, and she couldn't catch her breath.

"She's hyperventilating," Clare declared in disgust.

"It's a panic attack," Serena said. "Get a paper bag."

The next thing Tracey knew, her mouth was covered with a bag and someone was yelling, "Deep breaths! Deep breaths!" Her heart pounded harder, louder—she could hear the banging . . .

But the banging wasn't coming from her chest. Someone was rapping on the door.

"Quiet!" Mr. Jackson ordered them. In a softer voice, he asked, "Is the door locked?"

"Of course," Clare whispered back.

But the door opened anyway. Mr. Jackson raced toward it and collided with a speeding wheelchair.

It got him right in the stomach. "Ow!" he screamed.

But none of his comrades raced to his aid. They were all frozen as they watched the rest of the rescue team march in and close the door behind them.

Tracey felt her breathing ease as she took in the new arrivals. Ken, Jenna, and Amanda followed Charles. Emily, Martin, and Sarah came in next. Madame brought up the rear.

Serena began chanting at Carter, and the boy's eyes were becoming even more glazed than they were normally. Tracey suddenly realized that she might be trying to hypnotize him permanently, so that he couldn't ever testify against them.

"Charles!" Tracey yelled and pointed toward the hypnotist. But Charles only glanced at Serena. He focused on the paper bag that had been used on Tracey and sent it flying across the room. It fell over Serena's head and covered her face. But Serena continued to chant.

"I'm going to have to knock her out," Charles declared.

Tracey looked around the room. She didn't see anything particularly heavy. "With what?"

Charles grinned. Suddenly, a big frying pan sailed into the room. It flew through space toward Serena. Since she couldn't see it coming, she couldn't duck—and it hit her in the head. That stopped her chanting.

Martin gasped. "Where did that pan come from?"

"From the kitchen," Charles said with a smug expression. "I don't have to see things to move them anymore."

Madame was clearly impressed. "Charles, you're improving!" But her attention was diverted when Stuart Kelley began moving toward the door. She turned to Sarah.

"Make him stop!"

But Sarah looked absolutely terrified and didn't move.

"Martin, stop him!" Jenna yelled.

Martin cringed. Jenna groaned and spoke rapidly. "Oh, that's right, I forgot—you're a weakling, you're hopeless, you can't do anything, you puny feeble little nobody."

Martin went into action. Seconds later, Stuart Kelley was on the ground, knocked unconscious. Jenna looked down at his prone body.

"Hi, *Daddy*," she said sarcastically. "What's new?"

Clare stood very still, taking in the scene. Then she started toward the kitchen. Jenna watched her.

"Don't even think about it," Jenna said. "Charles can get a weapon out of your hand before you can get a firm grip on it. He could even turn it around and use it on you."

Charles's eyes widened. "Gee, you're right! I never thought of that."

Mr. Jackson had recovered from his encounter with the wheelchair. He stood there stiffly and spoke to Madame.

"What do you think you're going to do now?"

"I've called the police," she replied. "And when they arrive, I'll accuse you of kidnapping Tracey."

"We didn't kidnap Tracey," Clare objected. "She came here of her own free will."

"Then I'll accuse you of kidnapping Carter," the teacher said.

Mr. Jackson didn't blink. "Call his foster parents. He has their permission to be with me. You have no proof of anything illegal going on here, Madame. And I sincerely doubt that you really called the police." He actually smiled.

Jenna whispered in Tracey's ear. "She didn't. She's just

360

trying to scare him."

The principal continued. "It seems to me, Madame, that you have more to fear from the police than we do."

"What do you mean?" she asked.

"I'm the principal of Meadowbrook Middle School. I'm a respected member of this community. If you have me arrested, there will be publicity. And I'll have a platform to tell the world all about your gifted class."

Tracey looked at Madame. Was that fear in her eyes? If so, it vanished quickly.

"And I'll have no option but to instruct my students to use their gifts against you. You know what they can do." As if to make her point even clearer, she put a hand on Sarah's shoulder. Sarah flinched, but she didn't contradict Madame.

Mr. Jackson fell silent for a moment. "Then it looks like perhaps we should make a deal," he said finally.

"Go on," Madame said.

"You say nothing to anyone about this. And I won't expose your students."

Ken spoke. "That's not much of a deal. He wouldn't tell people about us, Madame. It's like you always say—nobody believes we have gifts."

"And why would the police believe *you*?" Clare countered. "You have no evidence against us."

"But there *is* evidence, Madame," Tracey cried out. "You can tell the police about the project. You can show them the plans."

"What project?" Madame asked.

"It's what they want to use us for. It's in a folder, in that desk."

"I'll get it," Charles said quickly. He looked at the desk, and all the drawers opened. And all the papers came flying out. Telephone bills, bank statements—hundreds of documents floated through the air.

"Oops!" Charles murmured. "Sorry."

"The police are here!" Emily announced.

"Madame, they'll see Serena," Ken pointed out.

"Sarah, move Serena," Madame ordered.

There was a knock on the door. "Police! Open up!"

Mr. Jackson turned to Clare.

"Open the door."

"Sarah!" Madame exclaimed. "Do it!"

But Serena remained where she was, with the paper bag on her head and unconscious. And Clare was already beginning to open the door.

"Sarah, quick!" Madame hissed.

"Oh, Madame," the girl whispered in an agonized voice. But she looked at Serena. And as if by her own free will, the woman got up and walked out of the room into the kitchen.

Two police officers stood in the doorway. "Excuse me, ma'am," one of them said to Clare. "But we've had a complaint of some kind of disruption going on here."

The other officer looked at the papers lying all over the floor. "What's going on here?"

Mr. Jackson strode forward. "Good afternoon, officers." He introduced himself and shook their hands. One of the officers looked at him with interest.

"We've met before. You're my kid's school principal."

"That's right," Mr. Jackson said, beaming. "We're working on a school project here." He looked at the papers and smiled ruefully. "I'm afraid we had a little accident and made a mess. But I don't quite think it's in the category of anything criminal!" He laughed at his own little quip.

The police officers didn't laugh, but they didn't seem concerned, either. "I guess you made some noise and a neighbor complained," one said. "Just keep it down, okay?"

"Of course, officers," Mr. Jackson said smoothly.

Madame spoke up. "Actually, the meeting has ended and we were about to leave. Come along, everyone."

Eight of the nine gifted students gathered around her.

"Come along, Carter," Madame called.

"No, Madame," Jenna whispered frantically in her ear. "He's the spy!"

But the teacher ignored her. "Carter?" she called again.

In zombie mode, the boy rose from his seat at the dining table and joined them. Madame ushered them all past the policemen and out the door. She turned back to the people still in the house and spoke.

"This was an interesting meeting. Highly enlightening." She paused and then added, "I'll get back to you, Mr. Jackson, and we can continue negotiations."

Chapter Fourteen

AS THE LAST CLASS period began on Monday afternoon, room 209 was unusually quiet. Everyone seemed to be lost in their own thoughts as they waited for Madame to arrive.

There had been rumors and phone calls the day before and whispered conversations in the hallways of Meadowbrook today. But no one else knew what was really going on.

Ken spoke quietly to Tracey. "So you didn't find out what this project is all about."

Tracey shook her head. "I didn't get that far."

Amanda overheard them. Her comment was directed to Emily: "Why can't you just look into the future and tell us?"

"I don't even know what to look for," Emily told her. "I have to know what the project *is* before I can see if it's going to happen."

"Well, I'll never be able to read it in their minds," Jenna

grumbled. "Not if they know I'm around." She turned to Tracey. "Too bad we can't combine our gifts."

"Maybe we can figure out a way," Tracey said. "Do you guys realize, this was the first time we've all pooled our gifts? Everyone did something." She counted them off on her fingers. "I got into the house, Charles made the locked door open. Martin stopped Stuart from escaping, Jenna read Clare's mind, Emily told us the police had arrived, and, and, oh yeah, Sarah moved Serena out of the dining room before the police could see her."

"Yeah, right," Jenna muttered. "After Madame asked her *three* times."

"But she did it," Tracey said stoutly, and she smiled at Sarah. "Thanks, Sarah."

"You're welcome," Sarah whispered, but she didn't seem proud of it, and she looked away.

Amanda was offended. "You left me out. I provided the information about Mr. Jackson."

That was information that Tracey could have provided, but she let Amanda take the credit. "That's right."

"And you left out Ken," Amanda added. She smiled warmly at the boy.

Tracey grinned. So that "sort-of" relationship was on again. "Ken did a lot."

"Not with my gift," Ken said. He turned slightly and

366

eyed the small boy at the back. "What about him?"

Silence fell over the room again as they all turned to look at Carter.

"It wasn't his fault," Tracey declared. "He was hypnotized." But the looks that Carter was receiving from his classmates were less than friendly. The boy, as always—almost always—seemed oblivious. But now they all knew he took in everything they said, everything that happened in the class. They could never trust him.

Madame walked in. She wasn't alone.

"Good afternoon, class. I'd like to introduce Dr. Paley. He'd like to say a few words to you."

The plump, balding man faced them. "Hello. I met one of your classmates recently. She told me about her gift."

A gasp went up from practically every student.

Jenna groaned. "Knock it off, guys. It was me, okay? I had to tell him or I'd have gotten tossed into a mental institution. But I didn't tell him about anyone else."

"That's right," the man said. "Logic tells me that you all must be special in some way, but I have no idea what your gifts are, and I'm not going to ask you about them. Maybe, someday, you'll trust me and you'll want to tell me. But I won't be pressing you for information."

Charles looked suspicious. "Why are you here if you're not trying to find out stuff about us?"

"I'm here because you have a classmate in need," he said simply.

"Carter," Madame called softly. "Could you come up here, please?"

Obediently, the boy rose and came to the front of the room. He stood silently by her desk.

"I have permission to take Carter back to Harmony House," Dr. Paley said. "I'm going to try to help him there."

"Just keep him away from the rest of us," Charles said bitterly. "He's a traitor."

"Don't jump to conclusions," Madame said. "It may turn out that Carter can help us."

"He doesn't have a gift," Tracey told her.

Madame smiled. "There are gifts, and there are gifts. There's a lot we don't know about Carter. Thank you, Dr. Paley."

The doctor left with Carter. As soon as the door closed behind them, people had questions.

"Can we trust that Paley guy?" Charles wanted to know.

"He got me out of Harmony House," Jenna replied. "He's okay—I read his mind."

"But what if Carter tells him everything about us?" Emily asked anxiously.

The conversation was stopped by a shrill buzz from the intercom on the wall behind Madame's desk. Then they heard the voice of Ms. Simmons, the office secretary.

"May I have your attention? I have an important announcement to make. The Board of Education regrets to inform you that your principal, Mr. Jackson, will be leaving his position due to personal reasons. Mr. Jones from the history department will be acting principal until the position is filled. I am sure you all join me in bidding Mr. Jackson a fond farewell and offering him our best wishes for future success."

The intercom went silent, and silence remained in the classroom. But only for a few seconds. Then a couple of people let out a cheer, and everyone was talking at once.

"Was that part of the deal, Madame?"

"Is he leaving town?"

"Where's he going?"

"Does this mean we're safe?"

Madame rapped on her desk, and the voices died down.

"This isn't the end," she said. Her voice was calm but serious. "And there's no reason to cheer. Mr. Jackson is only one piece of what I think may be a very big puzzle. Even if he's out of the picture, you are not safe. There will be more challenges, bigger challenges, and we have to get ready to face them."

"What kind of challenges?" Jenna asked.

"I don't know," Madame replied simply.

"Then how can we get ready if we don't know what we're going to face?" Ken wanted to know.

"We're going to work on the gifts," Madame said. "Harder and faster than we've ever worked before. It's not simply a question of control anymore, of fitting in, of being comfortable. You're never going to be like other people, and there's no point in trying. It's a question of getting better at being yourself."

"I'm getting better," Martin piped up. "At that house, Jenna barely had to tease me at all to make my gift come out."

"That's true," Jenna admitted.

Madame nodded. "Yes, you're improving, Martin. ou're all improving. But you can't just get a little better. You have to find the extent of your gifts—your true potential." She paused and gazed at the room.

"You can't waste your gifts on trivialities." She looked at Charles.

"Or run away from your gift." She looked at Ken.

"Or fear it." She looked at Sarah.

"Or—"

She was interrupted by the opening of the door. Tracey caught her breath. Mr. Jackson was standing there.

"Just wanted to say goodbye," he said and smiled broadly. Nobody smiled back.

Madame eyed him evenly. "Stay away from us."

"Oh, I will," he assured her. "That's part of the deal. But you know, Madame . . . you can't protect them forever." He was still smiling as he retreated and shut the door.

Madame turned to the class. "You won't need protection, from me or anyone else. Okay, let's move on. Are you ready?"

Heads were bobbing. Madame smiled a little sadly.

"No, you're not. But you will be."

Tracey wanted to believe her. But deep in her heart she knew that in the end they only had to believe in themselves.

Gifted

SPEAK
NO EVIL

Chapter One

THE BOY KNOWN AS Carter Street was dreaming.

In his dream, he was in an empty space. There were no windows and no lights, but it wasn't dark, just a dull, bland gray. He was standing because there was nowhere to sit—no chairs, no sofa. He couldn't even sit on the floor because there didn't seem to be a floor. Maybe it wasn't a room at all. He could have been hanging in the air. Or he might have been inside his own head.

But the room, the space, wherever he was—it wasn't completely empty. There was a big television. And an unseen hand turned it on.

What he saw on the screen was vaguely familiar, like a rerun of a show he'd seen before. A young boy, maybe 11 or 12 years old, was riding on a roller coaster. He was accompanied by two shadowy, larger figures sitting on either side of him—the boy's parents? The boy was laughing, throwing his arms up in the air as his car went into a steep descent.

The vision on the screen dissolved and was replaced by another image. The same boy, with the same shadowy figures, at a dining table. Then he saw the boy splashing in a swimming pool. And now the boy was running around a baseball diamond. Then, abruptly, that unseen hand turned off the TV and the screen went dark.

That was when he woke up. For a moment he just lay in the bed very still and stared at the white ceiling above him. That boy in the dream . . . Did he know him? Maybe, maybe not. But there was definitely a connection. Whoever he was, the boy had been turned off, and Carter Street could relate to that.

He sat up and looked around. There was no television in this room, but it wasn't dark and empty. Light streamed in from a window. There was a desk, a chest of drawers, a sink with a mirror over it. There was even a picture on a wall—a small brown puppy lapping water in a bowl. Did the boy in his dream have a dog? No, because his mother was allergic to dog hair.

But he couldn't have known that, could he? Not if he didn't know the boy. Anyway, it was just a dream. He shook his head vigorously as if he could shake out the memory of it, but he knew it would linger. They always did, those dreams.

He didn't want to remember dreams—he had to concentrate on the present. His name, for example. Carter Street. At least, that was what everyone called him. And his location . . . He wasn't in the home of his foster family, the Grangers. And he wasn't in Madame's "gifted" class at Meadowbrook Middle School. Then it came back to him: he was in a place called Harmony House, a special place for teenagers who were in trouble. Was he in trouble? He didn't know and he didn't care. He wasn't in danger, that much he knew for sure, and that was all that mattered. He wasn't cold, and he had a roof over his head and a bed to sleep in. He wasn't hungry—well, maybe he was, just a little, but he knew that he'd be having food very soon. So everything was okay.

He got out of bed, went to the sink, and filled a plastic cup with water from the faucet. He took the cup over to the windowsill, where a plant was sitting. The plant hadn't been there when he arrived. It had been sent by his teacher, Madame, with a note that read, "We miss you."

The words didn't make much sense to him. How could anyone miss him? Even when he was physically in that class, he wasn't really there. He barely existed, no matter where he was. He made no impact on the class, and no one paid any attention to him. They wouldn't notice if he wasn't there.

Another paper had come with the plant—instructions for how to take care of it. He had to keep it warm, and he had to give it water every day. It had no other needs, just shelter and nourishment. Just like Carter Street.

After watering the plant, he continued with the same routine he'd been following since he'd arrived three days earlier. He washed his face, brushed his teeth, and got dressed. Then he left the room, closing the door behind him. He turned to the right and walked to the corner. He was aware of other boys coming out of rooms and moving in the same direction, but he didn't speak to any of them. He couldn't, even if he'd wanted to.

He descended a flight of stairs. At the bottom of the stairs, he went into the room on his left. At the entrance, a smiling man said, "Good morning, Carter." It wasn't a question or a demand, so Carter didn't have to do anything. He walked on to the serving area.

He joined a line of residents to pick up his breakfast tray, and when he received it, he took it to a table and sat down. There were others at the table. On his first day, a couple of them had spoken to him, but now, after three days of no responses, they'd stopped. He didn't particularly want to look at them, but they were in his range of vision, so he couldn't avoid seeing them. A tall boy, light brown hair, glasses. Another boy, darker hair, wearing a green shirt. A girl, blond hair. She had tiny sparkling stones in the lobes of her ears. None of this was important. He just registered the facts. They were talking, but their words meant nothing to him. Not until the boy in the green shirt spoke directly to him.

"Could you pass the salt?"

He understood this as a question that demanded an action. He picked up the salt shaker and handed it to him.

"Thanks," the boy said.

He knew what that meant—the boy was expressing appreciation for Carter's effort. But the word wasn't important, it didn't require a response, and now he could address his food. Food was important. He knew what was in the bowl—cereal, milk, fruit—but that didn't matter. All that mattered was the fact that he could eat it and then he wouldn't be hungry.

When he finished eating, he remained in his seat and watched the big clock on the wall. When it displayed a particular time, he rose, carried his tray to a conveyor belt, and left the dining room. He couldn't go back to his room, though. He had an appointment.

Turning a corner, he went to a door and opened it. A woman at a desk spoke to him. "Hello, Carter. You can go right in. Doctor Paley is waiting for you."

Carter went through the inner door.

"Hello, Carter," the doctor said. "Sit down."

Carter did as he was told and waited while the plump, balding man adjusted the video camera on a table. At the first meeting, the doctor had asked Carter if he would mind if their sessions were recorded, and Carter had offered no objection. Why would he? Being recorded didn't hurt.

"How are you today?" Dr. Paley asked.

Carter was stumped. He couldn't deal with questions like that. After three days of meetings, hadn't the man figured that out? His foster family, Madame, his classmates—none of them asked him this question anymore because they knew he couldn't answer it. And why should he? Surely the doctor could look at him and see that he wasn't in pain, that he was breathing, that he was physically intact. Nothing about him was any different than it was the day before.

When he didn't respond, Dr. Paley didn't press the question. He just went on speaking.

"I don't know very much about you, Carter. Nobody does. And that's because you don't know much about yourself, do you?"

Carter didn't answer, and Dr. Paley didn't seem to expect him to. He continued talking without a pause.

"The big question, of course, is why? It's possible that you have a condition known as amnesia, an inability to remember. You don't even seem to know your own name." He shuffled through some papers on his desk. "According to your history, you were found here in this city on Carter Street and brought to a hospital. The authorities at the hospital needed a name for you, so this is the name that was decided on."

Carter gazed at him steadily and waited for him to say something Carter didn't already know.

"There's no indication as to how this amnesia developed," Dr. Paley went on. He picked up another folder and opened it. "The authorities finally sent over your medical records, and I've studied them. Some cases of amnesia occur when the subject receives a severe blow to the head, but the scans you were given show no indication of any trauma. It's possible that you experienced some sort of an infection—a high fever, perhaps, or a virus that affected the part of your brain that stores memory. But blood tests gave no indication of recent illness."

He turned a page and continued. "You were given a battery of tests to determine general intelligence and motor skills. You responded appropriately. Your hearing was tested, and it appears to be normal." He looked up. "But you can't speak. This puzzled the examiners, since they couldn't find anything wrong with your vocal cords or your larynx."

Dr. Paley studied Carter thoughtfully. "But now we know that you *are* physically capable of speaking. A classmate witnessed this. You spoke to a woman . . ." he glanced down at the paper. "Serena Hancock."

The mere sound of the name made Carter want to flinch. Serena . . . yes. She could make him speak. He didn't know how she did it, but he remembered the ease with which the words left his mouth. He wished he couldn't remember what he said.

He hadn't intended to answer her questions, but he didn't seem to have any control when he was with her. And he wasn't capable of lying. So when Serena asked him about his classmates, he told her what he knew, despite the fact that the information was supposed to be kept secret. In class, Madame was always telling them not to reveal anything about their special gifts. Carter didn't have to worry about himself—he had no gift. But they weren't supposed to talk about each other. That's what he'd done, and he knew it was wrong. He had disobeyed.

Dr. Paley closed the folder. "Your teacher has told me that this woman, Serena Hancock, is a member of a group that has a special interest in your gifted classmates. These people have some sort of plan to use the students for criminal purposes. Now, I have a question for you, Carter.

Do you *want* to help these people?"

Want . . . It was one of those words that puzzled Carter. He knew what it meant, because he'd wanted things before: food when he was hungry, water when he was thirsty, warmth when he was cold. But the way Dr. Paley had just used the word—he didn't understand.

Dr. Paley sighed. "Let me ask you something else. Do you like your classmates? Or do you *dislike* your classmates?"

Like, dislike . . . Carter just looked at the doctor blankly. What was he talking about? He knew the words, he knew the dictionary definitions, he'd heard people use these words in conversation. But they didn't apply to him.

"Carter, I want to know what you're feeling."

Feeling . . . Carter knew the feeling of hunger, thirst, cold, heat, pain. He wasn't having any of those sensations at that moment.

"Are you sad? Are you angry? Are you sorry?"

Now Carter sort of understood what the doctor was asking, and he knew he couldn't provide an answer. Dr. Paley might just as well have been asking a blind person what he was seeing.

Carter Street didn't have those kinds of feelings.

Chapter Two

I F AMANDA BEESON WAS forced at gunpoint to say something nice about the gifted class, she'd have to admit that it was rarely boring, unlike geography or algebra. This class was unpredictable. Sure, sometimes Madame would go on and on about how they had to control their gifts, how they shouldn't reveal the nature of their gifts, blah, blah, blah, but there was always the chance something could happen during the class. Jenna might reveal something truly bizarre that she'd read in someone's mind. Like the time she told them she'd read the mind of a waiter in a fast-food hamburger place who wanted to pluck a strand of hair from his head and mix it into the ground beef. Or Emily could tell them who would win that season's American Idol. Something exciting or even dangerous could happen. Charles might decide to rearrange the desks with his telekinetic powers. Someone might tease Martin and he'd respond by kicking a hole in the wall. In a room full of people with extraordinary talents, there was always the possibility of a surprise or two.

Of course, this didn't mean Amanda *liked* the class. Her main objection to it was the fact that she didn't belong there. She'd known this the first time she was sent into the room, and she became more and more convinced of this every day. Nothing that went on in this class really applied to *her*.

For example, at that very moment, Madame was encouraging them to participate in a discussion that was completely irrelevant to Amanda.

"Class, we've spent a lot of time talking about how you can control your gifts, how you can stop these gifts from emerging and interfering with your own lives. You've practiced techniques involving concentration, meditation, special breathing rhythms. Some of you have made excellent progress. Martin, you've seen changes in your behavior, haven't you?"

Amanda glanced without much interest at the wimpy kid she'd never paid much attention to, and it dawned on her that he was becoming less wimpy. He'd grown over the past few months. His face had lost its babyish look, and he hadn't been whining so much lately. When he spoke, she realized his voice was deeper now, too.

"Well, yeah. My grandfather nags me a lot, and sometimes I can feel a lot of anger building up inside me.

I know I could let it out and really hurt him. But I don't."

"That doesn't count," Ken declared. "I mean, he's your grandfather, for crying out loud. You're not going to hit your own grandfather."

"You don't know my grandfather," Martin retorted. "And right this minute, I'm not feeling very kindly toward *you*."

Amanda hid a smile as Ken seemed to flinch slightly. Ken was a former athlete, still in great shape, but he knew as they all did that Martin could send him flying out of the window with a single blow.

"But," Martin added, "the point is, I can control my gift when my grandfather teases me."

"Very good," Madame said with approval. "There's another aspect to your gifts that we need to take into consideration. From our discussions, it seems that most of you—maybe *all* of you—were not born with these gifts. The gifts seem to have emerged as a response to a situation, an experience, or a feeling. Tracey, you understand this, don't you?"

Tracey nodded. "People ignored me, so I felt invisible. And I felt it so strongly that I started to disappear."

"Charles, would you like to comment on how feelings brought about your gift?"

Charles shrugged. "It's not a feeling, it's the situation.

I'm in a wheelchair. I can't walk, so I move stuff with my mind."

Madame smiled. "A lot of people are in wheelchairs, Charles, but they don't develop telekinetic powers. Do you remember the first time you were aware of your gift?"

"Yeah, I was in bed, and I wanted this comic book that was on the other side of the room. And I was too lazy to get into my wheelchair, so I made it come to me."

"And how did you feel when you realized what you could do?" Madame asked.

"Good," Charles said promptly.

"Why?" Madame asked.

"Because . . . because I hated not being able to do some stuff for myself. And now I could."

Madame nodded. "You see, Charles, feelings *are* involved. If you'd been content with your situation, you might not have developed the gift."

Ken broke in. "Madame, what's the point?"

Amanda looked at him gratefully. This was exactly what she was wondering, too. Thank goodness for Ken—the one person in the class she could connect with.

Madame raised her eyebrows. "Excuse me, Ken?"

"Okay, I get it, we got our gifts because we had strong feelings about something. I felt guilty about my best friend getting killed when we crashed into each other on the

387

football field, so I started hearing his voice from beyond the grave. And then all these other dead people jumped in and started talking to me. But I don't care how I got the stupid gift. I just want to control it so I don't have to listen to these—these ghosts, or whatever they are."

"But you can't control your gifts unless you understand them," Madame argued. "You have to dig deeper into your feelings if you want to manage these gifts. And you can't all do this in the same way. Not only because each gift is different, but also because each of you is at a unique level in terms of control. Some of you, for example, can summon your gifts at will."

Some students must have looked confused, because she explained.

"What I'm saying is that some of you can call on your gifts when you need them. Like Charles."

Charles beamed. "I can make anything move whenever I want it to move." To illustrate this, he stared at Madame's purse, which hung on the back of her chair. The bag began to rise.

"Charles," Madame warned.

The purse went back to its place.

"Others of you are less capable of bringing your gifts out when you want to. Tracey, you don't have complete control yet, do you?"

"But I'm getting better at it," Tracey said.

Whatever, Amanda thought. This is such a total waste of time.

"Amanda thinks this is a waste of time," Jenna piped up.

Amanda shot her a dirty look. She knew how to block Jenna from reading her mind, but she'd let her guard down.

"Jenna, you know you're not supposed to read your classmates' minds," Madame scolded. "But this is another example of my point. Did Amanda's thought just come to you?"

"No," Jenna replied. "She looked like she wasn't paying much attention, so I was curious to know what she was thinking about."

"In other words," Madame said, "you read her mind intentionally—which, of course, is wrong, because Amanda's thoughts are her own and none of your business. But you did provide an example of what I'm talking about. You have control of your gift. You can decide whether or not to read someone's mind."

Jenna nodded. "Yeah, I can pretty much do it whenever I want. Unless someone knows how to block me. And remembers to do it," she added, with a wicked glance at Amanda. Amanda ignored her.

"I suspect," Madame said, "that all of you are capable of calling upon your gifts when you want them to appear. But some of you haven't yet achieved that level of control."

This is so not interesting for me, Amanda thought. She kept the thought in the back of her mind so Jenna couldn't read it, but Madame was getting very good at reading her students' expressions.

"Amanda, do you really think this discussion is a waste of time?"

Amanda now had to admit to herself that there was another decent aspect of the gifted class. You could say what you really thought and not get into trouble.

"For me, it's a waste of time," she declared honestly. "I know how to control my gift. As long as I don't feel sorry for someone, I won't take over that person's body. And I hardly ever really want to do it, so I don't need to learn how to bring it out."

Emily gazed at her curiously. "Really? You're never tempted to live someone else's life for a while?"

"Like whose?" Amanda asked.

"I don't know . . ." Emily considered this. "Okay, Lady Gaga. I bet she's got a pretty fabulous life."

Amanda sniffed. "I'd rather make my own life fabulous."

Madame's eyes swept the room and settled on another student. "Sarah, do you think this discussion is a waste of time?"

Amanda was actually curious to hear the girl's response. Of all the classmates, Sarah talked the least about her gift.

The girl with the curly dark hair and the heart-shaped face spoke softly. "I think it's dangerous, Madame."

"How do you mean?" Madame asked.

"If we have total control of our gifts, if we could use them whenever we wanted to, we could end up doing bad things."

Madame gazed at her thoughtfully. "Can you give us an example?"

Everyone turned to look at Sarah, and there was real curiosity in their expressions. Amanda knew why. Supposedly, Sarah had the most powerful gift of all—she could make people do whatever she wanted them to do. None of them had seen much evidence of this remarkable gift, but they knew she had it.

But Sarah didn't use herself as an example. "Well, take Martin, for example. If he could call on his power whenever he wanted to . . ." Her voice trailed off.

"Go on, Sarah," Madame encouraged her.

With clear reluctance, the girl continued. "Maybe . . . maybe Martin doesn't like someone. So he . . . he makes something fall on that person's head and kills him."

"I wouldn't do that," Martin said indignantly.

"Are you sure about that?" Sarah asked. "I mean, what if someone was really, truly getting on your nerves?"

"You're not talking about Martin," Jenna said suddenly. "You're worried about yourself."

"Jenna!" Madame snapped.

Jenna sank back in her seat. "Sorry."

Tracey looked confused as she turned toward Sarah. "Are you afraid Martin is going to drop something on *your* head?"

"No," Sarah said. She looked at her watch and fidgeted, which struck Amanda as very unusual. Sarah was famous for being the perfect student who never behaved inappropriately in any classroom.

Madame glanced at the clock on the wall. "We only have a few more minutes. For tomorrow's class, I want you all to think about this: if you had complete control over your gift, how could you use them in positive ways? How could you help people, maybe even use your gifts to benefit mankind?" She gave them a moment to jot down the assignment.

"Now, does anyone have anything to say before the bell rings?"

Emily raised her hand. "Do you know how Carter is doing at Harmony House?"

Amanda was mildly curious about that, too. Their

former classmate had been sent to the institution for troubled teenagers more than a week ago.

Madame nodded. "I've been talking to Doctor Paley regularly. Carter hasn't spoken, but he's cooperating. Doctor Paley believes that eventually he'll be able to make a real connection with him. Oh, and I should tell you, he's not allowed any visitors yet."

Jenna snorted. "Who'd want to visit him? The guy was spying on us! He was consorting with the enemy. As far as I'm concerned, he can spend the rest of his life at Harmony House in solitary confinement."

"Try to keep an open mind about Carter," Madame urged her. "We don't know what his real intentions were."

The bell rang and Madame dismissed them. Amanda took her time gathering up her things, but all the while she kept an eye on Ken. He had already gotten up and was on his way to the door. The big question was—would he be waiting for her outside the class?

He'd been there yesterday when she emerged, and he'd walked her to her locker. If he did this today, she was going to ask him if he wanted to come home with her for a snack.

He was there! And as soon as she arrived, he began walking by her side.

"Do you think Carter knew what he was doing when

he was reporting on the class to Serena?" he asked as they strolled down the hall.

Amanda shrugged. "Who knows?"

Ken finished the comment for her. "And who cares? You know, this class is really starting to annoy me."

"No kidding," Amanda said with feeling. "I mean, what are we really getting out of it?"

Ken nodded. "I'm no better at stopping the voices than I was before. And I sure don't want to invite any more dead people to talk to me."

"And I don't want to be Lady Gaga," Amanda declared. "Personally, I think she looks kind of sleazy."

"And what Madame said about doing something good with our gifts—okay, maybe for some of the others that could work. But the best thing that ever came out of my gift was helping that kid find the lottery ticket his father had hidden before he died—and that was just a fluke. It's not going to happen again."

"We don't belong in that class, Ken," Amanda said.

"I know," Ken said. "But how are we going to get out of it?"

This was the perfect opportunity to invite him over to her place to discuss the matter. But they were approaching her locker now, and Amanda's heart sank when she saw Nina standing there, obviously waiting for her.

It was a funny thing about Nina. She'd been part of Amanda's clique since forever, but she wasn't exactly a friend. What was that word she'd heard on *Gossip Girl*? *Frenemy*. That's what Nina was. They hung out together, but Amanda didn't trust her.

Still, she forced a thin smile to greet the girl. "Hi, what's up?"

"My mom's picking me up to go to the mall. Want to come?"

Amanda groaned inwardly. If she said "yes," she couldn't invite Ken over. If she said "no," she'd have to give Nina an excuse, that she already had plans—which meant she couldn't invite Ken over.

"Yeah, okay," she said without much enthusiasm. She opened her locker.

"How ya doing, Ken?" Nina asked.

"Okay," Ken said.

"I was just thinking about you," Nina went on.

"Yeah? Why?"

Nina shook her head sadly. "Meadowbrook's soccer team is so pitiful this season. They'd be doing so much better if you were still playing."

Ken gave her a modest smile. "I don't know about that. I wish I could play, but I can't get the medical clearance. Because of my ankle."

"Ken was in a bad accident in September," Amanda told Nina.

"I know, I remember," Nina said, glancing at her briefly. Then she turned her full attention back to Ken. "I was so worried about you."

Ken seemed surprised. "Yeah?"

Amanda was more than surprised. Nina had never said one word about Ken's accident. She eyed Nina suspiciously. Was she flirting? And what was that flush spreading across Ken's face? Was he enjoying this? She slammed her locker door shut.

"I'm ready," she said shortly. "Let's go. See ya, Ken."

"Bye, Ken," Nina said. She linked her arm through Amanda's arm. Amanda turned her head to give Ken a private, parting smile, but he'd already turned in the opposite direction. What was he thinking after that little encounter? she wondered.

She could certainly see where Jenna's gift could come in handy . . .

Chapter Three

O N TUESDAY MORNING, CARTER woke up. He got out of bed, he went to the sink, he filled the cup and watered the plant. He brushed his teeth, he got dressed, and he went to the dining room. He ate his breakfast, he watched the clock, and when the time was right, he went to Dr. Paley's office.

"Good morning, Carter." The doctor's back was to the boy as he adjusted the video camera. "I want to try something new with you today." He turned to face Carter. "There is a procedure in which a sleeplike condition is induced in the subject. In this condition, the subject is highly susceptible to the suggestions of the doctor. This condition is called hypnosis."

Carter stiffened. He knew that word. That word could make bad things happen. Dr. Paley's eyebrows went up.

"Ah, I see that word disturbs you, and I think I know why. Serena Hancock used hypnosis to make you talk. But it's possible that what Serena used was a counter-hypnosis

397

process. Let me explain my theory."

He pulled out the chair that he normally sat on from behind the desk and placed it in the center of the room. Then he turned the chair that Carter always sat in to face it, and he motioned for Carter to sit down.

Carter didn't move. His entire body seemed to be on alert.

"Sit down, Carter," Dr. Paley said firmly.

He had to obey. He had no choice. Carter sat down.

"This is my theory," Dr. Paley said. "You may believe that Serena hypnotized you, but I believe that you are currently functioning in a state of trauma, and she was able to bring you *out* of that state. That's why you were able to communicate with her."

He leaned back in his chair and studied Carter thoughtfully. "I don't know how she was able to do this. I have tried to locate her, but she seems to have disappeared or changed her name. So what I would like to do is try my own form of hypnosis on you, with the hope that I can somehow cause your current state of hypnosis to end. I know this all sounds very confusing, but you must trust me. Carter? Carter, what are you looking at?"

Carter had been distracted by a sudden movement. It came from the far corner of the office where a filing cabinet stood. Dr. Paley followed the direction of Carter's eyes.

"Oh, no," the doctor snapped. He got up, grabbed a book from his desk, and tossed it in that direction. A very small mouse retreated behind the cabinet.

"Mice," the doctor murmured. "They're all over the building. I've complained, but it's an old structure and there are bound to be holes in the walls . . . Now, where were we? Ah, yes, I was about to attempt hypnotic therapy." He returned to his seat facing Carter.

"Let's begin." From his shirt pocket he withdrew what looked like a pen, but when he clicked it, a small white light appeared. "I want you to look at this light."

Carter looked at the light.

"The subject is looking at the light," Dr. Paley said quietly. Carter knew he was speaking for the recording device. Dr. Paley recorded or videotaped all the sessions.

Then, in a normal voice, Dr. Paley continued. "Now, don't take your eyes from the light, but listen to my voice very carefully. I want you to empty your mind. Your mind is like a room full of furniture. The pieces of furniture are your thoughts. I want you to pack your thoughts in boxes, one by one, and take them out of the room."

Carter didn't feel comfortable. Boxes . . . The image bothered him. A sensation began to creep over him. It wasn't hunger, it wasn't cold . . . but something else, something just as disturbing. He knew this sensation but he couldn't put a name to it.

But he did as he was told. He took a thought: Harmony House. He put it in a plain brown box. He carried the thought out of his mind. Then he did the same with the gifted class, the Granger home, and the house where he had met Serena and the other people.

"I'm going to count back from ten," Dr. Paley said. "Close your eyes. You will feel yourself getting sleepy. When I reach the number one, you will be in a deep sleep, but you will continue to hear my voice. Ten . . . nine . . . eight . . . seven . . ."

Carter searched his mind. It was empty—every thought had been packed up and taken out. There hadn't been that much there in the first place. But was he getting sleepy? He didn't think so.

". . . three . . . two . . . one. You are now in a deep sleep and you will do as I say."

Carter knew he wasn't asleep, but it was easy to follow Dr. Paley's commands.

"Raise your right hand. Put your right hand down. Raise your left hand. Put your left hand down. Very good. The subject appears to be in a trance. Now, Carter, let's bring up a memory."

This wouldn't be so easy. Memories were thoughts, and all his thoughts had been removed. But he continued to listen.

"Let's go back to the day you were discovered, on Carter Street. It's night, and you're huddled in a doorway. A policeman finds you. He asks you questions. You don't answer him. You're feeling something, Carter. What are you feeling? Maybe you're lonely. Maybe you're sad."

Lonely . . . sad . . . He couldn't connect to those words.

"Cold . . ." Dr. Paley suggested.

Yes . . . *yes*! He knew that sensation. The chill of the night crept over him, and he was very uncomfortable.

"The subject appears to be shivering," Dr. Paley murmured. "Carter . . . perhaps you haven't eaten in a while. So you are hungry. Are you hungry, Carter?" After a moment, he said, "The subject is licking his lips."

Cold, hungry, cold, hungry . . . This was bad. Carter didn't want to be there.

"And something else, too, Carter. You're feeling something else. Are you afraid?"

Afraid, afraid, afraid . . . The words rang in his ears, and suddenly all those thoughts he'd pushed out of his head came rushing back in, and more, more thoughts, thoughts he didn't know he had, horrible thoughts . . . Yes, that was the sensation he couldn't remember. He was afraid, and it was horrible, terrible, he had to shut it out, turn it off, go away, go far, far away, to a place where he wouldn't be cold or hungry or frightened . . .

Images, sounds, they flashed across his mind so rapidly, he couldn't identify anything . . . Lights and noises, lights and noises, they went on and on and on, louder and brighter, and the sensation grew stronger . . . Hunger, cold, fear—he had to make them stop! But he couldn't make them stop, so he had to escape. There was a way: he did it before, he could do it again . . .

"Carter. Carter! I'm going to count to ten, and when I reach ten, you will wake up. One, two, three . . ."

With the doctor's voice, the lights and the noises began to change. Colors faded, and the sounds were softer. Slowly, all became silent and gray again. Safe.

Carter opened his eyes. He didn't understand what had just happened to him, and he looked at Dr. Paley in bewilderment.

Dr. Paley was looking at him with an odd expression, too. As if he'd just seen something he'd never seen before.

"Carter. How do you feel?"

Pain . . . There was pain . . . Carter put his hands to his head in an effort to squeeze out the pain.

"You'd better go back to your room and lie down for a while," Dr. Paley said.

Carter rose and went to the door.

"But I want to see you again later today," Dr. Paley

told him. "After I've had a chance to study the videotape and talk to some colleagues. This is very important, Carter. Do you understand me?"

Carter turned his head and looked back at the doctor. Dr. Paley smiled.

"You see, Carter . . . You, too, have a gift."

CHAPTER FOUR

AS AMANDA APPROACHED room 209, she spotted Nina lingering just outside the door of the class.

"What are you doing here?" she asked her "frenemy."

Nina fluttered a thin strip of paper in the air. "You left this in my mother's car yesterday. It must have fallen out of your bag."

Amanda took the paper and examined it. It was the receipt for a pair of shoes she'd bought at the mall the day before.

"You'll need this if you want to return the shoes," Nina pointed out.

"I love those sandals, I'm not going to take them back," Amanda replied. Then she frowned. "Why are you giving me this now? Why didn't you give it to me at lunch today?"

Nina smiled sweetly. "I forgot."

Amanda doubted that. Nina knew that Ken was in this class with Amanda. She was just looking for an excuse to hang out in front of the room and "accidentally" run into him.

"Thanks," she said, tossing the receipt in her bag. "Bye."

But just as she suspected, Nina remained by the door. From her seat in class, Amanda could see Ken arrive and Nina stopping him. They weren't able to talk long—the bell was about to ring—but Amanda fumed anyway.

She knew she shouldn't be surprised. Ken was a highly desirable guy, popular and good-looking. And Nina had always competed with Amanda for everything from leadership of their clique to being the first with the current "It" purse, so why not with boys, too? It was only natural that Nina would go after the same one Amanda wanted.

Nina knew that Amanda was interested in Ken. Ever since he'd kissed her underwater at a pool party last summer, she'd had feelings for him. (Okay, the kiss was the result of a dare from some other guys, but even so, it *was* a kiss.) In her efforts to get a relationship going, Amanda had had ups and downs, but right now, things seemed to be going well. There was no way she'd let Nina intrude.

She flashed her most brilliant smile at Ken as he took his seat, but there was no opportunity to talk. Madame called for everyone's attention.

"Yesterday, I asked you to think about how you could use your gifts in positive ways. Does anyone have any thoughts on the subject?"

Charles spoke. "I've done that. I got the gun away from that woman Clare, when she had Emily in her car."

"Yes, I remember," Madame said. "But I'm interested in discussing how you can help others—not just the people in this class, but society in general."

Martin piped up. "You mean, like a superhero? If I could get a handle on my power whenever I wanted, I could run around saving people from bullies."

"Let's not jump that far ahead," Madame cautioned. "I'm not telling you to become superheroes. We're just trying to explore the potential of your gifts. If you did have control, you might have opportunities to benefit mankind."

Emily had a question. "But how? Like, what if I had a vision of a plane crashing and I called the airline to warn them? They'd want to know how I knew about it."

"What good would it do anyway?" Jenna asked. "They wouldn't believe you."

"And if they did believe you," Tracey chimed in, "you'd be revealing your gift. Which we're not supposed to do." She looked at Madame. "Right?"

Amanda was mildly surprised that Madame didn't make her usual quick response to that question. The teacher actually seemed uncertain. Finally, she spoke.

"There may be situations where you will be able to safely

reveal yourselves," she said slowly, "to certain people, and under certain conditions. But that's not what I want us to discuss now. At this point in time, I want you to think about ways in which you could use your gifts discreetly. To help people without calling attention to yourselves."

What's the point of that? Amanda wondered. We wouldn't get any credit for our good deeds.

Jenna suddenly burst out laughing. Madame looked startled.

"What's so funny about that, Jenna?" she demanded to know.

"Sorry, Madame. But I was just trying to imagine Amanda doing a good deed when she wouldn't get any credit for it."

"She was reading my mind, Madame!" Amanda complained. Then she realized she'd just affirmed what Jenna had said, and she sank back in her chair. From the corner of her eye she could see Ken looking at her, and it wasn't exactly in admiration. Did he really think she was the kind of person who would never do anything for anyone else?

Madame was angry. "Jenna, how many times do I need to remind you? You have absolutely no right to eavesdrop on your classmates' thoughts! It's rude, and you're invading their privacy."

"But I wasn't reading her mind," Jenna protested. "It was my own thought."

Liar, Amanda thought. And she didn't care if Jenna heard her.

Tracey spoke. "Jenna, you're not being fair. Remember when Amanda was in my head? She did a lot of nice things for me."

"Yeah, because she was afraid she was stuck being you forever," Jenna retorted. "Look, all I'm saying is that Amanda won't ever be a superhero. She's too selfish."

Madame was losing patience. "Could we please get back to the subject? Charles . . . can you think of a way you could use your gift discreetly to help people?"

Charles thought about it. "Okay, what about this? I'm in a grocery store, and there's this little old man who wants to buy a can of soup. Only it's on a really high shelf and he can't reach it. So when he's not looking, I make the can of soup come off the shelf and into his shopping basket."

Martin looked at him scornfully. "You think getting a can of soup off a shelf benefits mankind?"

Ken had a problem with this, too. "And when the old man sees the can in his basket and he doesn't know how it got there, he'll be afraid he's losing his mind."

Madame smiled. "It was a positive thought, Charles, but you can see there are ramifications and consequences to every action. Sarah, you haven't spoken. Do you have a comment to make?"

"No, Madame," Sarah said.

"For this class, I asked you to think about how you could use your gift in a positive way. Did you do this?"

"No, Madame."

Amanda was shocked. She'd had other classes with Sarah, and the girl was widely known as Little Miss Perfect who always did what teachers told her to do. It was weird that she would actually not do the assignment. Amanda herself hadn't done the assignment either, but if Madame asked, she would say that she'd thought and thought about it but hadn't been able to come up with an example. Sarah was such a goody-goody, she wasn't even capable of lying!

"Well, Sarah, think about it now." Madame's tone was kind but firm. "You have a very powerful gift. More than anyone else here, you have the ability to help people. Sarah, are you listening?"

Sarah had lowered her head, and no one could see her face. "Yes, Madame."

"Then answer me. What could you do to benefit mankind?"

"I can't," Sarah replied in an almost inaudible whisper.

"Why not?"

Sarah raised her head, and now Amanda could see tears streaming down her face. "I can't, Madame. I can't!"

Amanda was taken aback. The girl looked and sounded unbelievably upset, like she was on the verge of a nervous breakdown or something. It was awful. Amanda could feel her pain . . .

Uh-oh, this was dangerous! Quickly she concentrated on coming up with another emotional reaction. Silly girl, why is she freaking out? What a wimp . . .

But now Sarah was sobbing hysterically, and Amanda couldn't drown out the sound. She had to make this stop before pity overwhelmed her.

"Leave her alone," she said loudly. "She hasn't done anything wrong. She's doesn't have to benefit mankind if she doesn't want to!"

"You would say that," Jenna declared. "You're so selfish, Amanda!"

Madame hurried over to Sarah and put a hand on her shoulder. "Sarah, you need to calm down."

But Sarah continued to cry, and Madame turned to Emily. "Could you take Sarah to the infirmary, Emily?"

"Sure," Emily said. She got up and went to Sarah's desk. "Come on, Sarah."

Still sobbing, Sarah rose from her desk and left the room with Emily.

For a moment, the room was silent. Then Martin asked, "Why does she get so upset when we ask about her gift, Madame?"

Before Madame had a chance to reply, the chiming of three bells sounded from the intercom. It was followed by the voice of the school secretary.

"Madame, could you come to the office, please?"

Madame sighed and went to the door. "Class, continue discussing positive ways in which you can use your gifts," she ordered them before walking out.

Naturally, everyone started talking about anything but that.

"Do you think Carter is telling that doctor all about us?" Charles asked.

"He can't talk," Martin pointed out.

"But he *can*," Tracey piped up. "Remember? I told you guys—I saw him talking to that Serena."

Amanda didn't care what Carter was doing. She was more concerned about what Ken might be thinking after that little exchange with Jenna. Did he think she was selfish, too?

"Ken . . ."

He was staring straight ahead, and he didn't seem to have heard her. Or maybe he was intentionally ignoring her. Nervously, she nudged him. "*Ken.*"

He turned. "Oh, sorry. I was listening to someone."

Immediately, she turned on her most sympathetic expression. "A dead person?"

He nodded. "You remember that sweet old lady I told you about? The one who was hooked on a soap opera before she died?"

She didn't remember, but she nodded anyway.

"She wanted to know what happened in the last episode."

It came back to her. "Oh, right. You've been watching it for her." She wrinkled her nose. "Isn't that a drag? I mean, it's a really stupid show."

"Yeah, it's awful. But it meant a lot to her."

"Well, you're doing a good deed, I guess," Amanda said. "Are dead people still considered part of mankind?"

Tracey interrupted their private conversation. "Ken, what do you think?"

"About what?" Ken asked.

"Carter. Do you think he's talking about us?"

"He might be telling the doctor," Ken suggested.

"I'm not worried about that," Jenna said. "Doctor Paley's a good guy. He already knows about me. And Madame wouldn't be talking to him every day if she didn't trust him. But there are a lot of creepy people living at Harmony House. Serious losers, kids with bad connections. I hope he's not talking to them."

"Yeah, I wish I knew what was going on over there," Charles commented. "Too bad he's not allowed to have any visitors."

Martin turned to Jenna. "Couldn't *you* get into the place? They know you there."

Jenna shook her head. "Doesn't make any difference—they're really strict. There's a guard who won't let anyone past the reception area unless they've got a pass."

"I could get in!" Tracey declared. "The guard wouldn't see me if I'm invisible. I could follow Carter around and find out what he's up to."

"Forget it," Jenna said. "Remember what happened when you tried to spy on him before? And you became visible again? No offense, Tracey—I know you're improving, but you just don't have enough control of your gift. You could get into serious trouble if you're caught there."

"I've got an idea," Martin said.

Jenna rolled her eyes. "Let me guess. You'll punch out the guard."

"Jenna, don't tease him," Tracey hissed.

But Martin really did seem to be developing some control. "I'm thinking Amanda could get in."

Aghast, Amanda turned to him. "Me?"

"Like Jenna said, the place is full of losers," Martin said.

"There's got to be someone checking in who you could feel sorry for. You could do your bodysnatching thing, take over, and go in as that person."

Amanda stared at him in horror. What kind of insane idea was that? Then she caught Ken's eye. He was looking at her with interest.

"You think you could do that?"

"She could," Jenna broke in, "but she wouldn't. Do you really think Amanda's going to do something to help us?"

Amanda swallowed hard. "Don't speak for me, Jenna. I could try . . ."

"Today?" Jenna asked.

"Um . . . let me think . . . I don't even know where Harmony House is . . ."

"I'll take you there," Jenna declared. "Right after class."

That was definitely admiration on Ken's face. Amanda swallowed again and smiled thinly.

"Great."

Chapter Five

THE PAIN IN HIS head was gone by the time Carter returned to Dr. Paley's office. Even so, something in his head was different. It was like the TV in his dreams was embedded somewhere in his brain. At some point during the last session, it had been turned on. It was off again now, and Carter preferred this state of mind. Now that he was entering Dr. Paley's office, he had the sensation it could be turned on again, and he didn't want that. But he'd been told to return, and he did what he was told.

Dr. Paley seemed different, too. His eyes were brighter, and his smile was wider. Change meant danger. Carter began to shiver.

"Sit down, Carter. I want to show you something." He wheeled a trolley to the middle of the room and positioned it in front of Carter's chair. On top of the trolley stood a television, smaller than the one in his dreams, but still a television. Carter felt his heartbeat quicken.

Dr. Paley didn't notice his discomfort. "I want to show you the tape I made of our session this morning." He touched a button and slipped a disk into an opening. Then he sat down behind his desk, where he, too, could see the screen. He held a remote control toward the TV, it flickered to life, and Carter saw himself, sitting in this same chair. He couldn't see Dr. Paley on the screen, but he heard his voice.

"I'm going to count back from ten," Dr. Paley said. "Close your eyes. You will feel yourself getting sleepy. When I reach the number one, you will be in a deep sleep, but you will continue to hear my voice. Ten . . . nine . . . eight . . . seven . . ."

The pain was coming back. Carter covered his ears. Quickly, Dr. Paley took the remote control. The tape continued, but Carter didn't hear anything.

"Actually, we don't need the sound," Dr. Paley said. "You never spoke. Now, watch carefully, Carter. Here it comes."

Carter didn't have any expectations as to what he might have done under the spell of the doctor's hypnosis, but even so, it was a shock to see himself get smaller and smaller.

Dr. Paley had said Carter had a gift. Was it a gift like Tracey's? Then he realized that the chair on the screen wasn't vacant. A small white rabbit sat there, twitching its nose.

"That's not really a rabbit, Carter," Dr. Paley said softly.

"That's you."

He picked up the remote control. "I'm going to fast-forward for a minute. There, now watch this."

The rabbit on the chair seemed to puff up. Then it became fuzzy, almost impossible to identify as a rabbit. As it enlarged, it changed form. The form became too blurry to see anything in detail, but then Carter could see the outline of arms, legs, a torso . . . The focus returned. It was Carter, in the same position as before, still sitting in his chair. And all this happened in less than a second.

"You're suffering from Acute Faculative Allomorphy, Carter, commonly known as shapeshifting," Dr. Paley said.

Carter took his eyes off the screen and looked at the doctor. His whole body began to tremble.

Dr. Paley came out from behind his desk and drew another chair closer to Carter. He placed a warm hand gently on Carter's shoulder.

"Don't get upset, Carter. You're going to be all right. You're safe here. Nobody is going to hurt you. As I told you this morning, you have a gift. It's a very unusual gift—very few cases have been recorded, and these cases have been kept secret. My own interest in extraordinary abilities has given me access to information that has long been hidden from the public."

His voice was calming, and Carter stopped shaking. But

417

was he really safe? How could he be sure?

The doctor continued. "You must know by now that uncommon gifts like this exist. Think about your classmates."

Carter stiffened. He could hear Madame's voice. "Never tell, never tell." He'd told Serena, and he'd been sent away from the class.

It was almost as if Dr. Paley could read his thoughts. "You're not in trouble, Carter. No one is going to hurt you, or any of your classmates. I know everything because I've been talking with Madame. She has always suspected that you, too, may have some kind of special ability. We both have your best interests at heart. We want to help you."

The words rang true, and Carter had always trusted Madame.

"I've learned from Madame that many of your classmates' gifts arose through extreme situations—a trauma, a crisis of some sort—and I believe this may be true of you, too. We need to know why you became a shape shifter. From your reaction in watching the tape I could see you were shocked, but I don't think that was the first time you've ever shifted. Your state of amnesia has erased all memories of your gift. But the explanation for your ability is buried deep within your subconscious. I can't reach you through traditional hypnotic procedures, so I need to try something else."

Carter's eyes followed the doctor as he rose and went to the white cabinet in the corner of the room. He opened a drawer.

"I'm going to give you an injection. It's perfectly safe—it's just a sedative that will help you relax completely and allow you to overcome the inhibitions that are preventing you from speaking. Hopefully, you will recover some memories and be able to tell me about your past. Would you roll up your sleeve, please?"

It was a direct order. Carter had to obey. But Dr. Paley must have sensed the fear that engulfed him, because his voice became even more soothing.

"You'll only feel a little prick, and retrieving the memories shouldn't be painful. You may not even remember what you tell me. But I'm taping you so you'll be able to watch it all later. I'm keeping no secrets from you. You have to trust me, and you must not fight the need to express yourself."

It was just as Dr. Paley said—the injection was just a little sting in his arm, and then he felt nothing.

"We're going back in time, to six months ago. Close your eyes, Carter."

Carter closed his eyes, but what he saw wasn't darkness. At first he thought he was dreaming, because he could see the boy of his dreams. But then it was as if he was inside the boy, and it wasn't a dream. The boy was him.

He looked around, and everything he saw was familiar and comforting. The room held a sofa, two armchairs, a bookcase. At one end of the room, there was a large wooden table and chairs. On the floor, there was a colorful rug. There were windows, and through the windows he could see flowers.

He knew this house. He knew about things he couldn't even see, like the basketball hoop over the two-car garage. He knew that through the archway there was a big kitchen. He knew that if he went past the table and through another archway he'd be in a hallway, and off the hallway were three bedrooms. One of those bedrooms belonged to him.

Someone was singing. He could hear a woman's voice drifting out from another room. He knew the voice. It belonged to his mother.

A man sat in one of the armchairs with a newspaper in his hands. He knew this man. He was called "Dad."

The man looked at him. "I'm sorry, Paul. It's just not possible."

Paul. That was the boy's name. Not Carter. Paul.

My name is Paul.

He knew what his father was talking about, too. Paul

had just asked him if they could buy one of the puppies that had been born to their neighbor's dog.

"But it's so tiny, Dad. And Mrs. Robbins says he won't get much bigger."

His father smiled, but he shook his head. "Your mother is allergic to dog hair, Paul. It wouldn't matter whether the dog was big or small. Your mother can't visit the Robbinses' house for more than a few minutes. If we had a dog living in this house, even if you kept him in your room, she'd get sick. You wouldn't want that."

"No," Paul said. He turned to see his mother standing in the archway.

"I'm so sorry, sweetie-pie," she said. That was her special name for him, "sweetie-pie." He was grateful for the fact that she never used it when any of his friends were around. Not that he had many friends, not yet. They'd just moved here a few weeks ago.

They moved a lot. Every now and then, serious men came to talk to his parents. Soon after that, they would move. Years ago, Paul had asked his father who the men were and why they were always moving. His father told him that the men were from the government, and they were protecting them. They were part of something called a "witness protection program." His parents had witnessed a crime, and so had Paul, even though he couldn't

421

remember it. He'd only been four at the time. But ever since then they all had to be protected from the criminals, who had never been caught. His parents told Paul they had nothing to worry about as long as they did what the government men told them to do. And Paul didn't worry, because he trusted his father and his mother.

Right now, though, his mother looked a little worried. But it had nothing to do with criminals.

"Sweetie-pie, I hope you don't hate me for this," she said.

"I don't hate you, Mom," Paul replied.

"I'm going to see a specialist next week," she told him. "Maybe there's a new medicine for my allergy."

"Thanks, Mom," Paul said. "But it's okay, I don't have to have a dog. How about a couple of gerbils?"

"That might be just fine," his mother said. "I'll ask the doctor." She looked at her watch. "I need to run to the grocery store before dinner. Paul, could you empty the dishwasher?"

"Sure." He went into the kitchen. Just as he opened the dishwasher door, he heard a knock on the front door. His mother must have opened it, because he heard her cry out.

"What do you want?"

Then his father's voice: "What do you think you're doing?"

And then a horrible loud bang, followed by the sound of a body falling down. Then another bang, and another body hit the floor.

A gruff voice muttered, "We gotta find the kid."

Paul heard the footsteps coming down the hall. He knew they wouldn't find anyone in the bedrooms, and the next place they'd look would be the kitchen. Frantically, he looked around for a place to hide.

He ran into the little pantry and shut the door. But there was no lock to keep the men from opening it, and he could hear them coming.

His parents couldn't help him. There was no escape. In seconds the men would open the door and shoot him, just as they had shot his mother and his father. Danger—he was in terrible danger. There had to be some way, *some way* to save himself. If only he could become invisible . . .

He couldn't. But he could do something else. He didn't know he could do it—it just happened, and when it did, it felt like the most completely natural reaction he could have to the situation.

And when one of the men pulled open the door to the pantry, he didn't see Paul. He couldn't even see the small gerbil hiding behind a box of cereal.

From way off in the distance came the sound of sirens.

"The neighbors must have heard the shots," a man said.

"Let's get out of here."

From behind the box, Paul waited until he couldn't hear any voices. Then, slowly, he crept out of the pantry.

How odd the kitchen suddenly seemed to him. Such a big space . . . he knew he could scamper across it but he was afraid to move too quickly. He could imagine the sight he would encounter in the living room, and he wasn't ready for that. He wasn't ready for anything. Huge structures loomed ominously over him. He knew what they were—a refrigerator, a dishwasher—but his perspective made them frightening. He inched his way across the cold linoleum floor, and he'd almost reached the archway when the door to the living room burst open.

Frantically, he ran behind the stove. Peering out, he saw men in police uniforms. They were holding guns.

If he ran out the way he was, would they shoot him? He couldn't turn back into himself, not while he was behind the stove—he wouldn't fit into the space, he'd be crushed. And if he ran out and then transformed, the police might think he was one of the bad guys and kill him.

He heard one of them speak. "We need an ambulance immediately."

Enormous boot-clad feet were directly in front of him. "Kitchen's clear," a voice rang out.

Another voice. "Bedrooms and bathroom are clear."

And then another voice. "It looks bad. I'm not getting a pulse on either of them."

Paul knew whom they were talking about.

He stayed where he was. Time passed. There were new voices, new sounds.

"The house wasn't ransacked. This doesn't look like a burglary. Someone had it in for these folks."

"They must have been pros. We're not going to find any fingerprints."

"Headquarters says don't touch anything. They're calling in the FBI."

"Why?"

"No idea."

"Can we move the bodies?"

"Yeah."

Bodies. Paul knew what that meant. His parents were dead.

He remained behind the stove, and he had no idea how long he was there. There were more voices, more sounds. And then, finally, there was silence.

He came out and moved into the living room. There were some dark stains on the carpet, and he sniffed them. Blood. His parents' blood. Vaguely, he wondered why he wasn't crying. Maybe gerbils couldn't cry.

And now what was he supposed to do?

CHAPTER SIX

WHEN MADAME RETURNED TO the class, she was visibly excited.

"Good news, class! I've just had a conversation with Doctor Paley. Carter has had a breakthrough. He's talking!"

"What's he saying?" Tracey asked.

"He's just beginning to remember who he is, where he came from. Doctor Paley couldn't talk long, so I don't have any details yet."

"Is he talking about us?" Jenna wanted to know.

"Doctor Paley didn't say." Madame's eyes swept the room. "Class, I know you're all concerned, not only for Carter but for your own safety as well. And I can understand that. But Doctor Paley is a medical person, a specialist. He accepts the possibilities of abilities that cannot be explained by science. He is a man of integrity. I trust him, and I believe he can help us."

Jenna wasn't satisfied with that. "But what if Carter

starts talking to other people at Harmony House? Some of the kids who stay there are bad news."

The bell rang. "I'll bring this concern up with Doctor Paley," Madame promised as she dismissed them.

As she rose from her desk, Amanda was hoping that Jenna might have forgotten about their afterschool plans. No such luck. Jenna made it to the doorway first and practically blocked Amanda from leaving.

"Let's go."

"I need to stop by my locker," Amanda protested. She didn't really, but she'd do anything to postpone this adventure. She had a sudden inspiration. "I'll meet you by the back entrance."

Jenna looked at her skeptically, but she nodded and took off. Ken joined Amanda, and they walked together to her locker.

"That's really cool, what you're doing," Ken said. "Are you scared?"

"A little nervous," Amanda admitted. "I don't know if it'll work. And even if I can take someone over, I always worry about being able to get back into myself."

"Want me to come along with you guys?"

Of course she would have loved to have him come along, but she knew it wasn't a good idea. Jenna would only entertain him with tales of Amanda's selfishness.

She smiled sweetly. "It's so nice of you to offer, Ken. But if you're there, it might make it harder for me to take over someone."

"Why?"

This was risky, but she had to take a chance. She lowered her eyes demurely. "Because I have to concentrate really hard to do it. And if you're there . . . well, it might be hard to concentrate on anyone else."

Was she coming on too strong? She cast a sidelong glance at him. It was hard to say, but she could swear she saw a little blush creep up his face. Then he smiled. Unfortunately, he wasn't looking at her anymore.

"Hi, Nina."

And there she was, the frenemy, waiting by Amanda's locker. Like a cat waiting for a mouse and ready to pounce.

Nina acted like she was happy to see both of them, but Amanda knew a performance when she saw one.

"Hi, guys!" Nina chirped. "Have you seen how nice it is outside? It's like summer! I am so totally up for an ice cream. Who wants to come with me?"

Amanda rolled her eyes. Nina never ate ice cream. She was one of those idiots who never consumed anything nice for fear it might add an ounce to her scrawny frame.

And to make matters worse, Jenna chose that precise

moment to appear. "Are you ready to go?" she asked Amanda.

Amanda should have known Jenna wouldn't wait long by the back door. She was probably worried Amanda would sneak out of the front entrance—which was exactly what she had been considering.

Nina, of course, was staring at Jenna with her mouth open. Amanda didn't have to be a mind reader to know what was going on in her so-called friend's head. The notorious goth girl had plans with Queen Beeson?

"Class project," Amanda offered by way of explanation. She raised her hand in a casual salute to the others. But inside she was tormented as she left Ken alone with Nina to get ice cream.

Was Nina really a threat? Okay, she was cute, but Amanda knew she herself was cuter. Looks weren't everything, though. And Nina did have something Amanda didn't have. Nina was normal. She didn't have any weird gift to deal with. Ken wanted to be normal. Would he be intrigued with the notion of hanging out with a normal girl?

Of course she said nothing about this to Jenna. Not that Jenna would care. As soon as they were out of the building, she started to give instructions.

"We'll take the bus to City Hall and walk from

there. There are usually three or four new admissions to Harmony House every day, and we can check them out in the reception area."

"Whatever," Amanda mumbled. They crossed the street and went to the bus stop.

Jenna continued. "It's important that you're very careful about whose body you take over. Boys and girls live in separate sections, so it's best to pick a boy. You'll be able to hang around Carter more. If you're a girl, you'll only be able to see him in the dining hall, the TV room, and the game room. You won't be able to get into Carter's room."

Amanda tried to tune her out. *Blah, blah, blah . . .* She didn't want to listen to Jenna's instructions. All she could do was concentrate on blocking Jenna from hearing her own thoughts, mainly the thought that she did not want to be doing this at all.

Chapter Seven

THE BOY FORMERLY KNOWN as Carter Street had been in Dr. Paley's office for hours now. This was the third time he'd watched the video and listened to himself tell his story under hypnosis, but it wasn't getting any easier for him. He still couldn't get used to the sound of his voice. He sounded so normal—even if the story he told wasn't ordinary at all.

"I didn't know where to go. I stayed at home."

From off screen, the voice of Dr. Paley could be heard. "Why did you choose to be a gerbil?"

"It was the first thing that came to my mind, because I'd just asked my mother about getting some gerbils."

"Were you shocked to realize you could do this?"

"No. It felt natural. I had to be something very small to hide."

"How did you survive?" Dr. Paley asked. "Were you able to eat anything?"

"I found some crumbs behind the stove. That was a

surprise. My mother was always sweeping the floor."

"Where did you sleep, Paul?"

That name . . . He'd completely forgotten it. It still wasn't familiar, but strangely enough, it sounded right.

"The bottom drawer of my chest of drawers was open. I was able to jump in and sleep on a sweater."

"How long did you stay in the house?"

"I don't know. I couldn't see a clock. I couldn't even tell if it was day or night."

"Why did you leave?"

So many questions . . . Paul watched his own face on the screen. He looked tired, but he kept on talking.

"Some people must have come. I heard them close the drawer of the chest of drawers. I could feel it moving. I couldn't get out. I was in a dark place with no food. I was hungry." He stopped talking, and Paul could see that his body had begun to tremble.

"Keep talking, Paul. What happened next?"

"The chest of drawers stopped moving. It was in another place—a cold place. I got hungrier and colder. Then the drawer was opened. I was weak, but I got out of the drawer. People must have seen me—someone yelled, someone threw something at me. I was surprised. I thought people liked gerbils. They keep them as pets."

"Yes, yes, but perhaps they were startled because

432

they didn't expect to see a gerbil in a storage unit. Then what did you do?"

"I got away. I was outside. But it was still cold, and I was so hungry. I became a boy again."

"And that was when you were found," Dr. Paley said.

"I guess so."

"Why didn't you say anything?"

"I turned myself off."

"What do you mean?"

"Like a TV. I was off."

There was a moment of silence. Then he heard Dr. Paley's voice again, only this time it wasn't from the screen. The real Dr. Paley was in the room, and he'd paused the videotape.

"You've been turned back on now, Paul." The doctor moved his chair so he could be directly facing him. "I've done some research on your family. You were four years old when you and your parents witnessed an act of organized crime in New York—a murder. Your parents testified against the criminals, and that put their lives in danger. Your life was in danger, too. You couldn't testify, but you were still a witness. So the government put your family in a witness protection program. Your name was changed, and you were moved to another city. But the crime syndicate discovered your whereabouts and you were moved again, and then again. You have a memory of many homes, don't you?"

Paul nodded. In his mind he saw a small house, a large house, a hotel, an apartment. He dimly recalled many times when his parents were talking quietly, worriedly, and then abruptly falling silent when he entered the room. They must have tried so hard to keep him from feeling the danger they were all in.

"It wasn't easy tracking you," Dr. Paley continued. "Your name was changed many times. Your birth name was Paul, but you've been called Daniel, Sam, and Jonathan. It was in your last home that your parents went back to your original name, Paul."

So that was why Paul sounded natural, but not familiar. A lot of things were making sense now.

"And your last names—you've been Fletcher, O'Malley, and Kingston. Do you have a preference for one over the other?"

Paul shook his head.

"Well, I don't want to give you a name that the criminal syndicate might recognize. How about if we call you Paul Carter?"

Paul nodded.

"How do you feel, Paul?"

Feel—the word made more sense now. He could

remember feelings. He remembered feeling excited on the roller coaster. He remembered feeling happy when he made it all the way around the baseball diamond. He remembered feeling disappointed when he learned he couldn't have a dog.

And he remembered horror, terror, when those men killed his parents. He remembered feeling frightened.

He was still frightened. He didn't have to speak—Dr. Paley must have read it in his expression.

"You're scared, aren't you?"

Paul nodded.

"You have a gift, Paul," Dr. Paley said. "Just like your classmates. How does that feel, knowing you have a gift?"

It was hard trying to decide what to say about that, and even harder actually saying it. He managed to get some words out. "I . . . don't . . . know."

"Do you feel good?"

That wasn't the word. Paul shook his head.

"Are you afraid of your gift?"

That was closer to what he felt. Paul nodded.

"Don't be," Dr. Paley said. "I can help you."

Chapter Eight

THE BUS ARRIVED, AND Amanda reluctantly followed Jenna up the steps. Now that they were among other people, Jenna lowered her voice. "Remember to keep an eye on the resident assistants. When I was there, a real goon tried to blackmail me. He's been fired, but there might be other creeps around. Don't trust anyone."

Amanda fumbled in her bag and pulled out her iPod. Without even looking at Jenna, she stuck the plugs in her ears and turned it on. Jenna glared at her, but Amanda closed her eyes.

She wasn't lying when she admitted to Ken that she was a little nervous. She knew she was getting better and better at bodysnatching, but there was always the chance something could go wrong. She could get stuck being a juvenile delinquent forever. But this would definitely impress her classmates. Nobody could call her selfish again.

Quickly, she amended her thoughts. Of course she

didn't really care what any of those weirdos thought about her, and the only person she wanted to impress was Ken.

Jenna poked her in the arm when it was time to get off the bus. "Don't do that," Amanda snapped. "I'll get a bruise." Which made her think of something else.

"Do these kids at Harmony House get into physical fights?" she asked nervously. She took the plugs out of her ears.

Jenna shrugged. "The resident assistants break up the fights."

That wasn't much comfort.

"How long does it take for you to get into someone?" Jenna asked.

"That depends," Amanda replied. "If I feel really sorry for someone, if someone's super-pitiful, it can happen pretty quickly."

Jenna looked at her curiously. "You were Sarah for a while, weren't you? How did you make that happen? There's nothing pitiful about Sarah."

Amanda looked at her scornfully. "Are you kidding? She's a goody-goody. I don't think she knows what fun means. She dresses like a ten-year-old. And have you ever seen her with a boy?"

Jenna met Amanda's scorn with her own scorn. "So what?"

Amanda knew Jenna would never understand, so she didn't even try to explain. "I don't think it will be very difficult for me to take over someone at Harmony House. Considering the kind of people who end up there . . ." She gave Jenna a meaningful look, but Jenna didn't catch it. She was staring at someone across the street.

"Look at that girl," Jenna said.

Amanda gave her a quick once-over. She seemed to be in her mid-teens, average height, with long blond hair and a backpack hanging from her shoulders. What Amanda found most interesting about her were her jeans. She recognized the super-skinny, washed-out style immediately—she'd been thinking about them ever since she saw them in *Seventeen*, and she was waiting for them to show up in one of the local boutiques. Where had that girl found them?

But surely that wasn't what interested Jenna. "What about her?" Amanda asked.

"She's hitchhiking!"

Sure enough, Amanda saw the girl stick out her thumb as a car passed. "That's dangerous."

"No kidding," Jenna said. "She shouldn't get into a car with a stranger."

Amanda shrugged. "Maybe someone nice will pick her up."

Jenna shook her head. "Most people don't stop for hitchhikers. I mean, the hitchhiker could end up being a carjacker or something. It's dangerous for both of them."

"Someone's pulling over for her," Amanda said.

Jenna stared at the driver. Then, under her breath, she swore.

"What's the matter?" Amanda asked.

"I'm getting his thoughts. He thinks she looks hot . . . I don't think he just wants to give her a ride."

From what Amanda could see, the guy in the car looked pretty ordinary, but of course that didn't mean anything. She'd seen enough photos of criminals to know that they could look like perfectly nice people.

Both girls watched as the hitchhiker ambled toward the car.

"We gotta stop her," Jenna declared.

There was no way they could get across the busy street before the girl reached the car. Then Amanda had an idea.

"Wait, I think I can do something." She stared at the hitchhiker. *You stupid idiot, what are you doing?* . . . No, that was scorn, not pity. She tried again.

You poor thing, you have no idea what kind of danger you're in, you're going to suffer . . . Pity for the girl swept over her. She was getting closer to the car now, she was in big trouble . . .

It was a pretty new car, and she recognized the brand from the name on the back fender. The driver wasn't from around there—she could tell by the words on the license plate. She saw all this very clearly because she was there, close enough to touch the car. She had become the hitchhiker.

A man leaned out the window on the driver's side. "Need a ride, honey?"

Amanda-Hitchhiker glared at him grimly. "No, thank you. And I've seen your license plate number, so don't even think about trying to pick up anyone else, because I'm going to—"

She wasn't able to complete her threat. The car sped away.

Well, at least that part of the mission was successful. Now for the next part. Could she get back into herself without too much difficulty?

She looked back to the other side of the road, where Jenna and Other-Amanda were standing, and concentrated on the figure that looked like her.

Me—that's me. She closed her eyes and chanted the words over and over. She visualized herself as she really was, imprinting the image on her mind. And when she opened her eyes, she was thrilled. It worked! She was back in her own body and feeling totally normal. Amazing! She was getting really good at this—she was in complete control of her gift. Or maybe this experience was just a fluke and it wouldn't be as easy next time. Even so, clearly, she'd made real progress.

Not that she really cared, she reminded herself. She was more interested in removing the gift than improving it. But still, at least now she'd feel more confident about taking over someone at Harmony House.

Naturally, there wasn't a word of congratulations from Jenna. She was already halfway across the street, making her way to where the hitchhiker stood. Amanda followed her.

The hitchhiker wore a dazed expression.

"You okay?" Jenna asked.

"I feel a little dizzy," the blond-haired girl murmured. She blinked a couple of times. "Who are you? What happened to my ride?"

"He took off," Jenna said. "You lucked out."

The girl looked at her blankly. "Huh?"

Amanda wasn't about to let Jenna get the credit for this. "Do you have any idea how dangerous hitchhiking is? Didn't your mother ever tell you never to get into a car with a stranger?"

"I don't take advice from *her*," the girl declared. "She just took off with her boyfriend—she doesn't care about me."

441

That was kind of sad, Amanda thought. She caught herself before she could feel too sorry for the girl. She didn't want to be her again, even if she did have the jeans Amanda craved. "Where are you going?"

"I'm supposed to be spending the week at my dad's."

"You think he'd want you to be hitchhiking?" Jenna asked.

The girl grinned. "Actually, he sent me money to take a taxi. But I spent it on these jeans."

"I can't blame you," Amanda said. "They're fantastic, I love the stitching."

Jenna shot her a withering look. "That was really stupid. You have to take a taxi the rest of the way. I'm sure you can hail one here."

"Glad to," the girl replied. "Only I don't have any money to pay for one."

Jenna fished around in her pocket. "I've got two bucks." She turned to Amanda. "What about you?"

Reluctantly, Amanda took out her wallet. Looking inside, she said, "Five dollars."

Jenna peered into the wallet. "You've got a ten." She pulled it out.

"Hey!" Amanda cried in outrage.

Jenna stepped out in the street and waved her hand in the air. A taxi pulled up, and a moment later the hitchhiker was safely on her way to her father's.

"I can't believe you stole my money!" Amanda exclaimed.

Jenna just shrugged, but she looked at Amanda with actual interest. "It's funny. I always thought your gift was pretty worthless, but you might have just saved that girl's life."

It was Amanda's turn to shrug, but Jenna had a point. And this would make a very good story to tell Ken. It would certainly top any story Nina might be telling him right now.

Harmony House was just around the next corner. Together the girls went up the driveway and through the wide double doors into the reception area. Amanda had expected to see a room full of lowlife teens, but with the exception of a woman behind a desk, the area was vacant.

"There's no one here," Amanda murmured.

Jenna nodded toward some chairs. "We'll hang around—someone will show up. They get new admissions every day."

But the receptionist was watching them, and before they could sit down, she spoke. "Can I help you girls?"

"We're just waiting for someone," Jenna replied.

"Who?"

Jenna opened her mouth but nothing came out. Amanda looked around. A handsome young uniformed man was coming out of one of the doors that led into the institution.

"Him," she said.

The receptionist looked in the direction Amanda was pointing. "Officer Fisher? These girls want to see you."

The man looked in their direction and smiled. "Jenna!"

Jenna didn't smile back. "Hello. I, uh, I was just visiting someone. I have to go now." And before Amanda's astonished eyes, she hurried out of the building.

"I guess she didn't really want to see me," the man sighed. "Hi, I'm Jack Fisher, the police representative to Harmony House."

Now Amanda understood. Jenna didn't like cops. Too many nasty memories from her bad-girl days.

"I'm Amanda Beeson."

"Are you a friend of Jenna's?"

No, Amanda wanted to shout. But she withheld her instinctive response. "Um, kind of."

"And I presume you didn't come to see me." He smiled as he spoke, which made Amanda relax. But she still had to come up with a reason for being there.

"We, um, came to see a classmate. I guess—I guess Jenna must have remembered another appointment or something."

444

"Who are you here to see?"

"Carter Street."

Jack Fisher's forehead puckered. "Carter Street . . . Oh, yes. I don't think he's permitted to have visitors yet."

Amanda pretended that this was news to her. "Oh, that's too bad. How's he doing?"

"I don't really know," the man said apologetically. "I haven't had much to do with him."

Amanda nodded. "Well . . ." No one had come into the area for admission, and she wasn't about to sit around all day for nothing. "I guess I'll go then."

"Hang on a minute. Let me see if I can put you in touch with someone who's working with your friend. What was your name again?"

"Amanda Beeson."

Jack Fisher went over to the receptionist's desk. "Could you check and see if Doctor Paley is available for a moment? One of Carter Street's classmates is here."

The receptionist picked up a phone and made a call. A moment later the police officer returned to Amanda.

"Doctor Paley's coming out to see you. I have to go now. It was nice to meet you, Amanda."

"Nice to meet you," Amanda echoed. She sank down in a chair and mentally cursed Jenna for getting her into this business. What was she going to say to this

Dr. Paley?

A plump, balding man in a white coat came into the reception room. Since Amanda was the only person waiting, he strode toward her with a smile.

"Amanda?"

Amanda forced a smile. "Hello."

"I'm Doctor Paley. Are you from Carter's class?"

Amanda nodded. "How is Carter doing?"

"He's making progress. I can't tell you very much, of course. Do you know what doctor-patient confidentiality means?"

"I'm not sure," Amanda replied.

"It means that everything Carter says or does is just between him and me. Everything's completely private. I can't talk about him, not to you, not to anyone."

Amanda shrugged. "Okay." She wondered why the doctor was telling her this. It wasn't like she was bugging him for information.

"Madame has told me a little about your special class," Dr. Paley went on. "You're each quite unique."

Amanda hated talking about the class. She wanted to get out of there. But she couldn't be rude.

"Yes, I guess so."

He smiled. "Don't worry, I'm not going to ask you about your gift. I know it's not easy for any of you, though.

446

Having any kind of special talent can be difficult to live with. I bet sometimes you hate being gifted."

No kidding, Amanda thought. She couldn't help smiling.

"I just want to let you know, Amanda, that I'm always available to talk with you about it. And, of course, anything we discussed would be kept completely private, just between us. I wouldn't even tell Madame, if you didn't want me to."

"Really?"

He nodded. "Call me anytime, or stop by. Okay?"

"Okay," she replied.

He left her, and Amanda went out of the building. The doctor was nice, she thought. And Madame said he could be trusted.

Maybe this adventure hadn't gone according to plan, but she'd come away with something to think about.

447

Chapter Nine

D R. PALEY MUST HAVE canceled all his other appointments that day. He brought in sandwiches for himself and Paul, and then it was back to the videotape. The doctor left him in the room to watch it alone.

"So you left your home as a gerbil and became a boy again," the doctor was saying. "Why did you decide to switch back to your real shape?"

"I don't know," the boy on the screen replied. "It just happened. One minute I was a gerbil, and then I was a boy."

"Interesting," Dr. Paley murmured. And even though he was off camera and Paul couldn't see him on the screen, he had the feeling the doctor was making notes. "And then what happened?"

"I walked. But I was so hungry . . . I went by a construction site, and some workers were outside eating lunches. There was an open lunch box, and I saw a sandwich inside. No one was looking so I took it. I had a bite, but then this man saw me. And he hit me."

Watching, Paul saw himself flinch, as if he could still feel the blow.

"And then . . . ?" the doctor's voice prompted.

"I ran. He chased me, but he didn't catch me." He paused. "I think maybe I turned into something that could run faster than me. Yeah . . . I was a squirrel for a while. Then I was me again, and I was cold. I saw a store, and there was a coat in the window. I went inside . . ." The boy in the video began to shake.

"What happened?" Dr. Paley asked.

"I tried to take the coat. A man—he started to yell at me. Then he took out a gun. He was going to kill me, just like those men killed my parents. I was really scared. But then I turned into a rat and got away."

"Where did you go next?"

"I found some trash cans. There was food on top of the garbage. I ate some of it. Someone saw me. He threw something at me . . . I think it was a brick. I jumped off the trash can and turned back into myself. There was a grate in the sidewalk behind the trash cans, and it was a little warmer there. I must have fallen asleep. A policeman woke me up."

"Yes, I have the police notes here," Dr. Paley said. "The officer reported that you didn't respond verbally to his questions, but that you obeyed his directions when he told you to get up and come with him. He took you to the police station, where you were given something to eat."

Paul saw a twitch of the lips on his face, almost as if he'd wanted to smile. "A ham sandwich. A bag of potato chips. Two cookies—chocolate chip."

Dr. Paley continued. "The police were unable to identify you. You didn't match any descriptions of missing persons. A representative from social services took you to a youth shelter. Her notes are almost identical to the police officer's notes. You didn't communicate at all, but you followed her directions. At the youth shelter, you were examined by doctors and psychologists. It was determined that you were in some sort of state of shock and that you'd eventually recover. You were then assigned to a foster family—a Mr. and Mrs. Granger, who were already sheltering two foster boys. Is that correct?"

"Yes," Paul said.

"Have you shapeshifted while living with the Grangers?"

"No."

"Why not?"

"I'm not afraid of them. And they might not feed me if I were a rat or a squirrel."

"The Grangers . . . Were they kind to you?"

"Yes."

"They didn't hit you, or yell at you, or threaten you in any way?"

"No."

"But you didn't speak to them, either. Or to the other boys in the house. Why is that, Paul?"

"I couldn't. I was turned off."

As he watched the video, Paul realized that the real Dr. Paley had returned to the room, and he must have heard that last part. He picked up the remote control. "Turned off like this?" he asked, and the screen went blank.

Paul tried to say "yes," but it was too much effort. He simply nodded.

Dr. Paley pulled his chair around to face Paul. "I think I understand, Paul," he said quietly. "It was easier to just stop—stop *being*. To be a thing instead of a person. Am I right?"

Paul nodded again.

Dr. Paley looked at his watch. "That's enough for now, Paul. Why don't you go out into the garden for a while? I think you could use a little fresh air. Then we'll watch more of the video."

Paul left the office and went downstairs. What the people here called "the garden" wasn't really a garden— at least, there weren't any flowers or plants. It was just a paved outdoor area with a couple of benches and some

451

lawn chairs, and it was surrounded by high wire fences. But the weather was warm, no one else was around, and the lawn chair was more comfortable than the hard chair in Dr. Paley's office. Paul sat back, closed his eyes, and pondered what he'd remembered. He had a lot to think about.

"Hey, get up."

Paul opened his eyes. Three teenage boys, older and bigger than him, had arrived in the garden. Two of them had plopped down in the other two chairs, and the third seemed to want the chair Paul occupied.

"I said, get up!" the boy barked.

Paul did as he was told. He rose from the chair. The boy pushed him aside and sat down.

"Now beat it."

Automatically, Paul turned to leave. But then something inside him made him stop. It was nice out there, the sun was shining, he didn't want to go back to his little room. He didn't want to leave the garden. Why had he just given up his chair so easily? Because the other boy was bigger, and Paul was afraid of him?

"Beat it!" the boy yelled. "Get outta here!"

And a realization hit Paul hard. He didn't have to do what he was told to do. He didn't have to be afraid. Because he had a gift. And now was the time to use it.

He allowed a soft, shivery sensation to engulf him. A moment later a shriek went up from the boys as a huge wolf took over the space where Paul had been standing. The animal opened its mouth, baring large, sharp teeth, and let out a howl. The three boys fled the scene and ran back into the building.

A window flew open. "Omigod!" someone screamed. "Quick, call animal control! There's a wolf in the garden!"

Paul let out another howl, louder this time. It felt wonderful, like a cry of freedom. He ran around the garden, leaping over the chairs and benches. Now more people were looking out the windows and screaming.

"Get the security guard," someone yelled. "He's got a gun!"

Paul froze. He ducked around to the side of the garden, where no one could see him. And he turned back into a boy.

When the security guard appeared, all he saw was a small, thin boy sitting on a lawn chair.

"Did you see a wolf?" the guard asked.

Paul shook his head. Then he got up and went back into the building.

CHAPTER TEN

IN THE MEADOWBROOK MIDDLE School cafeteria, it was traditional for boys to sit with boys and girls to sit with girls. Even if they were friends, even if they were going together, boys and girls separated at lunch. It wasn't a law, it wasn't school policy—that's just the way it was.

But this was an opportunity to talk to Ken, and Amanda was going to have to break the unwritten rule. So when she picked up her tray she didn't go directly to her usual table, where Nina and her other friends were sitting. She waited until Ken emerged from the line.

"I have to tell you about Harmony House," she said.

He didn't ask why the story couldn't wait for class. His eyes searched the room. "There's a table."

Amanda knew people were looking at them as they sat down at the empty table together, and she knew that she'd have to answer for this later, but it was unavoidable. She was impressed that Ken didn't even look embarrassed. He really was too cool for words.

"What happened?" he asked. "Did you get inside?"

Amanda shook her head. "There wasn't anyone checking in. But I talked to Doctor Paley."

"About Carter?"

"Not really." She reported the conversation she'd had with the doctor. "I got this feeling he knows all about the kind of gifts we have. And I think he can help us."

"Help us do what?"

She hesitated. She really had no proof of what she was about to say. But she couldn't help herself. It seemed like a possibility, and Ken would be just as interested as she was.

"Help us lose our gifts."

Ken's eyebrows shot up. "You really think so?"

"He's a doctor, Ken. I bet he knows more about our conditions than Madame does."

"Wow," Ken breathed. "Wouldn't that be something . . ." His eyes shifted. "Hi, Nina."

"Hi, Ken. Amanda, Britney's got a big problem. We need you!"

Amanda gritted her teeth. What could she do? Ken might think she was selfish if she didn't rush to the aid of her friend.

"See you in class," Ken said. He picked up his tray and strolled over to a table where some of his friends were sitting. Amanda took her tray back to her usual table, where Britney, Sophie, and Katie were sitting.

Nina hadn't been lying. Poor Britney looked like she was on the verge of tears.

"He hasn't even spoken to me today," she whimpered. "He acts like I'm not even there."

"Who are you talking about?" Amanda asked.

Sophie answered for her. "Tommy Clerk, of course."

Amanda's brow furrowed. "Tommy Clerk?" She looked at the others. "Why is she crying over him?"

Katie frowned at her. "Amanda, where have you been? Britney's been talking about Tommy for weeks!"

Amanda recovered a dim memory of Britney's latest crush. "Oh yeah, right. Sorry, Britney, I forgot."

Real tears began to flow. "How could you forget?" Britney wailed softly. "I'm in *love* with him!"

It was on the tip of Amanda's tongue to remind her that she'd been in and out of love with half a dozen boys since September, but she managed to keep this to herself. Britney looked up to her, the way Nina used to, and Amanda didn't need any more frenemies. She had to be sympathetic and offer some advice.

"Tell me what happened," she ordered Britney. At the same time, she handed her a tissue.

Britney blew her nose. "He always goes to his locker

just before lunch. So I went by there, and I said 'hi.'"

"And then?"

"He said 'hi.'" Fresh tears began to flow. "And that was all! He closed his locker and walked away!"

"Boys can be so cruel," Katie muttered. "Forget about him, Brit. You can do better."

"But I want Tommy!" Britney sobbed. She appealed to Amanda. "What should I do?"

The other girls, even Nina, looked at Amanda and waited expectantly for the Queen Bee to speak. Amanda's status was on the line, and she needed to show them she was still in charge of the clique.

"You're not flirting, that's the problem," she told Britney firmly. "Saying 'hi' isn't enough. You have to come on a little stronger."

Nina raised her eyebrows. "But you're always saying we should play hard to get. You said boys don't like girls who show how they feel."

Amanda met Nina's doubtful eyes. "Up to a point," she declared. "Tommy might think Britney's out of his league. He could be afraid to speak to her. Boys can be insecure, you know."

Britney gazed at her in amazement. "Really?"

"Absolutely," Amanda said. "You should go over to his table right now. Don't sit down, just ask him something.

You've got a class with him, don't you?"

"Biology."

"Okay. Say something about that, ask him something."

"Something like what?"

"It doesn't matter! Just make sure you make eye contact, and when you walk away, look back and give him a little smile. Not too big. Like this." Amanda demonstrated her well-practiced "I'm just a little bit into you" smile.

"And then what?" Britney wanted to know.

"Then it's his turn. Make sure you run into him after the last bell, and I bet he'll ask you if you want to hang out."

"You really think that will work?" Nina asked skeptically.

"Of course it will," Amanda snapped. But even as she spoke, she wasn't really all that sure. Britney had never been able to flirt easily. If she went over to speak to Tommy now, she'd probably start giggling and fumbling with her words. And if Amanda wanted her crew to respect her, she had to show that her advice would result in success for Britney.

There was only one way to guarantee this. As Sophie, Katie, and Nina debated Amanda's proposal, Amanda kept her eyes fixed on Britney. *Poor Britney, so shy, she can be really pathetic when it comes to boys . . .*

That was all it took. In less than a second, Amanda was

458

looking across the table at Other-Amanda. She had taken over Britney's body.

She rose from the table, turned, and searched the cafeteria for Tommy Clerk. She spotted him at a table with some other guys and sauntered over.

She acted as if she was just walking past the table and then stopped, as if an idea had struck her. "Tommy . . ."

The boy looked up. "Yeah?"

"Do you understand that stuff about plants? What's it called—photo, photo something."

"Photosynthesis?" Tommy asked.

"Yeah, that. Do you know what it is?"

"It's the process when plants turn carbon dioxide and water into carbohydrates and oxygen."

Amanda-Britney had no idea what he was talking about, but this sounded good. "Oh, okay. Thanks!" She turned as if to walk away, and then looked back, aiming her special smile at Tommy. She hoped the smile looked as flirtatious on Britney's face as it did on her own. From the way Tommy's eyes widened, she had a feeling it did.

She sashayed back to her own table, sat down, and fixed her gaze on Other-Amanda. Almost instantly, she found herself back in her own body.

"That was good, Britney!" she exclaimed.

Britney seemed dazed. "Huh?"

"What you just did!"

Britney looked at her blankly. "What did I do?"

"Britney!" Katie exclaimed. "You talked to Tommy!"

"I did?"

Amanda turned to the others and rolled her eyes. "Can you believe her? She must have been so nervous, she blanked out!"

The girls grinned knowingly, and Amanda wasn't surprised when even Britney bought this.

Britney had never been the sharpest crayon in the box.

Chapter Eleven

"YOU TURNED INTO A wolf outside just now, didn't you, Paul?"

Paul nodded.

"Why?"

Paul looked at him helplessly. He wanted to tell Dr. Paley, but the words just wouldn't come.

"Were there other people out in the garden?"

Paul nodded.

"Did they frighten you? Is that why you shapeshifted?" Dr. Paley smiled. "This makes perfect sense, Paul. Many of your fellow students developed their gifts as a response to something uncomfortable."

Paul had mixed feelings about this. He wasn't proud of the fact that he'd been afraid. But he liked being compared to his classmates, knowing he had this in common with them.

"Let's watch some more of your hypnosis video," Dr. Paley said, and he turned on the TV. Paul looked at

461

himself and listened to the off-screen doctor's voice.

"Let's talk about Serena, Paul."

Paul watched his own face contort on the screen. He looked like he was in pain.

"I don't want to talk about her."

Dr. Paley's voice was gentle but firm. "You must, Paul. You betrayed your classmates. It wasn't your fault—she put you under some kind of spell. But you need to face up to what you did. How did you first meet Serena?"

"Mister Jackson brought me to see her."

"Mister Jackson . . . Ah yes, the former principal of your school. Serena hypnotized you and asked you questions. Do you remember this?"

"Yes."

"What did she ask you?"

"She asked me about the gifted class. She asked questions about the students. She asked me what kind of gifts they have."

"And you told her?"

"Yes."

"But Madame had warned the class never to reveal their gifts, isn't that right?"

"Yes." Paul was clearly in great distress. "I didn't want to tell her. I wanted to keep our secret."

"It's all right, Paul," Dr. Paley said. "She probably gave you some kind of posthypnotic suggestion. You couldn't

462

stop yourself. And you were probably afraid of those people. For good reason, too. They were dangerous people. You have nothing to be ashamed about, Paul. Your classmates will forgive you."

The boy on the screen seemed to relax a little.

Dr. Paley hit the pause button and turned to Paul. "There's one thing that puzzles me, though, Paul. We were talking about your shapeshifting ability as a response to fear. If you were afraid of Serena, Mister Jackson, and the other people in that group, why didn't you shift? You could have become some kind of large animal. You could have attacked them. Or you could have become a small animal and escaped. Why didn't that happen, Paul? Why didn't you shift?"

Again, Paul could only look at him helplessly. This time, the doctor had no speculations to offer. "You're not sure. You probably don't even remember. Well, let's get back to the video."

But Paul knew perfectly well why he hadn't shifted when he was with those bad people. He didn't know then that he *could*. It was true that he'd shifted before, at home, when the bad guys shot his parents. But back when he was turned off, he didn't know he could do it on purpose—he didn't know that he had some control over this strange and mysterious gift.

But he knew now.

Chapter Twelve

I N THE GIFTED CLASS, Ken ran in at the last
minute so Amanda didn't get a chance to talk to him
before Madame called for everyone's attention.

But before Madame had even said "good afternoon,"
Ken's hand shot up. Madame looked at him in surprise.

"Yes, Ken?"

"Madame, could I ask the class something? There's
something I've been thinking about a lot lately."

"Of course, Ken. What's on your mind?"

His classmates turned to look at him.

Ken was clearly uncomfortable at being the center of
attention, but he persevered. "I want to know . . . If you
could get rid of your gift, would you? I mean, most of
you guys know how I don't like hearing these voices. And
I was just wondering if I was the only one who doesn't
like having a gift."

"It's not always comfortable having a gift, Ken," Madame
said.

"Yeah, yeah, I know that," Ken interrupted. "I'm sorry, Madame, but I'm not talking about getting used to the gift. I want to know if anyone else wants to get rid of their gift."

An uncomfortable silence fell over the room. Amanda hastened to break it. "I'd like to get rid of my gift. I know there's no way I can," she added hastily, "but if I could, I would."

"Sometimes I wish I didn't have my gift," Emily offered. "When I get these images of terrible things about to happen . . ." She shuddered.

"You just have to learn to control it," Jenna declared, "so you don't see the future unless you want to. That's what I do. I mean, if I had to hear everyone's thoughts all the time, I'd go crazy. But I'm okay with it now."

Tracey agreed. "It's like Madame says—we need to figure out ways to use our gifts well."

"That's right," Madame said.

"No," came a quiet voice from the back.

Everyone turned to look at Sarah.

"I'd give anything to lose my gift," Sarah said.

Amanda thought Madame looked very upset. The teacher's lips tightened, and she folded her arms across her chest. She seemed to be gathering her thoughts and choosing her next words carefully.

"Class . . . I want you to listen to me. I know there are

many times when your gifts may seem like burdens—or curses, even. But they're not, you know. Each one of your gifts is a blessing."

"Yeah, that's what I think," Charles said. "It makes my life a lot easier."

"It's not just that, Charles," Madame continued. "You were given these gifts for a reason, and we don't really know what that reason is. But they're not to be wished away! They have a purpose, and our goal is to discover the purpose. You're here to learn, not to give up."

"It's not like you have a choice, anyway," Martin commented. "You can't lose your gift."

"But if we *could*—" Ken began.

"No!" Madame interrupted, and Amanda was startled by the tone of her voice. This was unusual. She always let the students have their say. And her voice was almost shrill. "You can't! It would be like losing your heart—your brain. This gift is part of who you are. You must cherish it, even if you can't understand it! Ken, I know you care about people, and with your gift you can help them. Amanda . . ." She practically glared at her. "Amanda, if you could stop thinking about your gift as a personal inconvenience, maybe you could help people, too!"

Amanda couldn't remember ever hearing Madame sound so emotional. It was weird. And how dare she pick on Amanda like that! Strong, conflicting emotions filled her, and she didn't know which was stronger—her pity for Madame's distress or her anger at being singled out.

Pity must have been the stronger one, because suddenly she was looking at the class through Madame's eyes.

"Madame, are you okay?" Jenna asked.

Quickly, Amanda blocked her thoughts so Jenna couldn't read them. Not that Jenna would even try— Madame was an expert at blocking Jenna.

"I'm fine," she said. She glanced at Other-Amanda, who had taken out her makeup bag and was now examining her face in a mirror. Sometimes she wondered why others were so easily fooled by the robot version of herself. She wasn't *that* vain.

The whole class was watching her expectantly. Amanda-Madame pulled her shoulders back, held her head high, and hoped she was doing a good imitation of Madame's erect posture. It was time to have some fun!

"Now, class, we're going to test the level of control we have over our gifts. We will begin with Tracey. Tracey, make yourself invisible right now."

"Um, I can *try*," Tracey said. "It doesn't always work."

"Just do it!" Amanda-Madame snapped.

Tracey didn't seem very happy about the order, but she obediently closed her eyes and scrunched up her face, as if she was concentrating very hard. Seconds later, she vanished.

"Very good," Amanda-Madame pronounced. "Now come back."

Nothing happened.

Jenna spoke. "She doesn't have as much control coming back as she has disappearing."

"Obviously," Amanda-Madame said. "Emily . . . Look into the future and tell us when Tracey will reappear."

Emily stared at Tracey's empty desk for a moment. "Tracey will be back before the bell rings," she predicted.

"All right." The fake teacher turned to Charles. "Charles, we know you can make things move. I want to know how precise your gift is. Please move my desk six inches to the left."

Charles looked at the desk and shrugged. "Sure." The heavy wooden desk rose slightly and moved to the left.

"Does anyone have a ruler or measuring tape?" Amanda-Madame asked.

"I think there's a measuring tape in your top drawer," Emily said.

For a second, Amanda-Madame was confused and looked at the desk in which the robot was sitting. She recovered quickly. "Yes, of course, that's right." She went into the drawer of the teacher's desk and took out a measuring tape.

"Hmm . . . You seem to have only moved the desk four inches, Charles. You must improve."

"Two inches, big deal," Charles protested.

"Charles! We aim for perfection here!"

Charles shrank back in his wheelchair. "Yes, Madame," he murmured.

It was getting very hard for Amanda not to burst out laughing. This was fun!

"Now we'll test Jenna. Class, do not block her. Jenna, what is Ken thinking about right now?"

"Wait a minute," Ken said quickly, but Jenna was too fast for him. She grinned.

"He's thinking about Amanda."

Amanda could only hope her face didn't reveal the pleasure she felt. Fortunately, Tracey chose that moment to reappear and distracted the class's attention.

"I'm back," she announced unnecessarily.

Amanda-Madame frowned. "It took too long. You need to work on that."

"My prediction was correct," Emily pointed out.

"Yes, yes, very good." She moved on. "Martin, let's test your strength." She looked around the room. The heaviest thing was the desk, but they'd already used that. She needed something more original.

Inspiration didn't fail her. "Martin, pick up Sarah and

469

hold her over your head."

Martin was startled. "Really?"

"Yes," Amanda-Madame stated.

"That's not much of a test," Jenna protested. "Sarah's not very heavy."

Amanda-Madame looked at her sternly. "He can't just lift her, he has to hold her over his head. That would be impossible for a normal person his size."

Martin got up and went to the back of the room. Sarah watched him apprehensively as he approached her.

"Madame, is this really necessary?" she asked.

"Don't worry, Martin won't drop you," Amanda-Madame assured her.

Martin didn't look all that confident. He stood very still for a moment, as if he was summoning his gift. Then he lifted Sarah out of her chair. The whole class watched as he raised her higher and higher, until his arms were stretched out straight and she was way over his head.

Sarah had gone as stiff as a board, and she did not look happy. "Okay, he's done it," she said. "Put me down now, Martin."

Amanda-Madame shook her head. "Martin, don't put her down. Sarah, you have to *make* Martin put you down. Use your gift."

"No!" Sarah cried out.

Amanda-Madame pretended to be shocked. "Sarah, are you disobeying your teacher? Make Martin put you down, *now*!"

"No, no, I don't want to do that!"

"Wait a minute!" Jenna suddenly shouted. "I can read your mind! You're not Madame, you're Amanda!"

Amanda wanted to kick herself. She'd let her guard down. "I am not," she said, but the denial sounded feeble, even to her ears.

Martin placed Sarah back in her chair. "Sorry about that," he mumbled. But he looked at Amanda-Madame with admiration in his eyes. "That was pretty cool," he said.

Ken was grinning, too. Clearly, he wasn't too displeased with having had his thoughts revealed. And Charles was laughing. "Hey, before you let Madame come back, can you dismiss us early?"

"And don't give us any homework," Martin added.

"Amanda, you get out of Madame right now!" Jenna yelled.

"I'll leave her when I'm ready," Amanda retorted.

The voice from the back of the room was tremulous. "No, you'll leave her now," Sarah said.

Amanda felt something she'd never felt before. It was like her mind, her consciousness, her spirit was forcibly

471

pulled out of the body she'd taken over. And it hurt.

Then she was herself again, in her own body, in her own chair. She looked at Sarah in wonderment. "You did that."

Sarah didn't reply. She stared down at her desk, and her expression was grim. Amanda couldn't stop looking at her. She'd known about Sarah's gift, but now she'd felt it. It was so powerful. And for the first time she had a clue as to why the girl was so afraid to use it.

No one else was looking at Sarah, though. They were watching Madame. The teacher had put her hand to her head.

"Madame?" Tracey asked worriedly. "Do you feel okay?"

"Did I . . . Did I faint?" Madame asked.

"Yes," Amanda said quickly. Too quickly. Madame's eyes became steely, and they were fixed on Amanda.

"You took over my body."

Amanda opened her mouth to deny it, but no words came out. What was it about Madame that made it so hard to lie to her?

So she took the other route. "I'm sorry," she murmured. "I was fooling around, and . . . I'm sorry."

Madame's voice could have cut glass. "You will never, never do that again, Amanda. Do you understand?"

"Yes, Madame."

At least the teacher didn't go on and on about it. She gave them a reading assignment, the bell rang, and she dismissed them.

Amanda turned to Ken. "We have to talk," she said urgently. She glanced at the door, which someone had already opened. Nina wasn't there—not yet, at least. "And we have to talk *alone*."

Ken got the message. He got up and followed Amanda out. She led him down the corridor and into the first empty classroom they came to.

She knew there was a custodian who came around to make sure rooms were empty, so she didn't waste any time, even if it meant coming off as a little pushy.

"I don't care what Madame says," she declared flatly. "If someone like this Doctor Paley can get rid of our gifts, I'm totally up for it."

"Me, too," Ken agreed. "Though I have to say that was pretty funny, what you pulled back in class."

"I guess it was kind of mean, what I did to Sarah," she confessed.

"Not really," Ken said thoughtfully. "She needed a push. She has big problems dealing with her gift. She has to confront it sooner or later. I think you did her a good deed."

Amanda preened. "I just thought I'd have one last crazy fling before giving up this gift for good. Do you want a long last talk with any ghosts?"

Ken's smile faded.

"What's the matter?"

"I'm thinking about Jack."

"Oh." She knew who Ken was referring to. Jack Farrell had been Ken's best buddy, and he'd died in that accident on the field. His was the first voice from beyond the grave that Ken had heard. "You still talk to him?"

"Not that much," Ken admitted. "Not like before. I guess he's comfortable now, wherever he is. He doesn't need me like he used to."

"So if you lost your gift and Jack couldn't reach you anymore, that would be okay?"

"Yeah, I guess so."

She wished he sounded more sure of himself. "Just think about it, Ken. No more ghosts asking you to check on their grandsons or watch soap operas."

"And no more gifted class," Ken added.

"Exactly. We could be normal, Ken. Wouldn't that be nice?"

He looked at her and smiled. "Yeah. Really nice. But we don't know for sure if Doctor Paley can do this."

"No, not for sure," Amanda admitted. "But we can try. I feel like this is right for us. Don't you?"

"Yeah." Then he fell silent, but Amanda didn't mind at all, because he was looking deeply into her eyes.

The custodian came in. "Out," he said.

They left the room—and ran right into Britney.

"There you are!" Britney exclaimed. "Nina was looking for you. And so was I. Guess what? It worked!"

Amanda looked at her blankly. "What worked?"

"What you made me do at lunch. Tommy just asked me to meet him at the mall! It happened, just like you said it would."

"Great," Amanda replied.

"It's funny, though," Britney went on. "I still can't remember actually talking to him in the cafeteria."

"You were nervous," Amanda told her.

Britney grinned. "I guess. But I'm not nervous now! I gotta go and meet Tommy. I'll call you tonight and tell you what happened."

She took off, and Ken turned to Amanda. "You did it, didn't you? You took over her body and came on to Tommy."

Amanda lowered her eyes modestly. "I kind of had to. She'd never do it on her own."

Ken smiled. "That was nice of you."

She loved the way he was looking at her. It occurred to her that she had a connection with him that Nina could never have. And when they lost their gifts together . . . it would link them in a way that could last forever.

475

Chapter Thirteen

PAUL CARTER WAS DREAMING, but not about a boy or a TV. He was dreaming about animals. He dreamed about an elephant, a tiger, a monkey. And they were all him.

He was hanging from the limb of a tree and swinging his legs. He leaped from branch to branch, and he could actually feel the motion. But then bad men approached, and they were carrying guns.

So he dropped from the tree and became an elephant. With his trunk, he swept the men off the ground and flung them far, far away. And then he became a cat, a soft, fuzzy cat, curled on someone's lap, being petted . . . That felt really nice. And then he was a lion, running for the pure pleasure of running, happy and unafraid. Who could hurt the king of the jungle?

When he woke up on Thursday morning, something struck him. For the first time in a long, long time, he didn't feel frightened. And he didn't go immediately into his morning routine of watering the plant, brushing his teeth, getting dressed. He stayed in his bed and had some wide-awake dreams.

He pictured himself back at Meadowbrook Middle School, in his gifted class. Charles talked about moving things with his mind. Jenna reported on what someone else was thinking. Emily predicted something that was going to happen.

And Carter—no, *Paul* Carter—told them how he'd been a bird that morning. How he'd flown to school. How he was planning to fly to Mexico . . .

What would it be like, to actually have a story to tell? All these months, he'd listened to tales of the others' gifts. He always felt like an outsider, like he wasn't supposed to be there. He'd been stuck in the class only because nobody knew what to do with him.

But now he could belong in the class. He could be part of the group. He was gifted, too.

Suddenly, he wanted to test his gift. He got out of bed and considered the possibilities. The first image that came to mind was the pet he always wanted.

He could feel it, the changes in his body, but it didn't hurt at all. And now he was a dog, a big dog. A German shepherd. He leaped back up on the bed so he could see himself in the mirror over the sink. He was beautiful! And in joy, he opened his mouth and let out a howl.

Immediately, there was a pounding on his door. "What's going on in there? Open this door!"

Paul shifted back. He went to the door and opened it. An angry resident assistant stood outside.

"Do you have a dog in here?"

Paul shook his head.

The guy looked at him suspiciously and pushed him aside. *I could become a snake and bite him*, Paul thought. He didn't—but it was nice knowing he could.

The resident assistant went to Paul's closet and looked inside. Then he bent down and checked under the bed. Finally he gave up, and with one last dark look at Paul, he left.

Paul suddenly realized that his face felt funny, like it was twitching or something. He went to the mirror, looked at his reflection, and realized why. He was smiling.

A glance at the clock on the wall told him he was late. Quickly, he watered the plant, washed his face, and got dressed.

At breakfast, he didn't join in any conversations, but he found himself listening and paying more attention to the others at his table. One of the older boys was bragging about the act that had sent him to Harmony House.

"So this lady is holding her purse really tightly, and I figure there's gotta be a reason. She's carrying something valuable. So I come up from behind and tap her on the shoulder. 'Excuse me,' I say, real polite and smiling, 'could you tell me where the First National Bank is?' She starts to think, and I grab the purse and take off. She's like so freaked out, I'm halfway around the corner before she even starts yelling!"

Paul imagined himself on the street and watching the event occur. What would he have done? If the thief was a fast runner, Paul could have become a cheetah. Wasn't that the fastest animal? Or he could shift into a tiger, pounce on the thief, take the purse in his teeth, and bring it back to the lady.

He felt himself smiling again. It was exciting, thinking about all the possibilities. He noticed that people at the table were looking at him oddly. Had he shifted without even trying? No, he decided, it was probably because they'd never seen him smile before.

He was still smiling when he arrived at Dr. Paley's office. Dr. Paley smiled back at him.

"I can see you're feeling well, Paul. But if I ask, 'How are you?' would you be able to answer me?"

It took a lot of effort and a few false tries, but finally Paul managed to murmur something that sounded pretty close to "fine."

Dr. Paley nodded with approval. "It's going to take a while before you'll be able to speak normally when fully conscious. You'll have to practice. I'm going to see if I can arrange for a speech therapist to work with you."

Paul was pleased. He wanted to be able to speak easily. When he was allowed to go back to school, he wanted to tell his classmates how he'd turned into a dog that morning and alarmed the resident assistant. He remembered Charles telling a funny story once, about how he teased his brother by moving his chair just as he was about to sit down. People laughed . . .

Madame had scolded him, though. She'd said Charles shouldn't use his gift for silly reasons. Paul would have to start seriously listening to what Madame said now. But maybe it was okay, just once in a while, to do something silly with a gift . . .

"Are you thinking about your gift?" Dr. Paley asked.

Paul nodded.

"It must be pretty shocking to suddenly realize how much power you have," the doctor said.

Paul nodded again, though *shocking* didn't seem to be the right word to describe his reaction. Maybe at first, when he saw himself as a rabbit on the TV screen. Now he was more . . . *interested*.

"These kinds of gifts . . . They can be frightening," the doctor continued. "You must have heard your classmates talk about that."

Paul thought back to the discussions in the gifted class. Yes, some people talked about being scared. Amanda worried that she might get stuck in the body of someone she'd taken over. Sarah . . . She was definitely scared, she wouldn't even talk about her gift.

"You know, with your gift you could become very dangerous."

Paul could see how that could happen. Animals can hurt people. Of course *people* could hurt people, too. But if you were a good person—or a good animal—you wouldn't do that. Madame talked a lot about controlling the gifts . . . He'd have to pay attention to her so he could learn how to use his gift well.

"Madame believes that most of your classmates developed their gifts as a reaction to something. Or perhaps as a compensation. They developed these gifts because they needed them to survive. Martin was small and weak. People teased him, and he dealt with this by becoming unnaturally strong. Charles felt trapped in his wheelchair and unable to do things on his own. So his mind became so strong that he could move objects with it. As for you . . ."

The doctor leaned back in his chair and studied Paul.

"Your gift emerged through fear. Are you still afraid, Paul?"

Paul worked at forming the word, and he was pleased

that it came out almost clearly. "No."

"Good!" Dr. Paley said. "Then perhaps you don't really need your gift. The goal, Paul, is to become normal. For example, Madame tells me that Martin has been growing, and he's just about reached a normal height and weight. I believe that when his subconscious accepts the fact that he doesn't need superstrength to fight his battles, he may naturally lose his gift."

That made sense to Paul.

"Madame told me about . . ." he studied some papers on his desk. ". . . Emily. She predicts the future, right? And do you know when she discovered this gift?"

The word that came from Paul's mouth sounded like "fahzer," but Dr. Paley understood.

"That's right. Her father was killed in an accident, and Emily claims to have seen it in her head before it happened. But my theory is that Emily subconsciously created that memory after the fact. And this triggered an actual ability to predict the future." He gazed up at the ceiling. "Is this a good thing? I don't think so. It could have grave consequences if Emily's visions become clearer and more accurate. This could change the course of history. Emily doesn't need this gift. I don't think any of you really need your gifts."

Paul didn't agree. He got some words out. "Charles

. . . chair." They sounded like "Shar" and "sheer," but Dr. Paley got the picture.

"You're saying Charles needs his gift because it's not likely that he'll ever be out of a wheelchair. But most people in wheelchairs don't have supernatural gifts, Paul, and they function perfectly well." He smiled. "Now, I don't know Charles personally, but I wonder if perhaps his gift emerged simply because he's too lazy to learn how to do things on his own. I do believe you'd all survive very well without your gifts. You'd probably be happier."

Paul wasn't so sure about that. *Happy* . . . It wasn't a word he normally associated with himself. But since discovering his gift, he might be tempted to call himself happy.

Dr. Paley looked at his watch. "That will be all for today, Paul." He rose and opened the door. Halfway out, Paul remembered something he wanted to ask the doctor. When would he be able to leave Harmony House? But before he could formulate words, the phone on the secretary's desk rang.

"Doctor Paley's office. Yes, send them in." She hung up the phone. "Ken Preston and Amanda Beeson have arrived for their appointment."

"Good," Dr. Paley said. "I'll see you tomorrow, Paul."

But Paul was curious. Why were two of his classmates coming to see Dr. Paley? Did it have something to do with what the doctor was just talking to him about?

Before, Paul wouldn't have cared about Ken and Amanda. But now that he was one of them . . .

The secretary had her back to him. Paul shifted. And fortunately, Dr. Paley was studying his notes—so he didn't notice the cockroach that crawled under his desk.

Chapter Fourteen

THE SECRETARY TOLD KEN and Amanda that Dr. Paley was expecting them. Sure enough, when they entered the inner office, the plump, balding man in the white coat was standing by his desk and smiling.

"Come in, Amanda. And you must be Ken. Have a seat."

Amanda surveyed the room, and what she saw was reassuring. It looked like any doctor's office, with an examining table, a cabinet holding medical equipment, and a tall weighing scale. It was all spotlessly clean, even the floor, so she felt okay about dropping her purse there when she sat down.

"So, are you kids cutting class?" the doctor asked jovially.

"We have excuses," Amanda assured him. She didn't want him thinking she and Ken were the kind of people who were residents of Harmony House. "I told the school secretary we had doctors' appointments."

"Which is absolutely true," Dr. Paley said. He indicated a framed diploma on the wall behind his desk. "I *am* a doctor."

Amanda had no doubts about that. If Madame trusted this man, he had to be what he said he was. Madame was no fool.

"Now, tell me what I can do for you."

Amanda looked at Ken.

"You go first," Ken said.

She faced the doctor. "When I saw you yesterday, you said you might be able to help us. And . . . and we need help."

"Help with what?" Dr. Paley asked.

Amanda glanced at Ken again. Ken nodded, clearly encouraging her to go on.

"Help us to get rid of these gifts."

"Ah." The doctor opened a folder and turned some pages. "Now, let me see. Amanda, you're suffering from psycho-transitional corporeality—you're a 'body snatcher,' is that correct?"

Amanda grimaced. "That makes me sound like a criminal."

Dr. Paley smiled. "It's just the term that's used for what you're capable of doing. You can inhabit the consciousness of others."

"It started when I was a little kid. I saw a woman begging

486

on a street, and I felt sorry for her. And then, suddenly, I *was* her."

"You didn't *try* to become her?"

"No! Who wants to be some poor, dirty beggar? It just happened, I couldn't do anything about it. I was looking through her eyes. I could even see myself, staring at her. Me. Whatever."

Dr. Paley regarded her thoughtfully. "You were in two places at once?"

"Not exactly," Amanda told him. "It wasn't like I could feel myself being me. But the girl . . . She acted like me, she talked like me. She wasn't like, *dead*, or a zombie. Every time this happens to me, when I can see myself, I'm acting like me. Does that make sense?" She looked at Ken for support.

"It's sort of like she has a clone," Ken offered. "Or she's a robot that's been programmed to be her."

"I see," Dr. Paley said, making some notes. "And you say this has happened other times?"

Amanda nodded. She described the time she became Tracey, back when Tracey was a major nerd and loser. She told him about the young woman she'd met at a séance, who was depressed because her mother had died. She didn't mention the time she'd become Ken. They never talked about that—it was just too creepy.

487

"And this happens because you feel sorry for the people. Can you stop it from happening?"

"Sometimes," Amanda said. "If I try really hard, I can think of them as absurd instead of pitiful."

Dr. Paley understood. "You treat them with scorn instead of pity."

"I guess. Sort of. Just so I don't, you know, body-snatch."

Ken jumped in. "That's how she got her reputation. Some kids call her the Queen of Mean."

Amanda was taken aback. "Where did you hear that?" she asked him.

"Nina told me."

Amanda gritted her teeth. That figured.

"Does this ever happen if you *want* to be someone else?" Dr. Paley asked.

"No, I like being me. Why would I want to be someone pitiful?" And then she realized she had an opportunity to salvage her reputation for Ken's sake. "Actually, I did do it on purpose recently. To save someone."

"What happened?" Ken and the doctor asked simultaneously.

Amanda preened. It was cool, having all this attention and a story to tell that would make her look like a really nice person.

She told the story of the hitchhiker. Ken was totally

blown away.

"Wow! You might have saved that girl's life!"

Amanda smiled modestly. "Yes, that's what Jenna said."

But Dr. Paley didn't look very impressed. "And you might have found yourself being abducted in the hitchhiker's place."

Amanda stopped smiling. "I didn't think of that," she admitted.

"Your gift has dangerous implications," Dr. Paley noted. "Ken, what about your gift? How do you feel about it?"

"It's mainly annoying," Ken said. He explained to the doctor how it all began, when he collided with his best friend Jack on the playing field. "It wasn't so bad when it was just Jack contacting me. But then I started hearing from all these other dead people. Some of them just wanted to talk, but a lot of them asked me to do favors for them."

"And did you do these favors?"

"Once in a while," Ken said. "Like, I've been watching a soap opera so I can tell this old lady what's happening on it. But sometimes, people want me to get involved in their lives. This one guy, he wanted me to contact his granddaughter and tell her that her boyfriend was no good. I said no." He paused. "I kind of felt bad about it, though."

"So your gift doesn't bring you any pleasure," Dr. Paley commented.

Ken shook his head. Amanda noticed he didn't mention the time he was able to save a young boy's impoverished family by talking to the boy's late father and finding out where the man had left a winning lottery ticket. She couldn't blame him for not telling the doctor. One decent experience didn't make up for a zillion obnoxious ones.

"Your gift could be dangerous, too," Dr. Paley told Ken.

"How?" Ken asked.

"You might feel very sympathetic to someone's plight and get involved in something that could harm you."

Ken considered this. "Yeah, I guess that could happen."

Dr. Paley gazed at them both seriously. "I can see that your gifts cause both of you a lot of problems. And I agree, your lives would be easier without them."

"Is it possible?" Amanda asked. "Is there any way we can get rid of our gifts?"

"It's . . . possible," Dr. Paley said slowly. "There's research going on now, and there are indications that a type of brain surgery could erase this kind of ability."

Amanda made a face. "Brain surgery? That sounds pretty scary."

"Actually, it's not as dramatic as it sounds," the doctor told her. "It's a totally noninvasive procedure."

"What does that mean?" Ken asked.

"Special scans identify the brain element that's

responsible for the gift. The area is treated with a laser beam. No cuts or incisions are made. The patient wouldn't even need an anaesthetic."

Amanda still didn't feel comfortable with the idea. "Would they have to shave your head?"

Dr. Paley smiled. "No, that wouldn't be necessary."

"Does it cost a lot?" Ken wanted to know.

"Actually, it's all experimental at this point. The patients who have received the treatments were all volunteers, part of a research study. So there was no charge." After a moment, he added, "I'm a member of this research team."

Amanda drew in her breath. "So does that mean you could do this laser thing to us?"

"I would have to consult with the other members of the team, of course. But, yes, it is possible that the procedure could take place right here in this office."

Amanda didn't know what to say. Ken was speechless, too.

"Now, as I said, this is all experimental," Dr. Paley went on. "There are no guarantees. But no one has been injured by the procedure *yet*."

The word yet hung in the air. Amanda tried to ignore it.

"How come Madame never told us about this?" Ken wanted to know.

"Madame doesn't know about it," the doctor said. "Very few people do. Let me ask you something. Do you tell many people about your gift?"

"No, of course not," Ken said. "No one would believe it."

"And if they did," Amanda added, "they'd think we were weird."

"Exactly," Dr. Paley said. "Most people don't believe that these abilities exist. And most people aren't intellectually or emotionally capable of dealing with such knowledge. Therefore, procedures to correct the problem have also been kept highly confidential. And that's why you must not tell anyone about this procedure."

"Not even Madame?" Ken asked.

Amanda answered before Dr. Paley could. "Especially not Madame. She'd try to talk us out of it. Remember, she told us we've been blessed."

"Madame is a very fine person," Dr. Paley said, "but she is not gifted. No matter how much she cares for you all, she can't really understand you."

Amanda thought of another reason. "And don't forget, if there weren't any so-called gifted students to teach, she wouldn't have a job."

"Are there other students in your class who'd be interested in losing their gifts?" Dr. Paley asked.

Ken and Amanda looked at each other. "Sarah," they said in unison.

Dr. Paley looked at his notes and frowned. "Sarah . . . I don't think Madame has mentioned her."

"She's got the most powerful gift of all," Ken told him. "She can make anyone do anything."

"But she never does," Amanda said. "Well, maybe once or twice. She stopped a man from getting his hands on a gun. But I've never seen her do anything really big."

"Interesting," Dr. Paley murmured. He made a note. "Well, I give you permission to tell Sarah about the procedure. And if she's interested, you can bring her along on Friday."

"Friday," Ken repeated. "You mean—tomorrow?"

Dr. Paley nodded. "I'm going to talk to my colleagues today, and if all goes well, we should be able to perform the procedure tomorrow. Leave me your cell phone numbers and I'll send you text messages later."

Amanda was stunned. She had no idea everything could happen this fast. "Don't we need to get our parents' permission?"

"Do your parents know about your gifts?" Dr. Paley asked.

Amanda and Ken both shook their heads.

"Do you want to tell them about your gifts?"

They looked at each other, and then both of them shook their heads again.

"Well, then . . ."

They gave the doctor their phone numbers. Amanda picked up her purse, and they left the office. Walking back through the building, she still felt like she was in a state of shock. Ken finally broke the silence.

"Wow."

And Amanda responded: "Yeah."

They entered the reception area, but before they could reach the door, a voice called out. "Well, hello again!"

Amanda turned. That good-looking police officer from the day before, Jack Something, approached her with a smile. Somehow, even though she was feeling dazed, she managed to smile back.

"Hello. This is my friend, Ken."

"Hi, Ken, I'm Jack Fisher. What are you guys doing here?"

Amanda thought rapidly. "Um, I thought maybe I could try again. You know, to see Carter. We have to get back to school now." She tugged at Ken's arm.

"You're at Meadowbrook Middle, right? I'm going in that direction, I'll give you a lift."

They walked outside together. "Hey, this is cool," Ken said. "I hope people see us getting out of a police car at school."

Jack started the car. "Your friends will think you guys are the new Bonnie and Clyde."

"Who?" Amanda asked.

"They were a couple of bank robbers in the 1930s," Jack told her.

"Oh. I wasn't born then."

Jack laughed. "Neither was I." Just then, there was a loud buzzing sound, and a voice came out over the car radio.

"All cars in the vicinity of Dover and Crane, proceed to incident in the five-hundred block. I repeat . . ."

Immediately, Jack made a U-turn and took off at high speed. The intersection of Dover and Crane was less than a minute away. When they reached the scene, just outside a tall office building, they saw an ambulance. Another cop came over to the car, and Jack rolled down the window.

"What's going on?" he asked.

"Suicide," the other cop said. "Guy who was just fired from his job jumped from the top of the building."

"Oh, that's bad," Jack murmured.

"Gets worse," the cop said. "He left a note. It says he left a bomb in the building and it's set to go off in fifteen minutes. We're trying to evacuate all the buildings on the street, but I don't know if we can get everyone out in time. And we have no idea where in the building the bomb is located." His face was grim. "Fifteen stories, Jack."

Jack jumped out of the car and opened the back door. "Sorry, you two, I won't be able to give you a lift. And I need you to leave the area immediately."

Amanda didn't need any encouragement. She climbed out of the back seat, and Ken followed her. More police cars were arriving, and they hurried to get out of the way.

"Omigod, I can't believe this," Amanda exclaimed. "There have to be hundreds of people in all those buildings. Maybe thousands! This is terrible!"

When Ken didn't respond, she turned to look at him. He'd stopped running, and he was several yards behind her. "Ken! Hurry up!"

"Wait," he said.

"Are you crazy?" she shrieked. "Wait for what? For the bomb to go off?"

Ken held up his hand, like he was telling her to stop talking. She knew the expression on his face. One of his dead correspondents had just checked in.

"Ken, tell the soap opera lady you'll call her back!" she wailed.

"Okay," Ken whispered. But Amanda didn't think he was speaking to *her*. Then he blinked.

"Amanda, I have to find Jack. You go on without me."

How many shocks could a girl take in one day? Amanda watched Ken move in the direction of the building. People were pouring out of it now, and there was panic in the air. She knew she should get as far away as she could, as fast as she could. But she just stood there, watching Ken walk closer and closer to the danger. And then she ran after him.

When she caught up with him, he'd just spotted Jack. The police officer saw him, and he looked angry. "What are you kids doing? I told you to get out of here!"

"I know where the bomb is," Ken said.

Jack stared at him. "What?"

"I know where the bomb is. It's in the men's bathroom on the tenth floor."

Jack's eyes narrowed. "How could you possibly know this?"

"I can't—I can't explain it now. There's still time—you can find the bomb and dismantle it. It's a simple timing device. You just have to switch it off."

Jack frowned. "Look, if you're playing some kind of game—"

"I'm not, I'm telling the truth, you gotta believe me!" Ken pleaded.

Jack grabbed the arm of another cop passing by. "Put these two in a car," he ordered. And he took off.

The cop grabbed Ken's arm with one hand and Amanda's arm with the other.

"Hey, that hurts!" Amanda cried in outrage.

The cop ignored her. He opened the back door of a police car and pushed them both in. Then he slammed the door. Amanda had seen enough police shows on TV to know they wouldn't be able to get out on their own.

She was pretty sure she knew what had just happened. She turned to Ken. "Did the suicide guy contact you?"

He nodded. "He was really upset about losing his job, but it wasn't just that. He was having a rough time in lots of ways. And he was angry at all his coworkers for something—I don't know what. So he planted the bomb and then he jumped out the window. But now he feels bad about it. He doesn't really want to hurt anyone."

Ken sank back in his seat and started rubbing his forehead. Instinctively, Amanda reached out and took his other hand. Maybe she was being pushy, but for once she didn't care. This felt like the right thing to do.

They sat there together in silence. From the window, Amanda could see a couple of guys in what looked like space suits go into the building. She didn't know how much more time passed—it felt like an eternity, but when she looked at her watch, she realized it had only been 20 minutes since they left Dr. Paley's office.

Suddenly, the back door of their car opened. A very weary-looking Jack Fisher stood there. "Okay, you can get out."

"Did you find the bomb?" Ken asked.

"Yes. It's been dismantled."

Ken let out his breath. "Okay."

Jack's eyes bore into him. "What I need to find out now is how you knew where the bomb was."

Ken scratched the side of his head. "It's—it's kind of hard to explain."

"You're coming to headquarters with me," Jack said flatly. "You can explain it to me there." He turned to Amanda. "You go back to school. I'll have someone take you."

"Can't I stay with Ken?" she asked.

Ken shot her an appreciative look. "You go on," he said. "Tell Madame what happened."

Jack beckoned to another cop and told him to take Amanda to Meadowbrook Middle School. She'd turned to go off with him when Ken called to her.

"Amanda . . . just tell Madame what happened *here*. You know what I mean."

She did. She had no intention of telling Madame what they'd discussed with Dr. Paley.

Chapter Fifteen

COCKROACHES MUST HAVE *excellent hearing ability*, Paul thought. Despite the fact that he was encased in leather and practically buried under a lot of stuff, he'd understood everything that went on outside Amanda's purse.

It had been easy for Paul to get into Amanda's purse. She'd put it on the floor next to her chair in Dr. Paley's office, and it had a drawstring fastening. Paul didn't have any problem crawling in, and no one saw him. But now he had to make a fast decision: should he remain in Amanda's purse, wedged between her makeup bag and her wallet, or figure out a way to leave with Ken?

Amanda would be going back to school, and Paul was tempted to go along with her. He missed Madame, he wanted to see his classmates, to find out what they'd been up to—and to hear what they might say about him. Had they forgiven him, like Dr. Paley said they would?

On the other hand, Ken was heading for police headquarters, where he'd be questioned about the bomb. And that could be very exciting.

Who should he choose? Who was more interesting? He could feel the bag moving. Amanda was about to get out of the police car. He quickly climbed out of her bag and dropped out. Then he scrambled across the back seat and climbed into the pocket of Ken's jacket. Luckily, everyone was too distracted by what was going on to see the bug make his journey.

In the darkness of the pocket, Paul couldn't see anything, but he heard Jack the cop return to the car and start up the engine. There wasn't much else to hear, though. Jack didn't say anything, and Ken was silent, too. He was probably trying to come up with a way to explain how he knew about the bomb.

Paul recalled all those times in class when Ken said he thought his gift was worthless. He'd told Dr. Paley that he didn't get any pleasure from his gift. But he'd just saved the lives of a lot of people. *Surely he must be feeling something*, Paul thought.

He heard the car stop and the doors opening, and he felt Ken move. Then he heard the buzz of many conversations, phones ringing, people moving around. They must be in the police headquarters.

"We'll go into my office," Jack said.

He heard a door close, and then it was quiet.

"Sit down, Ken," the police officer said. "Now, tell me what happened back there."

"I didn't have anything to do with that bomb," Ken said.

"But you knew where it was," Jack declared.

"Yes. Well, no. I mean, I just sort of guessed."

"That's not true, Ken. You were very precise about the location."

Ken said nothing. Paul heard the rustle of papers, and then Jack spoke again.

"Did you know this Mister Patterson? Arnold Patterson?"

"Is that the man who jumped out of the building?" Ken asked.

"Yes. Isn't the name familiar to you?"

"No."

"You don't know him?"

"No. Well, not exactly."

"Explain what you mean, Ken." The police officer's tone wasn't harsh, but it was clear that he was determined to get an answer.

For a few seconds, Ken was silent. Then he let out a long sigh. "I never actually met him. But . . . he spoke to me."

"When?"

"Today."

"He called you on the phone before he jumped out of

the building?"

"No. Not on the phone. And not before he jumped."

Now Jack sounded exasperated. "Ken, you're not making any sense."

"I heard him. *After* he jumped."

"I don't understand. You weren't anywhere near Patterson. And according to the investigator, he died on impact. He couldn't have spoken to you after he jumped."

"He did," Ken said stubbornly.

"Ken, tell me the truth!"

"What's the point?" Ken cried out. "You won't believe me."

"Try me," Jack said quietly.

There was a pause, and then Ken spoke in a dull, flat voice. "I hear dead people."

"What?"

"Dead people talk to me."

There was another pause. "I think you can come up with a better story than that, Ken."

"It's true, I swear it!"

"How does that happen, Ken?"

"I'm not sure. I just hear them, in my head."

"So . . . this wasn't the first time?"

"It started in September," Ken said. "I was on the soccer field, and I ran into my best friend. His name was Jack, too.

Jack Farrell."

"Go on."

"We were both knocked out. I recovered. Jack died."

The pocket where Paul was resting must have been close to Jack's heart. He could hear it beating faster.

"After he died, Jack started talking to me."

"What did he say?"

"He said he didn't blame me for the accident. He asked me to look out for his girlfriend. He still talks to me once in a while. Mostly, he just wants to know what's happening at school, what his pals are up to, that kind of thing. But then other dead people started talking to me, too."

"What do they say to you?"

"Sometimes they ask me for a favor. Mostly, they just want to talk."

"I see," Jack said.

"You think I'm nuts, don't you?" Ken asked. "I'm not. But I don't like hearing these voices. That's what I was talking to Doctor Paley about at Harmony House. He might be able to help me."

"So this is what that gifted class is all about," Jack remarked.

"You know about the class?"

"I knew Jenna was in it, and I suspected there was something unusual about her. What about your friend Amanda? Does she have a gift, too?"

"I'm not supposed to talk about it," Ken said.

"That's okay, you don't have to tell me what their gifts are," Jack told him. "Everything's starting to make sense now. This Patterson guy, he had regrets about leaving the bomb behind, so he told you where it could be found."

"Exactly," Ken said. "You really believe me? You understand?"

"I won't say I understand," Jack said carefully, "but there's a lot in this world that can't be explained. I try to keep an open mind. Yes, I believe you, Ken. That's quite a gift you have."

"I don't like it," Ken blurted out. "It's creepy. Doctor Paley says maybe he can help me lose it."

"Well, it was certainly useful in this case," Jack remarked. "Of course, I'll have to come up with some sort of explanation for my fellow officers. They might not be quite so willing to believe in gifts like this."

"Maybe you could say I found a note that Mister Patterson left behind," Ken suggested.

"Mmm, that's not a bad idea. All right, Ken, you can go now. I'll have an officer take you back to school."

Paul was pleased. Now he'd be able to see what was going on in the gifted class, too. On the way to Meadowbrook, he pondered what he'd learned that day.

Ken was a hero, he thought. He used his gift, and he told

the police where to find the bomb. Without Ken's help, the bomb might never have been found. It could have exploded and killed who knew how many people.

Amanda had been a hero, too. Paul had heard the story she told Dr. Paley in the office, about the hitchhiker. He'd heard everything else they talked about, too. Ken and Amanda ... They had powerful gifts! Why did they want to lose them? He just didn't understand.

When they got back to Meadowbrook, Ken went to the administrative office to explain his absence. He was told to wait, and Paul worried that he wouldn't get to attend the gifted class after all.

"Amanda! What are you doing here?"

"I just wanted to see if you were back. What happened?"

There was another voice. "You may come in now, Ken. Amanda, what are you doing here?"

"Uh, just—uh, nothing."

"Then get right back to class." Then there was a gasp. "What's that?"

"What's what?" Amanda asked.

"I thought I saw a bug. It's gone now. Come in, Ken."

Back in Amanda's purse, Paul found a comfortable spot in an open packet of tissues. There wasn't much to listen to as Amanda went to her usual classes. She talked to her friends, but she didn't even mention the events of the morning. She couldn't, of course. Paul remembered how many times Madame told the class they shouldn't talk about their gifts to people who wouldn't understand. It gave him a thrill to think that this advice now applied to him, too.

But Amanda's conversations were so boring. He had to listen to her talk about some dumb TV show she had watched the night before, a sale at a shoe store, someone's new purse that was only a replica of a famous designer bag. And in the cafeteria, she made a huge fuss over chipping a fingernail. None of this made any sense to him at all.

He was getting hungry. He poked around through the contents of Amanda's purse and saw that most of the things weren't any more interesting than her converstions. He got a little case of lipgloss open with his nose. It smelled like raspberries, but when he licked the gooey pink stuff, it wasn't very tasty. A small bottle of perfume smelled nice, but he knew he wouldn't be able to get the top off, and the liquid inside would probably taste disgusting.

He lucked out when he found a granola bar. Working on the paper for some time, he finally managed to make a tiny tear in the wrapper. Amanda wouldn't be too happy when she took out her bar and found it had been nibbled by a bug, but he couldn't help himself. After satisfying his hunger, he curled up in a silky scarf and went to sleep.

He woke up at the perfect time. Through the purse, he heard another familiar voice.

"Good afternoon, class. Where's Ken?"

He heard Amanda speak. "He's in the office, Madame. You won't believe what happened to us!"

Paul listened to Amanda tell the story of the man who committed suicide and the bomb he left behind.

"Oh my," Madame murmured. "How did Ken explain to the police why he knew where the bomb was?"

"I don't know," Amanda replied.

"And what were you and Ken doing there?"

Uh-oh, Paul thought. *She can't tell Madame they were consulting Doctor Paley.* He needed to help her out, provide a distraction. And he knew exactly how he could do it.

He crept out of her bag and started crawling up her leg. As he expected, Amanda let out an ear-piercing shriek and leaped out of her chair. Paul dropped to the floor and scurried away before Amanda could step on him.

"It's a cockroach! There are cockroaches in my purse!"

Somebody picked up a book and threw it at him. Paul dodged it and frantically searched the floorboards for a hole to crawl into. Then it dawned on him that here was the perfect opportunity to introduce his gift to the class. He shifted back to his human form.

"Carter!" Madame gasped. The rest of the class stared at him in stunned silence. The unfamiliar attention unnerved him, and it took a lot of effort to formulate any words. They came out as "I haff uh giff," but he was pretty sure they got the meaning.

Madame gazed at him in wonderment. "So I see," she said.

There was a short rap on the classroom door, and then the door opened. Dr. Paley walked in.

"Excuse me for interrupting your class, Madame," he said. "Ah, Paul. I thought I might find you here."

Madame's eyes darted back and forth between the boy and the doctor. "*Paul?*"

"That's his real name, the name he was given at birth," Dr. Paley said. "We're not sure about his last name, so we're calling him Paul Carter."

"Paul Carter," Madame repeated. "Well. We're pleased to have you back here, Paul."

"I'm afraid he can't stay," Dr. Paley said. "As you can see, Paul has made a lot of progress. He's recovered his memory, and he's beginning to speak."

"And he has a gift," Madame added.

"Yes, Paul is a shape shifter. But he still requires some counseling and therapy before he can be released from Harmony House. You'll have to come along with me, Paul."

Paul looked at Madame beseechingly, and Madame smiled but shook her head. "I'm sorry, Paul. We're all very excited about this, and we look forward to having you back, but you'll have to leave with Doctor Paley now."

Paul understood. As he walked to the door with the doctor, he looked at his classmates. Tracey and Emily smiled at him. Most of the others were looking at him in a friendly way, too. Only Jenna was frowning.

And Amanda, who had emptied the contents of her purse on her desk, was clearly upset. "He nibbled at my granola bar, Madame! That's gross!"

Chapter Sixteen

THE THOUGHT THAT a cockroach had been in her purse—even if that cockroach was really a human being—made Amanda sick. It wasn't just the granola bar. He could have crawled over everything. By the time she left class, she had decided to toss out everything that had been in her purse and replace it all with new stuff. First of all, she'd go directly to the mall and buy cosmetics. She'd need a new wallet, a replacement for her cell phone cover . . .

But all plans to restock her purse were swept away when she found Ken waiting for her by her locker.

"Ken, are you okay? What happened?"

Ken looked totally wiped out. He tried to smile, but it came out looking more like a grimace.

"I've been in the office all day, waiting to get a note for my absence." He sighed. "I had to tell him, Amanda."

"Tell who what?"

"Officer Fisher. I had to tell him about my gift."

Amanda drew in her breath. "No . . ."

"He kept asking me all these questions. And I couldn't come up with a story that would explain how I knew where the bomb was. I mean, what could I say? That I knew the guy who committed suicide and he told me what he was going to do? I didn't even know the poor man's name!" He leaned against the wall and let out a deep sigh. "So I told him I talk to dead people."

"What did he say?"

"He thought I was joking." Ken gave her a half-hearted smile. "You can't blame him. He told me I would have to come up with a better story than that. And I ended up telling him everything." He clenched his fists, and he looked like he was in real pain. "Everything, Amanda. Not just about me."

Now Amanda felt *really* sick. "You told him about our class? About all our gifts?"

"Well, I didn't go into details. But he knows we're a bunch of freaks." He sighed. "Madame is going to kill me."

"But he actually believed in your gift?" Amanda asked.

"Yeah, I guess so. Weird, huh? And then he let me go . . . but you should have seen the way he looked at me. Like I was some kind of alien." Suddenly he slammed his fist against the locker. "I hate this damned gift!"

Amanda had never seen him so upset. She touched his arm. "It's okay, Ken. It won't be for much longer. Tomorrow we'll see Doctor Paley and get that laser thing. No more gifts. We'll be normal."

"Shh," Ken whispered. Amanda turned to see Sarah coming toward them. She approached them tentatively, and when she spoke, her voice was barely audible.

"That was a very brave thing you did, Ken," she said.

He looked at her in confusion.

"I told the class how you located the bomb," Amanda explained.

"Oh." Ken forced a smile. "I wouldn't call it brave."

"Of course it was," Sarah said. "You revealed your gift so you could save people. I don't know if I would have the guts to do something like that."

"Maybe you'll never have to make the choice," Amanda said. "If you could lose your gift . . ." She looked at Ken with a question in her eyes. He shook his head slightly.

Sarah shrugged. "Well, I just wanted to say . . . I admire you."

"Thanks, Sarah," Ken said, and the girl left them.

"Why didn't you want me to tell her about Doctor Paley?" Amanda asked.

"I don't know," Ken said simply. "I guess, maybe because her gift is so powerful. And maybe she should hang on to it, because she could *really* save people."

"But if she doesn't *want* to save people," Amanda began

and then clamped her mouth shut. Nina was there.

"Who's saving people?" she chirped.

Amanda had to press her lips together to keep herself from yelling "None of your business," but Ken actually smiled at Nina.

"The X-Men," he said. "We were just talking about what it would be like to have superpowers. What do you think?"

"Not a clue," Nina said blithely. "Anyone want to get an ice cream?"

Of course she was looking at Ken when she asked the question, but Amanda answered.

"No."

To her surprise—and extreme annoyance—Ken said, "Sounds good."

Amanda stared at them as they started toward the exit together. Then she hurried to catch up with them.

"I've changed my mind," she announced.

She didn't get it. Two minutes earlier, she and Ken had been having this intense, serious discussion. Now he was listening to Nina chatter about her day's activities—and actually paying attention.

"...then Mister Jones called on me in history, and I hadn't read the assignment, so I started coughing and he let me go out to get some water, but when I got back, he asked me about the reading again, and so I started coughing again, and then . . ."

Ken seemed to be hanging on to every word. He kept his eyes on her, he nodded and made the right comments, like "no kidding" and "wow." Amanda couldn't believe it. Here she and Ken had just experienced this incredible day, and now he was acting like Nina was telling him something exciting.

How many more ways could she feel sick that day? she wondered as she slid into the booth at the ice-cream place. Was it possible that Ken was really into Nina? She couldn't bear this—she had to do something to turn him off her. And it dawned on her that she had the means to do this. She just had to come up with a reason to feel sorry for Nina . . .

". . . and if I don't get at least a C in history," Nina prattled, "I'll have to go to summer school, which means I won't be able to go to the beach . . ."

A summer without a tan. That was all it took.

Chapter Seventeen

D R. PALEY WAS NOT happy with Paul. He didn't yell, and he didn't threaten to punish him, but on the way back to Harmony House, he gave Paul a lecture on what he should not do.

"You must not leave Harmony House without permission," he warned Paul. "You are not a prisoner there, but it is the one place where you are safe. Never forget that you are still in danger. The people who killed your parents are still out there, and they may still be looking for you. Do you understand?"

"Yes," Paul said, and he was pleased to hear the word come out correctly and clearly.

"And you must not shapeshift, except under controlled circumstances and in my presence. Your gift could put you in danger, too. If you became, say, a lion and went out into the street, people would become frightened. You would be shot. Do you understand?"

"Yes," Paul said again. Why did Dr. Paley keep asking him

if he understood? Paul wasn't stupid.

"Madame told me that you have always obeyed her orders," he continued. "You must obey my orders, too. Do you understand?"

"*Yes.*" The word came out louder this time. Dr. Paley took his eyes momentarily off the road to glance at him.

"Your voice is improving."

When they arrived back at Harmony House, Dr. Paley told him to go to his room. "I have an important meeting with my colleagues," he said. "I would like them to meet you. I'll send someone to get you when we're ready. And don't forget what I've told you."

Back in his room, Paul lay on his bed, stared at the ceiling, and thought about his little adventure. Visiting the gifted class had brought back all kinds of memories, mostly bad ones. He remembered himself sitting there day after day, not speaking, not thinking, responding to commands, following every order he was given, doing nothing on his own. He had been something not quite human.

Now he was human—and more. He could speak, he could think. He had a gift. And he didn't have to follow orders anymore.

Like the orders Dr. Paley gave him just now. He knew the doctor was trying to protect him, and there was a time when Paul only wanted to be protected. That was why he followed orders, because he was always afraid.

He wasn't afraid anymore. And he didn't want to stay in this room and wait for Dr. Paley to send for him. There was so much to see, so much to explore. And hear. He was curious about Dr. Paley's meeting with his colleagues—people who believed in unusual gifts and what could be done with them. He could learn more about himself. Clearly, Dr. Paley thought he wasn't terribly intelligent, or he wouldn't be constantly asking Paul if he understood. So he wasn't going to get a lot of information from him, not right away at least. He wanted to hear Dr. Paley and his colleagues speaking freely.

He considered his options. What could he become? He didn't particularly want to be a cockroach again. True, he had to be small so no one would notice him, but he wanted to try something new. A spider? No, he could easily be stepped on and crushed. A snake? No. A worm . . . but they couldn't move very fast. His plan was to go to Dr. Paley's office, listen to their conversation, and then, as soon as the doctor sent for him, return to his room and shift back.

He was going to have to be a mouse, he decided. There were mice all over this building—the doctor had said so himself. And they weren't all shapeshifting humans. If by any chance he was spotted, no one would be too shocked.

Maybe a white mouse, not the ordinary gray kind. White ones were nicer looking. After he shifted, he wished he could

518

get up to the mirror over the sink so he could admire himself, but it was just too high.

He slipped out under the door and looked around. No one was in the hall, but even so, he kept close to the wall. As he approached Dr. Paley's office, he heard voices coming from around the corner, so he dived under the door of the office next to the doctor's.

Big mistake. "Eek, a mouse!" someone screamed. So people were just as freaked out by white mice as they were by gray ones. Paul raced along the edge of the room until he came to a hole just big enough to squeeze through. He spotted another mouse in the cavity, but he didn't pay any attention to Paul. That was good—Paul had no idea how mice communicated with each other.

He could hear people chattering excitedly through the wall of the room he'd just left.

"Those traps we set are not working," one person said. "We have to call in some real exterminators."

Paul shuddered. Well, he didn't have to stay being a mouse forever. But he would have to keep an eye out for those traps. What was it people put in traps to attract mice? Cheese, right? Paul wasn't too worried. He didn't like cheese. It would be no temptation for him.

He followed a narrow tunnel in what he thought was the direction of Dr. Paley's office. Sure enough, after a moment, he was able to make out some other voices, including one that he recognized.

"It's a phenomenal situation," the doctor was saying. "Nine students, and each one has a different gift."

"Which ones are coming for the procedure tomorrow?" another voice asked.

"The bodysnatching girl and the boy who talks to the deceased."

"What about the controller? She's the most intriguing."

"Supposedly, according to the subjects I spoke with, she wants to lose her gift, too, and I encouraged them to bring her along."

Then a third voice, a woman this time. "Is it really necessary to perform the procedure? We could learn so much from these kids. And think of their potential for investigation, advances in medicine and psychology, diplomacy . . . These kids could end wars!"

"Or start them," Dr. Paley said. "They're too young and immature—they can't be trusted with these powers."

"But we could work with them," the woman said. "Keep them in a controlled environment, train them, so they'd want to use their gifts for positive purposes."

"That's what the teacher is trying to do," Dr. Paley said. "But it's impossible. The subjects are too strong; they can't be contained. Already the subjects have fallen into the wrong hands on several occasions. They're dangerous."

"The potential is frightening," the other male voice concurred. "We really have no option. Their gifts must be eliminated."

"And we need to begin immediately," Dr. Paley said.

He must have moved farther from the wall because his voice became fainter, but Paul could still hear him.

"Ms. Callow? Would you send a resident assistant to bring Paul Carter here?"

This was Paul's cue. He needed to take off, get back to his room, and shift before the resident assistant appeared.

But he didn't move. He had to hear more. And it was a good thing he did.

"I'm looking forward to observing the procedures tomorrow," the male voice said.

"Actually, I don't think that's a good idea," Dr. Paley told him. "I haven't requested approval for the procedure from the Harmony House administrators."

"Why not?"

"Because it's quite possible they would have refused. It's still a highly experimental surgery. My appointments with the two students are on the books, and it might look peculiar if I have all of you here, too."

"That's a shame," the other man said. "I wanted to see if there would be immediate results. And any possible side effects."

"You will," Dr. Paley said. "That's what we're going to find out right now. I'll do the procedure on Paul."

"Does he want to lose his gift?" the woman asked.

"He doesn't know what he wants," Dr. Paley replied. "I don't think he has any sense of what his gift really entails. Don't worry, he won't give us any problems. If he shifts, I'll have a tranquilizer gun ready to knock him out, whatever he becomes."

"But what about the others?" the woman asked. "You said that two of the students are coming for the procedure voluntarily tomorrow, but what about the other six students?"

"What about them?" Dr. Paley countered.

"Maybe they don't want to lose their gifts," the woman said. "What if they refuse to have the procedure?"

There was a moment of silence before Dr. Paley replied. His tone was grim.

"Then the subjects themselves must be eliminated."

Chapter Eighteen

"NINA?"

Amanda-Nina blinked rapidly. It always took her a minute or so to adjust to being in another body. "What?"

"Are you okay?" Ken asked.

"Sure. Anyway, let's see, what were we talking about?" She did what she hoped sounded like a typical Nina giggle. "I'm such a ditz sometimes!"

"About how you might have to go to summer school."

Could he really be interested in this? Amanda wondered. "Yeah, isn't that lame? What am I going to do? Maybe I can bribe someone to write the next essay for me. And there's this really nerdy girl in the class. I bet she'd let me cheat off her if I let her sit with my group at lunch one time."

She watched Ken carefully as she spoke. He was pretty much the honorable type—he'd rather fail an exam than cheat to pass it. And he'd never approved of the snobbishness of some cliques and the way the girls acted like they were superior to other people. This had to be turning him off Nina.

He got up. "I'm going to the bathroom. If the waitress comes, could you order me a chocolate milkshake?"

"Okey-dokey!" Amanda-Nina said brightly.

She took advantage of Ken's absence to check on her *own* body. Other-Amanda had taken out her makeup bag, and she was filing her nails. Why was she always doing that? Amanda wondered. Real Amanda didn't file her nails *that* much. And what if that disgusting bug had crawled over the file? Amanda-Nina shuddered.

It occurred to her that she'd never spoken to her robot-self before. She tried now.

"A cockroach was on that nail file," she informed her.

"Ick!" Other-Amanda exclaimed, and she dropped the file.

Not bad, Amanda-Nina thought. That was pretty much what she would have done in the same circumstances. And now what would the robot do?

Exactly what real Amanda would have done. "I have to wash my hands!" she cried out. She left the booth and practically ran toward the bathroom. Amanda watched with interest. She'd never had such a good view of that dress from the back. Maybe she'd ask her mother to hem it, make it a little shorter.

A waitress came to the booth. "Hi. What can I get for you?"

"My friend wants a chocolate milkshake. I'll have . . ." She was about to ask for a diet soda but thought better of it. "A hot fudge sundae." After all, she'd be packing the calories on Nina's body, not her own.

"And the other person?"

"Water." It wasn't like Other-Amanda could really taste anything. And she began to wonder if maybe she should continue occupying Nina through the next day. Dr. Paley had said the procedure wouldn't hurt, but Amanda wouldn't mind letting the robot endure it instead of her. But no, the last time Ken had been with Other-Amanda, the thing had completely turned him off. Besides, this was something they had to do together.

Which brought her back to the immediate situation. She had to hold on to Ken's attention now so he wouldn't realize that the person he thought was Amanda had become the robot. This would not be easy, to keep his attention and turn him off simultaneously.

He was returning to the table now, followed closely behind by Other-Amanda. They both got into the booth.

"Nina, I was thinking," Ken said. "I've got Jones for history, too, and I'm doing pretty well in his class. Maybe I could help you. We could study together."

Amanda-Nina tried very hard not to let Nina's face show what she, Amanda, was feeling. It was worse than she thought. Ken wanted to get close to Nina! This made no sense at all to her. Nina was everything Ken didn't like—snotty, shallow, and selfish. She forced herself to giggle.

"Study? Ick! Who has time to study? I'd rather go to the mall after school."

"In the evenings," Ken suggested.

The waitress appeared with their orders. She put the glass of water down in front of Other-Amanda, who reached into her purse, pulled out her iPod, and stuck the earphones into her ears. Then she dropped a straw into the glass and started to sip. Amanda-Nina wouldn't have to worry about her.

Ken barely glanced at his milkshake. The hot fudge sundae in front of Amanda-Nina looked delicious, but she couldn't waste time on it.

"In the evenings? And miss all my favorite TV shows?" She started counting them off on her fingers. "*America's Next Top Model. Real World. American Idol. The Real Housewives of New Jersey.*"

Finally, a glimmer of distaste crossed Ken's face. "You like those reality shows?"

"*Love* them! Don't you?"

"Well . . . I guess I've never actually seen any of them," Ken said. "Maybe we can watch them together."

Amanda-Nina stared at him in disbelief. Ken hated reality TV—he'd told her that before. He thought these shows were stupid, and he couldn't understand why so many of his classmates liked them.

And that was when it hit her. Their classmates . . . Their ordinary, normal classmates who did ordinary, normal things, like go to the mall and watch TV. Who didn't go around snatching other people's bodies or talking to dead people. Nina was one of those ordinary, normal people, and Ken wanted to be one, too. That was why he wanted to connect with Nina.

An enormous wave of sadness came over her. Nina might be ordinary, but Ken deserved so much better. He deserved her, Amanda. Not the robot, who was now sitting placidly in her seat, sipping her water and listening to her iPod. Real Amanda. She amended that. Real un-gifted Amanda. And if he could just hold on till they had their procedures, they'd both be normal and they could be normal *together*.

She was desperate. "Do you really want to hang out with me, Ken? I'm not that smart, you know. I don't read at all. I'm not interested in current events. All I ever want to do is shop, and . . . and style my hair, and stuff like that. I don't really think we're right for each other."

Ken looked confused, and Amanda-Nina couldn't blame him. Nina had been coming on to him for days now, and here she was telling him she wasn't interested in hanging out together! She couldn't go on like this. Quickly, she gobbled three big spoonfuls of the sundae. Then she focused on the robot.

Easy-peasy. Amanda pulled out the earphones. "Nina, are you feeling all right?"

A dazed-looking Nina stared at the hot fudge sundae in front of her. "Where did that come from?" She rubbed her head. "Did I faint or something?"

"You're not well," Amanda said firmly. "Come on, I'll walk you home." She gave Nina a little push, and Nina got herself out of the booth.

Ken's eyes darted back and forth between the two girls and settled on Amanda. Then suddenly he grinned. "That was you," he said.

"What's he talking about?" Nina asked.

"Nothing," Amanda said. She heard a little dinging sound that told her she had a text message on her cell phone. A second later, a ding came from Ken's, too.

Taking the phone out of her purse, Amanda looked for the message.

Please be in my office at 10:00 Friday morning.

She was pretty sure that Ken was reading the very same message on his phone. They looked at each other.

"Tomorrow?" Amanda asked.

He nodded. "Tomorrow."

Chapter Nineteen

PAUL CARTER, THE WHITE mouse, had been through a rough night. When Dr. Paley learned that Paul wasn't in his room, he'd become anxious. He'd had the institution locked down—no one could go in or out—and all the staff were alerted to be on the lookout for him. Paul didn't dare leave the wall cavity, not even as a mouse.

So Dr. Paley planned to take all the gifts away from the students. And if all the gifted students didn't voluntarily submit to his "procedure," the students would be eliminated. He didn't hear Dr. Paley explain how this would be done, but Paul didn't doubt that he would find a way. And Madame trusted this man. She wouldn't guess his intentions, and she would probably give him access to Paul's classmates.

In a strange way, Paul understood the doctor's plans. And he didn't even think the doctor was evil—not like Serena Hancock, or the kidnapper Clare, or Mr. Jackson, the former principal. Dr. Paley truly believed that the gifted students were dangerous, that they presented a threat to the world. And he believed he was doing what was best for society.

Only it wasn't the best for Paul, or Amanda, or Ken, or any of his classmates. Dr. Paley had to be stopped. And Paul was the only one who knew or cared about what Dr. Paley wanted to do. He would have to stop him.

But Paul was a mouse, a tiny, insignificant creature that couldn't do much worse than chew through a granola bar wrapper a little more efficiently than a cockroach could.

Throughout the night, he wandered the narrow tunnels and crevices in the walls. It was cold in there, and he was hungry. But for the first time in a very long time, cold and hunger didn't matter so much to him. He had more important things to think about.

He did have one other option. If mice had gotten into the building, there had to be a way out. If he could find an exit and get far enough away so no one from Harmony House could see him, he could shift back into himself. He could seek out Amanda or Ken or Madame and warn them. But even though he'd lost track of the time in his wanderings, he knew it had to be the middle of the night. His classmates, his teacher—none of them would be at school. He had no idea where any of them lived, or even how to contact them by phone—and even if he did manage to contact them, how could he make himself understood?

But at least you'd be able to escape Doctor Paley yourself, he thought. He could go anywhere. He could live in a zoo for a while. Become a bird and fly to a distant land. Or become a squirrel and live in a tree, feeding on berries and nuts. Nobody bothered squirrels.

Only he didn't want to run away. He wanted to stay who he was—well, not who he was at that very moment. He wanted to be a boy. He wanted to go back to his foster family. He'd never been able to talk to the Grangers, to have any real contact with them, but he knew they'd been kind to him. He wanted to find out what kind of people they were and why they took in foster children. He wanted to get to know the two other boys he'd been living with. Maybe they'd play games together. Maybe they could have fun.

And more than anything, he wanted to be back at Meadowbrook Middle School, in room 209. He wanted to know the other special gifted students, to become part of their world—to learn how they could all use their gifts to make the world a better place, so that the kind of people who killed his parents couldn't get away with their crimes. What was it Madame had told them they could do? Benefit mankind. They could do that together. Running away, he'd just be alone again. A thing.

No, he had to stay and find some way to stop Dr. Paley and his colleagues. So he made his way through the walls and back to the place where he knew he was just outside the office. And he waited.

He slept a little, off and on, but the hunger and the cold didn't let him stay asleep very long. When some light came through a crack in the wall, he knew that it must be morning. And soon after that, he heard voices.

"Ms. Callow, I've got two young people coming at ten, and I don't want to be disturbed while they're in the office with me. Not even if it's important."

"Yes, sir. Oh, and sir?"

"Yes, Ms. Callow?"

"The Carter boy still hasn't been located."

Dr. Paley let out a deep sigh. "Well . . . if a strange animal appears in the building . . . a lion, or a tiger, whatever it is . . . tell security not to shoot it. They can tranquilize the animal, but they shouldn't try to kill it."

There was a moment before the secretary choked out, "Sir?"

Dr. Paley must have been a quick thinker. "I just heard on the radio about some animals escaping from the zoo. That's all."

"I see. Yes, sir. I'll notify security."

He really doesn't want to kill us, Paul thought. *That's a last resort. It's because he's afraid of us.* He himself had spent such a long time being afraid. It was a strange sensation, thinking someone might be afraid of *him*.

He examined the wall, feeling his way along as he searched for a hole big enough to let him get into the office. He was in luck—another mouse came from the opposite direction. Obviously, that little guy knew the area well. He disappeared from the tunnel. A second later, he heard Dr. Paley curse.

"Ms. Callow, please send another memo to the director. Something has to be done about these mice."

"Yes, sir."

Paul made his way to the point where the other mouse had escaped from the tunnel. All thoughts of hunger and cold and fatigue had vanished. He perched on his hind legs and peered out.

He could see Dr. Paley's feet. The man was walking around the office. Paul could hear things being picked up, put down, moved around. *The doctor must be setting things up for the procedure*, Paul thought.

He settled down to wait.

CHAPTER TWENTY

"HE SAID IT WOULDN'T hurt, right?" Amanda asked Ken as they approached Harmony House. "Do you believe him? I remember when I was a little kid, that's what doctors always said before they gave you an injection. And it hurt."

Ken nodded. "I know. But my mother had laser surgery on her eyes to improve her vision. She said she couldn't feel a thing."

"Okay." She felt Ken take her hand, and a tingle went up her arm.

"It's going to be fine," he said. "We're doing the right thing. I think."

"Absolutely," Amanda affirmed. "This is what we want. To be normal."

"I mean, it's not like I'll be looking for hidden bombs set by dead people again," Ken went on. "And you're not going to run into hitchhikers every day."

"Of course not," Amanda assured him. "And remember

that boy who was looking for the lottery ticket his father had put away before he died? I bet he would have found it eventually, even without your help."

"Maybe," Ken said. "Probably." After a moment, he added, "No, you're absolutely, positively right. He would have found it."

They entered the building and went up to the receptionist. "We have an appointment with Doctor Paley," Amanda said and gave her their names.

The woman checked her computer screen. "Yes, you can proceed to his office."

Her actions and response put Amanda at ease. This was just like going to the dentist, she thought. Easier, in fact. No injections, no drilling. This was more like going to the hair salon. It was no big deal.

And the secretary in the doctor's outer office was equally reassuring.

"Doctor Paley is expecting you," she said with a nod. "Go right in."

The doctor greeted them with a warm and welcoming smile. "Hello, Ken, Amanda. How are you feeling?"

"A little nervous," Ken admitted.

"But we haven't changed our minds," Amanda added quickly.

"Good," Dr. Paley said. "As I told you before, it's

experimental surgery, but tests have indicated no side effects or problems associated with the procedure. You won't feel a thing. And since there's no an anaesthetic, you won't need any recovery time."

"When my mother had laser surgery on her eyes, she did it during her lunch break and went right back to work afterward," Ken said.

Dr. Paley nodded. "And you'll be able to go right back to school." Then he grinned. "Unless you want an excuse to cut classes. I'll even write you a note. There's always a very slight possibility you'll experience a mild headache later today, but nothing that can't be cured with a regular pain reliever."

Amanda turned to Ken. "We could buy some sandwiches and have a picnic lunch in the park."

"Okay," Ken said. Amanda thought he looked a little pale. He was still holding her hand, and she gave it a squeeze.

Dr. Paley moved a machine toward them. "First I need to take scans of your heads. You've both had scans before, haven't you? You know it's nothing to be afraid of."

That procedure took all of two minutes. Afterward, Dr. Paley studied the images of their heads on a lighted screen.

"Yes," he murmured, more to himself than to them. "This won't be difficult at all." He addressed them. "I'd like to run a little test first, just to make sure I've pinpointed the area accurately." He studied them both for a moment. "Amanda . . . you have more control over your gift than Ken does, don't you?"

Amanda hesitated. She didn't want to hurt Ken's feelings. She knew that some boys could get totally unnerved if they learned a girl could do something better than they could. Fortunately, Ken wasn't that kind of boy.

"Totally," Ken said. "It's hard to call a dead person. I usually have to wait for someone to contact me first. Amanda can pretty much snap her fingers and become another person."

Amanda lowered her eyes modestly. "Oh, it's not *that* easy, Ken. I mean, I have to concentrate. And I need to find something depressing about the person."

Ken grinned. "That wasn't too hard with Nina, was it? It must be pretty easy to feel sorry for someone that boring."

Amanda giggled.

Dr. Paley looked like he was getting impatient. "All right, then let's get on with the little test. Amanda, you need to feel pity for your subject. Did you notice my secretary, Ms. Callow?"

Amanda hadn't really paid any attention to the woman in the outer office. "What about her?"

"Ms. Callow has a sad life," the doctor told her. "She was very much in love with a man, and they were about to get married when he was killed in an accident.

In fact, this happened on the way to the wedding ceremony."

"How awful!" Amanda exclaimed.

"Now she lives in a tiny apartment with her elderly mother, who's always nagging her."

"Why doesn't she just move out?" Amanda wanted to know.

"Her mother is not well and requires a great deal of care."

"Can't she hire someone to do it?"

Dr. Paley shook his head. "Ms. Callow cannot afford a nurse, so she has to do everything herself. She takes care of her mother in the morning, works here all day, then goes home to take care of her mother in the evenings. She has no social life at all. She's never even had a vacation, since her mother can't travel and Ms. Callow can't leave her alone."

Amanda frowned. She thought doctors were rich. "Couldn't you give her some money so she could hire someone to stay with her mother?"

Dr. Paley seemed momentarily annoyed by the question, but he recovered quickly. "I've offered, of course. But she's very proud. She won't accept charity. So she suffers."

It all sounded pretty grim to Amanda. That poor woman—what a depressing life she led.

Dr. Paley watched her expression closely. Then he went to the door and opened it. "Ms. Callow, could you come in here for a minute?"

For the first time, Amanda gave the secretary a long, hard look. She was attractive, and her clothes were decent. Cute, even. The woman didn't seem all that miserable. But appearances were deceptive—she knew that. Ms. Callow probably put up a good front for her job. Maybe she wore that same suit every day. This image made Amanda feel even more sympathy for her.

Dr. Paley spoke quietly to the secretary. "Please remain very still and don't say anything. I'm running a test." He went to his table of instruments and picked up a thick tube with a rubbery tip. Amanda flinched as he approached her with it.

"This won't hurt," he assured her. "I'm only going to touch your scalp with it."

He was telling the truth. It didn't hurt at all—there was just a little pressure.

"Now, Amanda, take over Ms. Callow."

"What?" the secretary cried out in alarm.

"Be quiet," the doctor ordered. "Go ahead, Amanda."

Amanda looked at the secretary and tried to imagine her daily life. All alone, except for her old mother, who probably wasn't very good company if she was sick all the time. She pictured a dark, ugly apartment and empty closets. Pity overwhelmed her.

"Amanda?"

Amanda looked at the doctor in wonderment. "I'm still me!"

Dr. Paley removed the instrument. "Excellent. You may leave, Ms. Callow."

The confused-looking secretary retreated and closed the door behind her.

"I have accurately pinpointed the area we need to treat," the doctor said. "Ken, I wish I could test you, but . . . Ken? Are you listening to me?"

Amanda looked at Ken. She recognized the glazed expression on her classmate's face.

"He's hearing someone! Ken, is it the soap opera lady?"

Dr. Paley didn't wait for Ken's response. He hurried over to him and pressed the rubber thing against his skull.

Ken frowned. "Jack . . . ?" He blinked.

"That's his friend—the one who died after the collision," Amanda told Dr. Paley.

"Jack?" Ken murmured again.

Dr. Paley smiled in satisfaction and lifted the instrument. "I cut the connection, Ken. This is going to work very well. I have no doubts." He nodded toward the examining table. "Who wants to go first?"

Ken and Amanda looked at each other. "Ladies first?" Ken suggested.

"Oh, that's so old-fashioned," Amanda said quickly.

Dr. Paley smiled. "Okay, I'll decide. Come on, Ken, let's show the young lady there's nothing to be afraid of."

Ken climbed up on to the table and lay down.

"I'll use the scan to pinpoint the exact spot where I'll direct the laser beam," the doctor said. He wheeled the machine to the side of the table.

Amanda watched nervously, but a movement on the floor distracted her. "There's a mouse!" she cried out.

Ken sat up. "Where?"

Amanda couldn't answer him. She couldn't even speak. Before her eyes, the mouse began to expand, and its body changed form. Then it wasn't a mouse at all.

"Carter!" she exclaimed.

"His name's Paul," Ken reminded her.

"Whatever," Amanda replied. "What are you doing here?"

Dr. Paley was frowning. "Paul, you shouldn't be in here. Go to your room immediately."

The boy's mouth moved, as if he was trying to reply. The only word that came out was "No."

Amanda glared at the boy. "I can't believe you nibbled at my granola bar. That was so disgusting."

Dr. Paley went to the door and opened it. "Ms. Callow, would you please call a resident assistant to escort Paul Carter back to his room?

The secretary came to the door and stared at Paul in astonishment. "I didn't even see him come in!"

"Um, he was hiding in the cabinet," Dr. Paley told her. "It's not important. Just call for a resident assistant, please." Ms. Callow hurriedly went back out to her desk.

Paul looked at Ken. Amanda remembered how expressionless the boy usually looked. Now there was no mistaking the urgency on his face.

"Stop," Paul said.

"Stop what?" Ken asked.

He mumbled something that sounded like "dun loose ya giff."

"We can't understand a word you're saying," Amanda snapped impatiently.

A familiar voice came from outside the door. "He's saying, don't lose your gift."

"You can't go in there!" Ms. Callow yelled.

But as usual, Jenna didn't respond well to authority figures. She stomped right into Dr. Paley's office.

"What are *you* doing here?" Ken asked.

"If you want the procedure, you're going to have to wait your turn," Amanda snapped.

Jenna wasn't alone. The police officer, Jack Fisher, followed her into Dr. Paley's office.

The doctor was not pleased. "Excuse me, but we're in the

542

process of a medical procedure here!"

"No one's performing any procedures in here today," Officer Fisher declared. "This surgery has not been authorized by Harmony House officials."

"What are you talking about?" Dr. Paley sputtered. "I am a certified medical doctor. I don't have to ask permission to perform a simple procedure that doesn't require an anaesthetic."

"You do when it's an experimental operation," the policeman declared.

"And what makes you think I'm doing an experimental operation?" the doctor demanded to know.

"This young lady told me."

Dr. Paley stared at Jenna. Jenna stared right back at him.

"You weren't very careful, Doctor Paley," she said. "You know about my gift. You know what I'm able to do. But you didn't block me when you came into class yesterday. I read your mind."

Dr. Paley turned to the police officer. "And you believe this nonsense? Do you honestly think this girl can read minds?"

"Yes," Jack Fisher said simply. "Just as I believe that boy on the table can communicate with the dead."

And then another person came into the room. "Doctor

543

Paley, please don't bother my students," Madame said quietly.

The doctor dropped all pretense. "Madame, I have no choice. This is absolutely necessary."

"Why?" she demanded to know.

"Because your students are dangerous."

Madame corrected him. "My students have the *potential* to be dangerous, just as all people have. But my students also have the potential to do great and wondrous things. I will not allow you to take that potential away from them."

Amanda finally got a chance to get a word in. "But Madame," she wailed, "I don't want to do great and wondrous things. I want to be normal! And so does Ken!"

"Do you, Ken?" Jack asked. "Yesterday you saved lives. Maybe hundreds of them. Could a normal person do that?"

Amanda looked at Ken. He seemed torn. He clenched his fists, his eyebrows went up, and he mumbled, "Not now, Jack."

"Excuse me?" the police officer said.

"Not you, sir. I'm talking to my friend Jack. I'll get back to you later, buddy." Then he hopped off the table.

"Amanda, maybe they're right. Maybe we shouldn't give this up. Think about the hitchhiker you saved."

"But think about me!" Amanda protested. "I don't want to spend my life hopping in and out of other people!"

544

"Oh, come on, Amanda," Ken said. "You've got more control over your gift than half the people in our class. You can choose when to use it."

Amanda had to admit he had a point.

"And what's so great about being normal, anyway?" Ken continued. "Think of your friend Nina. You want to be like her?"

Another good point. And what he said cheered her. Clearly, he wasn't impressed with her frenemy.

"I wish I could arrest you," Jack said to the doctor. "I wish I could take you into custody right now. Unfortunately, I can't prove that you're doing anything illegal. But I'll be keeping my eyes on you from now on, Doctor."

"I'm taking my students back to school now," Madame told Dr. Paley. "Including Paul."

"He hasn't been released from Harmony House," Dr. Paley argued.

"That can be arranged," Jack Fisher said. "I do have some influence here, you know. And I'm going to get a court order to keep you away from the gifted students."

The doctor turned to Madame. "You're going to regret this. When these young people get a little older, when they begin making their own calculated decisions how and when and why to use these gifts, you'll find that you've enabled and released unimaginable horror."

Amanda expected Madame to defend them. But instead, the teacher sighed. "Perhaps. I don't blame you for being frightened. I've got students who are afraid of their own gifts."

"As well they should be," Dr. Paley declared.

Madame nodded. "I can only hope to influence them, to help them use their gifts wisely and well. Some of them may reject this, but it's a risk I'm willing to take."

Amanda's eyes went from Ken to Jenna to Paul and she shivered. Who knew what any of them could turn out to be? Good, bad—there was no way of knowing. But there was one thing she knew for sure: their lives wouldn't be boring.

"Come along, class," Madame said. And Dr. Paley stepped aside to allow the gifted students to leave.

Chapter Twenty One

O N MONDAY MORNING, PAUL Carter took his place in the gifted class, just behind Martin.

Martin turned around. "What did it feel like, being a cockroach?"

Paul tried to answer. "Like . . . a cockroach." The last word came out sounding more like "rush," but Martin got the idea.

"Gross," he said.

Paul nodded. He thought about Martin's gift, and wondered if he'd ever be able to use his strength whenever he wanted to. What would he use it to do?

He looked around the room at his other classmates. Charles . . . Someday he wouldn't be satisfied with using his gift just to make his life easier. Maybe he would stop a bullet from reaching its target and save a life. Or maybe he'd send two cars crashing into each other, just to amuse himself.

Emily . . . Could she rescue an entire city by warning the

inhabitants of an impending earthquake? Or would she refuse to focus her gift and just allow fragments of visions to pass through her head?

Jenna could know good intentions and evil intentions, and she could take action—or refuse to get involved. Tracey could be a spy, but for what purposes? Ken could channel the dead and learn from them to help the living . . . or maybe he'd just watch soap operas. Amanda could make someone's life better. She could also make it worse.

His eyes rested on Sarah. He felt like he understood her now and why she was so afraid. In a way, she was like Dr. Paley. She recognized the terrible possibilities of her gift. She didn't trust herself to be able to use it well. The temptations might be too great.

Paul could relate to that. So far, it had come easy for him. His gift had been used to hide and to escape. It grew out of fear. He'd learned over the past few days that it could be used to inspire fear. Not just Amanda's fear of cockroaches and mice—much greater fears than that.

So perhaps Dr. Paley was right to want them un-gifted, or even eliminated. Or maybe Madame was right in believing they could benefit mankind.

He hoped Madame would talk about this today. About all the dangers they faced—from people like Serena,

Mr. Jackson, Clare, the people who wanted to use their gifts for some terrible purpose. People like Dr. Paley, who wanted to take their gifts away. And people like themselves.

He had a lot to learn—about himself, about his classmates, about what they could do, individually and together. And as Madame entered the room and called the class to order, he sat back and began to listen.

Also available

VOLUME 1

Gifted

BOOKS 1, 2 & 3

MARILYN KAYE